RIZZOLI & I

"Tess Gerritsen brin
tive Jane Rizzoli and medical examiner Maura Isles to tackle another baffling mystery . . . weaving a thriller that slowly unfolds in unexpected ways. . . . Rizzoli and Isles feel like real people, and readers who are fans of either the book series or the former TV show know there's an emotional angle to the proceedings and care about everything that happens to the duo. . . . Gerritsen writes effortlessly, and this is another stellar entry in the series."

—*Associated Press*

"A must-read for thriller fans and one of the best works by Tess Gerritsen to date."

—*San Francisco Review of Books*

"Tess Gerritsen really knows how to draw the reader into her books with just a few words. . . . In the gifted hands of Tess Gerritsen, Rizzoli, Isles, and the rich cast of well-developed characters keep the fast pace zipping along through the entire novel. . . . I will definitely be watching for the next one."

—Fredericksburg *Free Lance–Star*

"The unforgettable team of Rizzoli and Isles are back working on a chilling and difficult case. . . . The twists and turns this novel takes will force Gerritsen's heroines to face difficult emotions and their own biases. As always, Gerritsen is a master storyteller!" —*RT Book Reviews*

"The characters converge in dynamic, diabolical ways and, in doing so, reveal past events that continue to haunt present day. . . . Gerritsen continues to surprise with the depth and range of her storytelling ambitions. . . . Like the best of big-screen boogeyman blockbusters, there's complex villainy, a distortion between appearance and reality, and a third-act plot twist that will both surprise and satisfy. This one's a tasty treat *with* substance."

—CriminalElement.com

"The latest in the Rizzoli and Isles series mixes martyrdom, murder, and mystery. . . . Gerritsen's fans won't be surprised at the grisly crimes or the graphic autopsies. . . . One character's statement that 'sometimes up really *is* down' applies to this complex and enjoyable story. It's a worthy addition to the series."

—*Kirkus Reviews*

"The bitterness of a Boston winter doesn't hinder a killer with a knack for gruesome murders, in bestseller Gerritsen's twisty twelfth Rizzoli & Isles mystery. . . . [She] smoothly blends her leads' domestic dramas with the hunt for the ruthless killer."

—*Publishers Weekly*

"Be prepared for an exciting ride with unexpected twists and terrific writing." —*Library Journal*

RIZZOLI & ISLES: I KNOW A SECRET

BY TESS GERRITSEN

RIZZOLI & ISLES NOVELS

The Surgeon
The Apprentice
The Sinner
Body Double
Vanish
The Mephisto Club
The Keepsake
Ice Cold
The Silent Girl
Rizzoli & Isles: Last to Die
Rizzoli & Isles: Die Again
Rizzoli & Isles: I Know a Secret

OTHER NOVELS

Girl Missing
Harvest
Life Support
Blood Stream
Gravity
The Bone Garden
Playing with Fire

RIZZOLI & ISLES:

I KNOW A SECRET

A NOVEL

TESS GERRITSEN

BALLANTINE BOOKS · NEW YORK

A 2018 Ballantine Books Premium Mass Market Edition

Published in the United States by Ballantine Books, an imprint of Random House, a division of Penguin Random House LLC, New York.

BALLANTINE and the HOUSE colophon are registered trademarks of Penguin Random House LLC.

Originally published in hardcover in the United States by Ballantine Books, an imprint of Random House, a division of Penguin Random House LLC, in 2017.

ISBN 978-0-345-54390-5
Export ISBN 978-0-525-61974-1
Ebook ISBN 978-0-345-54389-9

Cover design: Caroline Teagle Johnson
Cover image: © Karina Vegas/Arcangel

Printed in the United States of America

randomhousebooks.com

9 8 7 6 5 4 3 2 1

Ballantine Books mass market edition: April 2018

To the divine Ms. Margaret Ruley

RIZZOLI & ISLES: I KNOW A SECRET

ONE

WHEN I WAS SEVEN YEARS OLD, I LEARNED how important it is to cry at funerals. On that particular summer day, the man lying in the coffin was my great uncle Orson, who was most memorable for his foul-smelling cigars and his stinky breath and his unabashed farting. While he was alive, he pretty much ignored me, the way I'd ignored him, so I was not in the least bit grief-stricken by his death. I did not see why I should have to attend his funeral, but that is not a choice seven-year-olds are allowed to make. And so that day I found myself squirming on a church pew, bored and sweating in a black dress, wondering why I couldn't have stayed home with Daddy, who had flat-out refused to come. Daddy said he'd be a hypocrite if he pretended to grieve for a man he despised. I didn't know what that word, *hypocrite,* meant, but I knew I didn't want to be one either. Yet there I was, wedged between my mother and Aunt Sylvia, forced to listen to an endless parade of people offering insipid praise for the unremarkable Uncle Orson. *A proudly independent man! He was passionate about his hobbies! How he loved his stamp collection!*

No one mentioned his bad breath.

I amused myself through the endless memorial service by studying the heads of the people in the pew in front of us. I noticed that Aunt Donna's hat was dusted with white dandruff, that Uncle Charlie had dozed off and his toupee had slipped askew. It looked like a brown rat trying to crawl down the side of his head. I did what any normal seven-year-old girl would do.

I burst out laughing.

The reaction was immediate. People turned and frowned at me. My mortified mother sank five sharp fingernails into my arm and hissed, "Stop it!"

"But his hair's fallen off! It looks like a rat!"

Her fingernails dug deeper. *"We will discuss this later, Holly."*

At home, there was no discussion. Instead, there was shouting and a slap on the face, and that's how I learned what constituted appropriate funeral behavior. I learned that one must be somber and silent and that, sometimes, tears are expected.

Four years later, at my mother's funeral, I made a point of noisily shedding copious tears because that was what everyone expected of me.

But today, at the funeral of Sarah Basterash, I'm not certain whether anyone expects me to cry. It's been more than a decade since I last saw the girl I knew in school as Sarah Byrne. We were never close, so I can't really say that I mourn her passing. In truth, I've come to her funeral in Newport only out of curiosity. I want to know how she died. I *need* to know how she died. *Such a terrible tragedy* is what everyone in the church is murmuring around me. Her husband was out of town, Sarah had a few drinks, and she fell asleep with a candle burning on her nightstand. The fire that killed her was merely an accident. That, at least, is what everyone says.

It's what I want to believe.

The little church in Newport is packed to capacity, filled with all the friends that Sarah made in her short life, most of whom I've never met. Nor have I met her husband, Kevin, who under happier circumstances would be quite an attractive man, someone I might make a play for, but today he looks genuinely broken. Is this what grief does to you?

I turn to survey the church, and I spot an old high school classmate named Kathy sitting behind me, her face blotchy, her mascara smeared from crying. Almost all the women and many of the men are crying, because a soprano is singing that old Quaker hymn "Simple Gifts," and that always seems to bring on the tears. For an instant, Kathy and I lock gazes, hers brimming and wet, mine cool and dry-eyed. I've changed so much since high school that I can't imagine she recognizes me, yet her gaze is transfixed and she keeps staring at me as if she's spotted a ghost.

I turn and face forward again.

By the time "Simple Gifts" is over, I too have managed to produce tears, just like everyone else.

I join the long line of mourners to pay my last respects, and as I file past the closed coffin, I study Sarah's photograph, which is displayed on an easel. She was only twenty-six, four years younger than I am, and in the photo she is dewy and pink-cheeked and smiling, the same pretty blonde I remember from our school days, when I was the girl no one noticed, the phantom who lurked in the periphery. Now here I am, my skin still flush with life, while Sarah, pretty little Sarah, is nothing but charred bones in a box. I'm sure that's what everyone thinks as they look at the image of Sarah Before the Fire; they see the smiling face in the photo and imagine scorched flesh and blackened skull.

The line moves forward, and I offer my condolences to Kevin. He murmurs, "Thank you for coming." He has no idea who I am or how I knew Sarah, but he sees that my cheeks are tearstained, and he grasps my hand in gratitude. I have wept for his dead wife, and that is all it takes to pass muster.

I slip out of the church into the cold November wind and walk away at a brisk pace, because I don't want to be waylaid by Kathy or any other childhood acquaintances. Over the years, I've managed to avoid them all.

Or perhaps they were avoiding me.

It is only two o'clock, and although my boss at Booksmart Media has given me the whole day off, I consider going back to the office to catch up on emails and phone calls. I am the publicist for a dozen authors and I need to schedule media appearances, mail out galleys, and write pitch letters. But before I head back to Boston, there is one more stop I have to make.

I drive to Sarah's house—or what used to be her house. Now there are only blackened remains, charred timbers, and a pile of soot-stained bricks. A white picket fence that once enclosed the front garden lies smashed and flattened, wrecked by the fire crew when they dragged their hoses and ladders from the street. By the time the fire trucks arrived, the house must already have been an inferno.

I get out of my car and approach the ruins. The air is still foul with the stench of smoke. Standing there on the sidewalk, I can make out the faint glint of a stainless-steel refrigerator buried in that blackened mess. Just a glance at this Newport neighborhood tells me this would have been an expensive house, and I wonder what sort of business Sarah's husband is in, or if there's money in his family. An advantage I certainly never had.

The wind gusts and dead leaves rattle across my shoes, a brittle sound that brings back another autumn day, twenty years ago, when I was ten years old and crunching across dead leaves in the woods. That day still casts its shadow across my life, and it's the reason I am standing here today.

I look down at the makeshift memorial that's materialized in Sarah's honor. People have left bouquets of flowers, and I see a mound of wilted roses and lilies and carnations, floral tributes to a young woman who was clearly loved. Suddenly I focus on a bit of greenery that is not part of any bouquet but has been draped across the other flowers, like an afterthought.

It is a palm leaf. Symbol of the martyr.

A chill scrabbles up my spine and I back away. Through the thudding of my heart, I hear the sound of an approaching car, and I turn to see a Newport police cruiser slow down to a crawl. The windows are rolled up and I cannot make out the officer's face, but I know he's giving me a long and careful look as he passes by. I turn away and duck back into my car.

There I sit for a moment, waiting for my heartbeat to slow down and my hands to stop trembling. I look again at the ruins of the house, and I once again picture Sarah at six years old. Pretty little Sarah Byrne, bouncing on the school-bus seat in front of me. Five of us rode the school bus that afternoon.

Now there are only four of us left.

"Goodbye, Sarah," I murmur. Then I start the car and drive back to Boston.

TWO

EVEN MONSTERS WERE MORTAL.

The woman lying on the other side of the window might appear to be as human as all the other patients in this intensive-care unit, but Dr. Maura Isles knew only too well that Amalthea Lank was indeed a monster. Behind the cubicle window was the creature who stalked Maura's nightmares, who cast a shadow over Maura's past, and whose face foretold Maura's future.

Here is my mother.

"We'd heard that Mrs. Lank had a daughter, but we didn't realize you were right down the road in Boston," said Dr. Wang. Was that a note of criticism she heard in his voice? Disapproval that she'd neglected her filial duties and failed to turn up at the bedside of her dying mother?

"She is my biological mother," said Maura, "but I

was just an infant when she gave me up for adoption. I learned about her only a few years ago."

"You've met her, though?"

"Yes, but I haven't spoken to her since . . ." Maura paused. *Since I swore I'd have nothing more to do with her.* "I didn't know she was in the ICU until the nurse called me this afternoon."

"She was admitted here two days ago, after she developed a fever and her white count crashed."

"How low is it?"

"Her neutrophil count—that's a specific type of white blood cell—is only five hundred. It should be triple that."

"I assume you've started empiric antibiotics?" She saw him blink in surprise and said, "I'm sorry, Dr. Wang. I should have mentioned that I'm a physician. I work for the medical examiner's office."

"Oh. I didn't realize." He cleared his throat and instantly shifted to the far-more-technical language they shared as medical doctors. "Yes, we started antibiotics right after we drew blood cultures. About five percent of patients on her chemotherapy regimen get febrile neutropenia."

"Which chemo regimen is she on?"

"Folfirinox. It's a combination of four drugs, including fluorouracil and leucovorin. According to one French study, Folfirinox definitely prolongs life for patients with metastatic pancreatic cancer, but they have to be closely monitored for fevers. Fortunately, the prison nurse at Framingham stayed on top of that." He paused, searching for a way to pose a delicate question. "I hope you don't mind me asking this."

"Yes?"

He looked away, clearly uncomfortable with the subject he was about to broach. It was far easier to discuss blood counts and antibiotic protocols and scientific data, because facts were neither good nor evil; they did not invite judgment. "Her medical record from Framingham doesn't mention the reason why she's in prison. All we were told is that Mrs. Lank is serving a life term with no chance of parole. The guard assigned to watch her insists that his prisoner stay handcuffed to the bed rail, which seems pretty barbaric to me."

"That's simply their protocol for hospitalized prisoners."

"She's dying of pancreatic cancer, and anyone can see how frail she is. She's certainly not going to jump up and escape. But the guard told us she's far more dangerous than she looks."

"She is," said Maura.

"Why was she sent to prison?"

"Homicides. Multiple."

He stared through the window at Amalthea. "*That* lady?"

"Now you understand the reason for the handcuffs. And for the guard stationed outside her cubicle." Maura glanced at the uniformed officer who sat by the doorway, monitoring their conversation.

"I'm sorry," said Dr. Wang. "This must be difficult for you, knowing that your mother—"

"Is a murderer? Yes." *And you don't know the worst of it. You don't know about the rest of the family.*

Through the cubicle window, Maura saw Amalthea's eyes slowly open. One bony finger beckoned to her, a gesture as chilling as the command of Satan's claw. I should turn and leave now, she thought. Amalthea did not deserve anyone's pity or kindness. But Maura did share a bond with this woman, a bond that went as deep as their molecules. If only by DNA, Amalthea Lank *was* her mother.

The male guard kept a close eye on Maura as she donned an isolation gown and mask. This would be no private visit; the guard would be observing their every look, every gesture, and the inevitable gossip would surely make the rounds of this hospital. Dr. Maura Isles, the Boston medical examiner whose scalpel had sliced open countless cadavers, who regularly followed in the wake of the Grim Reaper, was the daughter of a serial killer. Death was their family business.

Amalthea looked up at Maura with eyes as black as chips of obsidian. Oxygen hissed softly through her nasal prongs, and on the monitor above the bed, a cardiac rhythm blipped across the screen. Proof that even someone as soulless as Amalthea possessed a heart.

"You came to see me after all," whispered Amalthea. "After you swore you never would."

"They told me you're critically ill. This may be our last chance to talk, and I wanted to see you while I still could."

"Because you need something from me?"

Maura gave a disbelieving shake of the head. "What would I need from *you*?"

"It's how the world works, Maura. All sensible creatures seek an advantage. Everything we do is out of self-interest."

"That may be how it is for you. Not for me."

"Then why did you come?"

"Because you're dying. Because you keep writing me, asking me to visit. Because I like to think I have *some* sense of compassion."

"Which I don't have."

"Why do you think you're handcuffed to that bed?"

Amalthea grimaced and closed her eyes, her mouth suddenly tightening in pain. "I suppose I deserved that," she murmured. Sweat glistened on her upper lip and for a moment she lay perfectly still, as though any movement, even drawing a breath, was excruciating. The last time Maura had seen her, Amalthea's black hair was thick and generously streaked with silver. Now only a few wisps clung to her scalp, the last survivors of a brutal round of chemotherapy. The flesh of her temples had wasted away, and her skin sagged like a collapsing tent over the jutting bones of her face.

"You look like you're in pain. Do you need morphine?" Maura asked. "I'll call the nurse."

"No." Amalthea slowly released a breath. "Not yet. I need to be awake. I need to talk to you."

"About what?"

"About you, Maura. Who you are."

"I know who I am."

"Do you, really?" Amalthea's eyes were dark and fathomless. "You're my daughter. You can't deny it."

"But I'm nothing like you."

"Because you were raised by the kind and respectable Mr. and Mrs. Isles in San Francisco? Because you went to the best schools, had the finest education? Because you work on behalf of truth and justice?"

"Because I didn't slaughter two dozen women. Or

were there more? Were there other victims that didn't show up in your final tally?"

"That all happened in the past. I want to talk about the future."

"Why bother? You won't be here." It was a heartless thing to say, but Maura was not in the mood to be charitable. Suddenly she felt manipulated, lured here by a woman who knew exactly which puppet strings to pull. For months, Amalthea had been sending her letters. *I'm dying of cancer. I'm your only blood relative. This will be your last chance to say goodbye.* Few words held more power than *last chance.* Let that opportunity pass, and what followed might be a lifetime of regret.

"Yes, I'll be dead," said Amalthea matter-of-factly. "And you'll be left to wonder who your people are."

"My people?" Maura laughed. "As if we're some sort of tribe?"

"We are. We belong to a tribe that profits from the dead. Your father and I did. Your brother did. And isn't it ironic that you do as well? Ask yourself, Maura, why did you choose your profession? Such a strange one to pursue. Why aren't you a teacher or a banker? What compels you to slice open the dead?"

"It's about the science. I want to understand why they died."

"Of course. The intellectual answer."

"Is there a better one?"

"It's because of the darkness. We both share it. The difference is, I'm not afraid of it, but you are. You deal with your fear by cutting it open with your scalpels, hoping to reveal its secrets. But that doesn't work, does it? It doesn't solve your fundamental problem."

"Which is?"

"That it's inside you. The darkness is part of you."

Maura looked into her mother's eyes, and what she saw there made her throat suddenly go dry. *Dear God, I see myself.* She backed away. "I'm done here. You asked me to come and I did. Don't send me any more letters, because I won't answer them." She turned. "Goodbye, Amalthea."

"You're not the only one I write to."

Maura paused, about to open the cubicle door.

"I hear things. Things you might want to know." She closed her eyes and sighed. "You don't seem interested, but you will be. Because you'll find another one soon."

Another what?

Maura hovered on the verge of walking out, struggling not to be sucked back into the conversation. Don't respond, she thought. Don't let her trap you here.

It was her cell phone that saved her, its deep-throated buzz trembling in her pocket. Without a backward glance, she stepped out of the cubicle, yanked off the face mask, and fumbled under the isolation gown for the phone. "Dr. Isles," she answered.

"Got an early Christmas present for you," said Detective Jane Rizzoli, sounding far too breezy for the news she was about to deliver. "Twenty-six-year-old white female. Dead in bed, fully dressed."

"Where?"

"We're in the Leather District. It's a loft apartment

on Utica Street. I can't *wait* to hear what you think about this one."

"You said she's in bed? Her own?"

"Yeah. Her father found her."

"And is this clearly a homicide?"

"No doubt about it. But it's what happened to her *afterward* that's making Frost freak out over here." Jane paused and added quietly, "At least, I *hope* she was dead when it happened."

Through the cubicle window, Maura saw that Amalthea was watching the conversation, eyes sharp with interest. Of course she would be interested; death was their family trade.

"How soon can you get here?" said Jane.

"I'm in Framingham at the moment. It might take me a while, depending on traffic."

"Framingham? What're you doing out there?"

It was not a subject Maura wanted to discuss, certainly not with Jane. "I'm leaving now" was all she said. She hung up and looked at her dying mother. I'm done here, she thought. Now I never have to see you again.

Amalthea's lips slowly curved into a smile.

THREE

BY THE TIME MAURA ARRIVED IN BOSTON, DARKness had fallen and a bone-chilling wind had driven most pedestrians indoors. Utica Street was narrow and already crowded with official vehicles, so she parked around the corner and paused to survey the deserted street. Over the last few days there'd been snow followed by a thaw followed by this bitter cold, and the sidewalk had the treacherous gleam of ice. Time to go to work. Time to put Amalthea behind me, she thought. Which was exactly what Jane had advised her to do months ago: *Don't visit Amalthea; don't even think about her. Let the woman rot in jail.*

Now it's over and done with, thought Maura. I've said my goodbyes and she is finally out of my life.

She stepped out of her Lexus and the wind whipped the hem of her long black coat, piercing straight through the fabric of her woolen trousers. She walked as quickly as she dared to on the slick sidewalk, past a coffee shop and a shuttered travel agency, and turned the corner onto Utica Street, which cut like a narrow canyon between red-brick warehouses. Once this had been a district of leather workers and wholesalers. Many of those nineteenth-century buildings had been converted to loft apartments, and what had once been an industrial part of the city was now a trendy neighborhood for artists.

Maura stepped around construction rubbish, which partially blocked the street, and spied blue cruiser lights ahead, flashing like a grim homing beacon. Through the windshield she could see the silhouettes of two patrolmen sitting inside, their engine running to keep the vehicle warm. A cruiser window rolled down as she approached.

"Hey, Doc!" The patrolman grinned out at her. "You missed the excitement. The ambulance just left." Though he looked familiar, and he clearly recognized her, she had no idea what his name was, something that happened all too frequently.

"What excitement?" she asked.

"Rizzoli was inside talking to some guy when he clutches his chest and keels over. Probably a heart attack."

"Is he still alive?"

"He was when they drove off with him. You should've been here. They could've used a doctor."

"Wrong specialty." She glanced at the building. "Rizzoli still inside?"

"Yeah. Just go up the stairs. It's a real nice apartment up there. Cool place to live, if you're not dead." As the window rolled up, she could hear the cops chuckling at their own humor. Ha-ha, death-scene joke. Never funny.

She paused in the biting wind to pull on shoe covers and gloves, then pushed into the building. As the door slammed shut with a bang behind her, she stopped dead in her tracks, confronted by the image of a blood-spattered girl. Hanging on the foyer wall like a macabre welcome sign was a poster for the horror film *Carrie,* a splash of Technicolor gore that would startle every visitor who walked in the door. A whole gallery of other movie posters adorned the red-brick wall along the stairway. As she climbed the steps she passed *Day of the Triffids, The Pit and the Pendulum, The Birds,* and *Night of the Living Dead.*

"You finally got here," Jane called down from the second-floor landing. She pointed to *Night of the Living Dead.* "Imagine coming home to that happy image every night."

"These posters all look like originals. They're not to my taste, but they're probably pretty valuable."

"Come in and get a load of something else that's not to your taste. Sure as hell not *my* taste anyway."

Maura followed Jane into the apartment and paused to admire the massive wood beams overhead. The floor still had its original wide oak planks, now polished to a high gloss. Tasteful renovations had transformed what was once a warehouse into a stunning brick-walled loft that was certainly unaffordable for any starving artist.

"Way nicer than my apartment," said Jane. "I could move right in here, but first I'd get rid of *that* creepy thing on the wall." She pointed to the monstrous red eye that stared from yet another horror-movie poster. "Notice the name of the movie?"

"*I See You*?" said Maura.

"Remember that title. It could be significant," Jane said ominously. She led Maura through an open kitchen, past a vase filled with fresh roses and lilies, a lavish touch of spring on this December night. On the black granite countertop was a florist's card with *Happy Birthday! Love, Dad* written in purple ink.

"You said she was found by her father?" said Maura.

"Yeah, he owns this building. Lets her live here rent-free. She was supposed to meet Dad for lunch today at the Four Seasons to celebrate her birthday. When she didn't show up and she didn't answer her cell phone, Dad drove here to check on her. Says he found the entrance unlocked, but everything else looked fine to him. Until he got to the bedroom." Jane paused. "About this point in his story, he turned white, clutched his chest, and we had to call the ambulance."

"The patrolman downstairs said the man was still alive when the ambulance left."

"But he wasn't looking good. After what we found in the bedroom, I was worried that Frost might need an ambulance too."

Detective Barry Frost was standing in the far corner of the bedroom, determinedly focused on what he was jotting in a notebook. His wintry pallor was more pronounced than usual, and he managed only a feeble nod as Maura entered. She gave Frost scarcely a glance; her attention was fixed on the bed, where the victim was lying. The young woman lay in a strangely serene pose, her arms at her sides, as if she'd simply settled on top of the bedspread, fully dressed, for a nap. She was all in black, in leggings and a turtleneck, which emphasized the ghostly whiteness of her face. Her hair was black as well, but the blond roots betrayed the fact that her raven color was merely a dye job. Multiple gold studs pierced her ears, and a gold hoop gleamed on her right eyebrow. But it was what gaped beneath the eyebrows that drew Maura's shocked attention.

Both eye sockets were empty. The contents had been scooped out, leaving behind only bloody hollows.

Stunned, Maura glanced down at the woman's left hand. At what were nestled like two gruesome marbles in her open palm.

"And *that's* what makes this a fun night, boys and girls," Jane said.

"Bilateral globe enucleation," said Maura softly.

"Is that some kind of fancy medical talk for *someone cut out her eyeballs*?"

"Yes."

"I love how you give everything a nice dry clinical spin. It makes the fact she's holding her own eyeballs somehow seem less, oh, totally fucked up."

"Tell me about this victim," said Maura.

Frost looked up reluctantly from his notebook. "Cassandra Coyle, twenty-six years old. Lives—lived here alone; no current boyfriend. She's an independent filmmaker, has her own production company called Crazy Ruby Films. Works out of a small studio on South Street."

"That's another building that her dad owns," added Jane. "Obviously there's money in the family."

Frost continued. "Her father says he last spoke to

the victim yesterday afternoon, around five or six P.M., just as she was leaving her film studio. We're gonna head over there next to interview her colleagues, try to nail down the exact time they last saw her."

"What kind of films do they make?" asked Maura, although the answer had already been apparent, based on the movie posters she'd seen hanging in the loft.

"Horror flicks," said Frost. "Her dad said they'd just finished filming their second one."

"And that goes along with her sense of fashion," said Jane, eyeing the victim's multiple piercings and raven-black hair. "I thought Goth had gone out of style, but this gal totally rocked the look."

Reluctantly, Maura focused again on what was cradled in the victim's hand. Exposure to air had dried the corneas, and blue eyes that once glistened were now dull and clouded. Although the severed muscles had shriveled, she could identify the recti and oblique muscles that so precisely control the movements of the human eye. Those six muscles, working in intricate collaboration, allowed a hunter to track a duck through the sky, a student to scan a textbook.

"Please tell us she was already dead when he did . . . that," said Jane.

"These enucleations appear to be postmortem, judging by the condition of the palpebrae."

"The what?"

"The eyelids. Do you see how there's almost no extraneous damage to the tissues? Whoever removed the globes took his time doing it, and that would be difficult if she were conscious and struggling. Also there's minimal blood loss, which indicates to me that she had no pulse. Her circulation was already shut down when the first cut was made." Maura paused, studying the hollowed-out sockets. "The symbolism is fascinating."

Jane turned to Frost. "Didn't I tell you she'd say that?"

"The eyes are considered the windows to the soul. Maybe this killer didn't like what he saw in hers. Or he didn't like the way she looked at *him.* Maybe he felt threatened by her gaze and reacted by cutting out the eyes."

"Or maybe her last movie had something to do with it," said Frost. *"I See You."*

Maura looked at him. "That poster was for *her* movie?"

"She wrote and produced it. According to Dad, it was her first feature film. You never know who might have watched it. Maybe some weirdo."

"Who might have been inspired by it," said Maura, staring at the two eyes cupped in the victim's hand.

"You ever seen a case like this, Doc?" asked Frost. "A victim with the eyes cut out?"

"Dallas," Maura said. "It wasn't my case, but I heard about it from a colleague. Three women were shot to death and their eyes excised postmortem. The killer's first excision was surgically precise, like this one. But by the third victim, he'd gotten sloppy. Which was how they caught him."

"So . . . a serial killer."

"Who also happened to be skilled in taxidermy. After he was arrested, police found dozens of women's photos in his apartment, and he'd snipped out all the eyes of the photos. He hated women and was sexually aroused when he hurt them." She glanced at Frost. "But that's the only case I've heard of. This sort of mutilation is unusual."

"It's a first for us," said Jane.

"Let's hope it's your first and only." Maura grasped the right arm, tried to flex the elbow, and found the joint immovable. "The skin is cold and she's in full rigor mortis. Based on the phone call with her father, we know she was still alive around five P.M. yesterday. That narrows the postmortem interval to somewhere between twelve and twenty-four hours." She looked up. "Any witnesses who can help us narrow down time of death? Security cameras in the area?"

"Not on this block," said Frost. "But I spotted a camera on the building around the corner, and it looks like it's pointed right at the entrance to Utica Street. Maybe it caught her as she was walking home. And, if we're lucky, it recorded someone else too."

Maura peeled down the turtleneck collar to check for bruises or ligature marks, but she saw neither. Next she pulled up the victim's black turtleneck to expose the torso and, with Jane's help, rolled the body onto its side. The back was a deep purple, where blood had pooled after death. She pressed a gloved finger against the discolored flesh and found that livor mortis was fixed, which confirmed that the victim had been dead for at least twelve hours.

But what had caused this death? Except for the mutilated eyes, Maura saw no evidence of trauma. "No bullet wounds, no blood, no evidence of strangulation," she said. "I see no other injuries."

"He cuts out the eyeballs, but he doesn't take them," Jane said, frowning. "Instead, he leaves them in her hand, like some sick parting gift. What the hell's that supposed to mean?"

"That's a question for a psychologist." Maura straightened. "I can't determine the cause of death here. Let's see what turns up at autopsy."

"Maybe it was an OD," suggested Frost.

"That's certainly high on the list. The drug and tox screen will give us that answer." Maura stripped off her gloves. "She'll be first on my schedule tomorrow."

Jane followed Maura out of the bedroom. "Is there anything you want to talk about, Maura?"

"I can't tell you more until the autopsy."

"I don't mean about this case."

"I'm not sure what you mean."

"On the phone, you said you were in Framingham. Please tell me you didn't go to see that woman."

Calmly, Maura buttoned up her coat. "You make it sound like I've committed a crime."

"So you were there. I thought we both agreed you should stay away from her."

"Amalthea's been admitted to the ICU, Jane. She had complications from her chemotherapy, and I have no idea how much longer she'll be alive."

"She's using you, playing on your sympathy. Geez, Maura, you're just going to get hurt again."

"You know, I really don't want to talk about this." Without a backward glance, Maura headed down the stairs and walked out of the building. Outside, a frigid wind funneled down the street, lashing her hair and face. As she walked toward her car, she heard the building door slam shut again. Glancing back, she saw that Jane had followed her outside.

"What does she want from you?" Jane asked.

"She's dying of cancer. What do you think she wants? Maybe a little sympathy?"

"She's messing with your head. She knows how to get to you. Look how she twisted her son."

"You think I'd ever be like *him*?"

"Of course not! But you said it yourself once. You said you were born with the same streak of darkness that runs in the Lank family. Somehow she'll find a way to use that to her advantage."

Maura unlocked her Lexus. "I've got enough problems on my plate. I don't need a lecture from you."

"Okay, okay." Jane held up both hands, a gesture of surrender. "I'm just looking out for you. You're usually so smart. Please don't do something stupid."

Maura watched as Jane strode back to the crime scene. Back to the bedroom where a dead woman lay, her body frozen in rigor mortis. A woman with no eyes.

Suddenly Amalthea's words came back to her: *You'll find another one soon.*

Turning, she quickly scanned the street, surveying every doorway, every window. Was that a face watching her from the second floor? Did someone move in that alleyway? Everywhere she looked, she imagined ominous silhouettes. This was what Jane had warned her about. This was Amalthea's power; she'd parted the curtain to reveal a nightmarish landscape where everything was painted in shadows.

Shivering, Maura climbed into her car and started the engine. Icy air blasted from the heater vent. It was time to go home.

Time to flee the darkness.

FOUR

FROM THE COFFEE SHOP WHERE I'M SITTING, I watch the two women talking just outside the window. I recognize both of them, because I've seen them interviewed on television and have read about them in the news, usually in connection to murder. The one with the unruly dark hair is a homicide detective, and the tall woman in the long, elegant coat is the medical examiner. I can't hear what they're saying, but I can read their body language, the cop aggressively gesticulating, the doctor trying to retreat.

Abruptly the detective turns and walks away. The doctor stands very still for a moment, as if not certain whether to pursue her. Then she shakes her head in resignation, climbs into a sleek black Lexus, and drives away.

I wonder what *that* was all about?

I already know what drew them here on this bitterly cold night. An hour ago, I heard it on the news: A young woman has been murdered on Utica Street. The same street where Cassandra Coyle lives.

I peer down the entrance to Utica, but there's nothing to see except the flashing lights of police cruisers. Does Cassandra now lie dead, or is it some other unlucky woman? I haven't seen Cassie since middle school, and I wonder if I'd even recognize her. Certainly she would not recognize the new me, the Holly who now stands straight and looks you in the eye, who no longer lurks on the periphery, envying the golden girls. The years have polished my confidence and my sense of fashion. My black hair is now cut in a sleek bob, I've learned to walk in stilettos, and I'm wearing a two-hundred-dollar blouse that I shrewdly bought from the 75 percent–off rack. When you work as a publicist, you learn that appearances count, so I've adapted.

"What's going on out there? Do you know?" a voice asks.

The man has materialized beside me so suddenly that I flinch in surprise. Usually I'm aware of everyone in my proximity, but I was focused on the police activity outside the coffee shop and I didn't notice his approach. *Hot guy* is the first thing I think when I look at him. He's a few years older than I am, in his mid-thirties, with a lean athletic build, blue eyes, and wheat-colored hair. I deduct a few points because he's drinking a latte, and at this time of night, real men drink espresso. I'm willing to overlook that flaw because of those gorgeous blue eyes. They aren't focused on me right now but on the activity outside the window. On all the official vehicles that have converged on the street where Cassandra Coyle lives.

Or lived.

"All those police cars out there," he says. "I wonder what happened."

"Something bad."

He points. "Look, there's the Channel Six van."

We both sit for a moment sipping our drinks, watching the action on the street. Now another TV news van arrives, and several other patrons in the coffee shop gravitate to the window. I feel them pressing in around me, jostling for a better view. The sight of a mere police car isn't enough to excite most jaded Bostonians, but when the TV cameras show up, our antennae perk up, because now we know that this is more than a fender bender or a double-parked car. Something newsworthy has happened.

As if to confirm our instincts, the white van from the medical examiner's office rolls into view. Is it here to fetch Cassandra or some other unlucky victim? The sight of that van makes my pulse suddenly kick into a gallop. Don't let it be her, I think. Let it be someone else, someone I don't know.

"Uh-oh, medical examiner's van," says Blue Eyes. "That's not good."

"Did anyone see what happened?" a woman asks.

"Just a lot of police showing up."

"Anyone hear gunshots or anything?"

"You were here first," Blue Eyes says to me. "What did you see?"

Everyone looks in my direction. "The police cars

were already here when I walked in. It must have happened some time ago."

The others stand watching, hypnotized by the flashing lights. Blue Eyes settles onto the stool right beside me and tips sugar into his inappropriate-for-the-evening latte. I wonder if he chose that seat because he wants a ringside view of the action outside or if he's trying to be friendly. The latter would be fine with me. In fact, I'm feeling an electric tingle up my thigh as my body automatically responds to his. I haven't come here looking for company, but it's been a while since I've enjoyed a man's intimate attentions. More than a month, if you don't count the quickie hand job last week with the valet at the Colonnade Hotel.

"So. Do you live around here?" he asks. A promising opening, though unimaginative.

"No. Do you?"

"I live in the Back Bay. I was supposed to meet friends at the Italian restaurant down the street, but I'm way too early. Thought I'd stop in for coffee."

"I live in the North End. I was here to meet friends too, but they canceled at the last minute." How easily the lie slips off my lips, and he has no reason to doubt me. Most people automatically assume that you're telling the truth, which makes life so much easier for people like me. I hold out my hand to shake his, a gesture that men find unnerving when a woman does it, but I want to set the parameters early. I want to make it clear that this is a meeting of equals.

We sit for a moment companionably sipping our coffees, watching the action. Police investigations are, for the most part, unexciting to watch. All you see are vehicles coming and going and people in uniforms walking in and out of buildings. You don't get a view of what's going on inside; you can only surmise, based on which personnel shows up, what the situation might be. There's a calmness, even boredom, on all the cops' faces. Whatever happened on Utica Street took place some hours ago, and investigators are simply assembling the pieces of the puzzle.

With nothing very interesting to watch, the other customers in the coffee shop drift away, leaving Blue Eyes and me alone at the window counter.

"I guess we'll have to check the news to see what happened," he says.

"It's a murder."

"How do you know?"

"I saw a homicide detective out there a few minutes ago."

"Did he come over and introduce himself?"

"It's a she. I don't remember her name, but I've seen her on TV. The fact she's a woman interests me. It makes me wonder why she chose that sort of job."

He eyes me more closely. "Do you, uh, follow this sort of thing? Murders?"

"No, I'm just good at remembering faces. But I'm lousy at remembering names."

"While we're on that subject of names, mine is Everett." He smiles, and charming laugh lines crease his eyes. "Now you're free to forget it."

"What if I don't want to forget it?"

"I hope that means you think I'm memorable."

I consider what might happen between us. Looking into his eyes, I suddenly know exactly what I *want* to happen: We go to his place in the Back Bay. We chase our coffees with a few glasses of wine. And then we rut all night like hot bunnies. What a shame he's supposed to meet his friends for dinner in the neighborhood. I'm not at all interested in meeting his friends, and I'm not going to waste any time waiting by the phone for him to call me, so I guess this is hello and goodbye. Some things aren't meant to happen, even if you want them to.

I drain my coffee cup and rise from my seat. "It was good to meet you, Everett."

"Ah. You remembered my name."

"Hope you have a nice dinner with your friends."

"What if I don't want to have dinner with them?"

"Isn't that why you're in the neighborhood?"

"Plans can change. I can call my friends and tell them I suddenly need to be somewhere else."

"And where might that be?"

He stands up too, and we're now eye-to-eye. That tingle in my leg spreads to my pelvis in warm, delicious waves, and all at once I forget about Cassandra and what her death might mean. My attention is only on this man and what's about to happen between us.

"My place or yours?" he asks.

FIVE

AMBER VOORHEES HAD VIOLET-STREAKED BLOND hair and polished black fingernails, but it was the nose ring that most unsettled Jane. As Amber sobbed, threads of snot hung from that gold hoop, and she kept dabbing at it delicately with tissue to catch the drips. Her colleagues Travis Chang and Ben Farney weren't crying, but they seemed just as shocked and devastated by the news of Cassandra Coyle's death. All three filmmakers wore T-shirts and hoodies and ripped jeans, the uniform of young hipsters, and none of them looked as if they'd combed their hair in days. Judging by the locker-room smell of the studio, they hadn't showered in days either. Every horizontal surface in the room was covered by pizza boxes, empty cans of Red Bull, and scattered pages from their film script. On the video monitor, a scene from their work-in-progress was playing: a blond teenager, sobbing and stumbling through dark woods, fleeing from some relentless and shadowy killer.

Travis abruptly turned to the computer and paused the video. The image of the killer froze onscreen, an ominous shadow framed between trees. "Fuck," he groaned. "I can't believe this. I *can't fucking believe this.*"

Amber wrapped her arms around Travis, and the young man gave a sob. Now Ben joined the hug and the three filmmakers clung to one another for a moment, their three-way embrace backlit by the glow from the computer monitor.

Jane glanced at Frost and saw him blink away a brief sheen of tears. Grief was contagious, and Frost had no immunity to it, even after years of delivering bad news and watching the recipients crumble. Cops were like terrorists. They tossed devastating bombs into the lives of victims' friends and families, and then they stood around to watch the damage they'd done.

Travis was first to pull away from the hug. He crossed to a sagging sofa, sank onto the cushions, and dropped his head in his hands. "God, just yesterday she was here. She was sitting *right here.*"

"I knew there was a reason she stopped answering my texts," said Amber, sniffling into her tissue. "When she went silent, I figured it was 'cause she was stressing out over her dad."

"When did she stop answering texts?" Jane asked. "Can you check your phone?"

Amber hunted around under the scattered script pages and finally uncovered her cell phone. She scrolled back through her messages. "I texted her last night, around two A.M. She didn't answer."

"Would you expect her to, at two A.M.?"

"Yeah, actually. At this stage of the project."

"We've been pulling all-nighters," said Ben. He too dropped onto the sofa and rubbed his face. "We were up till three, editing the film. None of us even bothered to go home, just crashed right here." He nodded at the sleeping bags wadded up in the corner.

"All three of you spent the night here?"

Ben nodded again. "We're under the gun because of deadlines. Cassie would've been working with us too, except she needed to pull herself together before she met her dad. Something she was definitely not looking forward to."

"What time did she leave here yesterday?" Jane asked.

"Around six, maybe?" Ben asked his colleagues, who both nodded.

"The pizzas had just been delivered," said Amber. "Cassie didn't stay to eat. Said she was going to get something on her own, so the three of us kept working." She wiped a hand across her eyes, leaving a thick smear of mascara on her cheek. "I can't believe that's the last time we'll ever see her. When she walked out the door, she was talking about the party we'd have for picture lock."

"Picture lock?" asked Frost.

"That's when all the edits are done," said Ben. "Basically, it's the finished movie but without sound effects or music. We're almost there, maybe another week or two."

"Plus another twenty grand," muttered Travis. He raised his head and his black hair stood up in greasy tufts. "Shit. I don't know how we'll raise it without Cassie."

Jane frowned at him. "Was Cassandra supposed to deliver that money?"

The three young filmmakers looked at one another, as if unsure who should answer the question.

"She was gonna ask her dad at lunch today," said Amber. "That's why she was stressing out. She hated having to beg him for money. Especially over lunch at the Four Seasons."

Jane surveyed the room, taking in the stained carpet, the ratty sofa, and the bundled-up sleeping bags. These filmmakers were well into their twenties, but they seemed far younger, just three movie-obsessed kids who were still living like dorm rats.

"Do you folks actually make a living as filmmakers?" she asked.

"A living?" Travis shrugged, as if the question were irrelevant. "We make movies, and that's the point. We're living the dream."

"Using money from Cassandra's father."

"It's not a gift. He's investing in his daughter's career. This movie could put her on the map as a filmmaker, and the story meant a lot to her personally."

Jane glanced down at the script lying on the desk. "*Mr. Simian*?"

"Don't be fooled by the title, or the fact it's a horror flick. This is a serious project about a girl who goes missing. It's based on a true event from her childhood and it's gonna find a way bigger audience than our first film."

"Would that first movie be *I See You*?" said Frost.

Travis shot a surprised look at Frost. "You saw it?"

"We saw the poster for it. The one hanging in Cassandra's apartment."

"Is that . . ." Amber swallowed. "Is that where you found her?"

"It's where her father found her."

Amber shuddered and hugged herself, as if suddenly chilled. "How did it happen?" she murmured. "Did someone break in?"

Jane didn't answer the question but asked one of her own: "Where have you all been in the last twenty-four hours?"

The three filmmakers exchanged glances to gauge who should speak first.

Travis answered, his words measured and deliberate. "We've been right here, in this building. All three of us. All night and all day."

The other two nodded in agreement.

"Look, I know why you're asking us these questions, Detective," said Travis. "It's your job to ask them. But we've known Cassie since we were all students at NYU. When you make a movie together, it's this—this incredible bonding experience like nothing else. We eat and sleep and work together. Yeah, we argue sometimes, but then we make up, because we're *family.*" He pointed at the computer screen, where the image of the killer was still freeze-framed. "We were gonna break out with this film. Prove to the world that we don't need to kiss some studio executive's ass to make a great movie."

"Can you tell us what your various roles were in making *Mr. Simian*?" asked Frost, dutifully jotting everything down in his tattered notebook.

"I'm the director," said Travis.

"I'm DP," said Benjamin. "Also known as the cinematographer."

"Producer," said Amber. "I hire and fire, do payroll, keep it all running like a well-oiled machine." She paused and said with a sigh, "Actually, I do pretty much everything."

"And what was Cassandra's role?"

"She wrote the script. And she's executive producer, which you could say is the most important job of all," said Travis. "Financing the production."

"With her father's money."

"Yeah, but we just need a *little* more. One more check, that's all she was going to ask him for."

A check that they would probably never see.

Amber sank onto the sofa next to Ben, and all three of them sat in silence. The room itself seemed to smell of stale food and failure.

Jane looked up at the movie poster hanging on the wall behind the sofa. It was the same poster that she'd seen in Cassandra's apartment. *I See You.* "That movie," she said, pointing to the image of the monstrous red eye peering from the blackness. "Tell me about it."

"It was our first feature film," said Travis. He added morosely, "And I hope it's not our last."

"Did all four of you work on it?"

"Yeah. It started as our film school project at NYU. We learned a lot, making that one." He gave a rueful shake of the head. "We also made a lot of mistakes."

"How'd it do in theaters?" asked Frost.

The silence was painful. And telling.

"We never got a distribution deal," Travis admitted.

"So no one saw it?"

"Oh, it was shown at quite a few horror-film festivals. Like this one." Travis displayed the SCREAMFEST FILM FESTIVAL T-shirt he was wearing under his hoodie. "It's also available on DVD and video on demand. In fact, we hear it's become something of a cult classic, which is, like, the best thing that can happen to a horror flick."

"Did it make any money?" asked Jane.

"That's really not the point."

"So the point would be?"

"We now have *fans*. People who know about our work! In the indie-film business, sometimes all it takes is word of mouth to build the audience for your next project."

"So it didn't make money."

Travis sighed and looked down at the filthy carpet. "No," he admitted.

Jane's gaze lifted back to the monstrous eye in the movie poster. "What happens in that movie? What's it about?"

"It's about a girl who witnesses a murder, but the police can't find any body or evidence, so they don't believe her. That's because the murder hasn't happened yet. She's telepathically linked to the killer, and she can see what he's *about* to do."

Jane and Frost glanced at each other. *Too bad we don't have that advantage. We'd solve this case in no time flat.*

"And I'm guessing the killer eventually comes after her," Jane said.

"Of course," said Ben. "That's, like, straight out of Horror 101. Eventually, the killer *must* come after the heroine."

"Does anyone in that movie get mutilated?"

"Well, yeah. Again, it's one of those rules of horror films. Straight out of—"

"Yeah, yeah. Horror 101. What sort of mutilations?"

"A few fingers get chopped off. A girl gets the number 666 carved into her forehead."

"Don't forget the ear," reminded Amber.

"Oh, yeah. One guy gets his ear sliced off, like van Gogh."

You people are sick.

"What about the eyes?" said Frost. "Do any of the characters get their eyes cut out?"

The filmmakers looked at one another.

"No," said Travis. "Why are you asking about eyes?"

"Because of the title. The movie's called *I See You.*"

"But you asked specifically about eyes getting cut out. Why? Did something like that happen to . . ." Travis paused, horror suddenly registering on his face.

Amber pressed her hand to her mouth. "Oh, God. Did that happen to *Cassandra*?"

Jane didn't answer but moved on to another question. "How many people saw that movie?" Again, she pointed to the poster.

For a moment, no one spoke. They were still stunned

by what they'd just learned. In their world, all the blood was fake and the limbs were rubber props, mere cartoon violence. *Welcome to my world. The real world.*

"How many?" Jane asked again.

"We don't really know," admitted Travis. "We did sell some DVDs. Made about a thousand bucks from video downloads. Plus, we showed it at those film festivals."

"Give me an estimate."

"Maybe a few thousand people saw it. But we have no idea who they are. The horror audience is worldwide, so they could be living anywhere."

"You don't think she was killed by someone who saw our *movie*?" said Amber. "I mean, that's crazy! Horror fans may look scary, but they're actually really nice and well-adjusted people." She pointed to the computer screen, where the killer's silhouette was still frozen. "Movies like *Mr. Simian,* they're all about helping us process fear, about working through our inner aggressions. They're therapeutic." She shook her head. "The nasties don't watch horror films."

"You know what the *real* assholes watch?" said Ben. "Romantic comedies."

Travis opened a desk drawer, pulled out a DVD, and handed it to Jane. "A copy of *I See You.* It's all yours, Detective."

"And the movie you're working on now? You have a DVD of *Mr. Simian* we can watch?"

"Sorry, we're still editing, so it's not ready to be seen yet. But take a look at *I See You* and tell us what you think. And if there's anything else you need, we're ready to help."

"If this really does have something to do with *I See You,* should we all be worried?" Amber said. "Will the killer come after *us*?"

There was a long silence as the three filmmakers considered that possibility.

It was Travis who said, softly: "It's Horror 101."

SIX

THE SEDATED PATIENT LYING IN THE HOSPITAL bed looked nothing like the man Jane had interviewed only a few hours earlier. This was a deflated version of Matthew Coyle, gray and shrunken, his jaw sagging open. In contrast to that colorless ghost, the woman seated at his bedside was a startling splash of color: flame hair, an emerald blouse, bright-red lipstick. Though Priscilla Coyle was fifty-eight, nearly as old as Matthew, she looked at least a decade younger, her skin burnished and Botoxed, her body as toned as an athlete's. Beside her sickly husband, she was the picture of vitality, and judging by her tailored dress and high heels, a vigil at his bedside was not what she'd planned to be doing this evening.

Priscilla glanced at her watch and said to Jane and Frost, "You'll have to come back in the morning to speak to him. He was so agitated the doctors had to sedate him, and he'll probably sleep straight through the night."

"Actually, we're here to talk to you, Mrs. Coyle," said Jane.

"Why? I can't really tell you anything. I spent the whole afternoon in a board meeting for the Gardner Museum. I had no idea anything was wrong until the hospital called to tell me Matthew was admitted."

"Can we step out of the room? There's a visitors' lounge down the hall where we can talk."

"I really should get home soon. There are so many people I need to notify."

"This shouldn't take long," Frost assured her. "We just need to confirm some details about what happened when."

Matthew Coyle had been admitted to Pilgrim Hospital's VIP wing, where the visitors' lounge featured a wide-screen TV, leather-upholstered furniture, and a well-stocked Keurig coffeemaker. Priscilla settled on the sofa, her Prada crocodile purse perched beside her, and casually slung her Cucinelli coat across the armrest. Jane had once sneaked a peek at a Cucinelli price tag, so she knew how expensive that cashmere coat was. If she ever owned such a coat, she'd keep it locked up in a safety-deposit box, not thoughtlessly toss it around as Priscilla did.

Frost pulled up a chair to face Priscilla and said, "Tell us what happened today, Mrs. Coyle." It was an easy, open-ended question, yet Priscilla seemed to consider her answer a long time before speaking.

"Matthew was supposed to meet Cassandra for lunch at the Four Seasons. When she didn't show up at the restaurant, he called me, asking if I'd heard from her. I hadn't. Then a few hours later, the hospital called to tell me that he'd been admitted with a heart attack."

"Did they often meet for lunch?"

"Hardly ever. Cassie's so busy, she scarcely even bothers to . . ." Priscilla paused. Corrected herself. "She had her own life, so we didn't see much of her. But today was a special occasion."

"Your husband told us it was a birthday lunch."

Priscilla nodded. "Her birthday's actually December thirteenth, but we were out of town. So they planned to celebrate today instead."

"You weren't going to join them?"

"I had that board meeting already scheduled, and I didn't think . . ." Priscilla's voice faded, and she looked down to fuss with the gold clasp of her purse. It was what she *didn't* say that intrigued Jane. Sometimes there was more meaning in silence than in words.

"How did you and your daughter get along?" Jane asked.

"Cassandra was actually my stepdaughter." She shrugged. "We weren't particularly close."

"Were you at odds?"

At this, Priscilla looked up. "I'll be honest. Matthew divorced Cassandra's mother to marry me. So you can understand why we had tensions. She's always held that against me, even though her parents' marriage was essentially over long before Matthew and I got involved. Now it's nineteen years later, and I'm still the *other woman,* even though *my* money paid for her tuition at NYU, and *my* money financed her ridiculous—"

Priscilla caught herself, and she stared down at her crocodile purse again, a purse that symbolized exactly what she'd brought to the marriage. Matthew Coyle had left his wife for a woman accustomed to Prada and Cucinelli, a financial inequality that could strain any relationship.

"Do you know anyone who might want to harm Cassandra?" asked Jane. "Any ex-boyfriends, any enemies?" *Aside from you.*

"I'm not aware of any. But, then, I didn't keep close tabs on her life. After Matthew and I married, Cassandra stayed behind with her mother in Brookline."

"Where is her mother now? We need to speak to her."

"Elaine's in London right now, visiting friends. She'll catch a flight home day after tomorrow. At least, that's what she said in her email."

"You emailed her the news about Cassandra?"

"Well, someone had to let her know."

Jane tried to imagine receiving such an email: *Your daughter's been murdered.* The hatred must run deep between these women for the news of a daughter's death to be delivered by a few cool taps on a smartphone.

"I really don't know what else I can tell you," said Priscilla.

"Do you know any of Cassandra's friends?"

Priscilla wrinkled her nose. "I've met those three kids she works with."

"Kids?"

"They graduated from college four years ago, and they look like they still sleep in their clothes. You'd think by now they'd have jobs. I have no idea how they feed themselves, making those movies."

"Did you happen to watch Cassandra's first movie?"

"I sat through maybe fifteen minutes of *I See You.* It was all I could stand." She looked in the direction of her husband's hospital room. "Matthew sat through the whole bloody thing. Talked himself into liking it, because what else could he do? He wanted to make his little girl happy. After all these years, he's still trying to make up for leaving her mother, and Cassie was happy to take whatever he offered. The free apartment, the studio space. But I don't think she ever really forgave him."

"Did they get along? Your husband and Cassandra?"

"Of course."

"Yet you say Cassandra never forgave him. Were there arguments, maybe about money?"

"Don't all kids fight about money with their parents?"

"Sometimes those fights get out of hand."

Priscilla shrugged. "They had issues. I'm sure the subject of money was going to come up at their lunch today. She's been hinting she needed more, to finish the new movie she's making. Just another reason why I didn't want to join them for lunch." She paused. "Why are you asking about Matthew? You can't possibly think he had anything to do with this?"

"Just routine questions, ma'am," Frost said. "We always have to look at the immediate family."

"He's her *father.* Don't you have any real suspects?"

"Do you know any, Mrs. Coyle?"

Priscilla considered the question. "Cassie was a pretty girl, and pretty girls attract attention. When you catch a man's eye, you have no idea what that might lead to. Maybe he'll get obsessed. Maybe he'll follow you home and . . . We all know what can happen to women."

Certainly Jane knew. She'd seen the evidence in the morgue, in the battered bodies and the pretty faces slashed by rejected suitors. She thought of the gaping sockets that had once contained Cassandra's eyes, eyes that must have seen the killer. Had she looked at him with disdain or disgust? Is that why he'd felt compelled to scoop out the eyes, so they would never again look at him?

Priscilla reached for her coat. "I need to go home. It's been an awful day."

"One last question before you leave, Mrs. Coyle," said Jane.

"Yes?"

"Where were you and your husband last night?"

"Last night?" Priscilla frowned. "Why?"

"Again, it's just a routine question."

Priscilla's lips tightened. "All right. Since you feel the need to ask it, I'll be happy to answer. Matthew and I were home last night. I cooked dinner. Salmon and broccoli, if it matters to you. And then we watched a movie on TV."

"Which movie?"

"Oh, for God's sake. It was some old movie on Turner Classics. *Invasion of the Body Snatchers.*"

"And after that?"

"After that, we went to bed."

—

"YOU EVER WATCHED *INVASION OF the Body Snatchers*?" asked Frost as he and Jane sat in the hospital cafeteria, wolfing down sandwiches. At that late hour, tuna salad and ham and cheese were the only choices left in the vending machine. Jane's tuna sandwich was soggy, but at least it was dinner—something they'd both skipped that evening.

"Hasn't that movie been remade about half a dozen times?" she asked.

"I'm not talking about the remakes. I mean the classic black-and-white version, the one with Kevin McCarthy."

"Black-and-white? That's kind of before our time, wasn't it?"

"Yeah, but that film's timeless. Alice calls it the perfect metaphor for alienation. She says that when someone transforms into a pod person, like in the movie, it's the same as your husband or wife turning into a stranger, someone who no longer loves you. That makes it more disturbing than your typical monster flick, because the fear hits you on this deep psychological level."

"Wait. Since when are you talking to Alice again?"

"Since . . . I don't know. A few weeks ago. Last night we watched *Body Snatchers* together. It was on TV at nine P.M., so Priscilla Coyle was telling the truth when she said she saw it with her husband."

"You spent the night with *Alice*?"

"We just had dinner and watched some TV. Then I went home."

"Remind me. Your divorce has been final for how many months now?"

"This doesn't mean we're getting back together."

Jane sighed and put down her soggy tuna sandwich. Why did everyone she cared about seem to be making such bad personal decisions lately? First there was Maura, going to visit that psycho Amalthea Lank. Now Frost, whom she thought of as her younger brother, was once again taking up with his ex-wife. She remembered his tearful late-night phone calls after Alice had left him for her law school classmate, nights when Jane had agonized about whether she should confiscate his weapon just to keep him safe. And she thought of the months that followed, of listening to his woeful litany of bad dates with women who were never pretty enough or brilliant enough to replace Alice, the bitch. Now she saw the tragic cycle repeating again, joy and heartbreak, joy and heartbreak. Frost deserved better than this.

It was time for some tough love.

"Since you two are talking again," said Jane, "did Alice happen to mention how her boyfriend's doing? That guy she met in law school?"

"She finished law school. She already has her degree."

"All the better to screw you in court."

"But she didn't screw me. Our divorce was civilized."

"Probably because she was feeling guilty about humping Mr. Law Student. Please tell me you're going to be careful."

Frost set down his sandwich as well and gave a deep sigh. "You know, life isn't as black and white as you seem to think it is. There's a reason I married Alice. She's smart, she's gorgeous, she's funny—"

"She's got a boyfriend."

"No, that's all over with. He got a job in D.C. and they broke up."

"Oh. So that's why she's running back to reliable old you."

"Geez, you don't know what the dating market's like these days. It's like swimming in a sea of sharks. I've been on two dozen dates and they've all been disasters. Women aren't like they used to be."

"No, we have fangs now."

"And no one wants to date a cop. They all seem to think we've got control issues."

"Well, you definitely do. You let Alice control *you.*"

"No, I don't."

"It's probably why she bounced back into your life, because she knows she can wrap you around her little finger." Jane leaned forward, intent on saving him from a mistake that would break his heart. "You can do better, really you can. You're a nice guy; you're smart. You're gonna get a *great* pension."

"Stop it. You always think you know better." Frost, usually so pasty-faced, had flushed an indignant red. "Why are we talking about Alice anyway? We were discussing *Body Snatchers.*"

"Yeah, yeah." She sighed. "The movie."

"The point is, it *was* on TV last night, just like Mrs. Coyle said, so she's telling the truth. And why would she kill her stepdaughter?"

"Because they hated each other?"

"When her husband wakes up, he'll confirm the alibi."

"Back to Alice. You do remember how much she hurt you? I don't want to see that happen again."

"That's it. We're done talking about this." Frost crumpled his sandwich wrappings and got to his feet. Suddenly his head snapped up as the hospital's paging system announced: *Code Blue, Room 715. Code Blue, Room 715.*

Frost turned to Jane. "Seven one five? Isn't that . . ."

Matthew Coyle's room.

She was right behind Frost as they dashed out of the cafeteria. *Seven floors. Too far to climb.* She slapped the elevator button once, twice. When the door slid open, she almost collided with a nurse stepping out.

"I thought he was gonna be okay," said Frost as the elevator whooshed up to the seventh floor.

"A heart attack is never okay. And we never finished interviewing him."

The door opened and a young woman in a scrub suit sprinted past, headed to Room 715. Through the open doorway, Jane could not see the patient, only the scrum of personnel crowded around his bed, an impenetrable wall of blue scrub suits.

"Vasopressin's not working," a woman called out.

"Okay, let's go again. Two hundred joules."

"I'm shocking on three. Everybody clear! One. Two. *Three!*"

Jane heard a thump. Tense seconds passed as all eyes turned to the cardiac monitor.

"Okay, we've got a rhythm! Sinus tach."

"And a BP. Ninety over sixty."

“Excuse me,” a voice said behind Jane. “Are you the patient’s family?”

Jane turned to see a nurse eyeing them. “We’re with Boston PD. This patient is a witness in a homicide case.”

“Please move away from the room.”

“What happened?” said Jane.

“Let the doctors do their jobs.”

As the nurse herded them back into the hallway, Jane caught a glimpse of Matthew Coyle’s bare foot. Against the white sheets, it was alarmingly blue and mottled. Then the door swung shut and that limp foot vanished from sight.

“Is he going to be okay?” Frost asked.

The nurse looked at the closed door and gave the only answer she could. “I don’t know.”

SEVEN

BLUE EYES IS STILL ASLEEP WHEN I CLIMB OUT of his bed the next morning. Our clothes are scattered all over the floor where we shed them, my blouse and his shirt by the door, my pants midway across the room, my bra coiled up like a lacy pink cobra by the nightstand. I gather up my clothes and purse and tiptoe into the bathroom. It's just the sort of bathroom a man would design, with stark black tiles and a chrome-and-glass shower. There's no tub in sight; men just don't seem to value a good long soak in a bathtub. I pee into the sleek Numi toilet and wash my face and brush my teeth at the white-onyx sink. I always carry a spare toothbrush in my purse, for just such impromptu sleepovers, although I can't remember the last time I spent the whole night in a man's bed. Usually I'm up and on my way before dawn. I must have been tired last night.

Or maybe it was the two bottles of Rioja we drank.

I see the aftermath in the mirror: my puffy eyes, my scarecrow hair. I wet my hair and smooth it down into a semblance of my usual black bob. As disheveled as I am, I also look sated and thoroughly content, something I haven't felt in a long time. *Thank you, Blue Eyes.*

I open the medicine cabinet and survey the contents. Band-Aids, aspirin, SPF-30 sunscreen, and cough syrup. There are also two prescription pill bottles, which I take out for closer inspection. Vicodin and Valium, both prescribed for back pain. The bottles are two years old and each still contains about a dozen tablets, which tells me that he hasn't been bothered by back pain recently.

He won't notice if a few pills go missing.

I shake out four of each and slip them into my pocket. I'm no addict, but when the opportunity presents itself, why not avail myself of free pharmaceuticals that might come in useful someday? He's obviously not in dire need of them. I replace the childproof caps and eye the name on the bottles. *Everett J. Prescott.* What a Brahmin-sounding name, surely someone who has a long and distinguished bloodline. Last night we never bothered to exchange full names. He has no idea what my last name is, which is for the best, since the chances are we'll never see each other again.

I get dressed in the bathroom and tiptoe back into the bedroom to put on my shoes. He sleeps through it all, one bare arm flung across the sheets. For a moment I pause to admire his arm, with its lean and sculpted muscles. They aren't the overly bulging biceps of a gym rat; these look like honest muscles built with real labor. Last night he told me he was a landscape architect, and I picture him building stone walls and hauling bales of peat, even though I doubt that's what landscape architects actually do. A shame I'll never get to find out.

It's well past time for me to leave. I want to be long gone when he wakes up. This is the way I've always handled the morning after, because I'm no fan of awkward goodbyes and halfhearted promises of second dates. I usually break them anyway. This is the reason why I never bring men home to my own apartment. If they don't know where I live, they can't come knocking on my door.

But something about Everett makes me reconsider my love-'em-and-leave-'em strategy. It's not just the fact he was an extremely attentive lover, who was so eager to please my every whim, or that he's easy on the eyes and he laughs at all my jokes. No, there's something more to him: a depth, a sincerity that I seldom encounter in other people.

Or maybe I'm just feeling that old oxytocin rush you get after a good and thorough fucking.

Outside on the street, I look back at the red-brick townhouse. It's a handsome building and no doubt historic, in a neighborhood that I could never afford to live in. Everett must be doing very well indeed, and for a moment I reconsider my decision to walk away so precipitously. Maybe I should have lingered a little longer. Maybe I should have told him my phone number, or at least my last name.

Then I think of the downside. The invasion of my

privacy. His inevitable expectations. The phone calls, ever more insistent, the clinging, the jealousy.

No, it's better just to walk away.

But as I do, I commit his address to memory, so I'll always know where to find him. Because you never know: A man like Everett Prescott might come in useful someday.

EIGHT

"HOW LONG DID THEY WORK TO RESUSCITATE him?" said Maura as she cut through the ribs of Cassandra Coyle. Jane winced at the snap of the bone shears as Maura kept cutting, *crack crack crack,* like a carpenter in her workshop. The rib cage that had protected Cassandra's heart and lungs was now just a bony palisade blocking their view of the secrets within, and Maura worked quickly and efficiently to clear away the barrier of ribs and breastplate.

"It took them about fifteen, twenty minutes," said Jane. "But they got his heart beating again. I called the hospital this morning and he's still alive. For now."

Maura snapped another rib, and Jane saw Frost grimace at the sound of cracking bone. While the sights and smells of the morgue were familiar territory for Maura, this room would always be no-man's-land to Frost, whose delicate stomach was legendary in the homicide unit. Cassandra Coyle was one of the fresher corpses they'd encountered, only a day old when she'd been discovered, but odors bloom quickly in a dead body at room temperature. Frost was getting enough of a whiff to make his face blanch, and he raised his arm to block the smell.

"Statistics show that you have about a forty percent chance of surviving a cardiac arrest in the hospital. A twenty percent chance of eventually leaving the hospital alive," said Maura, matter-of-factly quoting statistics as she cut through the last few ribs. "Is he awake yet?"

"No. He's still comatose."

"Then I'm afraid his prognosis is poor. Even if Mr. Coyle does survive, he probably suffered anoxic brain damage."

"Meaning he could be a vegetable."

"Unfortunately, that's a possible outcome."

The ribs were now split, and Maura pried up the breastplate. Frost backed away as the stench of body fluids rose from the exposed cavity, but Maura simply leaned closer to peer at the thoracic organs.

"These lungs look edematous. Heavy with fluid." Maura reached for a scalpel.

"And what does that tell us?" asked Frost, voice muffled.

"It's a nonspecific finding. It could mean a number of things." Maura glanced up and said to her assistant, "Yoshima, could you make sure the drug and tox screen is expedited?"

"Already done," Yoshima said, always the calm voice of efficiency. "I ordered both an AxSYM and

Toxi-Lab A, plus GC-MS for quantitation. That should cover pretty much every known drug."

Rooting deep inside the thorax, Maura lifted out the dripping lungs. "These are definitely heavy. I see no obvious lesions, only a few petechiae. Again, a non-specific finding." She placed the severed heart on a tray and, with gloved fingers, traced the coronary arteries. "Interesting."

"Aw, you say that to every corpse," said Jane.

"Because every corpse tells a story, but this one isn't revealing any secrets. The neck dissection and X-rays were normal. Her hyoid bone is intact. And look how clean her coronaries are, with no evidence of thrombosis or infarction. This was a perfectly healthy heart in what seems to be a perfectly healthy young woman."

A woman who looked lean and fit and certainly capable of putting up a good fight, thought Jane. Yet Cassandra Coyle had no torn fingernails, no bruises on her hands, nothing to indicate she'd offered any resistance whatsoever against her attacker.

Maura moved on to the abdomen. Methodically, she excised liver and spleen, pancreas and intestines, but it was the stomach she was most interested in. She lifted it out as gingerly as if she were delivering a newborn and set it on the dissection tray. This was the part of the postmortem that Jane always quailed from. Whatever the victim had last eaten would now be two days old, a putrid stew of stomach acid and partly digested food. Both she and Frost retreated a few paces as Maura picked up the scalpel. Above his paper mask, Frost's eyes narrowed in anticipation of the stench.

But when Maura sliced open the stomach, all that dribbled out was purplish liquid.

"Do you smell that?" Maura asked.

"I'd rather not," said Jane.

"I think it's wine. Judging by how dark it is, I'm guessing something heavy like a cabernet or a zinfandel."

"What, you're not gonna tell us the vintage? What about the label?" Jane snorted. "You're slipping, Maura."

Maura probed the stomach cavity. "I don't see any food in here, which means she hadn't eaten anything for at least a few hours before she died." Maura looked up. "Did you find open wine bottles in her apartment?"

"No," said Frost. "And there were no dirty wineglasses on the counter or in the sink."

"Maybe she had a drink somewhere else," said Jane. "You think she met her killer at a bar?"

"It would have been *just* before getting home. Liquids pass pretty quickly into the jejunum, yet she still has wine in her stomach."

Frost said, "She left her film studio around six P.M. It's only a ten-minute walk to her residence. I'll check the bars in the area."

Maura emptied the scant stomach contents into a specimen jar, then moved to the corpse's head. There she stood frowning at Cassandra Coyle's empty eye sockets. She had already examined the enucleated globes, which were now soaking in a jar of preservative, like two grotesque olives bobbing in gin.

"So she stops somewhere to have a glass of wine," said Jane, trying to piece together the sequence of events. "Then she brings her killer home. Or he follows her there. But what happens next? How did he kill her?"

Maura didn't answer. Instead, she once again picked up the scalpel. Starting behind one ear, she cut into the scalp and sliced all the way across the top of the head to behind the opposite ear.

How easily the most recognizable feature of a human being can be obliterated, thought Jane, as she watched Maura peel the scalp forward in one limp flap. Cassandra Coyle's pretty face collapsed in a fleshy mask, dyed black hair flopping forward to conceal it like a fringed curtain. The whine of the oscillating saw cut off any conversation, and Jane turned away at the smell of bone dust. The skull, at least, was impersonal. It could be anyone's cranium being sawed open, anyone's brain about to be exposed.

Maura pried off the cranial cap and revealed the glistening surface of gray matter. Here was what had made Cassandra a unique human being. Stored in this three-pound organ had been every memory, every experience, everything Cassandra had ever known or felt or loved. Gently, Maura lifted the lobes and sliced through nerves and arteries before easing the brain out of its cranial bed. "No obvious hemorrhages," she noted. "No contusions. No edema."

"So it looks normal?" asked Frost.

"Yes, it does. On the surface, at least." Maura gingerly lowered the organ into a bucket of formalin. "This is a young woman with a healthy-looking heart and lungs and brain. She hasn't been strangled. She hasn't been sexually assaulted. There are no bruises, no needle marks, no apparent trauma at all, except for the eyes. And those were removed postmortem."

"Then what happened to her? What killed her?" said Jane.

For a moment Maura didn't answer. Her gaze remained on the brain, submerged in the bucket of formalin. A brain that had offered up no answers. She glanced at Jane and said, "I don't know."

The cell phone buzzed in Jane's pocket. She stripped off her gloves, reached under the protective gown to fish it out, and saw a number she didn't recognize.

"Detective Rizzoli," she answered.

"Hey, sorry I didn't get back to you sooner," a man said. "But I just got home from Boca Raton and, man, I'm sorry I did. This weather sucks."

"Who is this?"

"It's Benny Lima. You know, the Lima Travel Agency? You left a message on my phone last night, asking about my security camera. The one that's pointed toward Utica Street."

"Is your camera operational?"

"Sure is. Last year we caught a kid throwing rocks through the window."

The word *camera* had caught Frost's attention, and he was watching the conversation with sudden interest.

"We need whatever footage you have from Monday night," Jane said. "Do you still have it?"

"It's right here, waiting for you."

NINE

FREEZING RAIN WAS SPITTING FROM THE SKY, and it pricked Jane's face like needles as she and Frost stepped out of their car and dashed across the street to the Lima Travel Agency. They ducked inside, and a bell tinkled as the door slammed shut, announcing their arrival.

"Hello?" Jane called. "Mr. Lima?"

The office appeared deserted. Judging by the dusty plastic philodendron and the faded cruise-ship posters, no one had bothered to redecorate in decades. On the desk computer, the screen saver cycled through seductive photos of tropical beaches, exactly where every Bostonian longed to be on this gray and miserable day.

Somewhere in back, a toilet flushed. A moment later a man waddled out of the rear office. Not merely a man—a mountain of flesh lumbered toward them, with one damp hand already extended in greeting.

"You're the Boston PD folks, right?" He gave Jane a doughy and enthusiastic handshake. "Benny Lima. I would've returned your call earlier, but, like I told you on the phone, I just got back from—"

"Boca," said Jane.

"Yeah. Went down for my uncle Carlo's funeral. Big deal, real big deal. He was like a celebrity in that retirement community down there. Anyways, I didn't hear your voicemail till I got in to the office this morning. I am delighted to help Boston PD in any way I can."

"You said you had security video, Mr. Lima?" asked Frost.

"Yeah. Our system only holds forty-eight hours of footage, but if you need something in that time frame, it should still be there."

"We need whatever was recorded on Monday night."

"Should still be on there. Come on back, let me show you our setup."

Benny led them at a maddeningly leisurely pace to the back office, which was scarcely large enough to hold all three of them. Frost squeezed past Benny's massive bulk and sat down at the computer.

"We had the system installed three years ago, after we had three break-ins in one month. It's not like we keep any cash in the place, but those assholes kept making off with our computers. Camera finally caught one of 'em in the act. Can you believe it—the kid lived right around the corner. What a little shit."

Frost tapped the keyboard, and the view from the surveillance camera appeared onscreen. The camera was pointed toward the entrance to narrow Utica Street, where Cassandra Coyle's residence was located. The view was only partial and not particularly high res, but of all the security cameras in the neighborhood, this was the only one that might have recorded anyone entering or leaving the south end of Utica Street. The video they were now looking at was taken in daylight, with three pedestrians in the frame. According to the time stamp, this was recorded on Monday at 10:00 A.M.

When Cassandra Coyle was still alive.

"That's the very beginning of the recording," said Benny. "As soon as I heard your message, I hit SAVE, so it wouldn't record over what you wanted."

Frost clicked on the FAST-FORWARD icon. "Let's move ahead to Monday evening."

Benny looked at Jane. "Is this about that gal who got murdered down the street? I saw the news on TV. Not the kinda thing that happens in this neighborhood."

"This kind of thing could happen in any neighborhood," said Jane.

"But I've been here forever. My uncle started this travel agency in the seventies, back when folks appreciated a little guidance in their travel planning. We used to book a lot of trips to Hong Kong and Taiwan, what with Chinatown right down the street. Now everyone just goes online and gets whatever crappy deal pops up on their computer. This is a safe neighborhood, and I don't remember any murders around here. I mean, except for that shooting across the way on Knapp Street." He paused. "And that guy who got whacked in the warehouse." Another pause. "And, oh, yeah, there was the time when—"

"Here we go," said Frost.

Jane focused on the screen, where the time stamp now said 5:05 P.M. "You see anything?"

"Not yet," said Frost.

"At that particular time, I was in Boca Raton," Benny said. "Got my airline receipts and everything, in case you want to see them."

Jane did not want to see them. She pulled up a chair next to Frost and sat down. Watching surveillance video was one of those mind-numbing tasks that promised hours of boredom and the occasional adrenaline jolt of *eureka*. According to Cassandra's three colleagues, she had left the Crazy Ruby Films studio at around 6:00 P.M., after spending all day working on the edits of *Mr. Simian*. From the studio, it was only a ten-minute walk home to Utica Street. If she entered Utica from Beach Street, she would have walked right past this camera.

So where was she?

Frost sped up the video, and the minutes ticked by in double time. Cars glided past. Pedestrians moved in and out of the frame in jerky fast-forward. No one turned onto Utica Street.

"Six-thirty," said Frost.

"So she didn't go straight home from work."

"Or we missed her," said Benny, as if he were now part of the team. He was looming right behind Jane, staring over her shoulder. "She could have entered the other end of Utica, from Kneeland Street. In which case my camera wouldn't catch her."

That was not what Jane wanted to hear, but Benny

was right; Cassandra might have entered Utica unseen by this or any camera.

Benny was breathing right on her neck, and his snuffling breaths made her think of winter viruses. She tried to ignore him and stay focused on the video. Monday night had been frigid, only sixteen degrees, and the pedestrians walking past the camera were all dressed for the cold in bulky coats and scarves and hats. If one of the passersby was Cassandra, would they even be able to identify her? As Jane leaned closer, so did Benny, spewing germs on her neck with every breath.

"Mr. Lima, could you do us a *big* favor?" she said.

"Yeah. Sure!"

"I noticed a coffee shop right down the street. My partner and I could really use some coffee right now."

"Whaddya want? Lattes? Cappuccinos? They got all kinds."

She dug a twenty-dollar bill out of her purse and handed it to him. "Black with sugar. For both of us."

"You got it." He pulled on a down coat that was so massive, he looked like a cumulus cloud rolling toward the door. "Happy to be of service to Boston PD!"

Don't hurry back, she thought, as the door swung shut behind him.

On the computer screen, the video time stamp advanced to 8:10 and the parade of pedestrians slowly thinned out. By now Cassandra should have made it home, which meant she'd entered Utica Street from the other direction. *Damn it, we missed her.*

"Bingo," Frost suddenly said.

Jane snapped to attention, her eyes back on the

screen, where Frost had captured an image in freeze-frame.

Two figures were fused into a single silhouette, caught just as they were turning onto Utica Street. Though Jane could not see the faces, it was clear by the height and width of the shoulders that the taller one was a man. The smaller figure seemed to be leaning into him, her head resting on his shoulder. Jane stared at the two-headed figure, trying to make out any identifying features, but the faces were obscured by darkness.

"Cassandra was five foot six. If that's her, then the man's got to be at least six feet tall," she said.

"This was at eight-fifteen P.M.," said Frost. "If she left the studio at six, where's she been? Where did she meet this guy?"

Jane focused on what was slung over one of the man's shoulders: a backpack. She thought of what he might be carrying in that pack. Latex gloves. Surgical instruments. Everything the well-prepared killer needed to perform his bizarre postmortem ritual.

The touch of Benny's hand on her shoulder almost made her jump out of the chair.

"Hey, it's just me! Got your coffees." Benny handed her a cup.

She settled back, heart thumping, and took a gulp of coffee that was so hot she burned her tongue. *Slow down. Take your time.*

"Is that him?" asked Benny.

Jane turned to see him staring at the screen. He, at least, they could eliminate as a suspect. No mere jacket could hide a man as big as a house. "Let's just call him a person of interest."

"And you saw him on my security camera! Cool."

But this glimpse was all too brief, just a shadow of two people flitting across the screen. "Fast-forward," said Jane. "Let's see if we can catch him as he leaves."

The time stamp spun forward—9:00 P.M.;10:00.

At 11:10 P.M., Frost froze the image.

"And there you are," said Jane softly. The man's face was shadowed by his jacket hood, so they could not make out his features. Once again, the backpack was slung over his shoulder.

"He enters Utica Street with the victim at eight-fifteen," said Frost. "Exits at eleven-ten. Three hours later."

Which gave him more than enough time to kill and mutilate. *What else were you doing in her apartment during those three hours? Enjoying the view?* She thought of Cassandra Coyle, so serenely posed in bed, the cause of her death still unknown. A drug, a toxin? How do you talk a victim into swallowing poison? Did Cassandra know that death was being offered to her?

"He doesn't show his face at all," said Frost. "We can't tell his age or his race. All we can assume is, he's a man. Or a *very* big woman."

"There's something else we know," said Jane.

"What?"

"This was no stranger." Jane looked at Frost. "She brought him home with her."

TEN

CASSANDRA COYLE'S FUNERAL WAS A WAR ZONE.

From her seat in the sixth pew of St. Ann's Church, Jane watched the poisonous looks fly back and forth like arrows between the enemy camps of Matthew Coyle's ex-wife, Elaine, and his current wife, Priscilla. In the pew behind Jane, women were gossiping about the second wife, and none too quietly.

"Look at her. Pretending like she actually cared about the poor girl."

"What on earth did Matthew ever see in her?"

"Her money, of course. What else? She's all plastic, from her face to her credit cards."

"Poor Elaine. Having to sit in the same church with her on such an awful day."

Jane glanced back to see two women in their fifties, their heads bent together, united in disapproval. Like Matthew Coyle's first wife, Elaine, they no doubt belonged to the sisterhood of wives who both feared and despised women like Priscilla, who swooped in and snatched away weak-willed husbands. That sisterhood had shown up today in full force, and some openly glared as Priscilla stood up to address the gathering of mourners. For this very public funeral, Priscilla had spared no expense, and her stepdaughter's coffin was crafted from gleaming rosewood and adorned with a lavish spray of white gladiolus. She stopped to touch the closed coffin, a theatrical pause that made even Jane cringe, and then moved to the microphone.

"Most of you have probably heard that Matthew can't be here with us today," said Priscilla. "I know he wants to be, but he's in the hospital, recovering from the shock of losing his wonderful daughter. So I must be the one to speak for both of us. We have lost—the world has lost—a beautiful and talented young woman. And our hearts are broken."

A snort erupted behind Jane, loud enough to be heard across the aisle, where Frost was sitting among the Team Priscilla mourners. She saw Frost give a disbelieving shake of the head and she wondered about the comments he was hearing from Priscilla's allies, who now aimed dark looks at the woman who'd just snorted.

"I first met Cassie when she was only six years old. She was a shy and skinny girl, all legs and long hair," continued Priscilla. If she'd heard the undercurrent of disapproval in the room, she steadfastly ignored it. She also avoided looking at the front pew, where her rival, Elaine, was sitting.

"Even though we were still new to each other, Cassie wrapped her little arms around me and gave me a hug.

And she said, 'Now I have another mommy.' That's the moment I knew we were going to be a real family."

"Bullshit," muttered the woman behind Jane.

A young woman lay dead in her coffin, her father was gravely ill in the hospital, and this was how the Coyle family grieved, with resentment and rage. Jane had seen it before, at other victims' funerals. Murder strikes without warning, and it leaves no chance to settle feuds or say goodbyes. It leaves conversations forever unfinished, and here was the result: a family that would always be split by loss.

Priscilla sat down and a familiar trio stood up to speak next. Cassandra's filmmaker colleagues had managed to clean up reasonably well, with both men now dressed in dark suits and ties. While Amber was somberly garbed in a black dress, her gold nose ring glinted startlingly bright under the altar lights. They looked like three dazed explorers who'd somehow wandered into the gathering and weren't quite sure how to blend in.

Amber was obviously too upset to say a word, and Ben simply stared down at his Reeboks. It was Travis Chang who spoke for all of them as he nervously blinked in the spotlight.

"We were the Four Musketeers, and Cassie was our D'Artagnan," said Travis. "She was a fighter, a leader. A storyteller who could spin gold out of childhood trauma. That was our Cassandra. The four of us met in a filmmaking class in NYU, where we learned that the most powerful stories emerge from the most painful episodes of our lives. We were in the process of bringing one of those stories to film, when we lost her." Travis's voice broke. As he paused to recover, Amber took his hand and Ben dropped his head even lower.

"If what we learned in that film class is true," said Travis, "if pain is what brings forth the best stories, then one *hell* of a story is coming out of this. Losing her is more pain than the three of us know what to do with. But we swear we'll finish what you started, Cass. This movie is your story and your baby. We won't let you down."

They left the podium and returned to their pew.

For a moment no one stood up to speak.

In the prolonged hush, the sudden creak of the pew seemed all the louder as Elaine Coyle rose to her feet. Today Cassandra's mother looked far more formidable than she had four days ago, when Jane and Frost had interviewed her and the shock of her daughter's death had left her barely able to speak above a whisper. Now she moved with grim resolve to the podium and stood for a moment, surveying the audience. Unlike Priscilla, whose face had been nipped and tucked into a sleek but plastic version of eternal youth, Elaine wore her age without apology, and she was all the more impressive because of it. Her upswept hair was streaked with gray and her face was etched by the passage of fifty-eight years, but she radiated strength.

And bitterness.

"My daughter didn't suffer fools gladly," she said. "She chose as her friends only people she believed in, and she returned their loyalty a thousandfold." She looked at the three young filmmakers. "Thank you, Travis and Ben and Amber, for being my daughter's friends. You know the obstacles that Cassie overcame. When the going got tough, *you* stood by her. Unlike some people who have no sense of loyalty. Who walk away from their responsibilities at the first whiff of temptation." Elaine's gaze shifted to Priscilla, and her eyes hardened.

Behind Jane, the Team Elaine women gave murmurs of approval.

"If Cassie were here, she'd tell you what real love is. She'd tell you it means not walking away from a child who's only six years old. You can't make up for that betrayal by throwing money and gifts at her. The child always knows. The child never forgets."

"God, can't somebody stop this?" a man whispered.

Priscilla stood up and walked out of the church.

It was the minister who gently took control of the situation. He stepped up to the podium, and the live microphone caught their murmurs.

"Shall we move on to the next speaker, my dear?"

"No. I still have something to say," Elaine insisted.

"But perhaps there's a better time for this? Please, let me help you back to your seat."

"No, I—" Elaine suddenly wobbled. Her face went white and she reached out to clutch the podium.

"Help! Can someone help me?" the minister pleaded as he tried to catch her beneath the arms. He was still holding on as Elaine's legs slid out from under her and she crumpled to the floor.

ELAINE SAT IN THE MINISTER'S office, sipping a cup of heavily sugared tea. Her color was back, and so was her steeliness; she'd refused the ambulance and decisively shut down any talk of a visit to the emergency room. Instead, she sat grim-faced and rigid as the minister scurried to refill the teapot with hot water. Behind her loomed a bookcase filled with volumes about compassion and faith and charity, none of which could be read in Elaine's eyes.

"It's been a week now," said Elaine, looking at Jane and Frost. "And you still have no idea who killed my daughter?"

"We're following every lead, ma'am," said Jane.

"What have you found out?"

"Well, we've learned that you have a very complicated family." *And there's nothing like seeing it in all its brutal glory.* Jane pulled up a chair and sat down so she was eye-to-eye with Elaine. "I have to say, you were pretty rough on Priscilla."

"She deserves it. What else can you say about a woman who steals your husband?"

"I'd say the husband had something to do with it."

"Oh, they both did. Do you know how it happened?"

I'm not sure I want to know.

"Matthew was her CPA. Did her taxes, kept track of all her various accounts. He knew how much she was worth. He knew she could give him the good life. When he started flying out of town on business trips, I had no idea that he was jetting off with *her.* There I was, at home with poor little Cassie, and it was an awful time for us to be left alone. A little girl had just been kidnapped in the neighborhood, and all the families were rattled, but did he give a damn? No. He was too busy chasing after that rich piece of ass."

The minister froze, steaming kettle poised over the teapot. Red-faced, he turned away.

Elaine looked at Jane. "You've spoken to her. I bet she gave you a completely different version of the story."

"She told us that your marriage was already in trouble," said Jane.

"Of course she'd say that. Home-wreckers always do."

Jane sighed. "We're not family counselors, ma'am. We're just trying to find your daughter's killer. Do you think Cassie's death might have something to do with the various conflicts in your family?"

"I know they hated each other."

"Your daughter hated Priscilla?"

"Another woman swoops in and steals your daddy. Try to imagine how that would feel. Wouldn't *you* hate her?"

It wasn't at all hard to imagine. Jane thought of her own father, who'd had a brief fling with a woman they now referred to as the Bimbo. She thought of how that affair had broken Angela's heart. Now that Frank's fling had ended and he had returned home, could those broken pieces ever really be put back together?

"If you're looking for a suspect who hated my daughter," said Elaine, "you should take a good long look at Priscilla."

"Is there anyone else we should be focused on?" said Frost. "A lot of people attended the funeral service today. Did you recognize most of them?"

"Why are you asking?"

"Because sometimes a killer will insinuate himself into the investigation. He'll attend the funeral to see the effects on a victim's family. He'll ask a lot of questions to find out if the police are on the right track."

The minister stared at Frost. "You think the killer might have been *here*? In my church?"

"It's always a possibility, sir. That's why we placed the surveillance camera at the entrance, to record the faces of everyone who walked in. If the killer was here, he could be on video." Frost looked at Elaine. "Did you see anyone who seemed out of place? Who didn't belong?"

"Aside from Priscilla's awful crowd?" Elaine shook her head. "I know most of the people. Cassie's classmates. A few old friends from Brookline, where she grew up. So many people loved her and came to pay their respects." She stared down at her cold tea with a frown of distaste. "Thank God I didn't have to see *him.*"

"Who?"

"Matthew. I hear he's in a coma and his prognosis isn't good." She set down her teacup with a triumphant clack. "If he does die, that's one funeral I *won't* be attending."

"THERE'S NOTHING AS WONDERFUL AS a big happy family, hey, Frost?" said Jane as they drove back to Boston PD, Jane at the wheel. "Her daughter's been murdered, her ex-husband is on life support, and she can't stop ragging on about the evil second wife. I thought Priscilla was a piece of work, but this lady?"

"Yeah, she's *epic.* How do you stay bitter at an ex for so long? I mean, it's been, what? Nineteen years since their divorce."

Jane pulled to a stop at a red light and looked at Frost, who had suffered through his own painful divorce, yet he'd never seemed bitter about it. Now he was back to watching movies and eating pizza with his ex-wife. If anyone lacked the gene for holding a grudge, it was Frost, whose legendary congeniality only served to make Jane look bad. The problem with being congenial was that people walked all over you. Growing up with two brothers had taught Jane that a swift kick to the shin generally worked faster than saying *pretty please.*

"You're not even a little bit mad at Alice?" she asked.

"Why are we back to talking about Alice?"

"Seeing as we're on the topic of angry exes."

"Well, I *am* mad," he admitted. "A little."

"A little?"

"But what good does it do to walk around angry all your life? It's not healthy. You've got to forgive and move on, like your mom did. She bounced back, right?"

"Yeah. The trouble is, my dad bounced back too. Straight back into her life."

"Isn't that a good thing, having them together again?"

"Come to the Rizzoli Christmas Eve dinner. You can see for yourself how well it's working out between them."

"Is that like a threat or an invitation?"

"My mom keeps asking when you're coming to dinner again. You're like the *nice* son she never had, and she'll always have a soft spot for you, after you changed her flat tire. You might as well come, because there's gonna be so much food. I'm talking *crazy* amounts of food."

"Geez, I would come, but I've got plans Christmas Eve."

"Don't tell me." She looked at him. "Alice?"

"Yeah."

Jane sighed. "Okay. I guess you can bring her."

"You see? *That's* why I can't bring Alice to dinner. She's really sensitive about your attitude toward her."

"I have an attitude because of what she did to you. I hate seeing you get hurt. And if she does it again, I'm gonna come over and kick her butt."

"And *that's* why I'm not bringing her to dinner. But tell your mom hi for me, okay? She's a nice lady."

Jane pulled into the Boston PD parking lot and shut off the engine. "Wish I could find an excuse not to show up. The way things are going between Mom and Dad, it's not gonna be a fun night."

"Well, you've got no choice. They're your family, and it's Christmas Eve."

"Yeah." Jane snorted. "Ho ho ho."

ELEVEN

"SO WHAT'S THE DEAL WITH THE GIRL WHO got her eyeballs scooped out?"

Jane frowned across the dining table at her brother Frankie, who was carving a generous slice off the roast leg of lamb. Their mother had spent all day in the kitchen, laboring over the meal that was now spread out in full glory on the Rizzoli family table. The leg of lamb was studded with garlic cloves and roasted to a perfect medium rare. Surrounding it were bowls of crisp rosemary potatoes, green beans with almonds, three different salads, and homemade dinner rolls. Angela sat at the end of the table, her face shiny with sweat from the kitchen, waiting for her family to compliment the magnificent feast she'd laid out for them.

But, no, Frankie had to go *there,* straight to murder, and he did it while slicing his meat, releasing a river of blood-tinged juices.

"This isn't the time or place, Frankie," Jane muttered.

"Angela, this meal is amazing," said Gabriel, as always the considerate son-in-law. "Every Christmas you manage to top yourself!"

"It's been more than a week," said Frankie, undeterred. "That's way past the first forty-eight." He turned to their father, Frank, and said, with an air of authority, "In case you haven't heard the term, Dad, the first forty-eight hours after a murder is when it's most likely to get solved. And it sounds like Boston PD doesn't even have a suspect yet."

Grimly, Jane cut up potatoes and green beans for her three-year-old daughter, Regina. "You know I can't talk about the case."

"Sure you can. We're all family here. Besides, it's been all over the news, what the perp did to that girl."

"First, that particular detail about her eyeballs was not supposed to be made public. Someone leaked it, and I'm trying to find out who the hell it was. Second, she was not a *girl.* She was twenty-six years old, and that makes her a woman."

"Yeah, yeah. You keep ragging on about that."

"And you keep ignoring it." She turned to Angela. "Ma, this roast turned out perfect. How did you get it to be so tender?"

"It's all in the marinade, Janie. I gave you the recipe last year, remember?"

"I'll have to find it. But it'll never turn out as good as yours."

"Carving out a girl's eyeballs, that's gotta have some deep psychological meaning," said Frankie, the all-knowing authority about everything. "Makes you wonder what the symbolism is. This guy must have an issue with the way girls—excuse me, *women*—look at him."

Jane laughed. "So you think you're a profiler now?"

"Janie," Frank, Sr., said, "your brother has every right to his opinion."

"About something he knows nothing about?"

"I know what I heard," said Frankie.

"And that would be?"

"The victim's eyes were cut out and the perp left the eyeballs in her hand."

Angela slapped down her knife and fork. "It's Christmas Eve. Do we have to talk about such horrible things?"

"This is their job," said Jane's father, shoveling potatoes into his mouth. "We gotta learn to deal with it."

"Since when is it Frankie's job?" said Jane.

"Since he started taking all those criminology courses over at Bunker Hill. You're his sister; you should encourage him. You can give him a leg up when it comes time for him to apply."

"But I'm not applying to Boston PD," said Frankie with a maddening note of superiority. "I'm already at stage three in the SASS. It's looking good, real good."

Jane frowned. "What's the SASS?"

"Your hubby knows." Frankie glanced over at Gabriel.

Up till now, Gabriel had occupied himself slicing Regina's meat into bite-size pieces. With a look of resignation, he answered, "It stands for Special Agent Selection System."

"Cool, huh?" said Frank, Sr., slapping his son on the back. "Our Frankie here's gonna be an FBI agent."

"Now, hold on, Pop," said Frankie, modestly raising both hands in protest. "It's still early in the process. I passed the first exam. Next I go for the meet and greet. That's where having my brother-in-law in the agency is gonna work in my favor. Right, Gabe?"

"It can't hurt" was Gabriel's noncommittal answer. He turned to Angela. "May I have some more green beans? Regina's gobbling them all up."

"That's why I want to keep track of current investigations," said Frankie. "Like this gal who got her eyes cut out. I want to watch how the case is handled at the local level."

"Well, Frankie," said Jane, "I don't think I have much to teach you. Seeing as I just work at the *local* level."

"What kinda attitude is that?" her father snapped. "Frankie's not good enough to be in your club?"

"It's not a matter of *good enough,* Dad. It's an active investigation. I can't talk about it."

"Did your creepy friend do the autopsy?" asked Frankie.

"What?"

"I hear the cops call her the Queen of the Dead."

"Who told you that?"

"I got my sources." Frankie grinned at their father. "Wouldn't mind a night in the morgue with *her.*"

Angela shoved her chair back and stood up. "Why do I even bother to cook? Next time I'm just gonna order pizza." She pushed through the swinging door, into the kitchen.

"Eh, don't worry about her. She'll be fine," said Frank, Sr. "Give her a few minutes to cool down."

Jane slapped down her fork. "Way to go, you two."

"What?" said her father.

"You and Mom just got back together. And this is the way you treat her?"

"What's the problem?" said her brother. "It's the way they've always been."

"And that makes it okay, does it?" Jane dropped her napkin and stood up.

"Now you're leaving the table too?" said her father.

"Someone's gotta help Ma poison the dessert."

In the kitchen, Jane found Angela standing by the sink, pouring herself a generous glass of wine.

"Want to share the bottle?" asked Jane.

"No. I think I deserve the whole damn thing." Angela took a desperate gulp. "It's back to the old days, Janie. Nothing's changed."

You've changed. The old Angela would have shrugged off her husband's thoughtless comments and soldiered on through dinner. But for this new Angela, those comments must have felt like a thousand small cuts to her soul. And here she was, trying to medicate the pain with Chianti.

"You sure you want to drink alone?" said Jane.

"Oh, all right. Here, join me," said Angela, and she filled a glass for Jane. They both gulped and sighed.

"You cooked a really wonderful meal, Mom."

"I know."

"Dad knows it too. He just doesn't know how to express his appreciation."

They took another sip. And Angela asked softly, "Have you seen Vince lately?"

Jane paused, startled by the mention of Vince Korsak, the retired cop who had made Angela briefly, deliriously happy. Until Frank returned to reclaim his wife. Until Angela's Catholic guilt and sense of duty forced her to end the affair with Korsak.

Frowning into her wine, Jane said, "Yeah, I see Vince every so often. Usually eating lunch at Doyle's."

"How does he look?"

"The same," she lied. The truth was, Vince Korsak looked miserable. He looked like a man determined to eat and drink himself to death.

"Is he . . . seeing anyone new?"

"I don't know, Ma. Vince and I haven't had a chance to talk much."

"I wouldn't blame him if he was seeing someone. He has a right to move on, but . . ." Angela set down her glass. "Oh, God, I think I made a mistake. I shouldn't have let him go, and now it's too late."

The kitchen door swung open and Jane's brother lumbered in. "Hey, Dad wants to know what's for dessert."

"Dessert?" Angela quickly wiped her eyes and turned to the refrigerator. She pulled out a carton of ice cream and handed it to Frankie. "There."

"Is this it?"

"What, you expected Baked Alaska?"

"Okay, okay. Just wondering."

"I got chocolate syrup too. Go scoop it out for everyone."

He started to leave the kitchen, then turned back to

Angela. "Ma, it's really good to have everything back to normal. You and Dad, I mean. It's the way things are supposed to be."

"Sure, Frankie," sighed Angela. "The way things should be."

Jane's cell phone rang. She dug it out of her pocket, took one look at the caller's number, and answered crisply: "Detective Rizzoli."

To Jane's annoyance, Frankie watched her conversation with eagle eyes, Mr. Would-be Special Agent ready to insinuate himself into the case. "I'll be right there," she said, and hung up. She looked at Angela. "I'm sorry, Ma. I have to leave."

"You got another case?" said Frankie. "What is it?"

"You really want to know?"

"Yeah!"

"Read tomorrow's paper."

"IS IT JUST ME, OR does it seem like we always get the weird ones?" said Frost.

They stood shivering on the pier at Jeffries Point, where the wind blowing in across the inner harbor felt like icicles piercing her face. She pulled up her scarf to cover her already numb nose. Only four days into what was officially winter, and already there were thin cakes of ice bobbing in the harbor. At nearby Logan Airport, a jet lifted into the sky, and the roar of its engines briefly drowned out the rhythmic slap of water on the pilings.

"All homicides are weird in their own ways," said Jane.

"This is not how I wanted to spend Christmas Eve. I had to leave Alice just as things were starting to get cozy." He stared down at the reason why he and Jane had been pulled away from their holiday meals to meet up at this desolate spot. "At least the cause of death shouldn't be hard to figure out on this one."

Under the glare of their flashlights lay a young white man, his bare chest exposed to the winter wind. He was otherwise well dressed, in wool slacks, an ostrich belt, and leather wing-tip shoes. Nice-looking fellow, maybe in his mid-twenties, thought Jane. Clean-shaven and well groomed, with a trendy haircut that featured a blond swoop of a forelock. He had no dirt under his fingernails, no calluses on his hands. Someone you might find working in a downtown business office.

Not lying shirtless on a windswept pier with three arrows protruding from his chest.

Approaching headlights made Jane turn as a Lexus pulled up behind the parked police cruiser. Maura Isles stepped out, her long coat flaring like a cape in the wind. She was dressed all in winter black: boots, slacks, turtleneck. Appropriate attire for Boston's Queen of the Dead.

"Merry Christmas," said Jane. "Got you a special present."

Maura didn't answer; her attention was focused on the young man lying at their feet. She pulled off her wool gloves, stuffed them in her pocket. The purple latex gloves she donned instead would be no protection in this wind, and before frostbite could set in, she quickly crouched down and studied the arrows. All three had entered the front of the chest, two on the left side of the sternum, one on the right. All three had pierced so deeply that only half the shafts were visible.

"Looks like someone got a brand-new bow and arrow for Christmas," said Jane. "And used this poor guy for target practice."

"What's the story here?" asked Maura.

"Security guard making his rounds found the victim. He swears the body wasn't here three hours ago when he last came by. It's a remote spot, so no security cameras in the area. I'm guessing witnesses are going to be hard to find, especially on Christmas Eve."

"These look like standard aluminum arrows, all with the same orange fletchings. You can probably buy these in any sporting-goods store," said Maura. "They entered at slightly different angles. I don't see any other wounds . . ."

"And that seems weird to me," said Frost.

Jane laughed. "That's the only thing that seems weird to you?"

"The guy gets shot with three arrows, all in the front of his chest. It takes a second or two to nock an arrow in the bow. Meanwhile, wouldn't you think this guy would turn and run? It's like he just stood there and let someone shoot him three times in the chest."

"I don't think these arrows killed him," said Maura.

"At least one of those arrows should have pierced a lung or something."

"Certainly, based on their locations. But look how little blood there is from any of these wounds. Shine your lights here." As Jane and Frost aimed their flashlights at the torso, Maura reached under the right armpit and pressed gloved fingers into the skin. "There's already some faint lividity in the right axilla, and it appears fixed." She stepped around to the other side of the body to examine the opposite armpit. "But there's no lividity on the left. Help me roll him onto his side. I want to get a better look at his back."

Jane and Frost both squatted beside the body. Careful not to dislodge any of the arrows, they logrolled the corpse onto its right side. Through Jane's latex gloves, the flesh felt cold, like chilled meat pulled straight from the refrigerator. Eyes stinging in the wind, she squinted down at the exposed back, now illuminated by Maura's flashlight.

"Has this body been repositioned since it was found?" asked Maura.

"Security guard says he didn't even touch it. Why?"

"Do you see how the lividity is only on the right side of the torso? Gravity made the blood settle there because he was lying on his right side for at least a few hours after death. Yet here he's lying supine."

"So he was killed somewhere else. Maybe brought here in the trunk of a car."

"The pattern of livor mortis would suggest that." Maura reached down to flex the arm. "Rigor mortis is just starting in the limbs. I would estimate time of death somewhere between two and six hours ago."

"Then he's moved here and left on his back." Jane stared down at the three arrows, the orange fletches quivering in the wind. "What's the point of sticking him with arrows, if he was already dead? This is some weird symbolic shit."

"It could be a rage killing," said Maura. "The perp

didn't get enough of an emotional release when he killed this man. So he killed him again and again, by piercing him with arrows."

"Or maybe the arrows *mean* something," said Frost. "You know what this makes me think of? Robin Hood. Steal from the rich, give to the poor. His belt's made of ostrich leather, and that's not cheap. This guy looks well off."

"Yet he ends up dead and shirtless on a pier," said Jane. She turned to Maura. "If the arrows didn't kill him, what did?"

At that moment, another jet lifted into the sky from Logan Airport. Maura stood silent, cruiser rack lights flaring blue and white on her face, as she waited for the jet's roar to fade.

"I don't know," she said.

TWELVE

MAURA COULD NOT REMEMBER A CHRISTMAS morning so cold. She stood at her kitchen window, a coffee mug cupped in her hands, looking out at the ice that glazed her backyard. The outdoor thermometer registered six degrees, not accounting for windchill, and the flagstone patio was now as slick as a skating rink. This morning when she'd stepped out to pick up her newspaper, she'd slipped on the front walkway and almost fallen, and her back muscles still ached from twisting around to catch herself. This was not a day to leave the house, and she was grateful she didn't have to. Today her colleague Abe Bristol was on call for the ME's office, and she could spend a lazy day catching up on her reading and tonight enjoy a quiet meal alone. Already, a lamb shank was defrosting in the sink and a bottle of amarone waited to be uncorked.

She refilled her coffee cup and sat down at the kitchen table to read *The Boston Globe.* The Christmas Day edition was so thin it was almost not worth paging through it, but this was her morning ritual whenever she had a day off: two cups of coffee, an English muffin, and the newspaper. A real newspaper, not pixels glaring from a laptop. She ignored the gray tabby, who kept mewing and rubbing against her ankles, demanding his second breakfast. A month ago, she'd adopted the greedy animal after finding it wandering at a crime scene, and not a day went by that she didn't regret bringing the Beast home. Now it was too late; the cat belonged to her. Or she belonged to the cat. Sometimes it was hard to tell who owned whom.

She nudged the Beast away with her foot and turned to a new page of the *Globe.* Last night's discovery of the body on the pier had not yet made it into the newspaper, but she saw an update on Cassandra Coyle's murder.

Cause of Woman's Death Remains Unknown

The death of a young woman found last Tuesday has been called "suspicious" by investigators. Cassandra Coyle, age 26, was found at home by her father after she failed to show up at a luncheon date. An autopsy was performed on Wednesday, but the medical examiner's office has not yet determined the cause of death. . . .

The cat jumped onto the table and sat down on the newspaper, its rump planted squarely on the article.

"Thank you for your comment," Maura said, and dropped the Beast back on the floor. It gave her a parting look of disdain and strutted out of the kitchen. So this is what it's come to, she thought. I'm now talking to my cat. When had she turned into another lonely cat lady, ruled by a feline? She didn't have to be alone on Christmas. She could have driven up to Maine and visited her seventeen-year-old ward, Julian, at his boarding school. She could have thrown a holiday party for her neighbors, or volunteered at a soup kitchen, or accepted any number of invitations to dinner.

I could have called Daniel.

She thought of the Christmas Eve when she had been so desperate to catch a glimpse of him, even from a distance, that she had slipped into a pew at the back of his church to hear him celebrate the holiday Mass. She, a nonbeliever, had listened to his words about God and love and hope, but their love for each other had led only to heartbreak for them both. On this Christmas morning, as Daniel stood before his congregation, did he scan the pews, hoping to see her again? Or would they grow old in parallel, their lives never again to intersect?

The doorbell rang.

She jerked straight, startled by the sound. She'd been so focused on thoughts of Daniel that of course he was the one she instantly pictured, waiting to see her. Who else would ring her bell on Christmas morning? *Hello, Temptation. Do I dare answer?*

She went to the foyer, took a deep breath, and opened the door.

It was not Daniel but a middle-aged woman who stood on the porch, holding a large cardboard box. Bundled in a puffy down coat and wool scarf, with a knit cap pulled low over her eyebrows, only part of her face was visible. Maura saw tired brown eyes and wind-chapped cheeks. A few wisps of blond hair had escaped the hat and fluttered in the wind.

"Are you Dr. Maura Isles?" the woman asked.

"Yes."

"She asked me to bring this to you." The woman handed the box to Maura. It wasn't heavy, but whatever it contained gave a clatter.

"What is this?" asked Maura.

"I don't know. I was just asked to deliver it to your house. Merry Christmas, ma'am." The woman turned and made her way down the steps, onto the icy walkway.

"Wait. *Who* asked you to bring it?" Maura called out.

The woman did not answer but headed toward a white van that stood idling at the curb. Perplexed, Maura watched the woman climb into the vehicle and drive away.

The bitter cold drove Maura back into the house, and as she nudged the door closed with her foot, she felt the box's contents shift and rattle. She carried it into the living room and set it on the coffee table. The top was sealed with weathered packing tape and there were no labels, nothing to identify to whom it belonged or what it might contain.

She went to the kitchen for a pair of scissors, and when she returned she found that the cat had climbed on the coffee table and was now pawing at the sealed box, eager to crawl inside.

She slit the tape and pulled open the flaps.

Inside was a jumble of random items that might have come from a thrift-store grab bag: An old ladies' wristwatch, the hands frozen at 4:15. A plastic bag with costume jewelry. A patent-leather clutch purse, cracked and peeling. Deeper down were a dozen photographs of people she didn't recognize, posing in various locations. She saw an old farmhouse, a small-town street, a picnic under a tree. Judging by the clothing and hairstyles, these photos had been taken sometime during the 1940s or '50s. Why would someone send these items to her house?

Reaching deeper, she found an envelope containing more loose photos. She shuffled through the images and suddenly stared at a face she recognized. A face that made the hairs stand up on the back of her neck. The photos dropped to the floor, where they lay like a poisonous snake at her feet.

She ran into the kitchen and called Jane.

"DID YOU SEE HER LICENSE plate?" asked Jane. "Can you tell me *anything* that might help me trace the vehicle?"

"It was a white van," said Maura, pacing her living room. "That's all I remember."

"Old, new? Ford, Chevy?"

"You know I can't tell the difference! All cars look alike to me!" Maura huffed out a breath and sank onto her sofa. "I'm sorry, I shouldn't have called you on Christmas, but I freaked out. I probably overreacted."

"Overreacted?" Jane gave a disbelieving laugh. "You just got a creepy Christmas gift delivered right to your front door, sent by a serial killer who's *supposed* to be locked up in maximum security. That should alarm the hell out of you. It alarms *me.* The question is, what does Amalthea want from you?"

Maura stared at the photo that had so rattled her. It was a dark-haired woman standing under a spreading oak tree, her eyes gazing at the camera with unflinching directness. Her white dress was sheer as gauze, showing off her slim waist and slender arms. If this were some stranger's photo, Maura would consider it a charming image, taken on a pretty country road. But she knew who that young woman was. She hugged herself and said softly, "She looked so much like me. . . ."

As Jane slowly shuffled through the photos, Maura sat silent, focusing instead on the Christmas tree that she'd halfheartedly decorated last week. She still hadn't opened the gifts underneath it, most of them from her colleagues at the ME's office. Jane's gift, wrapped in gaudy purple and silver foil, sat front and center. She had planned to open them all this morning, but the arrival of the cardboard box had swept away any Christmas spirit from this house. Was the box intended as some sort of peace offering? Perhaps Amalthea, using her own twisted logic, thought that Maura would want these keepsakes from her birth family. A family Maura wished she'd never heard of. A family of monsters.

The last of those monsters was now dying a slow and painful death from cancer. When Amalthea's gone, will I finally be free of them? Maura wondered. Can I go back to thinking of myself as Maura Isles, daughter of the respectable Mr. and Mrs. Isles of San Francisco?

"Jesus. Get a load of the happy family," said Jane, eyeing a photo with Amalthea, her husband, and their son. "Mommy, Daddy, and little Ted Bundy. The kid definitely looked like her."

The kid. My murderous brother, thought Maura. The first time she'd laid eyes on him was when she'd examined his corpse. Here in this photo was her bloodline, a family whose trade had been murder for profit. Did Amalthea send her these mementos to remind her that she could never escape who she really was?

"She's just playing head games again," said Jane, tossing down the photos. "She must've had this box stashed away somewhere, maybe in a storage unit. Then she got that woman to deliver it to you, on Christmas, no less. Too bad you can't tell me more about the van. Help me find out who that woman was."

"Even if you knew, what could you do about it? It's not illegal to drop off a box of photos."

"This is intimidation. Amalthea's stalking you."

"From her bed in the hospital?"

"Maura, this *must* have upset you; otherwise you wouldn't have called me."

"I didn't know who else to call."

"Like I'm your last resort? Jesus, I'm the *first* person you should call. You shouldn't be dealing with this all by yourself. And what is this, spending Christmas alone, just you and that damn cat? I swear, next year I'm gonna *drag* you to dinner at my mom's."

"Gee, that sounds like fun."

Jane sighed. "Tell me what you'd like me to do about this box."

Maura looked down at the cat, who was rubbing up against her leg, feigning affection in hopes of another meal. "I don't know."

"Well, I'll tell you what I *am* gonna do. I'll make sure Amalthea can't do this again. Obviously she's got people on the outside running errands for her. I'm gonna lock that woman down so tight, she won't ever be able to reach you."

A sudden thought made Maura freeze, a thought so disturbing it sent a chill up her neck. Even the cat seemed to sense the disturbance, and it watched her with new alertness. "What if Amalthea wasn't the one who sent this?"

"Who else would send it? Her husband's dead. Her son's dead. There's no one else alive in that family."

Maura turned to Jane. "Are we sure of that?"

THIRTEEN

THE WEEK AFTER CHRISTMAS IS NOT OFFICIALLY a holiday week, but it might as well be if you work in the PR biz as I do. No one is answering my phone calls or emails today. None of my usual newspaper contacts want to hear about the scandalous new memoir by the TV celebrity who just happens to be my god-awful client. This last week in December is a dead zone when it comes to selling books or pitching stories about books, but this happens to be the week that the memoir by Miss Victoria Avalon, reality-TV star, has been tossed into the marketplace. Of course, Miss Avalon did not really write her book, because she's close to illiterate. A reliable ghostwriter was hired for the task, a woman named Beth who turns in clean if uninspired copy and always delivers on time. Beth hates Victoria, or so it's rumored. As a book publicist, I'm privy to a lot of inside gossip, and this particular nugget is almost certainly true, because Victoria is eminently hateable. I hate her too. But I also admire her for her who-gives-a-fuck-what-you-think attitude, because that's exactly the attitude you need to get ahead in the world. In that way, Victoria and I are alike. I really don't give a fuck either; I just do a better job of hiding it.

In fact, I'm superb at hiding it.

And so I sit at my desk, a smile on my face, as I explain to Victoria over the phone why none of the hoped-for interviews we pitched to radio or TV have come through. *This is because it's only a few days after Christmas,* I tell her, *and everyone's still too stuffed with turkey and booze to return my calls. Yes, Victoria, it's an outrage. Yes, Victoria, everyone knows how big a name you are. (Your tits appeared in* Esquire*! You were married to a New England Patriots tight end for a grand total of eight months!)* Victoria thinks it's my fault the publicity isn't rolling in the door for her, my fault that those stacks and stacks of her (actually Beth's) book aren't moving in Barnes & Noble.

I keep smiling even when she starts to yell at me. It's important to smile even while on the phone, because people can *hear* the smile in your voice. It's also important because my boss, Mark, is watching me from his desk, and I can't let him see that our client is going ballistic and will probably fire Booksmart Media as her publicity firm. I'm smiling as she calls me *a stupid little Barbie.* I'm even smiling as she slams down the phone.

Mark says, "Is she upset?"

"Yes. She expected to be on the bestseller list."

He snorts. "They all expect that. You handled her well."

I don't know if he's flattering me or if he means it. We both know that Victoria Avalon is never going to be on any bestseller list. And we both know that I'll be blamed for it.

I need to get her some press coverage for her stupid book, ASAP. I turn to my computer to see if Victoria's name has turned up anywhere in any media. Even a gossip column will do. I wake up the screen and the *Boston Globe* home page lights up. That's when I spot the latest news—not about Victoria, who I suddenly don't give a fuck about. No, this is a front-page story about the dead young man found on the pier at Jeffries Point a few nights ago. On TV yesterday, they reported that the victim was shot with arrows. The police now know the man's name.

"Maybe we should pitch her book to Arthur again," says Mark. "I think he just needs a nudge. Her memoir *is* tangentially related to football, and I can see it showing up in his sports column."

I look up at Mark. "What?"

"Victoria was married to that football guy. It's an angle for a sports columnist, don't you think?"

"I'm sorry." I grab my purse and jump out of my chair. "I need to run out for a while."

"Okay. Nothing seems to be happening today anyway. But if you get a chance to review that press packet we're sending out for Alison Reeve's book—"

I don't hear the rest of what he says, because I am already running out the door.

FOURTEEN

THEY NOW KNEW THE DEAD MAN'S NAME. Stretched out on the autopsy table was Timothy McDougal, age twenty-five, an unmarried accountant who lived in Boston's North End. The tips of the three arrows were still embedded in his chest, but Yoshima had cut off the fletch ends with bolt cutters, leaving only metal stubs protruding from the flesh. Even so, cutting the Y incision was a challenge, and Maura's scalpel sketched a crooked line down the chest as she avoided cutting into the puncture wounds. The angle of each arrow's penetration had already been captured on X-ray, where it was obvious that one of the arrows had penetrated the descending aorta. It certainly would have qualified as a mortal wound.

Except for the fact this man was already dead when that arrow pierced his chest.

The morgue door opened and Jane walked in, tying on her face mask. "Frost won't be coming. He's visiting the victim's sister again. She's taking this pretty hard. Worst Christmas ever."

Maura looked down at the corpse of Timothy McDougal, who was last seen alive on the afternoon of December 24, when he'd cheerfully waved to his neighbor as he walked out of his apartment building. The next morning, he was expected at his younger sister's house in Brookline for Christmas brunch. He never appeared. By then the report of a young man's body on Jeffries Point was already on the news, and, fearing the worst, the sister called the police.

"Their parents are both dead, and he was her only sibling," said Jane. "Imagine being only twenty-two and having no family left in the world."

Maura put down the scalpel and picked up pruning shears. "What did you learn from the sister? Any leads?"

"She insists Tim had no enemies and he's never been in trouble. Best big brother ever. Everybody loved him."

"Except for whoever shot him with these arrows," Yoshima said.

Maura finished snapping apart the ribs, and she lifted the sternal shield. Frowning into the exposed cavity, she asked, "Any history of drug use?"

"Sister says absolutely not. He was a health-food nut."

"Any drugs turn up in his residence?"

"Frost and I went through his apartment inch by inch. It's just a studio, so there wasn't much to search. We found no drugs, no paraphernalia, not even a baggie of weed. Just some wine in the fridge and a bottle of tequila in the cabinet. This guy was so clean he would've squeaked."

"Or so everyone believes."

"Yeah." Jane shrugged. "You never know what the truth is."

Every human being had secrets, and too often it was Maura who uncovered them: The upstanding citizen found dead with child porn clutched in his lifeless hand. Or the perfect society wife with the syringe of heroin and a needle still embedded in her arm. Timothy McDougal almost certainly had secrets as well, and now Maura had to uncover the most baffling secret of all.

What killed you?

Staring into the open thorax, she could not yet discern the answer, although the cause of death had *seemed* apparent judging by the X-rays. Now that the chest was open, she could see the arrow itself, could feel the steel tip poking through the aorta wall. The descending aorta was the major highway through which all blood bound for the lower body flowed. Rupture it and blood will pulse out like a cannon, propelled by every heartbeat. If this man had died of internal exsanguination, she should be looking at a cavity filled with blood, but there was not enough pooled in here. Which told her that by the time the arrow penetrated his aorta, his heart had already stopped beating.

"I can see by your face that there's some kind of problem," said Jane.

Maura's answer was to reach for the scalpel. She did not like uncertainty, and she began to cut with new urgency. Out came a healthy young man's heart and lungs. She saw no coronary disease, no emphysema, no evidence that he had ever abused cigarettes. The liver and spleen were disease-free, and the pancreas should have provided him with a lifetime's worth of insulin.

She placed the stomach on the dissection tray and slit it open. Out spilled brown liquid with the strong stench of alcohol. She paused, scalpel hovering above the tray, suddenly struck by the memory of another incised stomach. Another whiff of alcohol. "Whiskey," she said.

"So he was drinking before he died."

Maura looked at Jane. "Does that remind you of another victim?"

"You're thinking of Cassandra Coyle."

"She had wine in her stomach. I couldn't find the cause of her death either. Is alcohol a common denominator here? Something delivered in a drink?"

"We canvassed all the bars in Cassandra's neighborhood. Every place within walking distance."

"And no one remembered seeing her?"

"One waitress said Cassandra's photo looked familiar, but she said the woman she thought was Cassandra was drinking with another woman. She didn't remember any man with her."

"Did these two victims know each other? Have the same circle of friends?"

Jane considered this. "I'm not aware of any connection. They lived in different neighborhoods, worked in completely different jobs." She pulled out her cell phone. "Frost should still be with Tim's sister. Let's find out if she knew Cassandra."

As Jane spoke with Frost, Maura spread open the stomach, revealing no trace of undigested food. When the victim was last seen, it was a holiday afternoon, when a single young man might meet friends for a drink before dinner. Cassandra Coyle's stomach had been preprandial as well, containing only traces of wine. Was *drinks with friends* the common factor?

She looked at Yoshima. "Do we have the tox screen back yet for Cassandra Coyle?"

"It hasn't been two weeks, but I marked it *expedite.* Let me check," he said, and crossed to the computer.

Jane hung up her phone. "Timothy's sister says she's never heard the name Cassandra Coyle. And I can't really think of any connection between these two victims, except for the fact they were both young, healthy, and drank booze before they died."

"And they were both mutilated postmortem."

Jane paused. "Well, yeah. There's that."

"Got it," called out Yoshima. "Cassandra Coyle's tox screen came back positive for alcohol. And for ketamine."

"Ketamine?" Maura crossed to the computer and stared at the report. "Blood alcohol's point zero four. Ketamine level is two milligrams per liter."

"Isn't that a date-rape drug?" said Jane.

"Actually, it's an anesthetic, sometimes used for date rape. But I found no evidence that Cassandra was raped."

"So now we know what killed her," said Jane.

"No, we don't." Maura looked up from the computer. "She didn't die from ketamine. This blood level is in the therapeutic range for anesthesia. It's enough to incapacitate but not high enough to kill a healthy young woman."

"Maybe she was given a drug you didn't screen for."

"I screened for everything I could think of."

"Then what killed her, Maura?"

"I don't know." Maura returned to the table and stared at Timothy McDougal. "I don't know what killed this man either. We now have two young victims with no apparent cause of death." Maura shook her head. "I'm missing something."

"You never miss anything."

"If our killer uses alcohol and ketamine to incapacitate his victims, what does he do next? They're unconscious and vulnerable. How does he kill them, without leaving any trace of—" Abruptly she turned to Yoshima. "Let's get out the CrimeScope. Before I do any more dissection, I want to examine his face."

"What do you think you're going to see?" said Jane.

"Put on the goggles and let's find out."

Details hidden to the naked eye under normal light could sometimes magically become visible under wavelengths from a forensic light source. Fibers and body fluids will fluoresce, and against a background of pale skin, otherwise invisible residues and inks will show up as dark patches. This search would not be entirely random; Maura already knew what she was looking for.

And where she would find it.

"Lights off," she said to Yoshima, and he flipped the switch.

The room went dark. Under the glow of the CrimeScope, a host of new details suddenly became visible as Maura tuned the instrument, altering the wavelength.

Strands of hair glowed on the floor, the detritus shed by multiple cops and ME staff. Gloves, gowns, and shoe covers were not 100 percent effective in preventing the shedding of hairs and fibers, and here was the evidence.

Maura focused the beam on Timothy McDougal's face.

"CSRU already searched him for trace evidence at the scene," said Jane.

"I know, but I'm looking for something else. Something I'm not even sure will turn up." She couldn't see it yet on the face, so she lowered the beam to the neck and once again tuned through different wavelengths, ignoring the dark pinpoints of blood spatter that she'd disseminated during her Y incision. She was looking for something less random. Something geometric.

And there, just above the level of the thyroid cartilage, she saw it. A faint band that encircled the throat and extended toward the back of the neck, where it vanished from sight.

"What the hell's that?" asked Jane. "A ligature mark?"

"No. I've already examined the neck and there's no bruising, no impressions on the skin itself. And his hyoid bone is intact on the X-ray."

"Then what made that pattern?"

"I think it's residue. Adhesive manufacturers sometimes add materials like titanium dioxide or iron oxide to their products. I was hoping this would show up under the CrimeScope, and here it is."

"Adhesive? You mean like duct tape?"

"Possibly, but this tape wasn't used to restrain him. See how the pattern extends only around the front of the neck? The tape was used to hold something in place, but it wasn't tight enough to leave bruises. If this man's tox screen also comes back positive for ketamine, then I have a pretty good idea what happened to him. And to Cassandra Coyle. Yoshima, lights."

Jane pulled off her goggles and frowned at Maura. "You think they were killed by the same perp?"

Maura nodded. "And I know how he did it."

FIFTEEN

Blue Eyes looks surprised to see me standing in his doorway. It's been nearly two weeks since we slept together, since I sneaked like a thief out of his bedroom. I haven't tried to contact him, not once, because sometimes a girl doesn't need any more obligations in her life. It's too much work trying to keep a man happy, and I have my own needs to look after.

Which is why I'm now standing on his doorstep: Because I need him. Not *him,* specifically, just someone who'll make me feel safe again after the unsettling news I read on the *Boston Globe* website. I'm not even sure why I chose to run to him. Maybe it's because instinct tells me he's reliable and utterly harmless, someone I can turn my back on without worrying about a knife sinking between my shoulder blades. Maybe because he's a relative stranger who won't know the difference between truth and the fiction I occasionally spin. All I know is, for the first time I can remember, I'm hungry for some human connection. I think he is too.

But he doesn't seem eager to invite me in. He just frowns at me as if I'm some pesky neighborhood evangelist he'd love to get rid of.

"It's cold out here," I say. "Can I come in?"

"You never even bothered to say goodbye."

"That was shitty of me. I'm sorry. I was going through a tough time at work and I wasn't myself. And that night I spent with you, it sort of overwhelmed me. I needed time to think about what happened between us. What it all meant."

He gives a resigned sigh. "Okay, Holly, come in. It's, like, ten degrees out there and I don't want you to catch pneumonia."

I don't bother to correct him that you can't catch pneumonia from the cold, and I just follow him inside. Once again I'm impressed by his townhouse, which feels like a palace compared with my dinky apartment. Everett is what my late mother would have called a *quality acquaintance,* a boyfriend worth cultivating. I fear I've already fouled things up between us, and he's too nice a guy to throw me out yet. He's wearing blue jeans and an old flannel shirt, so it must be his day off, which gives me time to make things right between us. We stand for a moment in awkward silence, regarding each other. I'm mesmerized by the blueness of his eyes. His hair's uncombed and his shirt's missing a button, but those details only make him seem more genuine to me. For once, a man I don't have to be wary of.

"I want to explain why I left without saying goodbye," I tell him. "That night we met, you—well, you took my breath away. I couldn't help myself. I jumped into bed with you way too soon. And the next morning, I felt . . . ashamed."

His gaze instantly softens. "Why?"

"Because I'm not that kind of girl." Actually, I *am* that kind of girl, but he doesn't need to know that. "When I woke up the next morning, I knew what you probably thought of me, and I couldn't face you. I was too embarrassed. So I climbed out of bed, put on my clothes, and . . ." I let my voice trail away and I sink onto his sofa. It's a beautiful black leather sofa, very comfortable and certainly expensive. Not something I could ever afford.

Another point in his favor.

He sits down next to me and takes my hand. "Holly, I understand exactly what you're saying," he says quietly. "I may be a guy, but I felt the same way, jumping into bed with you so soon. I was afraid you'd think I was just using you. I don't want you to think I'm some kind of jerk. Because I'm not."

"I never thought so."

He takes a deep breath and smiles. "Okay, shall we start over?" He holds out his hand. "Hello, I'm Everett Prescott. I'm pleased to make your acquaintance."

We shake hands and grin at each other. Instantly, everything's all better between us. I feel warmth flood through me, not a sexual flush this time but something deeper. Something that takes me by surprise. A connection. Is this what it's like to fall in love?

"So tell me, why did you come back?" he asks. "Why today?"

I look down at our hands, joined together, and decide to tell him the truth. "Something awful happened. I saw it on the news this morning."

"What happened?"

"There was a man murdered on Christmas Eve. They found his body on Jeffries Point pier."

"Yes, I heard about that."

"The thing is, I *knew* him."

Everett stares at me. "God, I'm sorry. Was he a good friend?"

"No, we just went to school together, in Brookline. But the news shook me up, you know? It reminded me that anything can happen to us. At any time."

He puts his arm around me and pulls me against him. I press my cheek against his soft flannel shirt and sniff the scent of laundry detergent and aftershave. Comforting smells that make me feel like a little girl again, safe in Daddy's arms.

"Nothing's going to happen to you, Holly," he murmurs.

It's something my father always says, and I don't believe him either.

I sigh against his shirt. "No one can make that promise."

"Well, I did." Everett tucks a hand under my chin and lifts my gaze to his. He's studying me, trying to understand what has shaken me so deeply. I've told him about Tim, but that's only part of the story. He doesn't need to know the rest of it.

He doesn't need to know about the others who've died.

"What can I do to make you feel safe?" he says.

"Just be my friend." I take a breath. "That's what I need right now. Someone I can count on." *Someone who won't ask too many questions.*

"Would you like me to go with you to the funeral?"

"What?"

"For your friend. If you're this upset about his death, you *should* go. It's important to acknowledge grief, Holly. It will give you closure, and I'll be right beside you."

There could be advantages to having him accompany me at Tim's funeral. He'd be an extra pair of ears to listen in on gossip, to gather information about how Tim died and what the police are thinking. But there'd be dangers as well. At Sarah Byrne's funeral, I'd been quick to slip away. At Cassie Coyle's funeral, I was able to pass myself off as a college classmate named Sasha, because no one recognized me. But Everett knows my name is Holly. He knows a bit of the truth, not all of it, and that's enough to complicate any lies I need to tell. There's an old poem that goes: *Oh, what a tangled web we weave when first we practice to deceive,* but that's all backward. Real problems don't come from deception; they come from the truth.

"I can be your rock, Holly, if you want me to be," he offers.

I look into Everett's eyes and see the definite gleam of infatuation. Yes, he could be useful, in ways I'm only now considering.

"What do you think?" he says.

I smile. "I think I'd like that very much."

But as our lips meet in a kiss, it suddenly occurs to me that a rock isn't just something to cling to, something to keep you safe. It's also something that can drag you down, down under the waves.

SIXTEEN

"THIS IS THE ONLY MECHANISM OF DEATH that makes sense to me," said Maura. "The problem is, it's almost impossible for me to prove."

Maura looked across the Boston PD conference table at forensic psychologist Dr. Lawrence Zucker, whose expression offered little indication whether she'd convinced him. Both Jane and Frost had remained silent, allowing Maura to present her theory without interruption. Now she had to defend it to a man whose face she'd never been able to read. A familiar visitor to the homicide unit, Dr. Zucker was the psychologist whom Boston PD consulted when they needed help understanding a perpetrator's behavior. While Maura respected him as a fellow professional, she had never warmed to him, and no wonder. With his coldly probing gaze, he seemed more android than human, a machine designed to drill deeply and dispassionately into the mind of whoever sat before him.

And that gaze was now focused on Maura.

"Do you have any evidence to support your proposed mechanism of death?" Dr. Zucker asked, pale eyes unblinking.

"The swab of the victim's neck turned up traces of polyisoprene as well as a C5 hydrocarbon component," said Maura. "Both of these are commonly used in duct-tape adhesives. Inorganic materials are also common components, and that's what made the residue visible under the CrimeScope."

Jane said, "You can see the residue outline in the photos of his neck," and she turned her laptop to face him.

Zucker squinted at the image. "It's pretty subtle."

"But it's definitely there. Evidence of tape adhesive on his skin."

"Maybe the tape was used to restrain him."

"His neck showed no bruising and no scratches," said Maura. "There was nothing on his hands to indicate a physical struggle. I believe he was already unconscious when he was killed. The lab confirmed there was alcohol and ketamine in his blood, just like we found in Cassandra Coyle. But the blood levels weren't high enough to kill. Only to incapacitate."

"So what was the tape on his neck for, if not to restrain him?"

"I believe it was used to fix something in place against his skin. Something that needed a fairly airtight seal. When I realized that was adhesive residue on his neck, I immediately thought of Heaven's Gate. And I'm not referring to the Michael Cimino movie."

She paused, waiting to see if Zucker recognized the reference.

"I assume you're referring to the cult in San Diego?" said Zucker.

Maura nodded and looked at Frost. "It happened in 1997. Heaven's Gate was an oddball New Age cult led by a man named Marshall Applewhite, who believed he was descended from Jesus Christ. He told his followers that the world was about to be destroyed by aliens and the only way to survive was to leave earth. The comet Hale-Bopp happened to be approaching around that time, and Applewhite believed that in the comet's tail was an alien spaceship, waiting to beam aboard their souls. But to board that ship, they first had to abandon their earthly bodies." She paused. "I think you can all guess what that entailed."

"Suicide," said Frost.

"Thirty-nine cult members dressed themselves in identical black shirts, sweatpants, and Nike athletic shoes. They ingested just enough phenobarbital and vodka to sedate themselves so they wouldn't experience any anxiety or panic. Then they secured plastic bags over their heads. They died of asphyxiation."

"In that case, the cause of death was obvious," said Zucker.

"Of course. When a victim's found with a plastic bag over his head, the mechanism of death is apparent, and that's what they found in the Heaven's Gate mass suicide. But what if someone removes the plastic bag *after* the victim has died? It's very difficult to prove homicide, because that form of asphyxiation doesn't leave any specific pathologic changes. When I performed the autopsies on Cassandra Coyle and Timothy McDougal, all I found was a minor degree of lung edema and scattered lung petechiae. If it weren't for the fact they were both mutilated postmortem, I would have had a hard time classifying either case as homicide."

"Let me get this straight," said Zucker. "Someone commits the perfect murders. And then ensures that we *know* these are murders by mutilating the corpses?"

"Yes."

Dr. Zucker rocked forward in his chair, his reptilian-cold eyes lit with interest. "This is fascinating."

"What it is is sick," said Jane.

"Consider the message this killer is trying to convey," said Zucker. "He's telling the world how clever he is, saying, *If I want to, I can kill and get away with it. But I want you to* know *what I've done.*"

"So he's bragging," said Jane.

"Yes, but bragging to whom?"

"To us, of course. He's taunting the police, telling us he's too smart to be caught."

"Are you certain *we're* the ones he's trying to communicate with? Mob hits leave calling cards as well, designed to intimidate."

"We're not seeing any mob connections with either of these victims," said Jane.

"Then the message could be for someone else entirely. Someone who understands the symbolism of removing the eyes or stabbing with arrows. Tell me more about this second victim, the young man. You said he was found on the pier, but where was he killed?"

"We don't know. He was last seen leaving his apartment building in the North End around four P.M., five hours before his body was found. Dark-blue fibers collected from his pants are consistent with carpet commonly used in autos, so after he was killed, the body was probably transported by car to the pier."

Zucker leaned back, fingers tented, eyes narrowed in thought. "Our killer made a point of placing his victim in a public location. He could have dumped the body in the harbor or hidden it in the woods. But, no, he wanted it found. He wanted publicity. This is definitely a message of some kind."

"That's why I asked Dr. Isles to present her theory to you," Jane said to Zucker. "I think we're wading into some deep, dark psychological shit here. We want your take on what kind of weirdo we're dealing with."

This was precisely the type of case Zucker savored, and Maura saw excitement in his eyes as he considered the question. She wondered what manner of man chose to delve so enthusiastically into the darkness. To understand a killer's mind, did it take someone equally twisted? *What does that say about me?*

"Why do you believe these two victims were killed by the same perpetrator?" Zucker asked Maura.

"It seems pretty clear to me. Both of them had ketamine and alcohol in their blood. Neither had an apparent cause of death. Both were mutilated postmortem."

"Cutting out the eyeballs is very different symbolism from stabbing arrows into the chest."

"In either case, it takes a sick puppy to do it," said Jane.

"The mere presence of ketamine in the tox screen isn't all that unique," said Zucker. "It's a common-enough club drug. According to one recent study, even high school students are now using it."

"Yes," Maura conceded. "It's common enough, but—"

"Then there's the fact that the first victim's female, the second is male," said Zucker. "Is there anything that ties them together?" He looked at Jane. "Did they know each other? Have friends or jobs in common?"

"As far as we've determined, no," Jane admitted. "Different neighborhoods, different circles of friends, different colleges, different jobs."

"Online connections? Social media?"

"Tim McDougal didn't have a Facebook or Twitter account, so we can't connect them that way."

"I've also reviewed their credit-card statements," said Frost. "Over the last six months they didn't frequent the same restaurants, bars, or even grocery stores. Timothy's younger sister doesn't recognize Cassandra's name. And Cassandra's stepmother never heard of Timothy McDougal."

"So how and why did the killer choose *these* two particular people?"

There was a long silence. No one had the answer.

"They both had alcohol in their stomachs," said Maura.

Dr. Zucker had been silently jotting notes, and now he looked up from his yellow legal pad. "Spiking a drink with ketamine sounds like a common prelude to date rape."

"Neither victim was sexually assaulted," said Maura.

"You're certain?"

Maura stared straight back at him. "Every orifice

was swabbed. All the clothing was examined for traces of semen. There was no physical evidence of sexual assault."

"But it doesn't rule out a sexual motive."

"I can't comment on motive, Dr. Zucker. Only on the evidence."

Zucker's lips twitched into a faint smile. There was something deeply disquieting about this man, as if he knew details about Maura that she herself wasn't aware of. Certainly he knew about Amalthea. Everyone at Boston PD knew the painful fact that Maura had a mother serving a life sentence in prison for multiple homicides. Did he see some trace of Amalthea in her face, in her personality? Was that a smile of recognition he'd just given her?

"I didn't mean to offend, Dr. Isles. I'm aware that evidence is your stock in trade," said Zucker. "But my role is to understand why the killer chose these two victims in particular, if in fact it *is* the same killer. Because there are significant differences between these victims. Gender. Circle of acquaintances. Neighborhoods. Method of postmortem mutilation. A couple of weeks ago, when Detectives Frost and Rizzoli asked my opinion on Cassandra Coyle, we were working with a completely different psychological theory about why her eyes were removed." He looked at Jane. "You called it *see no evil.*"

"You agreed at the time," said Jane.

"Because removing the eyes is a powerfully symbolic act. It's also very specific. A killer chooses the eyes because they represent something to him and he gets a sexual thrill from excising them. I'm trying to understand why he'd then target a male victim and use a radically different method of mutilation."

"So you don't think these cases are related," said Jane.

"I'll need more to go on before I'm convinced." Zucker closed his notebook and looked at Maura. "Let me know when you have it."

As Dr. Zucker left the room, Maura remained in her chair, resignedly staring at the documents spread across the table.

"That turned into a harder sell than I thought," said Jane.

"But he's right," Maura admitted. "We don't have enough evidence yet to prove it's the same killer."

"But *you* see a connection, and that's good enough for me."

"I don't know why."

Jane leaned forward. "Because you don't normally believe in hunches. You're always going on about that pesky thing called evidence. The last time you had a hunch, I didn't believe you, but you turned out to be right. You saw the connection that no one else saw, including me. So this time, Maura, I'm going to listen to you."

"I'm not sure you should."

"Don't tell me you're doubting yourself now."

Maura stacked the pages. "We need to find something that these victims had in common. Something that brought them both into contact with this killer." She placed Timothy McDougal's crime-scene photos in a folder and was about to close the cover when she paused, staring at the image. A memory suddenly rippled to the surface, a memory of sunlight glowing through jeweled panes of glass.

"What?" said Jane.

Maura didn't answer. She pulled out a photo of Cassandra Coyle's corpse and placed it beside Timothy McDougal's crime-scene photo. Two different victims, one a man, the other a woman. The man skewered with multiple arrows, the woman with her eyes removed. "I can't believe I didn't see it," she said.

"Want to tell me what you're thinking?" said Jane.

"Not yet. Not till I've done some more research." Maura whisked the photos into her folder and headed for the door. "I need to consult someone."

"Who?"

Maura paused in the doorway. "I'd rather not tell you," she said, and walked out of the room.

SEVENTEEN

NEUTRAL GROUND. THAT WAS THE AGREEMENT, someplace public, where they'd both be obliged to behave as professionals. Certainly they could not meet in her house, where they had met so many times before, and where temptation would whisper from the bedroom. Nor could they meet at Our Lady of Divine Light, where church staff or parishioners might see them together again and wonder. No, this café on Huntington Avenue was far safer territory, and at 3:00 P.M., it was quiet enough for them to linger unnoticed and undisturbed.

She was the first to arrive, and she chose a booth at the rear of the café. She sat with her back to the wall, like a gunslinger waiting for the enemy to arrive, but the true enemy wasn't Daniel; it was her own heart. She ordered coffee. Even before her first caffeinated sip, her pulse was racing. She tried to distract herself by pulling out the case files and reviewing the crime-scene photos. How twisted was this, that scenes of violence and death were what calmed her? The dead were always good company. They made no demands, expected no favors.

Aroused no desires.

She heard the door open and her gaze snapped up as he stepped into the café. Bundled as he was in a winter coat and a scarf, he might be just another patron escaping the chill to warm up with coffee, but Daniel Brophy was not just any man. The waitress paused in the middle of laying out silverware to stare as he walked past, and no wonder. With his dark hair and long black coat, he looked like a somber Heathcliff striding in from the moors. Daniel did not notice the waitress's lingering look; he had spotted Maura, and his gaze was only on her as he walked straight to her booth.

"It's been too long," he said quietly.

"It wasn't so long ago. April, I think." In truth, she remembered the exact date, the time, and the circumstances when they'd last seen each other. So did he.

"Roxbury Crossing," he said. "The night that retired cop was killed."

Crime scenes were now the only places where they encountered each other. While she attended to the dead, Father Daniel Brophy's role as Boston PD chaplain was to administer to the living, the grief-stricken and the traumatized who were so often left in the wake of violent crime. They had their separate duties and no reason to speak to each other at death scenes, but she was always aware of him. Even when they exchanged not a glance, she knew whenever he was nearby and could feel the disturbance in her well-ordered universe.

Now that universe seemed to tilt around her.

He shrugged off his coat and unwound his scarf, exposing the priest's collar around his neck. That unforgiving band of white was merely starched fabric, but it had the power to keep apart two people who loved each other.

She avoided looking at the collar as she said, "Did you resign as police chaplain? I haven't seen you at any crime scenes."

"I've been in Canada for the last six months. I got back to town only a few weeks ago."

"Canada? Why?"

"For a spiritual retreat. I requested it. I needed to get away from Boston for a while."

She didn't ask the reason why he needed time away. She could see the deeper worry lines in his face, the new strands of silver in his dark hair. It wasn't Boston he had fled from; it was her.

"I was surprised when you called me today," he said. "The last time we spoke, you asked me never to contact you again. It hasn't been easy, but I want only what's best for you, Maura. That's all I've ever wanted."

"Daniel, this isn't about us. It's about—"

"Can I get you something, sir?"

They both looked up to see the waitress standing at their table, her pen and pad in hand.

"Just coffee, please," said Daniel.

They were silent as the waitress filled his cup and

warmed Maura's. Did the woman wonder about this odd couple sitting so glum and silent in the booth? Did she assume it was merely a counseling session, that Maura was seeking comfort from her priest? Or did she see more, understand more?

Only after the waitress had left did Maura say to Daniel, "I called you because something's come up in an investigation. I need your opinion."

"About?"

"Could you look at this? Tell me what immediately comes to mind." She slid a crime-scene photo across the table to him.

He frowned at the image. "Why are you showing this to me?"

"The victim's name is Timothy McDougal. He was found on a pier at Jeffries Point on Christmas Eve. So far the police have no leads and no suspects."

"I'm not sure how I can help you."

"Just keep that image in mind. Now look at this one." She slid him the photo of Cassandra Coyle's corpse. It was a close-up of her face, with two gaping holes where the eyes had once been. As he stared, she said nothing, waiting to see if he would be jarred by the same revelation. When at last he glanced up at her, there was astonishment in his eyes. "Saint Lucy."

She nodded. "That's exactly who I thought of."

"You never attend church, yet you recognize this symbolism?"

"My parents were Catholic, and . . ." She hesitated, reluctant to confess her secret. "You don't know this, but I used to sit in your church, just to meditate. Sometimes I was the only one there. The last pew on the left, that's where I'd always sit."

"Why? When you don't even believe?"

"I wanted to feel close to you. Even when you weren't there."

He reached across the table to touch her hand. "Maura."

"Next to the pew where I sat, along the left wall, there are these beautiful stained-glass windows with portraits of the saints. I used to stare at those windows, thinking about their lives. About the agonies they suffered as martyrs. Strangely enough, I found that comforting, because their pain made me count my blessings. I remember one window in particular. It shows a man with his arms bound to a post, and he's looking up toward heaven. A man who's been shot with arrows."

He nodded. "Sebastian, patron saint of archers and policemen. One of the most recognizable martyrs in medieval art. He was a Roman officer who converted to Christianity, and when he refused to honor the old gods, he was tied to a post and executed." He tapped on the photo of Timothy McDougal. "You think this is a re-creation of Sebastian's martyrdom?"

She nodded. "I'm glad you see the symbolism too."

He pointed to the photo of Cassandra Coyle. "Tell me about this victim."

"A twenty-six-year-old woman, found dead in her bedroom. Both her eyes were surgically removed postmortem. Her eyeballs were placed in her open palm."

"The classic portrayal of Lucy, patron saint of the

blind. She was a virgin who devoted herself to Christ, and when she refused to marry, the man she was betrothed to had her thrown in prison and tortured. The torturer dug out her eyes."

"Once you recognize it, the symbolism practically screams at you. One victim was stabbed with arrows, like Saint Sebastian. One victim had her eyes cut out, like Saint Lucy."

"What does Boston PD think?"

"I haven't mentioned the symbolism to them yet. I wanted to hear your reaction first. You know the history of the saints, so you'd have the answers."

"I know the liturgical calendar, and I'm familiar with the lives of most of the saints. But I'm not any sort of expert."

"No? I remember you explaining in great detail the iconography of sacred art. You told me that when you see an old man holding keys, it's almost certainly a depiction of Saint Peter, holding the keys to heaven. That a woman with an ointment pot is Mary Magdalene, and a man with ragged clothes and a lamb is John the Baptist."

"Any art historian can tell you that."

"But how many art historians are as well versed as you are in religious symbolism? You might be able to help us identify this killer's other victims."

"Are there other victims?"

"I don't know. Maybe we just haven't recognized them yet. And that's where we need your help."

For a moment he said nothing. She knew why he was hesitating. It was because of their history together as lovers. A year ago they had gone their separate ways, and the wound from that separation had not yet healed. It was still fresh, still painful. She both hoped and dreaded that he would agree to her request.

Calmly he reached for his coat and scarf. So this is his answer, she thought; a wise decision, of course. It was far better that he walk away now, but she was left heartsick as he rose to his feet. Would there ever be a day when she'd look at Daniel Brophy and feel nothing? Certainly this was not that day.

"Let's go now," he said. "I'll meet you at the church."

She frowned at him. "The church?"

"If I'm going to advise you, we should start with the basics. I'll see you there."

HOW MANY TIMES HAD SHE huddled in a pew in Our Lady of Divine Light, wallowing in her own misery? She was not a believer, yet she longed for guidance from some higher authority, and she drew comfort from the familiar symbols she saw everywhere in this building: The votive candles, flickering in the shadows. The altar, draped in rich red velvet. The stone Madonna, gazing down benignly from her alcove throne. How many times had she studied the figures of saints in the stained-glass windows and pondered their torments? Today the light that shone through those windows cast a cold and wintry gleam on Daniel's face.

"I haven't taken enough time to really study the glasswork in these windows, but they're beautiful, aren't they?" he said, as he and Maura stood admiring the first window. In each of the four corners was a different saintly figure. "I was told these aren't very old—only a hundred years, not much more. They were crafted in France, in the traditional style, similar to what you can find in medieval churches all across Europe."

She pointed to the top left corner. "Saint Sebastian."

"Yes," said Daniel. "He's easy to identify by the manner of his martyrdom. He's often depicted tied to a post, with his body pierced by arrows."

"And the man in the upper right corner?" she asked. "Which saint is he?"

"That would be Bartholomew, the patron saint of Armenia. Do you see the knife he's holding? It's the symbol of his martyrdom."

"He was stabbed to death?"

"No, his death was far worse. Bartholomew was flayed alive as punishment for converting the king of Armenia to Christianity. In some paintings, he's depicted with his own excised skin hanging over his arm like a bloody cloak." Daniel gave her a rueful smile. "Not surprisingly, he's the patron saint of butchers and tanners."

"Who is the saint in the bottom left corner?"

"That's Saint Agatha, yet another martyr."

"What's on the plate she's carrying? They look like loaves of bread."

"They're not, um, actually loaves of bread." He paused, his discomfort so apparent that she frowned at him.

"How was she martyred?"

"Her death was particularly brutal. When she refused to honor the old Roman gods, she was tortured. Forced to walk on glass and burned with live coals. Finally, they ripped off her breasts with pincers."

Maura stared at the objects resting on the plate, which she now knew weren't loaves of bread but the excised breasts of a mutilated woman. She shook her head. "God, these stories."

"They're horrifying, yes. But they can't be entirely unknown to you. Since your adoptive parents were Catholic."

"Only in the nominal sense. Attendance at Christmas Mass was about the extent of their involvement, and by the time I was twelve, I'd stopped going to church at all. I hadn't set foot in one in years until . . ." She paused. "Until I met you."

They stood silent for a moment, each avoiding the other's gaze, both of them staring ahead at the window, as if all the answers, the remedies to their pain, were etched in stained glass.

"I never stopped loving you," he said softly. "I never will."

"Yet we're not together."

He looked at her. "I'm not the one who said goodbye."

"What choice did I have when you believe so completely in *this*?" She nodded at the windows of saints, at the altar and the pews. "Something I can't believe in, won't believe in."

"Science doesn't have all the answers, Maura."

"No, it certainly doesn't," she said with a note of

bitterness. Science didn't explain why some people chose to be miserable in love.

"There's more to consider than just our happiness," he said. "There are people in this parish who depend on me, people in deep pain who need my help. And there's my sister. She's still alive, still healthy after all these years. I know you don't believe in miracles, but I do."

"Medical science cured her leukemia. Not a miracle."

"And if you're wrong? If I go back on my word, leave the Church, and my sister gets sick again . . ."

He'll never forgive himself, thought Maura. He'll never forgive me.

She sighed. "I didn't come here to talk about us."

"No, of course not." He looked up at the window. "You're here to talk about murder."

She refocused on the stained glass, on the fourth saint in the window, yet another woman who'd chosen misery. This saint she did not need help to identify; she already knew her name.

"Saint Lucy," she said.

He nodded. "Carrying a plate with her eyes on it. The eyes dug out by her torturers."

Outside, sunlight suddenly broke through the clouds and lit up the window, suffusing the glass with colors as rich as jewels. Maura frowned at the four figures gazing from the window. "They're both here, in the same window. Sebastian and Lucy. Is it possible he's been in this church and stood in this very spot?"

"The killer?"

"It's like we're looking at his storyboard, and here

are two of his victims. A man pierced with arrows. A woman with her eyes cut out."

"This window isn't unique, Maura. These four saints show up everywhere, and you'll probably find their images in Catholic churches all around the world. And, look, there are a dozen more saints here." He moved on to the next window. "There's Saint Anthony of Padua, holding bread and the lily. Saint Luke the Evangelist with his ox. Saint Francis with his wild birds. And that's the martyred Saint Agnes with her lamb."

"How was she martyred?"

"Like Saint Lucy, Agnes was a beautiful girl who chose Christ, refused to marry a suitor, and suffered for it. The rejected man was the son of a Roman governor, and he was so outraged, he had her beheaded. In paintings, she's often depicted holding a lamb as well as the iconic palm branch."

"What does the palm branch signify?"

"Certain plants and trees have special symbolism in the Church. The cedar tree, for instance, is a symbol of Christ. Clover is the Trinity, and ivy represents immortality. The palm branch is the symbol of martyrdom."

She moved to the third window, where she spotted the figures of two women standing side by side, both holding palm branches. "So those saints in the upper right corner, they're martyrs as well?"

"Yes. Since they died together, they're usually shown as a pair. Both were executed after they converted to Christianity. Do you see how Saint Fusca holds a sword? That was the instrument of their deaths. They were both stabbed and decapitated."

"Were they sisters?"

"No, the woman on the right is Fusca's nurse, Saint—" He stopped. Reluctantly, he turned to look at her. "Saint Maura."

EIGHTEEN

JANE SET A STACK OF PAPERS ON MAURA'S ROSEwood desk, which was freakishly tidy as usual. Jane's desk at the homicide unit looked like a place where work was actually being done, every square inch covered in files and Post-it notes. Maura's was a Stepford desk, too perfect to be real, with not a stray paper clip or a speck of dust to be seen. On that pristine surface, Jane's papers sat in an unruly pile, crying out to be straightened.

"We're working on your theory, believe me, Maura," said Jane. "Frost and I have been reading up on martyred saints, and, man, we are talking hardcore blood and guts." She pointed to the papers she'd brought Maura. "It's actually pretty disturbing stuff. I should've been paying more attention in catechism class."

Maura picked up the top page. *"Saint Apollonia, virgin and martyr,"* she read. *"Patron saint of dentists and people with toothaches?"*

"Oh, yeah, now *that* was a horrible death. They broke all her teeth, and in paintings she's usually depicted holding dental pincers." Jane nodded at the other pages in the stack. "In there you'll find beheadings, stabbings, stonings, crucifixions, drowning, burning, and clubbing. Oh, and my favorite: having your intestines pulled out with a windlass. If you can think of a horrible way to kill someone, it was probably done to some saint somewhere. And that's our problem."

"Problem?" Maura looked up from the page about Saint Apollonia.

"Maybe this perp's killed before, but we have no idea what method of mutilation he chose. We can't narrow down the victims by gender, since he's killing both men and women. We could waste a lot of time reviewing every unsolved beating, stabbing, and beheading."

"We know something far more specific than that, Jane. We know he uses ketamine to subdue his victims and suffocation to kill them. We know the mutilations are postmortem."

"Right, and those were the first things we searched for on the ViCAP database. Any victims with ketamine on board who were mutilated postmortem." Jane shook her head.

"Nothing?"

"Nothing."

Maura leaned back in her leather chair and tapped her silver pen on the desk. On the wall behind her hung a grotesque African mask, which seemed to mirror her look of frustration. Jane once asked Maura why she displayed so many creepy artifacts in her office and had received a lecture about the beauty and symbolism of ceremonial masks from Mali. But all Jane saw, when she looked up at that mask, was a monster ready to pounce.

"Then maybe he hasn't killed before," said Maura. "Or maybe the details we're searching for were missed on autopsy. Not every victim gets a comprehensive tox screen. And death by suffocation is sometimes impossible to determine. Even I missed it the first time, with Cassandra Coyle. I could kick myself for that."

"Actually, that's kind of a relief to hear," said Jane.

"A relief?"

"It's nice to know you're not perfect."

"I never said I was." Maura leaned forward in her chair and frowned at the stack of papers that Jane had brought, dozens of pages filled with some of the most gruesome episodes in Church history. "Our two victims, did they have any religious connection?"

"We chased that down too. Both Cassandra and Timothy were raised in Catholic households, but neither was observant. Timothy's younger sister said she can't remember the last time her brother attended church. And Cassandra's colleagues at her film studio said she despised organized religion, which goes along with her Goth vibe. I doubt either one of these victims met their killer in church."

"Still, there's *something* here, Jane. Something to do with saints and martyrs."

"Maybe you're seeing symbolism that doesn't actually exist. Maybe this has nothing to do with the Church and it's just some sicko who likes to randomly mutilate bodies."

"No, I feel certain about this. And I'm not the only one."

Jane studied Maura's flushed face and saw a brightness in her eyes, a new and feverish intensity. "I take it Daniel agrees with you?"

"He recognized it immediately. He's well versed in religious symbolism, and he can help us get into this killer's mind."

"Is that really why you went to him? Or was there some other reason to pull him into this?"

"Do you think I'm *looking* for an excuse to get involved with him again?" said Maura.

"You could've consulted an art history professor at Harvard. You could have asked a random nun or looked it up on Wikipedia. But, no, you called Daniel Brophy."

"He's worked with Boston PD for years. He's discreet and you know we can trust him."

"With this investigation, sure. But can he be trusted with *you*?"

"We've moved beyond that. We're keeping this purely professional."

"If you say so. But how was it for you?" Jane asked quietly. "Seeing him again?"

Maura's response was to turn away from Jane's gaze. Yes, that was typical Maura—avoiding conflict, as usual; shying away from any conversation that might stir up uncomfortable emotions. They had been friends and colleagues for years, had even faced death together, yet Maura had never really allowed Jane to see her deepest vulnerabilities. The woman's shields were always up, always shutting her out.

"Seeing him again was painful," Maura finally admitted. "All these months, I've struggled to not pick up the phone and call him." She gave an ironic laugh. "Then today I found out he hasn't even been in Boston for months. He's been in Canada on a retreat."

"Yeah, I guess I should have told you that."

Maura frowned at her. "You knew he left town?"

"He asked me not to tell you. He was going into seclusion, so you weren't supposed to contact him anyway. I thought he made a wise decision, going away. And to be honest, I was hoping you'd move on. That you'd find someone else, someone who can make you happy." Jane paused. "But it's not over between you two, is it?"

Maura looked down at the pages. "It's over. It *is* over," she repeated, as if trying to convince herself.

No, it's not, thought Jane, seeing the struggle on Maura's face. It's not over for either one of you.

Jane glanced down as her cell phone played a familiar ring tone: "Frosty the Snowman." "Hey," she answered. "I'm still with Maura. What's up?"

"Sometimes a guy just gets lucky," Frost said.

Jane snorted. "Okay, what's her name?"

"I don't know. But I'm starting to think our killer may not be a man."

—

"I WASN'T EVEN LOOKING FOR a woman. That's how I missed spotting her the first time I watched these surveillance videos," said Frost. "At the time, we had no idea the two cases might be linked, so I never thought to watch these in succession. But after Maura came up with her theory, I went back to these videos again. To see if there was anyone who attended both Cassandra's and Timothy's memorial services." He swiveled his laptop on his desk to face Jane. "And look what I found."

She leaned closer to study the image caught in freeze-frame on Frost's computer. It showed half a dozen people filing toward the camera, all of them somber-faced and dressed in wintry black.

"This is the video of Cassandra Coyle's memorial service," said Frost. "The camera was mounted right over the church entrance, so it captured everyone who walked in the door." He pointed to the laptop screen. "You remember those two women, right?"

"How could I forget? Team Elaine. They were sitting right behind me, making nasty remarks about Priscilla Coyle all through the service."

"And those three." Frost pointed at a familiar trio walking right behind the two older women. "Cassandra's colleagues from the film studio."

"Can't mistake 'em. No one else in that crowd had violet hair."

"Now look at this young woman here, just to the left of the filmmakers. Do you remember seeing her at the service?"

Jane leaned in to study the woman's face. She appeared to be about the same age as Cassandra, perhaps in her mid-twenties, a slim, attractive brunette with dark bangs cut in a blunt fringe. "Only vaguely. I may have seen her in the crowd, but there were two hundred people in that church. Why are you focusing on her?"

"The thing is, I didn't. Not the first time. When I went through this video and the video from Timothy McDougal's funeral, I was focusing on the men. I didn't pay much attention to the women. Then I happened to freeze the frame right at this point. This is the only clear view you get of the woman's face, peeking over Travis Chang's shoulder. You can't really see her again, because she ducks her head down after this shot. Keep her face in mind." Frost minimized the image and brought up a different image. It was another freeze-frame, showing a dozen people, again dressed in dark clothes. Again with somber faces.

"Different church," said Jane.

"Right. It's the video from Timothy McDougal's service. Now watch as these people walk into the church." Frost forwarded the video frame by frame and stopped. "Look who pops up at this service too."

Jane stared at the woman's dark hair, the heart-shaped face. "Are you sure it's the same woman?"

"It sure as hell looks like her. Same haircut, same face. And look closely at the plaid scarf she's wearing. Same colors, same pattern. That's her, all right. But it seems like she brought someone with her this time." Frost pointed to a sandy-haired man who stood at the woman's shoulder. They were holding hands.

"Did you see this man anywhere in the Cassandra Coyle video?"

"No. He's only at Timothy's funeral."

"So we finally have a link between these two murders," said Jane softly. She turned in astonishment to Frost. "And it's a woman."

NINETEEN

EVERETT IS GETTING TO BE A PROBLEM.

I knew this would happen. He's the sort of man who craves deep connections, who actually likes waking up in bed with the woman he fucked the night before. It has been my experience that 90 percent of men my age don't want to wake up with a woman. They'd rather hook up with a girl they found on Tinder, enjoy their quickie, then go their merry way. No dinner, no date, no need to rack their poor little brains for topics of conversation. We're all like billiard balls these days, briefly bouncing up against each other and then rolling away. For the most part, that's exactly the way I like it too. Uncomplicated and unencumbered. *Come on, baby, rock my world; now get out of here.*

This is not what Everett wants. He stands in my apartment doorway, holding a bottle of red wine, a tentative smile on his face. "You haven't returned my calls the last few days," he says. "I thought maybe if I dropped by, we might spend the evening talking. Or go out to dinner. Or just have a glass of wine."

"I'm sorry, but my life is crazy right now. And I'm just on my way out the door."

He looks at my coat, which I'm already buttoning, and sighs. "Of course. You've got places to go."

"Actually, I have to go to work."

"At six in the evening?"

"Don't, Everett. I shouldn't have to explain myself."

"I'm sorry, I'm sorry! It's just that I really *felt* something between us. And then suddenly you got skittish again. Did I do something? Say something wrong?"

I accept his bottle of wine, set it on the table by the door, and step out into the hallway. "I need a little breathing space right now, that's all." I lock the door behind me.

"I get that. You're independent; you told me that. I like my independence too."

Sure you do. That's why you were standing in my doorway, eyeing me like a worshipful puppy dog. Not that it's such a bad thing. A girl can always use a loyal hound, someone who'll adore her and overlook her faults and keep her happy in bed. A man who'll lend her money and fetch her bowls of chicken soup when she's sick. A man who'll do whatever she asks him to.

Even things he shouldn't do.

"Oh, look at the time. I really have to get going," I tell him. "I need to be at the Harvard Coop in half an hour."

"What's happening at the Coop?"

"One of my clients is doing a book-signing, and it's my job to make sure everything runs smoothly. You're welcome to come, but you can't be my date. You have to act like just another one of her fans."

"I can do that. Who's the author?"

"Victoria Avalon."

He gives me a blank stare, which makes me think better of him. Anyone who actually recognizes the name Victoria Avalon is, by my definition, a moron.

"She's a reality-TV star," I explain. "She was briefly married to Luke Jelco." Again he gives me a blank stare. "You know, the tight end? New England Patriots?"

"Oh, football. Right. So your client wrote a book?"

"Her name's on it anyway. In the publishing business, that's close enough."

"You know what? I'd love to come. It's been a while since I went to a book-signing at the Coop. Last year I met the woman who wrote the definitive biography of Bulfinch, the architect. It was kind of sad, because only three people showed up."

For a biography of Charles Bulfinch, three people would constitute a crowd.

"I hope to God more than three people show up tonight," I tell him as we walk out of the building. "Or I'll be out of a job."

EVEN SNOOTY HARVARD STUDENTS AREN'T immune to the siren call of celebrity tits and ass. They've shown up in droves, filling every seat in the small performance area on the third floor of the Harvard Coop bookstore. They're packed into the aisles of science and technology books and they even spill over onto the curving staircase. Hundreds of brainiacs, the future leaders of the free world, have come to worship at the feet of Victoria Avalon, who, and I swear this is true, once asked me: "How do you spell IQ?" The large crowd has made Victoria very happy tonight. Only last week she was yelling at me over the phone because I couldn't get enough media coverage for her new memoir. Tonight she's at her seductive best, beaming, wriggling, touching the arm of every fan who's come to get her autograph. Whether men or women, they're all enthralled. The women want to be her, and the men want to—well, we know exactly what the men want.

I stand at Victoria's left side, moving things along, flipping open the books to the title page, sliding them in front of her. She signs with a flourish, a big swirly *VA* in purple ink. The men ogle (there's a lot to ogle, because she's about to spill out of her low-cut bodice), and the women linger to chat, chat, chat. It's my job to bring the conversations to a quick close and nudge the fans along; otherwise we'll be in this bookstore all night. Victoria probably wouldn't mind that, because she feeds on adoration like a vampire, but I'm anxious to get this evening over with. Though I can't spot Everett among the crowd, I know he is patiently waiting for me to finish the event, and I feel the familiar tingle of anticipation between my legs. Maybe it's a lucky thing he stopped by to see me tonight. Sex is just what I need to relax me after a night of catering to this demanding bitch.

It takes two and a half hours for Victoria to greet all her fans. She's autographed one hundred eighty-three books, signing faster than a book a minute, but when we're done there's still a stack of sixty books left unsold. This of course makes Victoria unhappy. She wouldn't be Victoria if she was ever, for a moment in her life, satisfied with anything. As she signs the unsold stock, she whines about the venue ("more people would come here if they didn't have to drive into Cambridge!"), the weather ("it's too damn cold tonight!"), and the date ("everyone knows tonight's the final episode of *Dancing with the Stars*!"). I let her complaints roll off my back as I keep sliding her the books to sign. Out of the corner of my eye I spot Everett watching me with a sympathetic smile. *Yes, this is what I do for a living. Now you understand why I'm really, really looking forward to that bottle of wine you brought me.*

As Victoria signs the last book, I notice one of the store employees walking toward us with a bouquet of flowers in his arms. "Miss Avalon, I'm so glad you haven't left the store yet. These just arrived for you!"

At the sight of the bouquet, Victoria's pout instantly transforms into a thousand-watt smile. This is why she's a celebrity; she can turn it on and off like a switch. All she needs is a proper dose of adoration, and here it is, in the form of a plastic-wrapped bundle of roses.

"Oh, how lovely!" Victoria gushes. "Who sent them?"

"The deliveryman didn't say. But there is a card."

Victoria peels open the envelope and frowns at the handwritten message inside. "Well, this is kind of weird," she says.

"What does it say?" I ask.

"*Remember me?* That's all it says. And it's not signed." She hands me the card, but I scarcely look at it. My gaze is suddenly riveted on the bouquet itself.

On the foliage tucked in among the roses. This is not the usual fern leaf or aspidistra, bundled into bouquets by florists everywhere. While this bit of greenery means nothing to Victoria, who wouldn't know the difference between a hydrangea and a hydrant, a palm leaf does mean something to me.

Symbol of the martyr.

The card slips out of my fingers and flutters to the floor.

"These must be from one of my old admirers," Victoria says. "How weird that he didn't sign his name. Oh, well." She laughs. "A gal does love a little mystery in her life. He could have just come up and said hello. I wonder if he's here right now?"

I glance wildly around the bookstore. I see women browsing the shelves and three studious-looking young men hunched over their textbooks. And Everett. He notices I'm rattled, and he's frowning as he comes toward me.

"Holly? What's wrong?"

"I need to go home." I snatch up my coat. My hands are shaking. "I'll call you later."

TWENTY

THROUGH THE CLOSED DOOR OF THE CRAZY Ruby Films studio, Jane and Frost heard a woman's terrified shrieks, and Jane snorted. "If those kids want real nightmares, they should spend a night with us."

The door opened and a dazed-looking Travis Chang stood blinking at them. He was wearing the same ratty SCREAMFEST FILM FESTIVAL T-shirt he'd been wearing on their first visit, and his unwashed hair stood up in black tufts like greasy devil's horns. "Oh. Hey, you're back."

"Yeah, we're back," said Jane. "We need to show you something."

"Uh, we're right in the thick of editing."

"This won't take long."

Travis cast an embarrassed glance over his shoulder. "I just want to warn you, it's kinda ripe in here. You know how things get when you're, like, totally in the zone."

Judging by the condition of the studio, *in the zone* was not anyplace Jane cared to ever be. The room was even more disgusting than when they'd first visited, the trash cans overflowing with pizza boxes and Red Bull cans. Every horizontal surface was covered with wadded napkins, pens, notebooks, and electronics. The air smelled like scorched popcorn and dirty socks.

Slouched on the sofa were Travis's colleagues, Ben and Amber, who, judging by their sallow faces, hadn't been out of the building in days. They didn't even look up at their visitors but kept their eyes locked on the big-screen TV, where a buxom blonde in a low-cut T-shirt was desperately barricading a door against something that was trying to pound its way in. An ax blade splintered the wood. The blonde shrieked.

Travis hit the PAUSE button, freezing the blonde's face in mid-scream.

"What're you doing, man?" Ben protested. "We're up against the clock here."

"We're trying to make the deadline for horror-film festivals," Travis explained to Jane and Frost. "*Mr. Simian* needs to be submitted in three weeks."

"When can we see it?" asked Jane.

"Not yet. We're still editing and the soundtrack's in progress. Plus we've got a few special effects to tweak."

"I thought you guys ran out of money."

The three filmmakers looked at one another. Amber sighed. "We *are* out of money," she said. "So we all took out loans. And Ben sold his car."

"You kids are really going to gamble everything on this?"

"What else are we going to gamble on, if not our own creation?"

They were probably going to lose their filthy-looking shirts, but Jane had to admire their confidence.

"I watched *I See You,*" said Frost. "It wasn't bad. It should've made money."

Travis perked up. "You think so?"

"Better than a lot of horror films I've seen."

"Exactly! We know we can make as good a movie as any big studio. We just have to hang in there and keep telling good stories. Even if it means risking everything."

Jane pointed to the blonde on the TV screen. "I think I've seen that actress before. What else has she been in?"

"As far as I know, this was her first acting gig," said Ben. "She just has one of those universal faces."

"Standard hot blonde with perfect teeth," observed Jane.

"Yeah, they make the best victims." Ben paused. "Sorry. I guess that was in bad taste, considering . . ."

"You said you wanted to show us something," said Travis.

"Yeah. We want you to look at a photo." Jane glanced around the room for some open space to set down her laptop.

Travis swept away the pizza debris from the coffee table. "Here ya go."

Avoiding a clump of cheese that had congealed on the table, Jane set down her laptop and opened the photo file. "These are screen captures from Cassandra's memorial service. We had a surveillance camera set up at the entrance to videotape the faces of everyone who attended."

"You recorded the whole thing?" said Amber. "That's really creepy, recording people without their knowledge. It's like Big Brother watching us."

"It's like a homicide investigation." Jane turned the laptop screen to face them. "Do you recognize this woman?"

As the three filmmakers crowded around the laptop, Jane caught a powerful whiff of stale breath and dirty laundry, a stench that brought her straight back to her brothers' sleepovers, when every square inch of carpet was covered with sleeping bags and teenage boys.

Amber squinted through her black-framed glasses at the photo. "I don't remember seeing her, but there were a lot of people. Plus I was kinda weirded out about being in church."

"Why?" asked Frost.

Amber blinked at him. "I'm always worried I'll do something wrong and God'll strike me down with lightning."

"Hey, I think I remember this woman," said Ben. He leaned forward, absently stroking the week-old stubble on his chin. "She was sitting across the aisle from us. I gave her a good long look."

Amber punched his arm. "You would."

"No, no, it's 'cause she has an interesting face. I've got an eye for who'll pop on camera, and look at her. Nice cheekbones, great facial architecture, easy to light. And a big head."

"Is that good or bad?" said Jane. "A big head."

"Oh, it's good. A big head fills the screen, calls attention to itself. Gee, I wonder if she can act."

"We don't even know who she is," said Jane. "We were hoping one of you might recognize her."

"That was the only time I've ever seen her," said Ben. "At Cassie's funeral."

"You're sure you haven't seen her anywhere else? Did she come by this studio, ever hang out with Cassandra?"

"Nope." Ben glanced at his colleagues, and they shook their heads.

"Why are you asking about this woman?" said Travis.

"We're trying to find what her connection is to Cassandra and why she showed up at the church. Cassandra's stepmother doesn't know her. None of Cassandra's neighbors do either."

"What's the big deal? It's not a crime to show up at a stranger's funeral," said Amber.

"No. But it's odd."

"There were a lot of people at that service. Why are you asking about this woman in particular?"

"Because she showed up somewhere else." Jane tapped on the keyboard, and the second image of the mystery woman appeared onscreen. It was a harshly lit photo taken in the cold light of a winter morning.

"It's her again," said Amber.

"But different background, different light. Different day," noted Ben.

"Exactly," confirmed Jane. "This was from a surveillance video at a different memorial service. Notice there's a man holding hands with our mystery woman. Do you recognize him?"

All three filmmakers shook their heads.

"So what's the deal with this woman? Does she like to go to random funerals?" asked Ben.

"I don't think she chooses them at random. This second funeral was for a different homicide victim."

"Oh, wow. She's a murder junkie?" Ben looked at his colleagues again. "It's right out of *Kill Her Again, Sam.*"

"What?" asked Frost.

"It's a movie we worked on a few years ago, produced by a buddy of ours in L.A. About this Goth girl who goes to random funerals. She ends up catching the eye of a killer."

"Did Cassandra work on that movie as well?"

"We all did, but we were just part of the crew. It's not like the plot was special or anything. There really are people who go to the funerals of strangers. They feed off the grief. Or they want to be part of a community. Or they have an obsession with death. Maybe that's what she is. Just some oddball who never even knew Cassandra."

Jane looked at the young woman captured in the video. Dark-haired, beautiful, nameless. "I wonder what *her* reasons were for being there."

"Who knows? That's why we love making horror films, Detective," said Travis. "The possibilities are endless."

TWENTY-ONE

TIED TO A STAKE, SAINT POLYCARP THE MARTYR gazed serenely heavenward as the flames engulfed him, searing his skin and consuming his flesh. The man in this full-color illustration did not plead or shriek as he was burned alive on the pyre; no, he appeared to welcome the agony that would bring him straight to the arms of his Savior. Studying the image of Polycarp's demise, Jane thought of the time she'd splattered herself with hot grease while frying chicken, and she imagined the pain of that burn magnified a thousandfold, the flames lighting her clothes, her hair. Unlike Saint Polycarp, she wouldn't be gazing at heaven with a look of rapture. She'd be shrieking her head off.

Enough of this. She turned to the next page in the book, only to confront another martyr, another portrait of agony. The color illustration showed the death of Saint Erasmus of Formiae in all its bloody glory, with Erasmus stretched across a table as his torturers slit his belly open and wrapped his entrails around a windlass.

From her daughter's bedroom came the sound of Regina giggling as Gabriel read her a bedtime story, jarringly happy sounds that made the images in *The Book of Martyrs* seem all the more grotesque.

The doorbell buzzed.

Relieved to set aside the relentlessly gruesome illustrations, she left the kitchen to greet the visitor.

Father Daniel Brophy looked thinner and wearier than the last time she'd seen him, only seven months ago. His face reminded her of the martyrs she'd just been studying, a man resigned to his miseries.

"Thank you for coming, Daniel," said Jane.

"I'm not sure I can offer you much assistance, but I'm happy to try." As he hung up his coat, childish laughter erupted from Regina's bedroom.

"Gabriel's putting her to bed. Let's go talk in the kitchen."

"Is Maura joining us?"

"No. It's just you and me."

Was that disappointment or relief she saw in his eyes? She led him into the kitchen, where he surveyed the books and papers spread across the table.

"I've been reading up on the saints," she said. "Yeah, I know I should already know all this, but what can I say? Catechism class dropout."

"I thought you weren't convinced about Maura's theory."

"I'm still not sure I believe it, but I've learned it's not smart to ignore her theories. Because more often than not, she turns out to be right." Jane nodded at the

Cassandra Coyle and Timothy McDougal files on the table. "The problem is, I haven't been able to find anything that links these victims, except for the mystery woman who attended both their funerals. They had no friends in common; they lived in different neighborhoods, worked in different fields, and attended different colleges. But they were both drugged with ketamine and alcohol, and both were mutilated postmortem. Based on those mutilations, Maura believes the killer is obsessed with Catholic lore. That's where you come in."

"Because I'm your expert on saints and martyrs?"

"And you're also familiar with religious symbols in art. That's what Maura tells me."

"I've spent most of my life surrounded by sacred art. I'm somewhat familiar with the iconography."

"Then could you take another look at these crime-scene photos?" Jane slid her laptop across the table to him. "Tell me if anything new jumps out at you. Anything that might give us insight into this killer's mind."

"Maura and I have discussed these photos in detail. Shouldn't she be part of this conversation?"

"No, I'd rather hear from you separately." She added quietly, "It would be less complicated for you both, don't you think?"

She saw a flash of pain in his eyes, as stark as if she'd just thrust a blade into his chest. He sagged back in his chair and nodded. "When she called me, I thought I was ready to handle it. I thought we could both move forward as friends."

"Going on that retreat to Canada didn't help change things?"

"No. The retreat felt more like going under anesthesia. A long, deep coma. For six months I managed not to feel anything. Then when she called, when I saw her again, it was like suddenly waking up from that coma. And the pain was back. As bad as ever."

"I'm sorry to hear that, Daniel. Sorry for both of you."

From the bedroom came Regina's voice, calling out, "Good night, Daddy!" Jane saw Daniel wince, and she wondered: Does he regret never marrying, never having children? Does he ever pine for the life he could have had if he'd never donned that priest's collar?

"I want her to be happy," he said. "Nothing is more important to me than that."

"Nothing except your vows."

He looked at her with haunted eyes. "I made a promise to God when I was fourteen years old. I pledged that—"

"Yes, Maura told me about your sister. She had childhood leukemia, is that right?"

He nodded. "The doctors told us it was terminal. She was only six years old, and all I could do for her was pray. God answered my prayers, and today Sophie's alive and healthy. She has two beautiful adopted children."

"And you really believe your sister's alive only because of that deal you made with God?"

"You can't understand. You're not a believer."

"I believe we're each responsible for our own choices in life. You made your choice, for reasons that seemed right when you were fourteen. But now?" She shook her head. "Could God really be that cruel?"

The words must have stung, because he had no answer. He sat in silence, his hands resting on the illustrated book of saints and martyrs. Daniel too was a martyr, a man who'd accepted his fate as resolutely as Saint Polycarp, sacrificed to the flames.

Into that silence walked Gabriel, who came into the kitchen, saw their defeated-looking guest slumped in the chair, and gave Jane a questioning look. As a seasoned investigator, Gabriel was adept at assessing a scene, and he instantly understood that more than crime was being discussed in their kitchen. "Everything all right in here?" he asked.

Daniel glanced up, startled to see that Gabriel had joined them. "I'm afraid I don't have much to contribute."

"Intriguing theory, though, don't you think? A killer who's obsessed with religious iconography."

"Has the FBI joined the investigation?"

"No, I'm just the interested spouse on this one. Jane's spared me no details."

Jane laughed. "If a couple can't share a juicy murder, what's the point of being married?"

Gabriel nodded at the laptop. "What do you think, Daniel? Has Boston PD missed anything?"

"The symbolism seems apparent," said Daniel, clicking halfheartedly through the crime-scene photos. "The young woman's mutilation certainly looks like it's meant to represent Saint Lucy." He paused at a photo taken in Cassandra's kitchen, where the vase of flowers was displayed on the countertop. "And if you're looking for religious symbols, you can find plenty of them in this bouquet. White lilies represent purity and virginity. Red roses symbolize martyrdom." He paused. "Where did these flowers come from? Is it possible the killer—"

"No, that's a birthday bouquet from her father. So any symbolism you see there is purely incidental."

"She was killed on her birthday?"

"Three days later. December sixteenth."

For a moment Daniel stared at the birthday flowers, meant for a girl who would live only three more days.

"When was the second victim killed?" he asked. "The young man?"

"December twenty-fourth. Why?"

"And when was his birthday?" Daniel glanced up at her, and she saw a spark of excitement in his eyes. Gabriel had also picked up on the new tension in the room and he joined them at the table, his gaze fixed on Daniel.

"Let me find the autopsy report," Jane said, rifling through the file folders. "Here it is. Timothy McDougal. His date of birth was—"

"January twentieth?"

She looked up, startled. Said, softly: "Yes. January twentieth."

"How did you know his birthday?" Gabriel asked.

"The liturgical calendar. Each saint is commemorated on a particular day. On January twentieth, we honor Saint Sebastian, who's depicted in art with his body pierced by arrows."

"And Saint Lucy? Which day is she honored?" asked Jane.

"December thirteenth."

"Cassandra Coyle's birthday." Jane turned in astonishment to Gabriel. "That's it! The killer chooses the form of mutilation based on the victim's *birthday*! But how would he know what their birthdays are?"

"Driver's licenses," said Gabriel. "Young people at a bar, they almost always get carded. And both these victims had alcohol in their stomachs. So now you're talking bartenders. Servers . . ."

"Tim McDougal was stabbed with arrows," said Jane. "Did the killer have a stash of arrows handy, just in case he *happened* to run into someone born on January twentieth? He'd have to be a very well-equipped killer. Think of all the ways martyrs have been killed, with rocks and swords, cleavers and pincers. There's even one guy beaten to death with wooden shoes."

"Saint Vigilius of Trent, celebrated on June twenty-six," said Daniel. "He's often depicted holding the clog that killed him."

"Yeah, well, I doubt our killer packs a wooden shoe in the trunk of his car just in case he finds someone whose birthday is June twenty-six. No, our perp chooses his victim in advance, and *then* he gathers his tools. Which means he has access to their birth dates."

Gabriel shook his head. "You'll have to cast a very big net to find him. Birth dates are easy to find. Employee records, medical records. Facebook."

"But at least we've picked up his pattern! Mutilations that match the victims' *birth dates.* If this perp has killed before, now we can track it on ViCAP." She opened a new file on the laptop and turned the screen to Daniel. "Okay, I have a new job for you."

"What's this file I'm looking at?" he asked.

"These are all the unsolved homicides in New England this past year. Frost and I compiled a list of every victim who had postmortem injuries. After we eliminated firearm deaths, we were able to narrow it down to these thirty-two victims."

"Do you have their birth dates?" asked Daniel.

She nodded. "They would be on the attached autopsy reports. You know the liturgical calendar. Tell me if any of the victims' injuries match those of the saint celebrated on their birth date."

As Daniel slowly worked his way through the list, Jane stood up to make a fresh pot of coffee. This could be a very long night, but even without a new infusion of caffeine, her nerves were already humming. We've found it, she thought, the key to identifying the killer's earlier victims. Every new name, every new data point, improved their chances of finding some crucial link between the victims and the killer. She refilled everyone's coffee cup and sat down to watch Daniel click through the files.

An hour later, Daniel sighed and shook his head. "Nothing matches up."

"You've gone through them all?"

"All thirty-two cases. None of these injuries correlate with the victims' birth dates." He looked at Jane. "Maybe your two cases are his first kills. Maybe there aren't any other victims yet."

"Or we haven't searched widely enough," said Jane. "We should go back two years, even three. Expand the geographical region beyond New England."

"I don't know, Jane," said Gabriel. "What if Maura's

wrong and you're looking for connections that don't exist? This could end up being nothing but a huge distraction."

She scowled at the book of saints, which she'd pored over all evening, and suddenly focused on the cover image of Saint Polycarp, his flesh engulfed by flames. *Fire. It destroys everything. Bodies. Evidence.*

She reached for her cell phone. As Gabriel and Daniel watched in bewilderment, she called Frost.

"Do you still have that list of fire-related deaths?" she asked him.

"Yeah. Why?"

"Email it to me. Including all the cases that were classified accidental."

"We excluded the accidentals."

"I'm including them again. Every fire death involving a lone adult victim."

"Okay, I'm on it. Check your in-box."

"Accidental fire deaths?" said Gabriel as she hung up.

"Fire destroys evidence. And not every victim who dies in a fire gets a tox screen. I'm wondering if some of those accidental deaths weren't accidents at all."

Her laptop chimed with Frost's email.

She opened the attached file and a new list of cases appeared. Here were the two dozen victims who'd perished in accidental fires throughout New England in the last year. "Take a look," she said, and turned the laptop to Daniel.

"A ruling of accidental fire death usually means there's evidence of smoke inhalation at autopsy," said Gabriel. "That doesn't fit your perp's pattern. Not if he suffocates them with a plastic bag."

"If your victim's unconscious, you can let fire do the job. You don't need to suffocate him."

"Still, it's a different pattern, Jane."

"I'm not ready to give up on this theory yet. Maybe suffocation is a new technique for him. Maybe he's refining his—"

"Sarah Basterash, age twenty-six," said Daniel. He looked up from the laptop. "She died in a house fire in Newport, Rhode Island."

"Newport?" Jane peered over Daniel's shoulder to read the file. "November tenth, single-family home burned to the ground. Victim was alone, found in her bedroom. No evidence of trauma."

"Ketamine?" asked Gabriel.

She sighed in frustration. "A tox screen wasn't done."

"But look at her birth date," said Daniel. "It's May thirtieth. And she died in a fire."

Jane frowned at him. "Which saint is celebrated on May thirtieth?"

"Joan of Arc."

TWENTY-TWO

THE LAST TIME JANE HAD VISITED NEWPORT, IT was the height of summer, and the narrow streets were packed with tourists. She remembered trudging in shorts and sandals in the scorching heat as melting strawberry ice cream dripped down her arm. She had been eight months' pregnant with Regina, her ankles looked like swollen sausages, and she wanted nothing more than to take a nap. Still, the town had charmed her with its historic buildings and bustling waterfront, and no meal would ever top the rich lobster stew that she and Gabriel had devoured that night.

What a different town Newport was on this cold January day.

As Frost drove through the village, Jane peered out the car window at souvenir shops and restaurants that were now shuttered, at streets that winter had swept clear of all the tourists. One lone couple stood smoking cigarettes and shivering outside a pub.

"Did you ever go on a tour of the cottages when you were here?" said Frost.

"Yeah. I thought it was funny how they call them cottages. I could move my whole family into one of the closets."

"After we toured the Breakers, Alice went on a rant. I thought it was a really cool mansion, but she said it was an outrage that so much money was controlled by just one family."

"Oh, yeah. I forgot Alice was a commie."

"She's not a commie. She just has a strong sense of social justice."

Jane shot him a suspicious look. "You're sure talking a lot about Alice these days. Are you two really back together again?"

"Maybe. And I don't want to hear you say anything bad about her."

"Why would I say anything bad about your *lovely* ex-wife?"

"Because you can't help yourself."

"Apparently you can't help yourself either."

"Hey, look." He pointed to the pier. "There's a nice fish restaurant down there. Wonder if it's open? Maybe we could go there for lunch."

"Let me guess. You and Alice ate there."

"So what?"

"So I'm not in the mood to revisit all your happy memories with Alice. Let's just grab a burger on the way back." She eyed the GPS screen. "Turn left."

They drove down Bellevue Avenue, past the lavish homes that had lit the fires of Alice's socialist rage. In an earlier era, this was where tycoon families came to play during the summer, bringing their servants and carriages and ball gowns. And every autumn, those families returned to their equally lavish homes in the city, leaving these palaces empty and silent, awaiting next summer's round of parties. Jane had no illusions about where she would have stood in that social hierarchy. She'd be scrubbing pots in the kitchen or washing corsets and undergarments. Certainly she would not be one of the fortunate young ladies swaying to music in a gilded ballroom. Jane knew her place in the universe, and she'd learned to be satisfied with it.

"This is the street," she said. "Turn right."

They left behind the mansions and drove down a street where the homes were not as large but were still far more expensive than anything a Boston cop could afford. Sarah Basterash's husband worked for a major export firm, and Sarah would have enjoyed a comfortable life in this neighborhood where Lexuses and Volvos were parked in the driveways, where every front yard was impeccably landscaped. On this street of beautiful homes, it was a shock to suddenly come upon the blackened stone foundation.

Jane and Frost stepped out of the car and stared at the empty lot where the Basterash house had once stood. Though the charred remains had been hauled away, it was evident from the scorched bark on the trees that a fire had raged here, and when Jane inhaled, she imagined she could smell the stench of smoke and ash. The neighboring homes had not been touched, and they loomed on either side of the Basterash property like defiant survivors with perfect porches and manicured hedges. But the ruined foundation of their neighbor's home proved that tragedy could strike anyone. Fire made no distinction between rich and poor; the flames devoured them all.

"I WAS IN BEIJING ON a business trip when it happened," said Kevin Basterash. "My company exports agricultural products, and I was negotiating a deal to ship milk powder to China." His voice faded and he stared down at the beige carpet, which was so recently installed it still gave off the chemical smell of a new home. His apartment was spacious and sunlit, but everything about it struck Jane as temporary, from the bare walls to the empty bookshelves. Two months ago, Kevin Basterash had lost his house and his wife to the flames. Now this was what he called home, a characterless apartment complex five miles from the neighborhood where he and Sarah had once dreamed of children. In this soulless living room, not a single photograph was displayed.

The fire had taken everything.

"I got the news just before lunch, Beijing time," he said. "Our neighbor here in Newport called to tell me my house was in flames and the fire trucks had arrived. They hadn't found Sarah yet, and the neighbor was hoping she might be away and not in the house. But I already knew. I knew because Sarah didn't call me that morning, as usual. She always called me at the same time, every day." He looked at Jane and Frost. "They said it was an accident."

Jane nodded. "According to the fire investigators, your wife left candles burning on the nightstand and then she fell asleep. They found a bottle of scotch by her bed, so they assumed—"

"They assumed she was drunk and careless." Kevin gave an angry shake of his head. "That would not be Sarah. She was never careless. Yeah, she liked a drink or two at bedtime, but that doesn't mean she'd get intoxicated and sleep through a fire. That's what I told the police, the fire investigators. The problem was, the more I insisted it couldn't be an accident, the more they looked at *me.* They asked if I'd had any affairs, or if Sarah and I were arguing. The husband's always the prime suspect, right? So what if I was in China when it happened? I could have hired a killer to do it! After a while, I just had to accept that it must have been an accident. Because who'd want to hurt her? No one." He focused on Jane. "Then I got your call. And now everything's changed."

"Not necessarily," said Jane. "This is simply part of a larger investigation. We're looking at two homicide cases in Boston and trying to determine if they have any links to your wife's death. Does the name Timothy McDougal mean anything to you?"

Kevin shook his head. "I don't know that name."

"What about Cassandra Coyle?"

This time he hesitated. "Cassandra," he murmured, as though trying to conjure up a face, a memory. "Sarah did mention a friend named Cassandra, but I don't remember her last name."

"When was this?"

"Early last year. Sarah said she'd gotten a call from some girl she knew as a kid, and they were going to have lunch together. I never got the chance to meet the friend." He shook his head in self-disgust. "Probably because I was on some goddamn business trip."

"Where was your wife raised, Mr. Basterash?" asked Frost.

"Massachusetts. She moved to Newport after she found a job here, at the Montessori School."

"Did she visit the Boston area very often? Have friends or family there?"

"No, her parents are both dead, so there was really no one left for her to visit in Brookline."

Jane looked up from the notepad she'd been writing in. "Sarah grew up in Brookline?"

"Yes. She lived there until she graduated from high school."

Jane and Frost glanced at each other. Both Cassandra Coyle and Timothy McDougal had grown up in Brookline.

"Was your wife Catholic, Mr. Basterash?" asked Jane.

He frowned, clearly bewildered by Jane's question. "Her parents were Catholic, but Sarah left the Church years ago." He gave a sad laugh. "She said she was still traumatized by growing up Catholic."

"What did she mean by that?"

"It was just a joke. She used to say that the Bible should be rated R for violence."

Jane leaned forward, her pulse quickening. "How much did your wife know about Catholic saints?"

"A lot more than I do. I was raised agnostic, but Sarah could look at a painting and say, *That's Saint Stephen, who got stoned to death.*" He shrugged. "I guess that's what they teach kids in Sunday school."

"Do you know which church she attended as a child?"

"I have no idea."

"Which high school?"

"I'm sorry, I don't remember." He paused. "If I ever knew."

"Do you know any of her childhood friends from Brookline?"

For a long time he thought about this question but failed to answer it. Instead, he looked at the window, where curtains had not been hung, because this was not really a home yet. Perhaps it would never be a home but merely temporary lodging for Kevin Basterash, a place to grieve and heal before moving on.

"No," he finally said. "I blame myself for that."

"Why, sir?" Frost asked gently.

"Because I was never here for her. I was always traveling for business. Gone half the time, living out of a suitcase. Hammering out deals in Asia when I should have been home." He looked at them, and Jane saw guilt shining in his eyes. "Here you are, asking these questions about Sarah's childhood in Brookline, and I can't answer a single one."

Maybe someone else can, thought Jane.

SHE HAD NOT SPOKEN TO Elaine Coyle in weeks, and as Jane dialed the woman's number, she dreaded the question that Elaine would almost certainly ask her: *Have you caught my daughter's killer yet?* It's the one piece of news every victim's family wants to hear. They don't want more questions. They don't want excuses.

They want an end to their uncertainty. They want justice.

"I'm sorry," Jane had to tell Elaine. "We don't have a suspect yet, Mrs. Coyle."

"Then why are you calling?"

"Do you know the name Sarah Basterash?"

A pause. "No, I don't think so. Who is she?"

"A young woman who recently died in a fire in Rhode Island. She grew up in Brookline and I wondered if she knew Cassandra. She was about your daughter's age, so they may have attended the same school or the same church."

"I'm sorry, but I don't remember any girl with the last name Basterash."

"Her maiden name was Sarah Byrne. Her family lived less than a mile from—"

"Sarah Byrne? Sarah's *dead*?"

"Then you *did* know her."

"Yes. Yes, the Byrnes used to live down the road from us. Frank Byrne died of a heart attack a few years ago. And then his wife—"

"There's another name I need to ask you about," Jane cut in. "Do you remember Timothy McDougal?"

"Detective Frost asked me about him last week. That's the young man who was killed on Christmas Eve."

"Yes. But now I'm asking about a *boy* named Tim McDougal. A boy about your daughter's age, who may have gone to school with her."

"Detective Frost never told me the dead man grew up in Brookline."

"We didn't think it was relevant at the time. Do you remember him?"

"There was a boy named Tim, but I'm not sure what his last name was. And it happened so long ago. Twenty years . . ."

"*What* happened twenty years ago?"

There was a long silence. When Elaine finally answered, she spoke in barely a whisper. "The Apple Tree."

TWENTY-THREE

"When the Apple Tree Daycare abuse case went to trial, I was still in high school, so I don't know any more than you do. But you should be able to find what you need in these documents," said Norfolk County Assistant DA Dana Strout. Though she was only in her mid-thirties, gray roots were already peeking out in her hair, visible testimony to her stressful job as a prosecutor and a schedule too demanding for a much-needed visit to the hairdresser. "These boxes should get you started," Dana said as she dropped yet another load of files onto the conference room table.

Frost stared in dismay at the half dozen boxes that were already lined up on the table. "This is just to get us *started*?"

"The Apple Tree Daycare case was one of the longest criminal trials in the history of Norfolk County. These boxes contain the documents for just the pretrial investigation, which lasted over a year. So you've got a lot of homework. Good luck, Detectives."

Frost asked, with a note of desperation, "Can someone in this office give us the CliffsNotes version? Who was the prosecutor on the case?"

"The lead prosecutor was Erica Shay, but she's out of town this week."

"Is there anyone else who remembers the case?"

Dana shook her head. "The trial was twenty years ago, and the other attorneys on that case have all moved on. You know how it is in public service, Detective. Too much work for too small a paycheck. People move on to better jobs." She added, under her breath, "I'm thinking about it myself."

"We need to track down all the children who gave evidence in that trial. We can't find their names anywhere," said Jane.

"Because the victims' identities were probably sealed by the court to protect their privacy. That's why their names won't turn up on any Google search or media reports. But since you've got an active homicide investigation, I've given you access to all the records you need." Dana surveyed the boxes, then slid one across to Jane. "Here, this is probably what you want. It contains the pretrial interviews of the children. But, remember, their identities remain sealed."

"Absolutely," said Jane.

"Nothing leaves this room, okay? Take notes if you need to, and ask the clerk if you want photocopies. But the originals stay here." Dana went to the door, where she paused and looked back. "Just so you know, this office really doesn't want the case dragged back into the public eye. From what I've heard, it was a painful time for everyone involved. No one wants to revisit the Apple Tree."

"We don't have a choice."

"Are you certain this is relevant to your investigation? That trial was a long time ago, and I guarantee, Erica Shay is not going to be happy if it gets splashed across the front pages again."

"Is there some reason why she didn't want to share this information with us?"

"What do you mean? The boxes are right there."

"But we had to call the governor's office to access these files. We've never had to do that before during a homicide investigation."

Dana said nothing for a moment, just looked at the boxes lined up on the table. "I really can't comment."

"Did someone ask you not to?"

"Look, all I can tell you is, the trial was very sensitive. For weeks it was front-page news, and no wonder. A missing nine-year-old girl. A daycare operated by a family of pedophiles. Charges of murder and satanic-ritual abuse. Erica scored guilty verdicts for the abuse charges, but she couldn't convince the jury on the murder charge. So you can understand why she's not happy about this being dredged up again."

"We need to interview Ms. Shay. When will she be available?"

"As I said, she's out of town, and I don't know when she'll be able to talk to you." Dana turned to the door again. "Better get started. Office closes in two hours."

Jane regarded the boxes and sighed. "We're going to need a lot more than two hours."

"More like a month," grumbled Frost as he lifted an armload of files from the pretrial box.

Jane grabbed her own stack of folders and sat down across from him. Shuffling through the labels, she saw that they contained interviews, medical reports, and psychologists' evaluations.

The first folder she opened was labeled *Devine, H.*

She and Frost had earlier read the *Boston Globe* coverage of the trial, so they were already familiar with the basic facts of the case. The Apple Tree Daycare Center in Brookline, operated by Irena and Konrad Stanek and their twenty-two-year-old son, Martin, provided after-school supervision for children aged five to eleven. It also offered afternoon bus transportation straight from the local elementary school, a much-valued service for busy working parents. Apple Tree called itself *a place where both minds and souls are nurtured.* The Staneks were well-regarded members of the local Catholic church, where Irena and Konrad taught catechism classes. Martin had recently begun driving the Apple Tree school bus, and he liked to entertain the children with his magic tricks and balloon animals. For five years, Apple Tree Daycare operated without a single notable complaint.

Then nine-year-old Lizzie DiPalma vanished.

On a Saturday afternoon in October, Lizzie walked out of her house wearing a knit cap decorated with silver bugle beads, rode away on her bike, and was never seen again. Two days later, Lizzie's beaded hat was found on Martin Stanek's bus by one of the children. Since Martin was the only driver of that bus, he instantly became the prime suspect in Lizzie's disappearance. The case against him solidified when ten-year-old Holly Devine revealed a shocking secret.

Jane opened Holly Devine's file and read the psychologist's interview of the girl.

> *Subject is a ten-year-old female who lives with her parents, Elizabeth and Earl Devine, in Brookline, MA. She has no siblings. For two years she has attended the Apple Tree Daycare Center as an after-school student. On October 29, she reported to her mother that "bad things happened at Apple Tree," and she did not want to return. When pressed for more details, she said, "Martin and his mommy and daddy touched me where they're not supposed to."*

With growing horror, Jane read what the Stanek family had done to Holly Devine. The slapping, the fondling, the bruising. The penetration. She had to close the file and take a few deep breaths to calm herself. What she could not do was rid herself of the images of those three predators and their ten-year-old victim. Nor could she avoid thinking about her own daughter, Regina, who was only three years old. She thought of how she would react if she ever caught such monsters abusing her child. She thought of how little would be left of them after she finished exacting her revenge. If ever Jane broke the law, it would be for doing what mother bears do to anyone who threatens their cubs.

"Timothy McDougal was only five years old," said Frost. He looked up from the file he was reading with an expression of disgust. "His parents didn't even realize he was molested until the police called and said their son might be a victim."

"They had no idea he was being abused?"

"None at all. Same with Sarah Byrne. She was only six years old. It took half a dozen interviews by therapists before Sarah finally told them what happened."

Reluctantly, Jane refocused on Holly Devine's file.

> *. . . put his fingers inside me and it hurt. Then Irena did it to me, and the old man did it. Billy and I were screaming, but no one could hear us, because we were in the secret room. Sarah and Timmy and Cassie too. We were all locked up in the room, and they wouldn't stop . . .*

She set aside the file, flipped open her laptop, and searched online for the name *Holly Devine.* She found Facebook pages for two Holly Devines. One was forty-eight years old and lived in Denver. The other was a thirty-six-year-old in Seattle. There was no Holly Devine in Boston, or any who matched the age of the Holly Devine who'd been abused at Apple Tree. Perhaps she'd married and now had a different last name. Perhaps she simply had no online presence.

At least her name had not turned up in any obituaries.

In the psychologist's report, she found the phone number listed for Holly's family. Twenty years later, did the girl's parents still live at the same Brookline address, have the same phone number? She pulled out her cell phone and dialed.

Three rings later, a man answered: "Hello?" Deep-voiced and gruff.

"I'm Detective Jane Rizzoli, Boston PD. I'm trying to locate Holly Devine. Would you happen to know—"

"She doesn't live here."

"Can you tell me where she is?"

"No."

"Are you Mr. Devine? Hello?"

There was no response. The man had hung up.

Well, that was weird.

"Jesus," said Frost, staring at his laptop.

"What is it?"

"I'm looking at the file for Bill Sullivan, eleven years old. He's one of the kids who was abused by the Staneks."

Bill. *Billy.* She opened Holly Devine's folder again and spotted the name.

Billy and I were screaming, but no one could hear us, because we were in the secret room. . . .

"I googled the name," said Frost. "A young man named Bill Sullivan has just gone missing in Brookline."

"What? When?"

"Two days ago. This missing man is the same age, so he could be the same Bill Sullivan." He spun his laptop around for Jane to see.

Displayed on the screen was a brief article from *The Boston Globe.*

Detectives Probe Disappearance of Brookline Man

> *The vehicle owned by a missing Brookline man was found abandoned near the Putterham Meadow Golf Course early Tuesday morning. Thirty-one-year-old Bill Sullivan vanished Monday night and was reported missing by his mother, Susan, the next morning. He was last seen on surveillance camera leaving his office at Cornwell Investments. Bloodstains were found inside the vehicle, a late-model BMW, and police classify the disappearance as suspicious.*
>
> *Mr. Sullivan, an investment adviser, is described as six foot one and approximately 170 pounds, with blond hair and blue eyes.*

"Same name. Same age," said Jane.

"And the mother's name in the boy's file is also Susan. It's *got* to be the same kid."

"But this isn't a homicide; it's a missing-persons case. That doesn't fit the pattern." She looked at Frost. "What's the boy's birthday?"

Frost glanced at Bill Sullivan's file. "April twenty-eighth."

She pulled up the liturgical calendar on her laptop. "On April twenty-eighth, they honor Saint Vitalis of Milan," she said.

"Was he a martyr?"

Jane stared at the screen. "Yes. Saint Vitalis was buried alive."

That's why Bill Sullivan's body hasn't been found.

She jumped to her feet. Frost was right behind her as she walked out of the room and headed down the hall, straight to Dana Strout's office. The attorney was on the phone and she swiveled around, startled, as Jane and Frost invaded her space.

"The Staneks," said Jane. "Are they still in prison?"

"Do you mind if I finish this phone call first?"

"We need answers *now.*"

Dana said into the phone, "They're standing in my office right this minute. I'll call you back." She hung up and looked at Jane. "What is this all about?"

"Where are the Staneks?"

"Really, I don't understand the urgency."

"The Staneks went to prison because the children at their daycare center accused them of abuse. Three of those children are now dead. One has just gone missing. I'll ask you again. *Where are the Staneks?*"

For a moment Dana tapped a pen against her desk. "Konrad Stanek died in prison soon after the trial," she said. "His wife, Irena, passed away about four years ago, also while in prison."

"And their son, Martin? Where is he?"

"I just got off the phone with Erica Shay, the prosecutor. She says Martin Stanek served out his sentence. He's been released."

"When?"

"Three months ago. October."

TWENTY-FOUR

DADDY IS ON THE PHONE, HIS VOICE QUIET AND urgent.

"A woman's been calling here, asking about you," he says.

"Is it the same woman who called before?" I ask.

"No, this is a different woman. Claims she's a detective with Boston PD. Says it's urgent you get in touch with her because she's worried about your safety."

"Do you believe her?"

"I checked around. Found out Boston PD does have a Detective Rizzoli who works in homicide. But you never know. You can never be too careful, baby. I didn't tell her a thing."

"Thank you, Daddy. If she calls again, don't talk to her."

Over the phone I hear him coughing, the same stubborn cough he's had for months. I used to tell him that the damn cigarettes would kill him someday, and to stop me from nagging about it, he finally quit smoking, but the cough hasn't gone away. It's settled into his chest, and I hear the rattle of wet mucus. It's been far too long since I've visited. We both agreed I should stay away, because someone might be watching his house, but this cough worries me. He's the only one I really trust, and I don't know what I'll do without him.

"Daddy?"

"I'm all right, kitten," he wheezes. "I just want to keep my baby safe. Something has to be done about him."

"There's nothing I can do."

"But I can," he says quietly.

I pause, listening to my father's noisy breathing, and I consider what it is he's offering. My father does not make idle promises. He says exactly what he means.

"You know I'd do anything for you, Holly. Anything."

"I know, Daddy. We just have to be careful, and everything will be fine."

But everything is not fine, I think, as I hang up. Detective Rizzoli is looking for me, and I'm astonished by the speed with which she's connected me to the others. But she can't possibly know the whole story, and she never will.

Because I will never tell.

And neither will he.

TWENTY-FIVE

IT WAS THE SHABBIEST APARTMENT BUILDING ON the street, a three-story walk-up in Revere that was just a few rotten boards short of being condemned. Most of the paint had long since flaked off, and as Jane and Frost climbed the outside staircase to the third-floor unit, she felt the handrail wobble and imagined the whole rickety structure peeling away from the building and collapsing like a Tinkertoy ladder.

Frost knocked on the door and they waited, shivering and exposed, for someone to answer. They knew he was inside; Jane could hear the TV, and through the frayed curtains she glimpsed movement. At last the door opened and Martin Stanek stood glowering at them.

The photos of Martin taken at the time of his arrest two decades earlier showed a bespectacled young man with wheat-colored hair and a face that was still round and cherubic at the age of twenty-two. If Jane had seen young Martin on the street, she would have dismissed him as harmless, a man too meek to look her straight in the eye. She'd expected to see an older version of that man in the photograph, perhaps balder and flabbier, so she was taken aback by the man who now stood in the doorway. Two decades in prison had transformed him into a muscular machine with a gladiator's shoulders. His head was shaved, and there was no trace of softness left in that face, which now had the flattened nose of a boxer. A scar ran like an ugly railroad track above his left eyebrow, and his cheek was misshapen, as if the bone had been shattered and left to heal distorted.

"Martin Stanek?" said Jane.

"Who wants to know?"

"I'm Detective Rizzoli, Boston PD. This is my partner, Detective Frost. We need to ask you some questions."

"Aren't you about twenty years too late?"

"May we come in?"

"I served my time. I don't need to answer any more questions." He started to close the door in their faces.

Jane put out a hand to stop it. "You don't want to do that, sir."

"I'm within my rights."

"We can talk here and now, or we can talk at Boston PD. Which would you prefer?"

For a moment he considered his options, which he realized amounted to no choice at all. Without a word, he left the door open and turned back in to his apartment.

Jane and Frost followed him inside and shut the door against the cold.

Scanning the apartment, she focused on a painting of the Madonna and child, framed in gilt and hanging in a prominent place on the wall. Displayed on a table beneath it were half a dozen family photos: A smiling man and woman posing with a young boy. The same couple, middle-aged now, arms around each other's waists. The trio sitting around a campfire. All the photos were of the Staneks, before prison tore them apart.

Martin shut off the TV, and in the sudden silence they could hear the traffic through the thin walls, the rumble of the refrigerator in the kitchen. Although the stove and countertops were wiped clean and the dishes were washed and stacked on the drainboard, the apartment smelled like mold and rancid grease, an odor that probably came with the building itself, the legacy of tenants long gone.

"It's the only place I could rent," said Martin, reading the distaste in Jane's face. "Can't go back to my house in Brookline, even though it's still in my name. I'm a convicted sex offender, and the house is near a playground. I can't live anyplace where children might go. Had to put the house on the market just to pay the taxes. So this is it now. Home sweet home." He waved at the stained carpet, the threadbare sofa, and looked at them. "Why are you here?"

"We want to ask about your activities, Mr. Stanek. Where you were on certain days."

"Why should I cooperate? After what was done to me?"

"Done to *you*?" said Jane. "You think *you're* the victim?"

"Do you have any idea what happens to convicted pedophiles in prison? You think the guards try to keep you safe? No one gives a fuck if you live or die. They just stitch you up and throw you back to the wolves." His voice cracked. He turned away and sank into a chair at the kitchen table.

After a moment, Frost pulled out a chair and sat down as well. Quietly, he asked, "What happened to you in prison, Mr. Stanek?"

"What happened?" Martin raised his head and pointed at his own scarred face. "You can see what happened. The first night they knocked out three of my teeth. The next week they blew out my cheekbone. Then they smashed the fingers in my right hand. Then it was my left testicle."

"I'm sorry to hear about that, sir," Frost said. He *did* sound sorry. In the game of Good Cop, Bad Cop, Frost was always cast as Good Cop because the role was so natural to him. He was known as the Boy Scout of the homicide unit, friend to dogs and cats, kids and old ladies. The man you couldn't corrupt, so no one ever tried to.

Even Martin seemed to realize this was not an act. Frost's quiet note of sympathy made Martin suddenly look away, a sheen in his eyes. "What do you want from me?" he asked.

"Where were you on November tenth?" asked Jane, the Bad Cop. This time it was not merely an act; since becoming a mother, any crime against a child was a trigger point for her. Giving birth to Regina had made

Jane feel vulnerable to all the Martin Staneks in this world.

Martin scowled at her. "I don't know where I was on November tenth. Do you remember where *you* were two months ago?"

"What about December sixteenth?"

"Ditto. No idea. Probably sitting right here."

"And December twenty-fourth?"

"Christmas Eve? That I do know. I was at St. Clare's Church, eating dinner. They have a special holiday meal every year for people like me. People with no friends or families. Roast turkey and cornbread stuffing and mashed potatoes. Pumpkin pie for dessert. Ask them. They probably remember I was there. I'm ugly enough to be memorable."

Jane and Frost glanced at each other. If confirmed, it gave Stanek an alibi for Tim McDougal's murder. That would certainly present a problem.

"Why are you asking these questions?" he said.

"Remember those children you molested twenty years ago?"

"Never happened."

"You were tried and convicted, Mr. Stanek."

"By a jury who believed a pack of lies. By a prosecutor on a witch hunt."

"By children who dared to speak up."

"They were too young to know better. They said whatever they were told to say. Crazy things, impossible things. Read the transcripts; see for yourself. *Martin killed a cat and made us drink the blood. Martin took us into the woods to meet the devil. Martin made a tiger fly.* Do you think *any* of that happened?"

"The jury did."

"They were fed a load of crap. The prosecutors said we worshiped the devil—even my mom, who went to Mass three times a week. They said I picked up the kids in my bus and drove them to the woods to molest them. They even accused me of killing that little girl."

"Lizzie DiPalma."

"All because her hat was on my bus. Then that nasty Mrs. Devine went to the police and suddenly I'm a monster. I kill and eat kids for breakfast."

"Mrs. Devine? Holly's mother?"

"That woman saw the devil everywhere. Took one look at me and declared me evil. No wonder her little girl had so many tales to tell. How I tied kids to trees and sucked their blood and molested them with sticks. Then the prosecutors got the other kids to repeat the stories, and this is the result." Again he pointed to his face. "Twenty years in jail, a broken nose, a smashed jaw. Half my teeth gone. I survived only because I learned to fight back, unlike my dad. They said he died of a stroke. They said he popped a vessel and bled into his brain. The truth is, prison destroyed him. But it didn't destroy me, because I didn't let it. I'm gonna live long enough to see justice."

"Justice?" said Jane. "Or vengeance?"

"Sometimes there's no difference."

"Twenty years in prison gives you a lot of time to think, to build up a big head of rage. Time to plan how you'll get back at the people who put you there."

"You bet I want to get back at them."

"Even though they were just kids at the time?"

"What?"

"The kids you molested, Mr. Stanek. You're making them pay for telling the police what you did to them."

"I wasn't talking about the kids. I was talking about that bitch of a prosecutor. Erica Shay *knew* we were innocent, and she burned us at the stake anyway. When this journalist I've been talking to writes her book, it'll all come out."

"Interesting description you just used: *burned at the stake.*" Jane looked at the painting of the Madonna and child hanging on his wall. "I see you're a religious man."

"Not anymore."

"Then why hang that portrait of Mary and Jesus?"

"Because it was my mother's. It's all I have left of her. That and some photos."

"You were raised Catholic. I bet you know all your saints and martyrs."

"What're you talking about?"

Was that genuine bewilderment she saw in his eyes, the baffled response of an innocent man? *Or is he just a very good actor?*

"Tell me how Saint Lucy died," she said.

"Why?"

"Do you know or not?"

He shrugged. "Saint Lucy was tortured, and they cut out her eyes."

"And Saint Sebastian?"

"The Romans shot him full of arrows. What does that have to do with anything?"

"Cassandra Coyle. Tim McDougal. Sarah Byrne. Those names mean anything to you?"

He was silent, but his face had paled.

"Surely you remember the kids you picked up every day after school? The kids who rode in your bus? The kids who told the prosecutor what you did to them when no one was looking?"

"I didn't do anything to them."

"They're dead, Mr. Stanek, all three of them. All since you got out of prison. Isn't it interesting how you served twenty years in prison, you're finally released, and suddenly, *bam bam bam,* people start dying."

He rocked back in his chair as though slammed there by a physical blow. "You think *I* killed them?"

"Can you blame us for reaching that conclusion?"

He gave a disbelieving laugh. "Yeah, who else're you gonna blame? Somehow it always points to me."

"Did you kill them?"

"No, I did not kill them. But I'm sure you'll find a way to prove it anyway."

"I tell you what we're going to do, Mr. Stanek," said Jane. "We are now going to search your residence and your vehicle. You can cooperate and give us permission. Or we can do it the hard way, with a warrant."

"I don't have a vehicle," he said dully.

"Then how do you get around?"

"The kindness of strangers." He looked at Jane. "There are a few people like that left in the world."

"Do we have your permission to search, sir?" said Frost.

Stanek gave a defeated shrug. "It doesn't matter what I say. You'll search the place anyway."

As far as Jane was concerned, that counted as a yes.

She turned to Frost, who pulled out his cell phone to text the waiting CSRU team.

"Watch him," Jane said to Frost. "I'll start in the bedroom."

Like the living room, the bedroom was a grim and claustrophobic space. The only source of daylight was a single window that looked out on the narrow alley between buildings. Brown stains mottled the carpet, and the air smelled like stale linens and mildew, but the bed was neatly made and not even a stray sock was in sight. She went first into the bathroom and opened the medicine cabinet, hunting for a vial of anything that might be ketamine. She found only aspirin and a box of Band-Aids. In the under-sink cabinet, there was toilet paper but no duct tape, no rope, nothing from a killer's toolbox.

She returned to the bedroom and looked under the bed, felt between the mattress and box spring. She turned to the lone nightstand and opened the drawer. Inside were a flashlight, a few loose buttons, and an envelope filled with photographs. She shuffled through the pictures, most of them taken decades earlier, when the Staneks were still together as a family. Before they were wrenched apart, never again to see one another. She paused at the last photo in the envelope. It was an image of two women in their sixties, both wearing orange prison garb. The first woman was Martin's mother, Irena, her silver hair thinned to wisps, her face wasted to a ghost of her younger self. But it was the second face that shocked Jane, because it was a face she recognized.

She flipped over the photo and stared at the words written there in ink: *Your mother told me everything.*

Grimly, Jane returned to the living room and thrust the photo at Stanek. "Do you know who this woman is?" she asked him.

"That's my mother. A few months before she died in Framingham."

"No, the woman standing beside her."

He hesitated. "Someone she met there. A friend."

"What do you know about this *friend*?"

"She looked out for my mother in prison. Kept her safe from the other inmates, that's all."

Jane turned over the photo and pointed to the words written on the reverse. "*Your mother told me everything.* What does that mean? What did your mother tell her, Mr. Stanek?"

He said nothing.

"Maybe the truth about what happened at Apple Tree? Where Lizzie DiPalma's buried? Or maybe what you planned to do to those kids after you got out of prison?"

"I got nothing more to say." He shot so abruptly to his feet that Jane flinched away, startled.

"Maybe someone else does," Jane said, and she pulled out her cell phone to call Maura.

TWENTY-SIX

THE WOMAN STARED FROM THE PHOTO WITH A direct gaze that seemed to say: *I see you.* Her hair, half silver, half black, stood out like porcupine quills on her squarish head, but it was the eyes that gave Maura the deepest shock of recognition. It was like looking at herself in a future mirror.

"It's her. It's Amalthea," said Maura. In astonishment, she glanced at Jane. "She knew Irena Stanek?"

Jane nodded. "That photo was taken four years ago, just before Irena died at MCI–Framingham. I spoke to the warden, who confirms that Irena and Amalthea were friends. They spent almost all their time together, at meals and in the common areas. Amalthea knows all about the Apple Tree and what the Staneks did to those children. No wonder she and Irena were a pair. Monsters who understood each other."

Maura studied the face of Irena Stanek. Some might claim they could see evil shining in a person's eyes, but the woman standing beside Amalthea in this photograph seemed neither evil nor dangerous, merely ill and exhausted. There was nothing in Irena's eyes that would warn a victim: *Stay away. Danger here.*

"They look like two sweet old grannies, don't they?" said Jane. "Seeing them, you'd have no idea who they really are or what they've done. After Irena died, Amalthea mailed that photo to Martin Stanek, and since his release from prison, she's been writing him letters. Two killers communicating with each other, one on the outside, one on the inside."

Amalthea's words whispered from Maura's memory, their meaning suddenly, chillingly significant: *You'll find another one soon.*

"She knows what Stanek's been doing," said Maura.

Jane nodded. "It's time to talk to her."

ONLY A FEW WEEKS EARLIER, Maura had said her final goodbye to Amalthea Lank. Now here she was in the interview room at MCI–Framingham, waiting to confront the woman she had vowed never to see again. This time she would not have to face Amalthea alone. Jane would be watching from the other side of the one-way mirror, ready to step in if the conversation turned dangerous.

Jane spoke to her over the intercom. "Are you sure you're okay about this?"

"We have to do it. We have to find out what she knows."

"I hate putting you in this position, Maura. I wish there were some other way."

"I'm the one person she'll open up to. I'm the one with the connection."

"Stop saying that."

"But it's true." Maura took a deep breath. "Let's see if I can use that connection."

"All right, they're about to bring her into the room. Ready?"

Maura gave a stiff nod. The door swung open, and the clank of steel manacles announced the entrance of Amalthea Lank. As the guard shackled the prisoner's ankle to the table, Amalthea's gaze stayed on Maura, her eyes as focused as lasers. Since her first round of chemotherapy, Amalthea had regained some weight, and her hair was beginning to grow back in short, wispy strands. But it was her eyes that revealed the extent of her recovery. The canny gleam was back, dark and dangerous.

The guard withdrew, leaving the two women to silently regard each other. Maura had to resist the temptation to look away, to turn to the one-way mirror for reassurance.

"You said you weren't ever coming back to see me," said Amalthea. "Why are you here?"

"That box of photos you sent me."

"How do you know I'm the one who sent the box?"

"Because I recognized the faces in the photos. It's your family."

"*Your* family too. Your father. Your brother."

"A woman delivered that box to my house. Who was she?"

"No one important. Just someone who owed me a favor because I kept her safe in here." Amalthea leaned back in the chair and gave Maura a knowing smile. "When it suits me, I watch out for people. I make sure that nothing happens to them, both inside these walls and outside."

Delusions of grandeur, thought Maura. She's a pathetic old woman dying in prison and she believes she still has the power to manipulate. Why did I think she could actually tell us anything?

Amalthea glanced at the one-way mirror. "Detective Rizzoli's behind that window, isn't she? Watching and listening to us. I see you both on the news all the time. They call you 'Boston's First Ladies of Crime.'" She turned to the window. "If you want to know about Irena Stanek, Detective, you should come in here and ask me yourself."

"How did you know we're here about Irena?" asked Maura.

Amalthea snorted. "Really, Maura. Do you give me so little credit? I know what's happening out there. I know what you're up against."

"You were friends with Irena Stanek."

"She was just another lost soul I met in here. I looked out for her, kept her safe. Too bad she died before she could return any favors."

"Is that why you've been writing to Martin Stanek? Because he owes you?"

"I looked out for his mother. Why wouldn't he do me a few favors?"

"Like what?"

"Buy me magazines, newspapers. My favorite chocolate bars."

"He also told you things. Things he was planning to do."

"Did he?"

"When I visited you in the hospital, you said, *You'll find another one soon.* You meant we'd find another one of Martin Stanek's victims, didn't you?"

"Did I say that?" Amalthea shrugged and pointed to her head. "You know, chemo brain. It fogs the memory."

"Did Stanek tell you what he planned to do to the children who exposed him?"

"Why do you think he was planning anything?"

This was a chess game, Amalthea playing coy, bargaining for information. Giving away nothing for free.

"Answer me, Amalthea. There are lives at stake," said Maura.

"And this should matter to me?"

"If there's any trace of humanity in you, it should matter."

"Whose lives are we talking about?"

"Twenty years ago, five children helped send the Staneks to prison. Now three of those children are dead and one has gone missing. But you already know this, don't you?"

"What if those victims weren't so innocent? What if you have it all turned around and the Staneks were the real victims?"

"Up is down, black is white?"

"You didn't know Irena. I did. I took one look at her and I knew she didn't belong in here. People like to talk about stamping out evil, but most of you can't recognize it when you see it."

"I assume you can?"

Amalthea smiled. "I know my own kind. Do you?"

"I judge people by their actions, and I know what Martin Stanek did to those children."

"Then you don't know anything."

"What am I supposed to know?"

"That sometimes up really *is* down."

"You told me we'd find another victim soon. How did you know that?"

"You didn't seem to care at the time."

"Did Martin Stanek tell you? Did he share his plans for revenge?"

Amalthea sighed. "You're asking all the wrong questions."

"What's the right question?"

Amalthea turned to the one-way mirror and smiled at Jane, who was standing on the other side of the glass. "Which victim *haven't* you found?"

"IT'S ALL BULLSHIT. SHE TALKS in riddles just to string you along. Make sure you come back and visit her." Jane slapped the steering wheel. "Damn it, I should have talked to the bitch myself. I shouldn't have put you through that. I'm sorry."

"We both agreed it had to be me," said Maura. "I'm the one she trusts."

"You're the one she can manipulate." Jane scowled at the afternoon traffic, which had slowed their progress back to Boston. A line of cars stretched out before them, as far as they could see. "We got nothing useful out of her."

"She mentioned a victim you haven't found yet."

"She probably means Bill Sullivan, the young man who vanished in Brookline. If he was buried alive like Saint Vitalis, we may never find him. I just hope the poor guy was unconscious when Stanek started shoveling in the dirt."

"What if she was talking about a different victim, Jane? You still haven't found Holly Devine. Do you know if she's alive?"

"I keep calling her father, and he keeps refusing to talk to me. Maybe that's a good thing. If we can't find her, the killer can't find her either."

Maura looked at Jane. "You're so certain Martin Stanek is the killer. Why don't you arrest him?"

Jane's silence was revealing. For a moment she simply stared in silence at the traffic ahead. "I can't prove it," she finally admitted.

"You searched his apartment. You didn't find *any* evidence?"

"No ketamine, no duct tape, no scalpels, nothing. He doesn't have a car, so how did he move Tim McDougal's body to that pier? Plus, he has an ironclad alibi for Christmas Eve. He *was* eating dinner at the church soup kitchen. The nuns remember him."

"Maybe he's not your perp."

"Or he's working with a partner. Someone who's doing the killing for him. Stanek spent twenty years in prison, and who knows who he met in there? Someone *has* to be helping him."

"You're already monitoring his phone. Who does he talk to?"

"Just people you'd expect. His lawyer, the local

pizza joint. Some journalist who's writing a book. The realtor who's selling his parents' house."

"Anyone with a criminal record?"

"No. They all check out squeaky clean." Jane glared at the road ahead. "He's got to be working with someone he met in prison."

A minute passed. "What if Stanek is innocent?" Maura asked quietly.

"He's the only one with a motive. Who else would it be?"

"I just worry that we've settled on him too soon."

Jane looked at her. "Okay, tell me what's bugging you."

"Something that Amalthea told me. She said I'm too sure of myself and it makes me blind. Unable to see the truth."

"She was messing with your head again."

"What if we're *all* blind, Jane? What if Martin Stanek isn't guilty of anything?"

Jane gave a groan of frustration and abruptly turned the car onto the next exit ramp.

"What are you doing?"

"We're going to Brookline. I'm going to show you the old Apple Tree Daycare Center."

"It's still there?"

"It was in a wing of the Staneks' house. Frost and I walked the property yesterday. The place has been on the market for years, but there've been no offers. I guess no one wants a house with satanic vibes."

"Why are you taking me there?"

"Because Amalthea put that bug in your ear and

now you're doubting everything I tell you. I want to show you why I think Martin Stanek is guilty as hell."

By the time they arrived at the Stanek property, the sun was already setting, and the trees cast spindly shadows across the snow-covered front yard. The signpost still stood near the gate, but the shingle for Apple Tree Daycare was long gone, and the only evidence that children had once played in this yard was a dilapidated swing set. Maura lingered in the warm car for a moment, reluctant to trudge through the cold to that sagging front porch. The house was a traditional New England Cape with wooden shutters and double-hung windows, the clapboards now feathered with peeling flakes of paint. Disintegrating roof shingles littered the snow with flecks of asphalt.

"What exactly am I supposed to see in there?" said Maura.

"Come on in." Jane shoved open her car door. "I'll show you."

A path to the front porch had already been trampled through the ankle-deep snow during Jane and Frost's visit the day before, and they followed the same iced-over footprints to the porch.

"The stairs are coming apart, so be careful," Jane warned.

"Is the rest of the house in such bad shape?"

"The place is basically a teardown." Jane lifted a rock near the doorstep and retrieved a key. "I don't know why the Realtor even bothers to lock the door. She should invite vandals to torch the place and take care of the problem." Jane pushed the front door, and it gave a haunted-house creak as it swung open. "Welcome to Satan's Daycare."

It felt even colder inside the house, as if a chill had been permanently trapped within these walls. Maura stood in the shadowy foyer and surveyed peeling wallpaper printed with dainty pink roses, a floral print that probably graced the homes of countless grandmothers. A cracked mirror hung in the hallway, and the wide-plank pine floor was littered with dead leaves and other detritus that had been tracked inside or blown in by the wind whenever a visitor stepped through the front door.

"The stairs lead up to three bedrooms, where the Staneks lived," said Jane. "There's nothing to see up there, just empty rooms. Their furniture was auctioned off years ago, to pay for the family's legal bills."

"Martin Stanek still has title to the place?"

"Yes, but he can't live here because he's a registered sex offender. And he couldn't keep up with the property taxes, so he was forced to put the house on the market." Jane gestured down the hallway. "They operated the daycare center at that end of the house. That's what I want you to see."

Maura followed Jane past a bathroom with missing floor tiles and a toilet stained with rust and stepped into what had once been the Apple Tree playroom. Wide windows faced a backyard where saplings had sprung up, the woods marching ever closer to the house. Water had seeped through the roof, and the carpet stank of mold.

"Take a look at the wall," said Jane.

Maura turned and stared at the gallery of portraits, the faces now familiar to her.

"You recognize her, don't you?" said Jane, pointing to an image of a serene-faced woman holding two eyeballs in her hand. "Our old friend Saint Lucy. And, look, there's Saint Sebastian, skewered by arrows. Saint Vitalis. Saint Joan, burned at the stake. Irena Stanek taught catechism classes at her church, and she made sure the kids here learned all the saints' days. She even had them write their names under the saints who were honored on their birthdays. Look who wrote her name under Saint Lucy."

Maura frowned at the block letters, written in a childish hand. *Cassandra Coyle.*

"And there's Timmy McDougal's name, under Saint Sebastian. And Billy Sullivan's under Saint Vitalis. It's like these kids signed their own death warrants twenty years ago."

"You can find pictures of saints in any Catholic school classroom. This doesn't prove anything, Jane."

"This is the house where Martin Stanek grew up. Every day, he saw this wall of saints. He knew which kid's birthday was Saint Lucy's day or Saint Joan's day. And see how Irena marked the martyrs with gold stars? *Hooray for you, your saint died a gruesome death!* Stoning, crucifixion, flaying alive. The church's greatest hits are right here, and Martin lived with them. Maybe he was inspired by them."

Maura focused on the image of paired martyrs, one holding a sword. It was the same pair of martyrs she had seen in the stained-glass window in Our Lady of Divine Light. *Saint Fusca and Saint Maura. Beheaded.*

"And here's the name of our fifth child witness. The one we can't locate," said Jane. She pointed to the name

Holly Devine, printed neatly beneath the image of a man with blood streaming from his gaping mouth.

"Saint Livinus," said Maura.

"If we don't find Holly soon, that's how she's going to end up. Like poor old Saint Livinus, who had his tongue ripped out of his mouth to keep him from preaching."

Shivering, Maura turned away from the wall of horrors. In the deepening gloom, the house had grown even colder, and she felt the chill sink deep into her bones. She went to the windows and looked at the overgrown backyard, which was now receding into shadow.

"I keep thinking about Regina," said Jane. "What if I'd been one of the parents who sent a kid here? You do everything you can to keep your kid safe and protect her from monsters, but then you have to pay the bills and go to work. You have to trust *someone* with your kid."

"You're lucky you have your mom to watch her."

"Yeah, but what if my mom couldn't do it? What if I didn't have a mom? I'm sure some of these parents didn't have a choice, but couldn't they sense that *something* was wrong about this place?"

"You say that only because you know what happened here."

"Don't you feel the vibes?"

"I don't believe in vibes."

"Only because you can't measure them with one of your fancy scientific instruments."

"What I can measure is temperature, and I'm cold. If there's nothing else to see here, I'd like to—" Suddenly Maura paused, staring at the trees. "Someone's out there."

Jane looked out the window. "I don't see anyone."

"He was standing right at the edge of the woods. Facing this way."

"I'll take a look."

"Wait. Don't you think you should call for backup?"

But Jane was already running out the back door.

Maura stepped outside and saw Jane dart into a thicket of evergreens, where she was quickly swallowed up in the shadows. Maura could hear her moving through the underbrush, twigs snapping under her boots like sharp explosions.

Then silence.

"Jane?"

Heart thumping hard, Maura followed Jane's path across the yard and plunged into the gloom of the woods. The snow hid roots and fallen branches, and she was as noisy as a buffalo as she stumbled and crashed her way among the trees. She imagined Jane sprawled in the snow, imagined a killer standing over her, about to deliver a fatal blow.

Call for backup.

She pulled the cell phone out of her pocket and with chilled fingers tapped in the code to unlock it. Then she heard a shouted command:

"Freeze! Police!"

Maura followed the sound of Jane's voice and stumbled into a clearing, where Jane stood with her weapon drawn. Yards away stood a figure with arms raised to the sky, face hidden by the shadow of a jacket hood.

"Do you want me to call for assistance?" Maura said.

"First let's see who we have here," said Jane, and she barked at the figure, "State your name!"

"Can I lower my arms first?" came the calm reply. *A woman.*

"All right. Slowly," said Jane.

The woman lowered her arms and pushed back the hood of her jacket. Despite the fact that a gun was pointed at her, she appeared strangely unruffled as she regarded Jane and Maura. "What's this all about? Did I break some law just by walking around the neighborhood?"

Jane lowered her weapon and said in surprise, "It's you."

"I'm sorry. Have we met?"

"You were at Cassandra Coyle's memorial service. And Timothy McDougal's. What are you doing on this property?"

"I was looking for my dad's dog."

"You live around here?"

"My dad does." The young woman pointed at the faint glow of houselights beyond the trees. "His dog got out and I've been searching for him. I saw your car, and I wondered if someone was trying to break into the old daycare."

"You're Holly Devine, aren't you?" said Jane.

For a moment the woman didn't answer. When she finally did, her words were barely a murmur. "I haven't been called that name in years."

"We've been trying to find you, Holly. I kept calling your father, but he refused to tell me where you were."

"Because he doesn't trust anyone."

"Well, you're going to have to trust me. Your life may depend on it."

"What are you talking about?"

"Let's go someplace warm and I'll tell you."

TWENTY-SEVEN

THE SOUND OF A BARKING DOG GREETED THEM as they walked up the porch steps to the modest home of Earl Devine. It was a big dog, by the sound of it, and Maura hung back a few paces, imagining fur and teeth flying out at them as Holly opened the front door. The black Lab seemed far less interested in the visitors than in Holly, who knelt down to grasp its head in her hands.

"So you came home on your own, you bad boy," she scolded. "That's the last time I go looking for *you.*"

"Who are these people, Holly?" demanded a gruff voice. Earl Devine glowered from the hallway, where the lights cast a yellowish glow on his face. Judging by his clothes, which hung like drapes on his gaunt frame, he had recently lost a great deal of weight, but he faced Maura and Jane with arms flexed and hands closed in fists, as if ready to deliver blows in defense of his daughter.

"I went out searching for Joe and I ran into these ladies at the old daycare," said Holly. "I guess Joe decided to come back on his own."

"Yeah, he came back," Earl said, but his attention remained on Jane and Maura. "Who are you?"

"I spoke to you on the phone, Mr. Devine," said Jane. "I'm Detective Jane Rizzoli, Boston PD."

Earl looked at her outstretched hand and finally decided to shake it. "So you found my girl anyway."

"You could have saved me a lot of trouble by just telling me where she was."

Holly said, "I told them you don't trust people, Daddy."

"Not even the police?" said Jane.

"The police?" Earl Devine snorted. "Why should I? All I gotta do is watch the news. These days, we're as likely to be shot by a cop as helped by one."

"We're only trying to keep your daughter safe."

"Yeah, that's what you said on the phone, but how would I know if you were telling the truth? How would I know you're really a cop?"

"My dad's got a reason to be cautious," said Holly. "There's a guy who's been stalking me for a while. I had to change my last name from Devine to Donovan so he couldn't find me."

"He kept calling here, asking for her," said Earl. "He even got some woman to call, said she was a journalist who wanted to talk to Holly. I wasn't gonna trust you just because you claimed you were a cop."

"Who was this stalker?" asked Jane.

"Some young man Holly used to know. I never did like the looks of him. He kept coming by here asking about her, but I think I finally scared him off. If he knows what's good for him, he'll stay away from my girl."

"They're not here about my stalker, Daddy," said Holly.

"It's about the Apple Tree Daycare, sir," said Jane.

Earl frowned at her. "Why? That happened a long time ago. It's over and done with, and they sent those people to jail."

"Martin Stanek has been released. We think he wants revenge against everyone who sent him to prison, and we're afraid he might come after Holly."

"Has the man threatened her?"

"No, but three of the children who gave statements against Stanek have recently been murdered. A fourth has gone missing. You can understand why we're concerned about your daughter's safety."

He stared at Jane for a moment, then gave a grim nod. "Let's hear what you plan to do about him."

They sat in Earl Devine's cramped living room, where the frayed sofa and Naugahyde armchairs seemed as if they'd been part of the house for so long they were now melded to the floor. One of the chairs bore the permanent imprint of Earl's backside, which he now planted onto the cushion. Holly brought out mugs of coffee for the two visitors, but Maura took one look at the stained rim and discreetly set down her cup. She saw stains everywhere—rings on the area carpet from past doggie accidents, cigarette burns on the sofa armrest, a faint veil of mold on the ceiling where rain had once leaked in. There were no books or magazines in sight, only a stack of Pennysavers and newspaper coupons. Throughout the conversation, the television stayed on, an eternally glowing presence in the room.

"Those kids' names were sealed by the court. That's what the prosecutor promised us," said Earl Devine, his gaze hard on Jane's face. "How did you even know to come looking for Holly?"

"Actually, Mr. Devine, your daughter put herself into the picture." Jane turned to Holly. "You went to both Cassandra's and Tim's funerals. So you must have known they were both murdered."

Earl frowned at his daughter. "You didn't tell me you went to their funerals."

"I needed to find out if their murders were connected," said Holly. "No one was saying anything."

"Because at the time no one realized there *was* a connection between them," said Jane. "But *you* knew, Holly. You could have made my job a lot easier by just picking up the phone and calling the police. Why didn't you call?"

"I hoped it was a coincidence. I wasn't sure."

"Why didn't you call, Holly?" Jane repeated.

Holly stared back at her, momentarily silenced by the sharp tone of the question. Meekly, she dropped her gaze. "I should have. I'm sorry."

"If you had, Bill Sullivan might still be alive."

"What happened to Billy?" said Earl.

"He disappeared," said Jane. "Based on the circumstances of his disappearance and the blood in his car, we believe he's dead."

Maura stayed focused on Holly, and she saw the

young woman's head snap up at this latest revelation. Saw genuine shock in her eyes.

"*Billy's* dead?"

"You didn't know about that?" said Jane.

"No. No, I never thought he would be . . ."

"You said four children were dead," said Earl. "You've only told us about three."

"Sarah Byrne died in a fire in November. It was classified an accidental death, but it's now back under investigation. So you can see why we've been trying to contact your daughter." Jane looked at Holly. "Is there some reason you've been avoiding the police—"

"Now, wait a minute," Earl cut in.

Jane lifted a hand to silence him. "I want to hear from your daughter."

With everyone watching her, Holly seemed to reach deep inside herself for the courage to answer. She straightened and met Jane's gaze. "It was dead and buried and I wanted it to stay that way. I didn't want everyone to know."

"Know what?"

"About the Apple Tree. About what those people did to me. You don't seem to understand how something like that changes you. Or what it's like when everyone *knows* you were molested. When they look at you, the whole time they're imagining . . ." She hugged herself and stared down at the stained carpet. "To think it was my mom who made me go to that place. She said it wasn't safe for me to be home alone after school. She thought there were men lurking behind every bush, waiting to rape me."

"Holly," said Earl.

"It's true, Daddy. That's the way Mom was, imagining rapists everywhere. So every day I had to climb into his bus, and he drove us there. We were like lambs going to the slaughter." She raised her eyes to Jane. "You've read the files, Detective. You know what happened to us."

"Yes, I know," said Jane.

"All because my *mother* wanted me to be safe."

"Let go of the bitterness, Holly. Doesn't do you any good now." Earl looked at Jane. "My wife had a difficult childhood. Things happened to her when she was a little girl, things she was ashamed of. She had this uncle who . . ." He paused. "Anyway, it made her terrified that something like that could happen to Holly. She died a few months after the trial ended, probably from all the stress. Holly and I had to fend for ourselves, just the two of us, but I think we've managed okay. Look at my girl now! She went to college, got herself a good job. The last thing she needs is for people to dredge up that Apple Tree business again."

"This *is* for Holly's sake, Mr. Devine. We want her to be safe."

"So arrest the bastard."

"We can't, not yet. We need more evidence." To Holly, Jane said, "I know this is difficult for you. I know these are bad memories. But you can help us send Martin Stanek back to prison for good."

Holly turned to her father, as if for reassurance. These two seemed uncommonly close, a father–daughter bond forged by years of being alone together, the widower and his only child.

"Go ahead, sweetheart," said Earl. "Give them

what they need. Let's put that son of a bitch away for good."

"It's just that—it's hard to talk about what Martin—what he did to me—with my dad sitting here. It's embarrassing."

"Mr. Devine, would you mind giving us some privacy?" said Jane.

Earl pushed himself to his feet. "I'll leave you alone to talk. You need anything, sweetheart, you just shout." He walked away into the kitchen, and they heard water running. The clank of a pot on the stove.

"He likes to cook me dinner when I visit," said Holly, and added, with a wry smile, "He's actually a terrible cook, but it's his way of showing me he cares."

"We can see how much he cares," said Maura.

For the first time, Holly seemed to register Maura's presence. Up till now Maura had been silent, letting Jane conduct the interview, but there were strange emotional currents flowing in this house, and Maura wondered if Jane sensed them. If she had noticed how often father and daughter looked to each other for reassurance.

"For a few months I stopped coming here, because we were afraid my stalker was watching the house. That was really hard for Daddy, not having me visit. He's my best friend."

"Yet you can't talk about Martin Stanek in front of him," said Jane.

Holly glared at her. "Could you talk to *your* dad about how a man molested you? How he forced his penis down your throat?"

Jane paused. "No. I couldn't."

"Then you understand why he and I never talk about it."

"But *we* have to talk about it, Holly. You have to help us, so we can keep you safe."

"That's what the prosecutor said: *Tell us everything that happened, and we'll keep you safe.* But I was scared. I didn't want to disappear, like Lizzie."

"You knew Lizzie DiPalma?"

Holly nodded. "Every day, we rode Martin's bus together to Apple Tree. Lizzie was so much smarter than me, and so fierce. *She* would have fought back. Maybe killing her was the only way he could stop her from screaming for help. Or stop her from telling anyone what he'd done to her. She was kidnapped on a Saturday, so none of the kids were there to see it. We had no idea what happened to Lizzie." Holly drew in a deep breath and looked at Jane. "Until I found her hat."

"On Martin's bus," said Jane.

Holly nodded. "That's when I *knew* he did it. I knew I finally had to speak up. I'm just glad my mother believed me. After what happened to her when she was a little girl, she never doubted me. But some of the other parents didn't believe what their own children were saying."

"Because some of the other children's stories were pretty hard to believe," said Jane. "Timothy talked about a tiger flying in the woods. Sarah said the daycare had a secret basement where the Staneks threw dead babies. But police searched that building, and there was no basement. Certainly there were no flying tigers."

"Timmy and Sarah were just little kids. It was easy to confuse them."

"But you can see why some of those statements didn't pass muster."

"You weren't there, Detective. You didn't have to face the wall of martyrs every day and recite how each one died. Saint Peter of Verona, his head cracked with a cleaver. Saint Lawrence, burned on a gridiron. Saint Clement, drowned with an anchor around his neck. If your birthday fell on a martyr's day, you got the privilege of wearing the martyr's crown and holding the plastic palm leaf while everyone danced around you. Our parents thought it was perfectly wholesome! And that's what made it so insidious. Evil disguised as piety." Holly gave a shudder. "But after Lizzie vanished, I finally got up the courage to say something, because I knew that what happened to her could happen to me next. I told the truth. That's why Martin wants his revenge."

"We're going to keep you safe, Holly," said Jane. "But you have to help us."

"What should I do?"

"Until we have enough evidence to arrest Martin Stanek, it would be a good idea for you to leave town. Is there a friend you can stay with?"

"No. No, there's just my father."

"This isn't a good place. This is where Stanek will expect to find you."

"I can't leave my job. I have bills to pay." She glanced back and forth at Jane and Maura. "He hasn't found me yet. Shouldn't I be safe in my own apartment? What if I got a gun?"

"Do you have a permit to carry one?" said Jane.

"Does that matter?"

"You know I can't advise you to break the law."

"But sometimes laws don't make sense. What good are your stupid laws if I'm dead?"

Maura said, "What about police protection, Jane? Assign an officer to watch her."

"I'll see what I can arrange, but there's a limit to our resources." Jane looked at Holly. "In the meantime, the best way for you to stay safe is to be prepared. Know what to watch for. We believe Stanek is working with someone else, and his partner could be a man or a woman. You can't let down your guard under any circumstances. We know that two of the victims were drugged with alcohol and ketamine, and this may have happened in a bar. Don't accept drinks from people you don't know. In fact, just stay away from anyplace where people are drinking."

Holly's eyes widened. "That's how he does it? He puts something in their drinks?"

"But that won't happen to you. Now that you know."

Jane's cell phone rang, and she answered it with a brisk "Rizzoli." Maura was startled when, seconds later, Jane shot to her feet and strode outside to continue the call in private. Through the closed front door, she heard Jane demand, "How did this happen? Who the hell was watching him?"

"What's going on?" said Holly.

"I don't know. I'm going to find out." Maura followed Jane outside and closed the front door behind her. There she stood, shivering, waiting for Jane to finish the call.

"Jesus H. Christ." Jane hung up her phone and turned to Maura. "Martin Stanek's taken off."

"What? When?"

"We had a team watching his residence from the street. He slipped out the back door and no one's seen him since. We have no idea where he went."

Maura glanced at the window and saw Holly's face pressed up against the glass, watching them. Softly, she said, "You need to find him."

Jane nodded. "Before he finds her."

TWENTY-EIGHT

THROUGH THE LIVING-ROOM WINDOW, I WATCH Detective Rizzoli and Dr. Isles drive away from the house. I turn to my father and confess, “I’m scared, Daddy.”

“You don’t have to be.”

“But they have no idea where he is.”

Daddy pulls me against him and wraps his arms around me. Once, hugging my father was like hugging a sturdy tree trunk. He’s lost so much weight, it’s now like hugging a bag of bones, and through that brittle chest I can feel his heart beating against mine.

“If he comes after my little girl, he’s a dead man.” He lifts my face and looks into my eyes. “Don’t you worry. Daddy will take care of everything.”

“You promise?”

“I promise.” He reaches for my hand. “Now, come into the kitchen. There’s something I want to show you.”

TWENTY-NINE

"UNTIL WE FIND MARTIN STANEK, HOW DO we keep her safe?" asked Detective Tam.

That was the question on the mind of everyone seated around the Boston PD conference table. The investigation had broadened to include Detectives Crowe and Tam, and this morning Dr. Zucker had again joined them. They felt certain Holly was Stanek's next target, but they didn't know where or when he would strike.

"For someone whose life is in danger, she sure isn't acting particularly worried," said Crowe. "Yesterday morning, when Tam and I went to her apartment to check the building's security, she wouldn't even take the time to talk to us. Just told us she was late for work and walked out."

"Here's the good news," said Tam. "I found out her father has a permit to carry. Plus, Mr. Devine's a Navy veteran. Maybe we can talk her into letting him move in with her. Nothing like a daddy with a gun to keep a girl safe."

Jane snorted. "I'd shoot *myself* before I'd let my dad move in with me. No, Holly's not someone we can order around. She's got a mind of her own, and she's . . . different. I'm still trying to figure her out."

"Different in what way?" asked Dr. Zucker. It was exactly the type of question a forensic psychologist would ask, and Jane paused, trying to come up with an answer. To explain just what it was about Holly Devine that perplexed her.

"She seems weirdly cool and collected about the situation. She won't listen to any advice we have. Won't leave town, won't leave her job. That gal's in charge, and she doesn't let us forget it."

"You say that with a note of admiration, Detective Rizzoli."

Jane met Zucker's disturbingly reptilian gaze. Felt him studying her as he always did, a scientist probing for her deepest secrets. "Yes, I do admire her for that. I believe we should all be in control of our own lives."

"Sure does make it hard to protect her, though," said Tam.

"I've already warned her how the other victims were probably approached. How their drinks were spiked with ketamine. She knows what to watch out for, and that's the best protection of all." Jane paused. "And she might actually make our job easy. If she's willing to stay out there, in full view."

"We use her as bait?" said Crowe.

"Not *use* her, exactly. Just take advantage of the fact she's so damn headstrong. Even though she knows

Stanek's after her, she won't let it disrupt her life and she insists on sticking to her usual routine. If I were her, that's exactly what I'd do. In fact, it's what I *did* do, when I was in her situation a few years ago."

"What situation are you talking about?" said Tam. He had only recently joined the homicide unit, so he wasn't part of the investigation four years earlier, when Jane's hunt for the killer known as the Surgeon had suddenly twisted on her, turning her into the predator's target.

Frost said quietly, "She's talking about Warren Hoyt."

"When a perp forces you to change your life, then he's already beaten you," said Jane. "Holly refuses to surrender. Since she's so damn stubborn, I say we work with that. We keep her monitored, install security cameras in her building and her workplace. We wait for Stanek to make his move."

"You think she'd wear a bracelet monitor?" asked Tam. "It'd help us keep track of her."

"*You* try and get it on her."

"Why is this young woman so resistant?" asked Zucker. "Do you have any insights, Detective Rizzoli?"

"I think it's just her nature. Remember, Holly has a history of fighting back. She was the first child to step forward and accuse the Staneks of molesting her, and that took a lot of guts for a ten-year-old girl. Without Holly, there would have been no arrests, no trial. The abuse could have continued for years."

"Yes, I read her interview with the psychologist," said Zucker. "Holly was certainly the most precise and believable, while the other children's statements were obviously contaminated."

"What do you mean by that, Dr. Zucker?" asked Tam. "Contaminated?"

Zucker said, "The stories told by the younger ones were absurd. The five-year-old boy said tigers flew in the woods. One girl claimed that cats and babies were sacrificed to the devil and thrown into a cellar."

Jane shrugged. "Children do embellish."

"Or were they coached? Prodded into making statements by the prosecution? Remember, the Staneks' trial happened during an odd time in criminal justice, when the public was convinced there were satanic cults all over the country. I attended a forensic-psychology conference in the early nineties, and I heard a so-called expert describe vast networks of these cults abusing children and even sacrificing babies. She claimed that a quarter of her patients were survivors of ritual abuse. All around the country there were criminal trials going on, just like the Apple Tree case. Unfortunately, many of those trials weren't based on facts but on fear and superstition."

"Why would kids come up with such weird stories if they weren't at least partially true?" asked Tam.

"Let's consider just one of those ritual-abuse trials, the one involving the McMartin Preschool in California. The investigation started after a schizophrenic mother claimed her child was sodomized by a teacher at the school. Police sent out letters to all the other parents, alerting them that their children might be victims too, and by the time the case got to trial, the accusations had multiplied and grown outlandish. There were charges of wild sex orgies, of children being flushed down toilets into secret rooms, of attackers flying through the air like magic. The result was that an innocent man was convicted and spent five years in prison."

"You're not saying Martin Stanek was *innocent*?" said Jane.

"I merely question how the statements of these children at the Apple Tree were obtained. How much of it was fantasy? How much of it was coached?"

"Holly Devine had real physical injuries," Jane pointed out. "The doctor who examined her described bruises on her head, multiple scratches on her arms and face."

"The other children had no such injuries."

"A psychologist for the prosecution said that the children she spoke to showed emotional symptoms of abuse. Fear of the dark, bed-wetting. Night terrors. I can read you exactly what the judge said about it. He called the damage to these children profound and truly horrifying."

"Of course he said that. The whole country was swept up in the same moral panic."

"*Moral panic* didn't make a child vanish into thin air," said Jane. "Remember, a nine-year-old girl named Lizzie DiPalma *did* go missing. Her body's never been found."

"Martin Stanek wasn't convicted of her murder."

"Only because the jury refused to deliver a guilty verdict on that charge. But everyone *knew* he did it."

"Do you normally trust the wisdom of the mob?" Dr. Zucker responded, his eyebrow arched. "As a forensic psychologist, it's my role here to offer you different perspectives, to point out what you might miss. Human behavior isn't as black and white as you might like to believe. People have complex motives, and justice is meted out by imperfect human beings. Surely *something* about the children's statements must bother you."

"The prosecutor believed them."

"Your daughter's about three years old, isn't she? Imagine giving her the power to put a whole family in prison."

"The children at Apple Tree were older than my daughter."

"But not necessarily more accurate or truthful."

Jane sighed. "Now you sound like Dr. Isles."

"Ah, yes. The eternal skeptic."

"You can be as skeptical as you want, Dr. Zucker. But the fact is, Lizzie DiPalma *did* go missing twenty years ago. Her hat was found on the Apple Tree school bus, which made Martin Stanek the prime suspect. Now the children who accused him of abuse are being murdered. Stanek's looking pretty damn good as our killer."

"Convince me. Find the evidence to tie him to these murders. Any evidence."

"Every perp makes mistakes," she said. "We'll find his."

BILLY SULLIVAN'S MOTHER NOW LIVED in a handsome Tudor-style home only a mile from the more modest Brookline neighborhood where Billy had grown up.

This morning's freezing rain had glazed the shrubbery with ice, and the brick walkway leading to Mrs. Sullivan's porch looked slick enough to skate on. For a moment Frost and Jane remained in the car, watching the house and bracing themselves for the cold. And for the terrible conversation that lay ahead of them.

"She must already know that her son's dead," said Frost.

"But she doesn't know the worst of it yet. And I'm sure as hell not going to tell her how he probably died." *Buried alive, like Saint Vitalis.* Or had the killer been merciful and made certain that his victim was no longer breathing when he tossed the first shovelful of dirt onto the corpse? Jane did not want to think of the alternative: that Billy was still alive and conscious, trapped in a box as frozen clods thumped onto his coffin. Or bound and helpless in an open grave, choking on soil as it rained down on his face. This was where nightmares came from; it was what the job could do to her, if she let it.

"Come on. Sooner or later, we have to talk to her," said Frost.

At the front door, Frost rang the bell and they waited, shivering, as sleet tapped the pavement and shrubs. Inside, Billy Sullivan's mother would be terrified, anticipating bad news while desperately keeping alive some small flame of hope. Jane could always see that hope flickering in the faces of victims' families; too often, Jane was forced to snuff out that flame.

The woman who opened the door did not invite them in but stood barring the entrance for a moment, as if reluctant to let tragedy step into her house. Pale and dry-eyed, her face as stiff as molded wax, Susan Sullivan was desperately trying to stay in control. Her blond hair was swept back and lacquered in place, and her cream-colored knit pants and pink sweater set would have looked right at home at a country-club luncheon. Today, which could very well be the worst day of her life, she had chosen to wear pearls.

"Mrs. Sullivan," said Jane. "I'm Detective Rizzoli, Boston PD. This is Detective Frost. May we come in?"

The woman finally nodded and moved aside to let Jane and Frost step into the foyer. There was a painful silence as they removed their damp coats. Even with the threat of terrible news hanging over her, Susan did not neglect her duty as a hostess, and with brittle efficiency she hung up their coats in the closet and led them into the living room. Jane's attention was instantly riveted by an oil painting that hung above the fieldstone fireplace. It was a portrait of a golden-haired young man, his handsome face tilted toward the light, his lips curved in a quietly amused smile.

Her son, Billy.

This was not the only picture of him. Everywhere Jane looked in the room, she saw photos of Billy. There he was on the mantelpiece at graduation, a mortarboard angled jauntily on his blond hair. On the grand piano were silver-framed pictures of Billy as a toddler, as an adolescent, as a sunburned teen grinning from a sailboat. Nowhere did Jane see any photos of the boy's father; there was only Billy, who was clearly the object of Susan's adoration.

"I know it embarrasses him, having all these pictures of him here," said Susan. "But I'm so proud of him. He's the best son any mother could ask for."

She was talking about him in the present tense, that flame of hope still burning bright.

"Is there a Mr. Sullivan?" asked Frost.

"There is," Susan answered tersely. "As well as a second *Mrs.* Sullivan. Billy's father left us when Billy was only twelve years old. We almost never hear from him, and we don't need to hear from him. We've done just fine on our own. Billy's taken very good care of me."

"Where is your ex-husband now?"

"Living somewhere in Germany with his other family. But we don't need to talk about him." She paused and for an instant her composure cracked, revealing a glimpse of devastation in her eyes. "Have you found—do you know anything else?" she whispered.

"Brookline PD remains in charge of the investigation, Mrs. Sullivan," said Jane. "His disappearance is still classified as a missing-persons case."

"But you're with Boston PD."

"Yes, ma'am."

"On the phone, you told me you're with homicide." Susan's voice quavered. "Does that mean you believe . . ."

"It just means we're looking at all angles, considering all possibilities," said Frost, quick to respond to the woman's distress. "I know you've talked extensively to Brookline PD, and I know it's difficult to go through this again, but maybe you'll remember something new. Something that will help us find your son. You last saw Billy on Monday night?"

Susan nodded, her hands twisting in her lap. "We

had dinner together at home. Roast chicken," she added, smiling faintly at the memory. "Afterward, he needed to catch up on some work at his office. So he left, around eight o'clock."

"I understand he works in finance?"

"He's a portfolio manager at Cornwell Investments. He has some very-high-net-worth clients who demand a lot of attention, so Billy works hard to keep them happy. But don't ask me what he actually does there." She gave a sheepish shake of the head. "I scarcely understand anything to do with money, so Billy manages my investments, and he's done it very well. Which is why we were able to buy this house together. I never could have afforded it without his help."

"Your son lives here with you?"

"Yes. It's way too much house for just me. Five bedrooms, four fireplaces." Susan gazed up at the twelve-foot ceiling. "I'd be awfully lonely rattling around here by myself, and ever since his father left us, Billy and I have been a team. I look after him; he looks after me. It's a perfect arrangement."

No wonder her son never married, thought Jane. Who could possibly compete with this woman?

"Tell us about Monday evening, Mrs. Sullivan," Frost prompted gently. "What happened after your son left the house?"

"He said he'd be working late at the office, so I went to bed around ten. The next morning, when I woke up, I realized he never came home. He didn't answer his phone, so I knew something was wrong. I called the police, and a few hours later, they . . ." Susan paused. Cleared her throat. "They found his car, abandoned near the golf course. His keys were still in the ignition, and his briefcase was on the front seat. And there was blood." Her hands were twisting again in her lap, the only visible clue to her turmoil. If and when this woman finally lost control and allowed her grief to roar out, it would be unbearable to watch, thought Jane.

"The police said there's parking-lot surveillance video, and it shows Billy leaving his office around ten-thirty. But no one's seen or heard from him since," said Susan. "Not his colleagues at the office. Not his secretary. No one." She looked at Frost with haunted eyes. "If you know what happened, you have to be honest with me. I can't stand the silence."

"As long as he hasn't been found, there's always hope, Mrs. Sullivan," said Frost.

"Yes. Hope." Susan took a deep breath and straightened. Back in control. "You said the Brookline police are in charge. I don't understand where Boston PD comes in."

"Your son's disappearance may be linked to other cases we're investigating in Boston," said Jane.

"Which cases?"

"Do you remember the name Cassandra Coyle? Or Timothy McDougal?"

For a moment Susan sat very still, searching for some long-lost memory. When the revelation hit her, it was sudden, and her eyes abruptly snapped wide. "The Apple Tree."

Jane nodded. "Both Cassandra and Timothy were recently murdered, and now your son has gone missing. We believe these cases may be—"

"Excuse me. I'm going to be sick." Susan lurched to her feet and fled the room. They heard the slam of the bathroom door.

"Jesus," said Frost. "I hate this."

A clock ticked loudly on the mantelpiece. Beside it was a photo of Billy and his mother, both of them grinning from a motor yacht with the words *El Tesoro, Acapulco* emblazoned on the stern.

"These two were so close," said Jane. "Somehow she has to know. Deep in her heart, she must realize he's gone." She looked down at the coffee table, where issues of *Architectural Digest* were neatly splayed out, as though arranged by a stylist. It was a perfect living room in a perfect house in what had been a perfect life for Susan Sullivan. Now she was in the bathroom hugging the toilet bowl, and her son was almost certainly decomposing in a grave.

A toilet flushed. Footsteps approached in the hallway and Susan reappeared, her face grim, her shoulders bravely squared.

"I want to know how they died," she said. "What happened to Cassandra? To Timothy?"

"I'm sorry, Mrs. Sullivan, but these are active investigations," said Jane.

"You said they were murdered."

"Yes."

"I deserve to know more. Tell me."

After a moment, Jane finally nodded. "Please sit down."

Susan sank into the wingback chair. Although she was still pale, there was steel in her eyes, in her spine. "When did these murders happen?"

That much, at least, Jane could tell her. Dates were public knowledge, reported in the newspapers. "Cassandra Coyle was killed on December sixteenth, Timothy McDougal on December twenty-fourth."

"Christmas Eve," murmured Susan. She stared across the room at an empty chair, as if seeing her son's ghost lingering there. "That night, Billy and I cooked a goose for dinner. We spent all day in the kitchen, laughing. Drinking wine. Then we opened presents and watched old movies until one in the morning, just the two of us . . ." She paused, and her gaze snapped back to Jane. "Is that man out of prison?" She didn't have to say his name; they knew who she was talking about.

"Martin Stanek was released in October," said Jane.

"Where was he the night my son vanished?"

"We haven't established that yet."

"Arrest him. *Force* him to talk!"

"We're trying to locate him. And we can't arrest him without evidence."

"It's not the first time he's killed," said Susan. "There was that little girl Lizzie. He kidnapped her, killed her. Everyone knew it, except for that *stupid* jury. If they'd just listened to the prosecution, that man would still be in prison. And my son—my Billy—" She turned her head, unable to look at them. "I don't want to talk anymore. Please go."

"Mrs. Sullivan—"

"Please."

Reluctantly, Jane and Frost rose to their feet. They'd learned nothing useful here; all the visit had accomplished was to destroy any hope this woman might have clung to. It had not brought them any closer to finding Martin Stanek.

Back in their car, Jane and Frost cast one final look at the house where a woman was now alone, her life in ruins. Through the living-room window, Jane saw Susan's silhouette, pacing back and forth, and she was glad to be out of that house, glad to be breathing air that wasn't sodden with grief. "How did he do it?" she asked. "How did Stanek bring down a healthy six-foot man like Billy Sullivan?"

"Ketamine and booze. He used it before."

"But this time there must have been a struggle of some kind. The lab confirmed that the blood in the car was Billy Sullivan's, so he must have fought back." She started the car. "Let's take a drive to the golf course. I want to see where his BMW was found."

Brookline PD had already searched the site and found nothing, and there was nothing to see on this gloomy afternoon either. Jane parked at the edge of the golf course and surveyed the ice-crusted lawn. Sleet ticked the windshield and slid in melting rivulets down the glass. She saw no security cameras nearby; what happened on this stretch of road had gone unseen by any witness, electronic or human, but the blood inside Billy's BMW told a story, even though it had been only a few splashes on the dashboard.

"The killer abandons the car here, but where did he pick up the victim?" said Jane.

"If he followed the same pattern as the other two, alcohol would've been involved. A bar, a restaurant. It was late in the evening."

Once again, she started the engine. "Let's check out where he worked."

By the time Jane pulled into the parking lot of Cornwell Investments, it was 6:00 P.M. and the other businesses on the street were already closed, but the windows were lit in the building where Bill Sullivan had worked.

"Four cars in the parking lot," observed Jane. "Someone's working late."

Frost pointed to the security camera mounted in the parking lot. "That must be the camera that caught him leaving the building."

Surveillance video was how they knew that Bill Sullivan had walked into the building at eight-fifteen on a Friday night. At ten-thirty he walked out again, climbed into his BMW, and drove away. And then what happened? Jane wondered. How did Sullivan's bloodstained BMW end up abandoned a few miles away, at the edge of the golf course?

Jane pushed open her door. "Let's have a chat with his colleagues."

The front entrance was locked, and window blinds obscured their view into the ground-floor office. Jane knocked on the door and waited. Knocked again.

"I know someone's inside," said Frost. "I saw a guy walk past the window upstairs."

Jane pulled out her cell phone. "I'll give them a call, see if they're still answering the phone."

Before she could tap in the numbers, the door suddenly swung open. A man loomed before them, silent and poker-faced, and he eyed his visitors up and down, as if trying to decide if they were worth his attention.

He was dressed in standard business attire—white oxford shirt, wool slacks, a bland blue tie—but his haircut and his commanding presence gave him away. Jane had seen that same haircut on other men in his profession.

"This business is closed for the night," he said.

Jane looked past him, at the other people in the office. A man sat staring at a computer, his shirtsleeves rolled up as if he'd already spent hours at that desk. A woman in a skirt suit whisked past, carrying a cardboard box overflowing with file folders.

"I'm Detective Rizzoli, Boston PD," said Jane. "Which agency do you work for? What's going on here?"

"This is not your jurisdiction, ma'am." The man started to close the door.

She put up a hand to stop it. "We're investigating an abduction and possible homicide."

"Whose?"

"Bill Sullivan."

"Bill Sullivan no longer works here."

The door swung shut and a deadbolt thunked into place. Jane and Frost were left staring at the CORNWELL INVESTMENTS brass plaque mounted on the door.

"This just got a lot more interesting," said Jane.

THIRTY

I'M BEING WATCHED. PHIL AND AUDREY WHISPER and shoot furtive glances my way, the sort of looks you give to someone who's doomed with a terminal illness. Last week, Victoria Avalon fired Booksmart Media, and now she's signed on with some glitzy New York publicity firm. Although my boss, Mark, hasn't come right out and blamed me for losing our client, of course that's what everyone else is thinking. Even though I did everything I could to promote that stupid memoir, which Victoria didn't even write. Now I'm down to only eleven author-clients, I'm worried I'm about to lose my job, and the police won't stop tailing me.

And somewhere out there, Martin Stanek is circling in for the kill.

I notice Mark approaching my desk, and I quickly swivel toward my computer to work on the pitch letter for the *breathtaking new novel by Saul Gresham.* The letter's only half written, and so far all I've got are the usual tired superlatives. My fingers hover over the keyboard as I search for something new and fresh to say about this truly awful book, but what I really want to type is: *I hate my job I hate my job I hate my job.*

"Holly, is everything all right?"

I look up at Mark, who truly does look concerned. While that bitch Audrey just fakes her concern, and Phil's sympathy is about getting into my pants, Mark really does seem to worry about me. Which is good, because maybe it means he won't fire me after all.

"While you were gone at lunch, a Detective Rizzoli called here, wanting to speak to you."

"I know." I keep typing, an automatic stream of words pulled straight from every publicist's glossary. *Thrilling. Unputdownable. Pulse-pounding.* "Last week she came to see me while I was visiting my dad."

"What's going on?"

"There's a homicide investigation. I knew the victims."

"There's more than one victim?"

I stop typing and look at him. "Please, I can't talk about it. The police asked me not to."

"Of course. God, I'm sorry you have to go through this. It must be awful for you. Do the police know who did it?"

"Yes, but they can't find him and they think I might not be safe. That's why it's been hard for me to focus lately."

"Well, that explains everything. With all that going on in your life, no wonder things went off the rails with Victoria."

"I'm so sorry, Mark. I tried my best to keep her happy, but right now my life is a mess." I add, with a fetching tremble in my voice, "And I'm scared."

"Is there anything I can do? Do you need to take a leave of absence?"

"I can't afford to take time off. Please, I really need this job."

"Absolutely." He straightens and says loudly enough so that everyone in the office can hear it, "You have a job with us for as long as you need it, Holly. I promise." He raps my desk for emphasis, and I see Audrey scowling in my direction. *No, Audrey, I'm not going to be sacked, no matter how many nasty things you say behind my back.* But it's not Audrey who catches my attention; it's Phil, who's walking toward my desk, cradling a cellophane-wrapped bouquet of flowers.

"What's this?" I ask, bewildered, as he hands me the bouquet.

"What a nice idea, Phil," says Mark, clapping him on the back. "Good of you to think about cheering up our Holly."

"They're not from me," Phil admits, sounding annoyed that he hadn't thought of it himself. "The deliveryman just dropped them off."

Everyone watches as I peel back the cellophane and stare at a dozen yellow long-stem roses framed in baby's breath and exuberant foliage. With trembling fingers I sift through the foliage, but I find no palm leaves anywhere in the bouquet.

"There's a card," says Audrey. She's nosing around as usual, probably looking for something she can use against me. "Who's it from?"

As the three of them crowd around my desk, I have no choice but to open the envelope in front of them. The message inside is short and all too legible.

I miss you. Everett.

Phil's eyes narrow. "Who's Everett?"

"He's just a man I've been seeing. We've gone on a few dates."

Mark grins. "Ah, I sniff romance in the air! Now, come on, folks, let's all get back to work. Let Holly enjoy her flowers."

As they return to their desks, all the tension drains from my body. It's an innocent bouquet from Everett, nothing to worry about. I haven't seen him since the night of Victoria Avalon's book-signing, when I was so rattled that I broke off our evening together. The bottle of wine he brought me is still sitting unopened on my kitchen counter, awaiting his next visit. He's texted me every day for the past week, wanting to see me. The man won't give up.

Now another text message chimes on my cell phone. Of course it's from Everett.

Did you get the flowers?

I respond: *Yes, they're lovely. Thank you!*

Meet me after work for a drink?

I don't know. Things are crazy.

I can make them better.

I look at the yellow roses on my desk and suddenly think of the first glorious night that Everett and I slept together. How we feverishly clawed at each other like animals in heat. I remember what a tireless lover he was and how he seemed to know exactly what I wanted him to do to me. Maybe that's just what I need tonight, to lift my spirits. A hot, hunky dose of sex.

He sends another text message: *Rose and Thistle Pub? 5:30?*

After a moment I respond: *O.K. 5:30.*

See you there.

I set down the cell phone and focus again on the pitch letter I've been trying to write. In disgust I type: *I hate my JOB!!!,* then hit the delete key and send the draft into oblivion. There really is no point trying to work today. Anyway, it's already five o'clock.

I shut down the computer and gather up my notes on Saul Gresham's stupid novel. I'll work on this at home, where I won't have to put up with Audrey's catty remarks and Phil's moon-eyed stares. I open my purse and reach inside, just to assure myself that the gun is still there. *A lady's pistol,* my father called it when he handed it to me that night in the kitchen, small enough to not weigh you down but powerful enough to do the job without much kickback. The gun feels cool and alien but also reassuring. My little helper.

I sling the purse over my shoulder and walk out of the office, prepared to deal with whatever—or whoever—comes my way.

EVERETT IS NOWHERE TO BE seen in the Rose and Thistle. I choose a table in the corner and sip a glass of cabernet sauvignon as I survey the room. It's a cozy and clubby space, all dark wood and brass fixtures. I've never been to Ireland, but this is what I imagine their old country pubs must look like, with a fire crackling in the hearth and the Guinness golden harp hanging over the mantelpiece. But in this pub, the patrons are young and hip, a business crowd in oxford shirts and silk ties, and even the women wear pinstriped suits. After a long day of hammering out deals, they've come here to unwind, and already the pub is getting crowded and raucous.

I check my watch: 6:00 P.M. Everett has still not shown up.

At first all I notice is a faint tingle on my face, as if a breeze has brushed against it. I know that research has proven people can't really sense when someone is staring at them, but when I turn to see what triggered the sensation, I immediately spot the woman standing at the bar, eyeing me. In her late forties, with handsome streaks of silver in her auburn hair, she looks like an older, redheaded version of me, but with two extra decades' worth of confidence. Our gazes lock and a smile crooks up the right side of her mouth. She turns and says something to the bartender.

If Everett doesn't show up, there are certainly other tempting prospects in this pub.

I pull out my cell phone to check for new messages. Nothing from Everett. I'm tapping out a text to him when a glass of red wine suddenly appears on my table.

The waitress says, "It's the same wine you ordered earlier. Compliments of the lady at the bar."

I glance at the bar, and the auburn-haired woman smiles at me. I feel as if I've seen her before, but I can't remember where or when. Do we know each other, or does she just have one of those faces, those smiles, that invite a sense of familiarity? The glass of cabernet sits before me, as dark as ink in that firelit pub. I think of how many hands it took to deliver this wine to my table, from the farmer to the harvester, the vintner and the bottler. Then there's the bartender who poured it, the waitress who set it down before me, plus countless unseen others. When you think about it, a glass of wine is like the work of elves, and you can't possibly know if one of those elves wants to harm you.

My cell phone chimes with a text message from Everett.

Arghhh, sorry! Last-minute meeting with client. Can't make it tonight. Call you tomorrow?

I don't bother to answer him. Instead, I pick up the glass and give it a swirl. I've already tasted this cabernet, so I know it's pedestrian and not worth a second pouring, but it's not the wine I'm contemplating; it's what my next move should be. Should I invite her to my table and let the game begin?

THIRTY-ONE

"WHAT THE HELL DOES SHE THINK SHE'S doing?" said Jane.

Through Jane's earpiece, Tam's voice was almost lost in the background noise of the pub. "She's not drinking the wine. She's just sitting there, swirling it."

"We warned her. We told her his victims were drugged." She looked at Frost, seated beside her in the car. "Is this chick *trying* to get herself killed?"

"Okay, hold on," said Tam. "There's a woman moving toward her table. She's saying something to Holly."

Jane stared out her car window at the Rose and Thistle across the street. Half an hour earlier, Tam had reported that Holly was sitting alone in the pub, a development that sent both Jane and Frost scrambling to the scene. Not only had Holly refused to alter her daily routine, now she seemed to be actively courting disaster. Holly Devine hadn't struck Jane as a foolhardy woman, yet there she was, accepting drinks from strangers.

"The woman sat down at Holly's table," Tam informed her. "White female, middle-aged. Tall and thin."

"Has Holly tasted the wine yet?"

"No. They're just talking. Maybe they know each other. I can't be sure."

"Tam should move in," said Frost. "Get her out of that place."

"No. Let's see what happens next."

"What if she drinks the wine?"

"We're right here to keep an eye on her." Jane stared at the pub. "Maybe that's why she's doing it. She's trying to bring the killer to us. Either she's really stupid or she's really, really smart. I'm betting on smart."

"Now we've got a problem," came Tam's voice over the earpiece.

"What's happening?" snapped Jane.

"She took a sip."

"And the other woman? What's she doing?"

"Still sitting there. Nothing weird yet. They're just talking."

Jane glanced at the time on her cell phone. How quickly did ketamine work? Would they be able to tell if Holly was affected? Five minutes passed. Ten.

"Oh, shit. They're both getting up. They're leaving," said Tam.

"We're parked right in front. We'll catch them as they walk out."

"They're not going out the front door! They're heading to the back exit. I'm in pursuit. . . ."

"That's it," said Frost. "We gotta go in."

Almost simultaneously, Jane and Frost shoved open their doors and sprinted across the street. Jane was first through the front door and she plunged into the packed room, elbowing aside patrons as she shoved her way toward the rear exit. A glass shattered on the floor and she heard a *what the fuck, lady?* yelled in her direction, but she and Frost kept pushing forward, past three women waiting for the restroom, and slammed through the rear exit door.

An alley. Dark. Where was Holly?

From the far end of the alley came a woman's shouts.

They darted toward the sound, dodging crates and trash, and emerged on the street, where Tam had already pinned a woman against the wall. Nearby stood Holly, watching in bewilderment as Tam snapped handcuffs onto the woman.

"What the hell are you doing?" the woman protested.

"Boston PD," said Tam. "Stop resisting!"

"You can't arrest me! I didn't do anything!"

Tam glanced over his shoulder at Jane and Frost. "She tried to run."

"Of course I ran! I didn't know who the fuck you were, coming at us in the alley."

As Tam held the woman against the building, Jane did a pat-down and found no weapons.

Someone yelled from the sidewalk, "That was police brutality!"

"Smile, cops! You're on *Candid Camera*!"

Jane glanced around at the crowd that was rapidly coalescing around them. Everyone had a cell phone out, recording the arrest. Keep cool, she thought. Just do your job and don't let them rattle you.

"State your name," Jane ordered the woman.

"Who wants to know?"

"Detective Rizzoli, Boston PD."

Frost picked up the woman's purse, which had dropped on the sidewalk, and pulled out the wallet. "Her driver's license says she's Bonnie B. Sandridge, age forty-nine. Address is two twenty-three Bogandale Road." He looked up. "That's in West Roxbury."

"Sandridge?" Jane frowned. "You're the journalist."

"You know this woman?" Tam asked.

"Yeah. I spoke to her a few days ago. Her name turned up on Martin Stanek's phone log. She *claims* she's a journalist writing about the Apple Tree trial."

Tam turned the woman around to face them. The struggle had left a bloody scrape on her chin, and mascara was smeared down her cheek.

"Yes, I really am a journalist," said the woman. "And, trust me, I'm going to write about this arrest!"

"What's your relationship to Martin Stanek?" said Jane.

The woman glared at her. "Is *that* what this is all about? Instead of tackling me, you could have asked politely."

"Answer the question."

"I already told you. I've been interviewing him for my book."

"The book you claim to be writing."

"Talk to my literary agent. She'll confirm it. I'm a journalist and I'm just doing my job."

"And I'm just doing mine." Jane looked at Tam.

"Bring her in. I want every word she says recorded on video."

"Why's she being arrested? What'd she do?" someone yelled from the crowd.

"I'm a writer! I didn't do anything wrong!" Bonnie yelled back. "Except try to tell the truth about our corrupt criminal-justice system!"

"This video's going up on YouTube, lady. In case you need it for the lawsuit!"

Tam led away the defiant prisoner. Among the crowd of eager citizen-journalists stood Holly, who also had her phone out and was filming the events like everyone else.

Jane grabbed Holly by the arm and pulled her aside. "What the hell were you thinking?"

"Did I do something wrong?" Holly protested.

"You went to a bar, after I warned you what could happen."

"I was there to meet a friend."

"That woman?"

"No, a guy I'm dating. But at the last minute he canceled on me."

"So you sat there and accepted a drink from someone you don't know."

"She looked okay to me."

"They said that about Ted Bundy too."

"She's just a woman. What's a woman going to do to me?"

"I told you, Martin Stanek is not working alone. He has a partner helping him, and it might be this woman."

"Well, now you've got her, right? And you can thank me for helping you catch her."

"You're going home, Holly." Jane pulled out her cell phone. "In fact, I'm gonna make sure you go home."

"What are you doing?"

"I'm calling an officer to drive you."

"That's embarrassing. I'm not getting into a police car."

"What if she put something in your drink? You need to be driven home."

"No." Holly pulled away. "I feel perfectly fine. Look, there's a T station right over there. You've got your suspect; now I'm going home." She turned and walked away.

"Hey!" yelled Jane.

Holly just kept walking. Without a single backward glance, she headed down the steps and vanished into the subway station.

UNDER THE BRIGHT LIGHTS OF the Boston PD interview room, Bonnie Barton Sandridge looked even more disheveled than she had on the street. Her scraped chin was scabbed over and the streak of mascara was smeared like a bruise across her cheek. Jane and Frost sat facing her across the table, where all her belongings were laid out: A wallet with sixty-seven dollars in cash, three credit cards, and a driver's license. An Android cell phone. A key ring with three keys. Some wadded-up Kleenex. And, most interesting of all, a small spiral notebook, half its pages filled with detailed notes. Slowly, Jane flipped through the pages and stopped at the most recent entry.

She looked up at Bonnie. "Why were you stalking Holly Devine?"

"I wasn't stalking her."

Jane held up Bonnie's notebook. "You have her workplace address written in here."

"Booksmart Media is a business. Their address is public information."

"It's no accident that you just happened to show up at the pub where she was sitting. You followed her there from her job, didn't you?"

"Maybe I did. I've been trying to interview her for weeks, but she's a hard gal to pin down. Tonight was the first time I got close enough to say boo."

"So you bought her a glass of wine. Then tried to sneak her out the rear exit."

"Holly's the one who insisted we leave the back way. She said people have been following her, and she wanted to shake them off. And that glass of wine I sent her was just to break the ice. To get her to talk to me."

"About the Apple Tree?"

"The book I'm writing is about ritual-abuse trials. I plan to devote a whole chapter to the Apple Tree."

"The Apple Tree was twenty years ago. That case is old and dead, isn't it?"

"For some people, it's very much alive."

"Like Martin Stanek?"

"Is it any surprise that he's still obsessed by it? That trial tore apart his family. It destroyed his life."

"Funny how you don't mention the children's lives that were ruined."

"You just assume he's guilty. Did it ever occur to you that the Staneks might have been innocent?"

"The jury didn't think so."

"I've spent hours interviewing Martin. I've combed through the trial transcripts and read the accusations against him. They were absurd. In fact, one of the kids who accused him twenty years ago wanted to retract what she said. She was ready to sign a sworn affidavit that none of it was true."

"Wait. You *spoke* to one of the kids?"

"Yes. Cassandra Coyle."

"How did you find her? Did you stalk her too?"

"No, she found *me.* The children's names were sealed by the court, so I didn't know their identities. Last September, Cassandra got in touch with me after she read my articles on ritual-abuse trials. She knew I'd written about the McMartin case in Los Angeles and the Faith Chapel case in San Diego, and she urged me to write about the Apple Tree trial."

"Why?"

"Because she'd been having flashbacks. Remembering details that made her realize Martin Stanek was innocent. I began to look into the case, and it didn't take me long to conclude the trial was a farce, just as Cassandra thought. I don't believe the Staneks committed any crimes."

"Then who abducted Lizzie DiPalma?"

"That's the burning question, isn't it? Who really took that girl? The kidnapping set the stage for everything that followed. The hysteria, the satanic-abuse charges. That sham of a trial. Lizzie DiPalma's disappearance terrified the community, and they were ready to believe anything, even tigers flying through the air. That's what my book is about, Detective. How otherwise-reasonable people can be turned into a seething and dangerous mob." Her face had flushed a deep red. She released a breath and sank back in the chair.

"You seem pretty upset about this, Ms. Sandridge," observed Frost.

"I am. You should be too. We should *all* be upset when an innocent man spends half his life in prison."

"Upset enough to help him plan his revenge?" said Jane.

Bonnie frowned. "What?"

"A number of children claimed that the Staneks abused them. Three of those children are now dead and one is missing. Did you help Martin Stanek track them down?"

"I didn't even know their names."

"You knew Holly Devine's name."

"Only because Cassandra told me. She said Holly was the very first child to accuse the Staneks. Holly started it all, and I wanted to find out why."

"You do know that glass of wine you sent to her will be analyzed? And when it comes back positive for ketamine, you'll be pretty much screwed."

"What? No, you've got it all wrong! I'm just trying to expose the truth about American justice. About a time when hysteria sent people to jail for crimes that never even happened."

"Lizzie DiPalma's abduction certainly happened."

"But Martin didn't do it. Which means the real killer is still out there. *That* should worry you." Bonnie glanced up at the clock on the wall. "You've had me here long enough. Unless I'm under arrest, I'd like to go home."

"Not until you answer this question," said Jane. Leaning forward, she stared Bonnie straight in the eyes. "Where is Martin Stanek?"

Bonnie was silent.

"Do you really want to protect this man? After what he's done?"

"He hasn't done anything."

"No?" Jane opened the folder she'd brought into the room, pulled out an autopsy photo, and slapped it on the table in front of Bonnie. The woman flinched at the image of Cassandra Coyle's corpse.

"I knew she'd been murdered, but I didn't know about . . ." Bonnie looked at Cassandra's empty eye sockets and shuddered. "Martin didn't do that."

"Is that what he told you?"

"Why would he kill the woman who was trying so hard to exonerate him? She was ready to swear the abuse never happened, that she was coached by the prosecutor into telling those crazy stories. No, Martin wanted her *alive*."

"Or so he told you. Maybe you're just the world's biggest patsy. Maybe he used you to track down his victims. You find them, he kills them."

"That's ridiculous," she said, but there was now a note of doubt in her voice. Clearly this was a possibility that Bonnie hadn't considered: that Martin Stanek, the man she believed to be a tragic victim of injustice, had reeled her into acting as an accomplice.

"Martin never blamed the children," said Bonnie. "He knew they were only pawns in a bigger game."

"Then who does he blame?"

Bonnie's face hardened. "Who else but the adults? The ones who let it happen, who *made* it happen. That prosecutor, Erica Shay, used the trial as a springboard for her career, and, sure enough, she went on to bigger and better things. You should talk to *her.* You'll find out she never gave a damn about the truth. Only the scorecard."

"I'd rather talk to Martin Stanek, so I'm going to ask you again. Where is he?"

"He doesn't trust the police. He believes you all want him dead."

"Where is he?"

"He's scared! He had no one else to turn to."

"He's at your house, isn't he?"

Bonnie's face tightened in panic. "Please don't hurt him. Promise not to hurt him!"

Jane looked at Frost. "Let's go."

"THAT WOMAN WAS THE LAST piece of the puzzle," said Jane. "Bonnie tracked down the victims, followed them into bars. Spiked their drinks. And then he did the rest." She glanced at Frost. "Remember that cocktail waitress who recognized Cassandra Coyle's photo?"

"We thought she had to be wrong, because she saw Cassandra sitting with a woman."

"And she was right. Cassandra *was* sitting with a woman." Jane slapped the steering wheel in triumph. "We've got him. We've got them both."

"Unless that wine doesn't come back positive for ketamine."

"It will. It has to." Jane glanced in the rearview mirror and saw that Crowe and Tam were right behind them, their vehicle hugging close in heavy traffic.

"All thanks to that crazy Holly Devine," said Frost.

"Yeah, she's crazy like a fox. She knew we were watching her. She baited the trap, and look who walked in. A woman." Monsters came in all shapes and sizes, and the most dangerous are the ones you never suspect, the ones you think you can trust. Middle-aged women like Bonnie Sandridge were too often overlooked, so invisible that they failed to show up on anyone's radar. Everyone focused on the pretty young girls and the strapping young men. But older women were everywhere, hiding in plain view. Decades from now, would Jane be just another among the gray-haired legions of the invisible? Would anyone look closer and see the woman she really was, focused and formidable and perfectly capable of pulling a trigger?

They parked outside Bonnie Sandridge's house, and as she and Frost stepped out of the car, Jane was already unsnapping the holster at her belt. They didn't know if Stanek would resist when cornered, and they had to expect the worst. Across the street a dog barked, alarmed by this invasion of its neighborhood.

The lights were on inside, and a silhouette moved past the downstairs window.

"Someone's home," said Crowe.

"You two take the rear," said Jane. "Frost and I will go in the front door."

"How're you gonna approach this?"

"We'll try it the polite way. I'll just ring the doorbell

and see if Stanek—" She paused, startled by the unmistakable sound of gunshots.

"That came from inside the house!" said Tam.

There was no time to adjust their plans; they all sprinted for the front door. Tam was first into the house, with Jane barreling in right after him. In that first split second, she registered the blood in the living room. It was everywhere, a bright explosion of it on the wall, more splatters on the sofa. And on the floor, a pool of it was slowly spreading like a halo around the shattered skull of Martin Stanek.

"Drop it!" yelled Tam. "Drop your weapon!"

The man standing over Martin's body did not release his gun. Passively, he regarded the four detectives who stood with their weapons aimed at him, a firing squad ready to unleash a hail of bullets.

"Mr. Devine," said Jane. *"Drop your weapon."*

"I had to kill him," he said. "You know I did. You're a mother, Detective, so you understand, don't you? This was the only way to keep my Holly safe. The only way to be sure this piece of *crap* can't hurt her." He looked down in disgust at Stanek's body. "Now it's over and done with. I took care of the problem, and my girl doesn't have to be afraid."

"We can talk about it," Jane said quietly. Reasonably. "But first put down the gun."

"There's nothing more to talk about."

"There's a lot to talk about, Mr. Devine."

"Not for me." His gun came up a fraction of an inch. Jane's hand snapped taut, her finger primed to fire, but she didn't. She kept her aim on his chest, her heart thudding so hard she could feel every beat transmitted to the grip.

"Think about Holly," said Jane. "Think about what this will do to her."

"I am thinking about her. And this is one last gift I can give her." His mouth tilted up in a sad smile. "This takes care of everything."

Even as he raised his arms and pointed his gun at Jane, even as Crowe fired three bullets into his chest, Earl Devine was still smiling.

THIRTY-TWO

SO THIS IS HOW IT ENDS, THOUGHT MAURA, AS she watched morgue attendants wheel the pair of stretchers out of Bonnie Sandridge's home. Two final deaths, two last bodies. Frigid air swept through the open front door, but that rush of fresh air was not powerful enough to cleanse the stench of violence from the house. Murder leaves a scent of its own. Blood and fear and aggression release their chemical traces into the air, and Maura could smell it now, in this room where Martin Stanek and Earl Devine had died. She stood silent, inhaling the scent, reading the room. Police radios chattered and she heard the voices of CSRU personnel moving through the various rooms of the house, but it was the blood that spoke to Maura. She scanned the spatters and overlying drips on the wall, studied the two puddles on the wood floor where the bodies had fallen. The police might call this bloody conclusion to the case justice well served, but Maura felt unsettled as she regarded the twin pools of blood. The larger one came from Martin Stanek, whose heart had briefly continued to beat and pump blood from the mortal wound in his skull. Earl Devine had not lived or bled as long. All three of Detective Crowe's bullets had hit what would be the mid-chest bull's-eye on a firing-range target. Gold stars for Crowe's marksmanship. But after every fatal police shooting, questions followed, and the autopsy would have to address those questions.

"Trust me, it was a good shooting. We'll all swear to that."

Maura turned to Jane. "*Good shooting* is an oxymoron, if ever I heard one."

"You know what I mean. You also know that I'd be happy to throw Darren Crowe under the bus if I could, but this was definitely justified. Earl Devine killed Stanek. He confessed to it. Then he pointed his weapon at me."

"But you didn't fire at him. You hesitated."

"Yeah, and maybe Crowe saved my life."

"Or maybe your instincts told you Earl Devine wasn't really going to shoot you. Maybe you were better at reading his true intent."

"And if I was wrong? I might be dead now." She shook her head and snorted. "God, now I owe a debt to that jerk Crowe. I'd almost prefer getting shot."

Maura looked down again at the mingled blood, which was now congealed and drying. "Why did Earl Devine do this?"

"He said he was protecting his daughter. Said it was the last gift he could give her."

"Why did he then point his gun at you? He knew

what would happen next. This is a clear case of suicide by cop."

"Which spares everyone the ordeal of a trial. Think about it, Maura. If he lived and this ended up in court, his defense would be that he was protecting his daughter. That would dredge up the old Apple Tree case, and the whole world would learn that Holly was molested as a child. Maybe this was Earl's ultimate gift to his daughter. He kept her safe. And he protected her privacy."

"There's no privacy in murder. Those details will probably become public anyway." Maura peeled off her exam gloves. "Who has custody of Crowe's weapon?"

"He surrendered it."

"Please keep him away from the morgue tomorrow. I don't want any questions raised about my autopsy of Earl Devine. When *The Boston Globe* reports that a sixty-seven-year-old Navy veteran was gunned down by a cop, it's not going to go down well with the public."

"But that Navy veteran pointed a gun at me."

"A detail that won't show up until the second paragraph. Half the public doesn't read past the first." Maura turned to leave. "I'll see you tomorrow at the autopsy."

"Do I really need to be there? I know how these two men died, so there won't be any surprises."

Maura paused and looked back at the room. At the blood-spattered wall. "You never know what will turn up on an autopsy. I feel like this was all wrapped up too neatly, and there are still a lot of questions with no answers."

"Bonnie Sandridge can fill in the gaps. We just have to get her to talk."

"You have no proof she helped Stanek kill anyone."

"The proof has to be here in this house, or in her car. Hairs, fibers from the victims. A stash of ketamine. We'll find *something.*"

Jane sounded certain of herself, but Maura felt far less confident as she walked outside and climbed into her car. There she sat, staring at the brightly lit house. Silhouettes of crime-scene personnel moved past windows, searching for evidence to support what they already believed: that Bonnie Sandridge was the killer's accomplice. Confirmation bias had tripped many a scientist, and no doubt many a cop as well. You find only what you're looking for, which makes it far too easy to overlook everything else.

Her cell phone pinged with a text message and she glanced at the sender's number. At once she dropped the phone back into her purse, but that one glimpse made her stomach churn. Not now, she thought. I'm not ready to think about you.

On the drive home, that unanswered text message felt like a ticking time bomb in her purse. She forced herself to keep both hands on the steering wheel, to fix her gaze on the road. She should not have reopened the door between them, not even a crack. Now that they were speaking again, she wanted nothing more than to welcome Daniel back into her life, into her bed. *Bad move, Maura. Be strong, Maura. You must be your own woman.*

At home she poured herself a much-needed glass of zinfandel and served the Beast his belated dinner. The cat ate without so much as a glance her way, and when he'd licked up the last morsel of chicken, he simply walked out of the kitchen. So much for the joys of companionship, she thought. She received more love from this bottle of wine.

She sipped her zinfandel, trying not to look at the cell phone lying on the kitchen counter. It called to her the way opium calls to a junkie, tempting her back into a spiral of heartbreak. Daniel's text had been short: *Call if you need me.* There were only five words in that message, yet they had the power to paralyze her in this chair while she mulled over its true intent. What did those words—*if you need me*—really mean? Was he referring to the murder investigation and offering more expert advice?

Or is this about us?

She drained her glass of wine and poured a second. Pulled out the handwritten notes she'd jotted down at tonight's death scene and opened her laptop. Now was the time to organize her thoughts, while her memories were still fresh.

Her cell phone rang. *Daniel.*

She hesitated only a second before picking it up, only to see an unfamiliar number on the display. It was not Daniel's voice but a woman's on the phone, a woman who delivered the news that she'd both expected and dreaded. She left her laptop glowing on the kitchen table and ran to the closet to get her coat.

"THEY FOUND MRS. LANK COLLAPSED and unconscious in her cell," said Dr. Wang. "The prison nurse immediately began CPR and they managed to restore a pulse. But as you can see from the cardiac monitor, she's having frequent periods of ventricular tachycardia."

Maura stared through the ICU window at Amalthea, who was now deeply comatose. "Why?" she asked softly.

"The arrhythmia could be a complication of her chemotherapy. The drugs can be cardiotoxic."

"No, I meant, why did they even resuscitate her? They know she's dying of pancreatic cancer."

"But she's still listed as a full code." He looked at her. "Perhaps you don't know this, but Mrs. Lank signed a medical power of attorney document last week. She named you as her representative."

"I had no idea."

"You're her only relative. You have the authority. Do you want to change her status to *do not resuscitate*?"

Maura watched Amalthea's chest rise and fall with every whoosh of the ventilator. "Is she responsive to stimuli?"

He shook his head. "And she's not breathing on her own. No one knows how long she was unconscious, so there's a good chance she has anoxic brain damage. There may also be something else going on, neurologically. I haven't ordered a brain scan yet, but that would be the next diagnostic step, unless you decide . . ." He paused, watching her. Waiting for her answer.

"Do not resuscitate," she said quietly.

He nodded. "I think that's the right decision." He hesitated before giving her a pat on the arm, as if touching another human being did not come naturally to him, just as it did not come naturally to Maura. It was far easier to understand the mechanics of the human body than to know what one should say and do in times of grief.

Maura stepped into the cubicle and stood at Amalthea's bedside, surveying all the beeping and whooshing machinery. With a clinical eye she noted the scant urine in the collection bag, the flurry of premature beats on the screen, the lack of spontaneous breathing. These were all the signs of a body shutting down, a brain no longer functioning. Whoever Amalthea Lank had once been, all her thoughts and feelings and memories were now extinguished. Only this flesh-and-bone container remained.

An alarm on the monitor sounded. Maura looked up at the cardiac rhythm and saw a succession of jagged peaks. Ventricular tachycardia. The blood-pressure line plummeted. Through the window, she saw two nurses scrambling toward the cubicle, but Dr. Wang stopped them at the doorway.

"She's a DNR," he told them. "I just wrote the order."

Maura reached up and shut off the alarm.

On the monitor, she watched the rhythm deteriorate to ventricular fibrillation, the final electrical twitches of Amalthea's dying heart. The blood pressure cratered to zero, starving the last surviving brain cells of oxygen. *You gave birth to me*, thought Maura. *In every cell of my body I carry your DNA, but in every other way we are strangers.* She thought of the mother and father who had adopted and cherished her, both of them dead now. They were her real parents, because one's true family is defined not by DNA but by love. In that regard, this woman was no relation of Maura's, and as she watched Amalthea's final moments, she did not feel even the slightest twinge of grief.

The heart at last ceased its final twitches. A flat line traced across the screen.

A nurse stepped in and shut off the ventilator. "I'm sorry," she murmured.

Maura took a deep breath. "Thank you," she said, and walked out of the cubicle. She kept walking, out of the ICU, out of the hospital, into a wind so frigid that by the time she crossed the parking lot to her car, she could not feel her hands or face. A physical numbness to match what she felt inside. Amalthea is dead, my parents are dead, and I will probably never have a child, she thought. She had long felt alone in the world and had accepted it, but tonight, standing beside her car in the windswept parking lot, she realized she did not *want* to accept it. Did not have to accept it. She was alone only by choice.

I can change that. Tonight.

She slid into her car, pulled out the cell phone, and once again read Daniel's text message. *Call if you need me.*

She called.

DANIEL MADE IT TO HER house before she did.

When she arrived home, she saw him sitting in his parked car in her driveway, where the whole world could see him. Last year they'd been careful to conceal his visits, but tonight he'd cast aside all caution. Even before she shut off her engine, he was out of his car and opening her door.

She stepped out, into his arms.

There was no need to explain why she'd called him, no need for words of any kind. The first touch of his lips stripped away her last shreds of resistance. I'm right back in the trap, she thought, as they kissed their way into her house and down the hallway.

To her bedroom.

There, she stopped thinking at all, because she no longer cared about the consequences. All that mattered was that she felt alive again, whole again, reunited with the missing part of her soul. Loving Daniel might be foolish and ultimately star-crossed, but not loving him had been impossible. All these months she had tried to live without him, had swallowed the bitter pill of self-control and been rewarded with lonely nights and far too many glasses of wine. She'd convinced herself that walking away from him was sensible, because she could never claim him as her own, not when her rival was God Himself. But being *sensible* had not warmed her bed or made her happy or quelled the longing that she would always feel for this man.

In the bedroom they did not turn on the lights; they didn't need to. Their bodies were already familiar territory to each other, and she knew every inch of his skin. She could tell that he had lost weight, just as she had, as though their hunger for each other had been a true starvation. One night would not be enough to satisfy that hunger, and she did not know when they would have another, so she took what she could now, greedy for the pleasure that his Church had forbidden them. Here is what you've missed, Daniel, she thought. How petty your God must be, how cruel, to deny us this joy.

But later, as they lay together with the sweat cooling on their skin, she felt the old sadness creeping in. Here is our punishment, she thought. Not hell and brimstone but the inevitable pain of goodbye. Always a goodbye.

"Tell me why," he whispered. He didn't need to say more; she understood what he was asking. Months after she had unequivocally broken off their affair, why had she invited him back into her bed?

"She's dead," said Maura. "Amalthea Lank."

"When did this happen?"

"Tonight. I was there, at the hospital. I watched her last heartbeats on the monitor. She had cancer, so I knew she was dying, and I've known it for months. But still, when it happened . . ."

"I should have been there with you," he murmured, and she savored the warmth of his breath in her hair. "All you ever have to do is call me and I'll be here. You know that."

"It's strange. A few years ago, I didn't know Amalthea existed. But now that she's gone, my last living relative, I realize how alone I am."

"Only if you choose to be."

As if loneliness were a choice, she thought. She hadn't chosen the road to both joy and misery. She hadn't chosen to love a man who would always be torn between her and his promise to God. That choice had been made *for* them, by the killer who'd brought them together four years ago, a killer who'd turned his sights on Maura. Daniel had risked his life to save Maura's; what greater proof could he offer that he loved her?

"You're not alone, Maura," he said. "You have me." He turned her face toward his, and in the darkness she saw the gleam of his eyes, steadily focused on her. "You'll always have me."

Tonight, she believed him.

IN THE MORNING, DANIEL WAS gone.

She got dressed alone, ate her breakfast alone, read the newspaper alone. Well, not entirely alone: The cat sat nearby, licking his paws after a breakfast of fancy canned tuna.

"No comment, I take it?" Maura said to him.

The Beast didn't deign to look up at her.

As she rinsed her dishes and packed up her laptop, she thought of Daniel, who at this moment would be preparing for a new day of tending to the needy souls in his congregation. This was how their feverish nights together always concluded: with the mundane tasks of daily life, performed separately. In this way they were no different from married couples. They made love, they slept together, and in the morning off they both went to their jobs.

Today, she thought, this counts as happiness.

FROM A NIGHT OF LOVE to a day of death.

This morning it was the body of Earl Devine that waited to greet her when she walked into the autopsy room. Yoshima had already performed the X-rays, and the images were now displayed on the computer screen. As she tied on her gown, she studied the chest films and noted the position of the bullet that had lodged against the spine. Based on the exit wounds, which she'd examined at the death scene, two bullets had passed through the chest and out of the body. This was the sole bullet that remained, its trajectory halted by Devine's vertebral bone.

Jane walked into the autopsy room and joined Maura at the computer screen. "Let me guess. Cause of death is gunshot wounds. Can I be an ME too?"

"There's a bullet lodged in his sixth thoracic vertebra," said Maura.

"And we recovered the other two bullets at the scene. Backs up what I said last night. Crowe fired three times."

"An appropriate response to an imminent threat. I think he has nothing to worry about."

"Still, he's pretty rattled. We had to take him out for drinks last night, just to talk him down."

Maura shot her an amused look. "What is this I'm hearing? A note of sympathy for your old nemesis?"

"Yeah, can you believe it? It's like the world's turned upside down." Jane paused, studying Maura's face. "What'd you do to yourself?"

"Excuse me?"

"You're all bright and shiny this morning. Like you've been to a health spa or something."

"I don't know what you're talking about." But of course Maura did know; *bright and shiny* was exactly how the world looked to her today. Happiness left its telltale glow, and Jane was too observant to miss it. *If*

I tell her about last night, she'll certainly disapprove, but I don't give a damn. I choose not to care what Jane thinks, or what anyone thinks. Today I choose to be happy. With a defiant click of the mouse, she pulled up the next X-ray, and a lateral view of the chest appeared onscreen. Maura frowned at a coin-shaped lucency in the vertebral body, just above where the bullet had lodged. A lesion that should not be there.

"New makeup? Vitamin pills?" Jane asked.

"What?"

"*Something's* different about you."

Maura ignored her. She clicked back to the frontal view of the chest and zoomed in to study the fifth and sixth vertebrae. But the bullet-shredded lung had spilled air and blood into the chest cavity and forced the thoracic organs out of their usual positions. In this distorted landscape, she could not find what she was searching for.

"You see something interesting?" said Jane.

Maura clicked back to the lateral view and pointed to the lesion in the vertebral body. "I'm not sure what *this* is."

"I'm no doctor, but that doesn't look like a bullet to me."

"No, it's something else. Something in the bone. I need to confirm what I think it is." Maura turned to the autopsy table where Earl Devine was stretched out, awaiting her scalpel. "Let's open him up," she said, and tied on her mask.

As Maura started the Y incision, Jane said, "I hope you're not having doubts about how the shooting went down."

"No."

"So what are you looking for?"

"An explanation, Jane. The reason why this man chose suicide by cop."

"Isn't that a job for a psychiatrist?"

"In this case, the autopsy may give us the answer."

Maura cut swiftly and efficiently, moving with an urgency she hadn't felt before she'd viewed the X-rays. The cause of death and manner of death were both apparent, and she'd assumed this autopsy would merely confirm what she'd already been told about the shooting. But the lateral chest X-ray had added a possible twist to the tale, a tantalizing glimpse of Earl Devine's motives and his state of mind. A cadaver could reveal more than merely physical secrets; sometimes it offered insights into the personality once inhabiting the flesh. Whether clues were old slash marks on the wrists or needle tracks or cosmetic-surgery scars, every corpse told tales on its owner.

As Maura snapped through the ribs, she felt she was about to open the book containing Earl Devine's secrets, but when she lifted the breastplate and exposed the thoracic cavity, she found those secrets obscured by a chest full of blood. The three bullets fired by Detective Crowe had devastated their target, puncturing a lung and slicing through the aorta. The explosion of blood and leaked air had collapsed the right lung, deforming the usual landmarks. She plunged gloved hands into that cold pudding of blood and blindly ran her fingers across the surface of the left lung.

It did not take long to find what she was searching for.

"How can you see anything in there?" asked Jane.

"I can't. But I can already tell you this lung is not normal."

"Maybe because a bullet went through it?"

"A bullet had nothing to do with this." Maura reached again for the scalpel. It was tempting to take shortcuts and focus immediately on the lung, but that was how mistakes were made, vital details missed. Instead, she proceeded as she always did, first dissecting the tongue and neck, freeing the pharynx and esophagus from the cervical vertebrae. She saw no foreign bodies, nothing to distinguish Earl Devine's throat structures from those of any other sixty-seven-year-old man. *Slow down. Make no mistakes.* She felt Jane watching her with growing puzzlement. Yoshima set forceps on the tray, and the clang was as sharp as gunfire. Maura stayed on task, her scalpel slicing through the soft tissue and vessels of the thoracic inlet. With both hands deep in chilled blood, she freed the parietal pleura to separate the lungs from the chest wall.

"Basin," she requested.

Yoshima held out a stainless-steel basin, waiting for what she was about to drop into it.

She lifted the heart and lungs in a single organ bloc from the chest cavity, and the viscera plopped into the basin with a splash. The smell of cold blood and meat rose with the dripping offal. She carried the bowl to the sink and rinsed a slimy veil of blood from the organs, revealing what she had earlier felt on the surface of the left lung: a lesion that had been obscured on the X-ray by trauma.

Maura sliced out a wedge of lung. Staring at the

gray-white specimen glistening in her gloved hand, she knew how this tissue would almost certainly look under the microscope. She imagined dense whorls of keratin and strange, misshapen cells. And she thought of Earl Devine's house, where the smell of nicotine clung to the drapes, the furniture.

She looked at Jane. "I need a list of his medications. Find out who his doctor was."

"Why?"

Maura held up the wedge of tissue. "Because this explains his suicide."

THIRTY-THREE

"I HAD NO IDEA," SAID HOLLY DEVINE, HER hands calmly folded in her lap as she sat on her living-room sofa. "I knew Daddy was losing weight, but he told me he was just getting over pneumonia. He never said he was dying." She looked across the coffee table at Jane and Frost. "Maybe he didn't know either."

"Your father definitely knew," said Jane. "When we searched his medicine cabinet, we found prescription pills ordered by an oncologist, Dr. Christine Cuddy. Four months ago, your father was diagnosed with lung cancer. It had already spread to his bones, and when Dr. Isles studied the X-rays, she spotted a metastatic lesion in your father's spine. Your father must have been in a great deal of pain, because there was a recently prescribed bottle of Vicodin in his bathroom."

"He told me he'd pulled a muscle. He said the pain was getting better."

"It wasn't getting better, Holly. His cancer was already in his liver, and that pain was only going to get worse. He was offered chemotherapy but he refused. He told Dr. Cuddy that he wanted to live as fully as he could, while he could, without feeling sick. Because his daughter needed him."

It had been only two days since her father's death, yet Holly appeared composed and dry-eyed as she processed this new information. Outside, a truck rumbled by her apartment building, and the three teacups rattled on the flimsy-looking coffee table. Everything in Holly's apartment seemed cheaply made, the sort of furniture that usually came packed in a box with step-by-step instructions for assembly. This was a bare-bones apartment, for a career girl still perched on the bottom rungs of the ladder, but Holly was almost certainly on her way up. There was a slyness about her, a canny intelligence in her eyes that Jane was only now recognizing.

"I'm sure he didn't want me to worry. That's why he never told me about the cancer," said Holly. She gave a sad shake of the head. "He'd do anything to make me happy."

"He even killed for you," said Jane.

"He did what he thought had to be done. Isn't that what fathers do? They keep the monsters away."

"That wasn't his job, Holly. It was ours."

"But you couldn't protect me."

"Because you didn't let us. Instead, you practically invited the killers to strike. You ignored our advice and went to a bar. Allowed that woman to send you a drink. Were you *trying* to get yourself killed, or was it all part of the plan?"

"*You* weren't having any luck finding him."

"So you decided to do it yourself."

"What are you talking about?"

"What *was* the plan, Holly?"

"There was no plan. I went for a drink after work, that's all. I told you, I was supposed to meet a friend."

"Who never showed up."

"Do you think I lied about that?"

"I think we haven't heard the whole story."

"Which is?"

"That you went to the bar hoping to draw out Stanek and his partner. Instead of letting us find him, you chose to be a vigilante."

"I chose to fight back."

"By taking justice into your own hands?"

"Does it really matter how it happens, as long as it does happen?"

Jane stared at her for a moment, suddenly struck by the fact that, on some level, she actually agreed with this woman. She thought of the perps who'd walked free because some cop or attorney made a procedural error, perps that she knew were guilty. She thought of how often she wished there were a shortcut to bringing a killer to justice, a way to kick a monster straight into a prison cell. And she thought of Detective Johnny Tam, who had once resorted to just such a shortcut and delivered his own form of justice. Only Jane knew Tam's secret, and she would forever protect it.

But Holly's secrets couldn't be protected, because Boston PD knew exactly what she and her father had plotted. Holly had to be confronted.

"You drew them out," said Jane. "Made them reveal themselves."

"There's no law against it."

"There's a law against murder. You're an accessory."

Holly blinked. "Excuse me?"

"The last thing your father did on this earth was to protect his little girl. He was dying of lung cancer, so he had nothing to lose by killing Martin Stanek. And you knew he was going to do it."

"I didn't know."

"Of course you did."

"How could I?"

"Because you're the one who told him where to find Stanek. Moments after we arrested Bonnie Sandridge, you called your father's cell phone. A two-minute phone call, which is how he learned Bonnie's name and address. He went to her house armed and prepared to kill the man who threatened his daughter."

Holly took this accusation with surprising calmness. Jane had laid out the evidence that Holly was an accessory to Martin's murder, yet none of this seemed to fluster her.

Frost said, "Do you care to respond, Ms. Devine?"

"Yes." Holly sat up straighter. "I *did* call my father. Of course I called him. I'd just had an encounter with a woman who'd planned to abduct me, and I wanted to tell him I was safe. Any daughter would make that call. I may have mentioned Bonnie's name on the phone, but I didn't tell him to kill her. I just told Daddy not to worry, because you had her in custody. I didn't know that he'd go to her house. I didn't know he'd bring his gun." Holly took a deep breath and dropped her head. When she looked up again, her face was streaked with tears. "He gave his life for me. How can you talk about him as if he's a cold-blooded killer?"

Jane looked at those glistening eyes and trembling lips and she thought: Goddamn it, this gal's good. While Jane wasn't buying the act, others might be convinced. They had no recording of the phone conversation between Holly and her father, no proof that Holly actually knew what Earl planned to do. In court, this eerily poised young woman would easily sail through the toughest cross-examination.

"I need to be alone right now," said Holly. "This has been so hard, losing Daddy. Please, can you just *go*?"

"Of course," said Frost, and he stood up to leave. Was he actually buying this performance? Frost had always been a pushover for damsels in distress, especially if those damsels were young and attractive, but surely he could see what was going on here.

Jane held her silence as she and Frost left the apartment and walked out of the building. But as soon as they climbed into her car, she blurted, "*What* a load of crap. And what a hell of an actress."

"You think that was acting? She really did seem upset to me," said Frost.

"You mean those cute little tears she produced on command?"

"Okay." Frost sighed. "What's bugging you?"

"There's something not right about her."

"Care to be more specific?"

Jane considered what it was about Holly that bothered her. "Two nights ago, when we told her that Earl was dead, do you remember how she reacted to the news?"

"She cried. Like you'd expect a daughter to do."

"Oh, she cried, all right. Loud, honking sobs. But it felt staged to me, as if she was doing what we expected her to do. And I swear, just now she cried right on cue."

"What is your problem with her anyway?"

"I don't know." Jane started the car. "But I feel like I've missed something important. Something about *her.*"

Back in the homicide unit, Jane scanned all the file folders piled up on her desk, wondering if they contained some detail she'd overlooked, some explanation for why she felt so unsatisfied. Here were the case files she'd already combed through, covering the Boston murders of Cassandra Coyle and Timothy McDougal, the Newport death of Sarah Basterash, and the disappearance of Billy Sullivan in Brookline. Four victims in three different jurisdictions. Their deaths were so dissimilar that the decades-old connection between them could easily have been missed. Cassandra Coyle, her eyeballs scooped out and displayed in her hand like Saint Lucy. Tim McDougal, his chest pierced by arrows, like Saint Sebastian. Sarah Basterash, burned to cinders like Saint Joan. Billy Sullivan, almost certainly buried and moldering in his grave, like Saint Vitalis.

Then there was the child who was still alive, the one who'd been first to accuse the Staneks of abuse twenty years ago: Holly Devine, birthdate November 12. On that day, the church honored Saint Livinus, Apostle of Flanders, who died a martyr after being tortured by pagans. His tongue had been ripped out to stop him from spreading the word of God, but even after his death, according to legend, the amputated tongue of Livinus continued to preach. Did Holly ever lie awake at night, haunted by the bloody fate that was preordained by her birthdate? Did she shudder at the thought of her mouth being forced open, her tongue sliced away with a knife? Jane remembered her own fear when she'd been targeted by the killer called the Surgeon. She remembered startling awake in panic, drenched in sweat, imagining the killer's scalpel sinking into her flesh.

If Holly had ever felt such terror, she hid it well. Too well.

Jane sighed and rubbed her temples, wondering if she should reread the case files for these four victims.

No, not four victims. She sat up straight. *Five.*

She shuffled through the stack of folders and found the file for Lizzie DiPalma, the nine-year-old girl who'd vanished twenty years ago. Lizzie's disappearance was still classified as unsolved, but there'd been little doubt in the minds of investigators that Martin Stanek had abducted and killed her. Two decades later, the girl was still missing.

Frost returned from lunch, saw the files spread out across Jane's desk, and shook his head. "You're still going through those?"

"It's not settling right with me. It feels too neatly tied up, complete with a pretty bow. Our prime suspect conveniently ending up dead."

"Doesn't seem like a problem to me."

"And we never found out what happened to this little girl." She tapped on the folder. "Lizzie DiPalma."

"That was twenty years ago. It's not our case."

"But it feels like the *beginning* of everything. As if her disappearance was the first domino to fall, setting off what followed. Lizzie goes missing. Her hat turns up on Martin Stanek's school bus. Suddenly the accusations start flying. The Staneks are monsters! They've been molesting kids for months! Why didn't any of that come out earlier? Not even a hint of it?"

"Someone had to be the first to speak up."

"And the very first kid who did speak up was Holly Devine."

"The girl you keep insisting is strange."

"Whenever I talk to her, I feel like she's calculating every word. Like we're playing a chess game and she's five moves ahead of me."

Frost's phone rang. As he turned to answer it, Jane paged through the Lizzie DiPalma documents, wondering if any progress on the case was possible after so much time had passed. The grounds of the Apple Tree Daycare had been thoroughly searched for the girl's remains. While microscopic traces of her blood were found on the bus, it was explained by an injury a month earlier, when Lizzie had cut her lip. The most powerful evidence against Martin Stanek was Lizzie's beaded hat, found on the school bus. The hat she'd been wearing when she vanished.

The killer had to be Martin Stanek.

And now he's dead. End of story. With a sigh of finality, Jane closed the folder.

"You're not gonna like this," said Frost, hanging up the phone.

She turned to him. "What now?"

"You know that glass of wine that Bonnie Sandridge sent to Holly in the pub? The lab says there's no trace of ketamine." He shook his head. "We have to release her."

THIRTY-FOUR

ONLY TWO DAYS AGO, BONNIE SANDRIDGE HAD been handcuffed and booked as an accessory to murder. Now she swaggered into the Boston PD interview room as if she were the one in charge. Although her red hair was streaked with silver and decades of sun exposure had freckled her skin and etched wrinkles around her eyes, she carried herself with the athletic confidence of a woman who had always been handsome and knew it. She sat down at the interview table and regarded Jane and Frost with a look of scorn.

"Let me guess," she said. "That glass of wine turned out to be nothing but a glass of wine."

"We need to have a little chat," said Jane.

"After the way I was treated? Why should I cooperate?"

"Because we all want to know the truth. Help us figure it out, Bonnie."

"I think I'd rather expose your incompetence."

"Ms. Sandridge," Frost said quietly. "At the time of your arrest, we had every reason to think you were a threat to Holly Devine. The killer had already established a pattern, and when you sent Holly that glass of wine, it fit the pattern."

"What pattern?"

"On the night Cassandra Coyle was murdered, a waitress at a nearby cocktail lounge thought she saw Cassandra having drinks with a woman."

"And you thought I was that woman? Oh, dear, but you can't prove it, because that waitress couldn't ID me. Am I right?"

Jane said, "Still, you can understand why we arrested you. The night we saw you with Holly, we had to move in fast. We believed she was in imminent danger."

"Holly Devine in imminent danger?" Bonnie snorted. "That gal could slither out of anything."

"What makes you say that?"

"Why don't we ask a man?" Bonnie turned to Frost. "What do *you* think about Holly, Detective? Let's hear the first words that pop into your head."

He hesitated. "She's intelligent. Attractive—"

"Aha! Attractive. For men, it always comes down to that."

"Resourceful," he added quickly.

"You forgot seductive. Manipulative. Opportunistic."

"What are you getting at, Bonnie?" asked Jane.

The woman turned to Jane. "Holly Devine is a textbook sociopath. Not that I'm being judgmental or anything. Sociopathy must be within the range of normal human behavior, since there seem to be so many people like Holly in this world." She gave Jane a dismissive look that said: *You've got some catching up to do.* If there was anyone as dogged as a homicide cop, it was an investigative journalist, and Jane felt a grudging sense of respect for the woman. Bonnie wore her crow's-feet like battle scars, with pride and an attitude. "Don't tell me you didn't realize that yourself about Holly? Come on, you've talked to the girl."

"I found her . . . different," said Jane.

Bonnie gave a bark of a laugh. "That's a charitable way of putting it."

"Why do you think she's a sociopath? The only time you actually spoke to her was that night in the pub."

"Have you interviewed her colleagues at Booksmart Media? Asked them what they think of her? Most of the men in her office are just hot to get into her pants, but the women are wary. The women don't trust her."

"Maybe they're jealous," said Frost.

"No, they *really* don't trust her. Cassandra Coyle certainly didn't."

Jane frowned. "What did she say about Holly?"

"Cassandra's the one who brought her up. She bluntly told me not to trust Holly Devine. At Apple Tree, the other kids thought Holly was a strange girl and they avoided her. They sensed there was something not right about her. The only kid who played with her at all was Billy Sullivan."

"Why did Holly spook the other kids?"

"That's what I wondered. I wanted to see for myself why they thought the girl was strange, but no one knew how to find her. It took me months to track her down to Booksmart Media. I wanted to interview her for the chapter I'm writing about Apple Tree. She was the first child to accuse the Staneks, and I wondered if she told the truth."

"There was physical evidence," said Frost. "She had bruises. Scrapes."

"She could have gotten those anywhere."

"Why would she lie about being molested?"

Bonnie shrugged. "Maybe she did it to get attention. Maybe her crazy mother planted the idea in her head. Whatever the reason, Holly chose precisely the right moment to come forward. Lizzie DiPalma had disappeared and all the parents in the neighborhood were scared and searching for answers. Holly gave them one: The evil Staneks did it. Then Billy Sullivan claimed he'd been molested too, and the Staneks were doomed, just like *that.*" Bonnie snapped her fingers. "Frantic parents questioned their own kids, planting ideas in their heads. No wonder the other children began to repeat the stories. If you're asked about an incident again and again, you start to believe it happened. You actually start to *remember* it. The youngest kids were only five, six years old, and every time they were interviewed, their stories grew more bizarre. Flying tigers! Dead babies! The Staneks soaring through the air on broomsticks." She shook her head. "The jury sent that poor family to prison based on tales told by brainwashed children. Cassandra Coyle was already doubting her own memories of abuse. She said she'd contact the other children, see if they'd be willing to talk to me, but the only name she'd reveal to me was Holly Devine. Who's now the sole remaining source for my book."

"What's the point of this book you're writing? To exonerate Martin Stanek?"

"The more I learned about the case, the more angry I became. So, yes, proving his innocence was important. It's *still* important." Bonnie blinked and turned away. "Even if he's dead."

Jane saw a brief glimmer of tears in the woman's eyes. Quietly, she asked, "Were you in love with him?"

The question made Bonnie's chin snap up. She looked at Jane with an expression of surprise. "What?"

"It's obvious that you're emotionally involved."

"Because it matters to me. This story should matter to everyone."

"Why to you, in particular?"

Bonnie took a breath and sat up straighter. "To answer your question, no. I was not in love with Martin, but I did feel sorry for him. What was done to him, to his family, makes me so fucking—" She stopped, suddenly too agitated to speak, her hands balled into white, bony fists.

"Why does it make you so angry?" asked Jane.

Bonnie's fists balled tighter, but she didn't reply.

"There's got to be a reason why this matters so much to you. A reason you haven't told us."

For a long time Bonnie did not answer. When she finally spoke, it was barely a whisper. "Yes, it does matter. Because it happened to me too."

Jane and Frost exchanged startled looks. Frost asked gently, "What happened to you, Ms. Sandridge?"

"I had—I have—a daughter," said Bonnie. "She's

almost twenty-six. Her birthday's in three weeks, and more than anything I want to be there to celebrate with her. But I'm not allowed to see Amy, or call her, or even write to her." She squared her shoulders, as if preparing for battle, and looked at Jane and Frost. "When Amy was a freshman in college, she started having panic attacks. She'd wake up at night in her dorm room, convinced that someone was in her room, about to kill her. The attacks were so terrifying, she had to sleep with the light on. The student health service referred her to a therapist, a woman who claimed to be an expert in age regression. The therapist used hypnosis to explore Amy's childhood memories, trying to find the reason behind these panic attacks.

"For eight months, Amy returned again and again to that . . . doctor." Bonnie spat out the title like an epithet and ran a hand over her lips, as if to wipe away the taste of the word. "As the sessions continued, Amy started to remember things. Things that she'd supposedly suppressed. She remembered lying in bed as a child. Remembered the door opening and someone creeping through the darkness. Someone who pulled up her nightgown and . . ." Bonnie paused. Took another breath and plunged on. "These weren't vague memories. They were extremely detailed, right down to the objects that her molester used. A wooden spoon. The handle of a hairbrush. The therapist concluded that Amy's panic attacks resulted from years of abuse she'd suffered as a child. Now that Amy remembered it, it was time for her to confront her attacker." Bonnie looked up, lashes sparkling with tears. "Me."

Jane frowned. "Did you really—"

"Of course I didn't! *None* of it was true, not one goddamn detail! I was a single mom, and there was no one else living in our house, so of course the guilty party had to be *me.* I was the monster who sneaked into her room at night and molested her. The monster who turned her into such an emotional wreck. The more sessions Amy had with that therapist, the more anxious she became. I didn't realize what was going on until one night when it all came to a head.

"I got a call from the therapist to come in for a meeting. I went to her office thinking I'd hear an update on Amy's progress. Instead, I found myself in a room with my daughter. As the therapist sat listening, encouraging her, Amy proceeded to tell me all the horrible things I'd done to her when she was a child. She'd suddenly remembered the rapes, the abuse, the times I'd shared her with mysterious other people. I told her she'd imagined it all, that I'd never done any of those things, but she was convinced it happened. She *remembered* it. And then she . . ." Bonnie wiped away tears. "She told me she would never see or speak to me again, not for as long as she lived. When I tried to reason with her, tried to convince her that these memories were false, the therapist told me I was *lucky* to get off so easy. They could have called the police and had me arrested. She said Amy was being generous by letting it stay in the past. I was sobbing, pleading with my daughter to listen to me, but she just stood up and walked out of the room. And that was the last time I saw her." Bonnie ran her hand across her eyes, leaving wet smears on her face. "That's why the Apple Tree case matters to me."

"Because you think the same thing happened to the Staneks."

"Cassandra Coyle thought so too. She told me the case haunted her so deeply that she was inspired to write a movie about it."

"Her horror film? *Mr. Simian*?" said Frost.

Bonnie gave an ironic laugh. "Sometimes the only way to tell the truth is through fiction."

"But her colleagues told us *Mr. Simian* is about a girl who goes missing. It has nothing to do with kids being molested."

"The movie is also about how memories get twisted over time. How the truth is simply a matter of your point of view." Bonnie sat straighter. Back in control. "Have you heard of Dr. Elizabeth Loftus?"

"The psychologist?" said Frost.

Jane glanced at her partner. "How do you know that?"

"Alice told me about her," said Frost. "The subject came up in one of her law school classes, about witness testimony and whether it's reliable." He looked at Bonnie. "Alice is my wife."

Was your wife, Jane wanted to say but didn't.

"Back in the mid-nineties," said Bonnie, "Dr. Loftus published a groundbreaking article in *Psychiatric Annals*. It described an experiment she conducted using twenty-four adults. In the study, her subjects were reminded of four different events from their childhoods, as recounted by close relatives. But only three of those four events actually happened. One was purely fictional. The subjects were asked to recall details about each of the four events. As the weeks went by, they remembered more and more, and their details became quite elaborate. Even for the event that never happened.

"After the study was over, five of those twenty-four people could not identify which of the four events was the fictional one. They still believed it had really happened to them. In those five people, Dr. Loftus had successfully implanted a false memory. All it takes to implant a memory is to keep telling someone that an event actually occurred. Talk about it as if it's real, and refer to it again and again. Before long, your subjects will start filling in their own details, adding color and texture, until the memory is as vivid to them as real life. So vivid that the subjects *swear* it's true." She sank back in the chair. "Dr. Loftus's study was done on adults. Imagine how much easier it would be with children. You can make a young child believe almost anything."

"Like flying tigers and secret rooms in the basement," said Frost.

"You've read the children's interviews. You know how outlandish some of their claims were. Animal sacrifice. Devil worship. And, remember, some of those children were only five or six years old, hardly a reliable age, yet their testimony helped send the Stanek family to prison. It was the modern version of the Salem witch trials." She looked back and forth at Jane and Frost. "Have you met the prosecutor, Erica Shay?"

"Not yet," said Jane.

"The Apple Tree trial made her career. She couldn't

get a guilty verdict for the Lizzie DiPalma abduction, but she still managed to send the satanic Staneks to prison. Winning was all that mattered to her. Not the truth. Certainly not justice."

"That's a pretty serious accusation," said Frost. "You're saying the prosecutor knowingly sent innocent people to jail."

Bonnie nodded. "That's exactly what I'm saying."

"TRUST ME. MARTIN STANEK WAS guilty as hell," said Erica Shay.

At fifty-eight, the prosecutor looked even more formidable than she had in the news clippings from the Apple Tree trial twenty years earlier, when she'd cut a steely figure in tailored skirt suits, her blond hair swept back in a severe chignon. Two decades had whittled away any trace of softness from her face, carving it into sharp angles with jutting cheekbones and a beak-like nose, and her gaze was direct and battle-ready.

"Of course Stanek claimed he was innocent. All the guilty ones do."

"So do the innocent ones," said Jane.

Erica leaned back in her chair and gazed coolly across her oak desk at the two detectives sitting in her office. It was a nicely appointed room, one wall covered with her diplomas and awards and a gallery of photos: Erica with a succession of Massachusetts governors. Erica with two senators. Erica with the president. The wall announced to everyone who entered: *I know important people. I'm not to be trifled with.*

"I simply did my job. I presented the evidence against

Martin Stanek in court," said Erica. "And the jury decided he was guilty."

"Of molestation," said Jane. "But not of Lizzie DiPalma's abduction."

Erica's eyes flashed with annoyance. "That was the jury's mistake. I didn't doubt for an instant that he killed her. We all know he did it."

"Do we?"

"All you have to do is look at the evidence. Nine-year-old Lizzie DiPalma goes missing on a Saturday afternoon. She leaves her house, wearing her favorite knitted hat with silver beads. She gets on her bike, rides away, and she's never seen again. Her bike's found at the roadside a mile and a half away. Two days later, Lizzie's hat—very distinctive, bought during a family trip to Paris—is found on the Apple Tree school bus by one of the kids. Now tell me, how does that hat end up on a vehicle that only Martin Stanek drove? A vehicle that was supposedly parked and locked in the Stanek driveway the entire weekend? Traces of Lizzie's blood were found on the floor of that same bus."

"Lizzie cut her lip on the bus a month earlier. Her mother shared that detail at trial."

Erica gave a snort. "Lizzie's mother was an idiot. She never should have revealed that information."

"It was the truth, wasn't it?"

"All it did was put reasonable doubt in the minds of the jurors. It made them question everything else we presented. Then the defense concocted the absurd theory that someone *else* abducted Lizzie. That the girl might still be alive." Erica shook her head in disgust. "At least we got a guilty verdict for the abuse charges. Twenty years in prison was less than I hoped for, but that's twenty years when Stanek couldn't hurt anyone. As soon as he walked free, it didn't take him long to go right back to killing. He wanted revenge. Those children told the truth, and it sent him to prison."

"The truth? Some of the claims were pretty far-fetched," said Frost.

"Children exaggerate. Or they get a few details wrong. But they don't lie, not about abuse."

"They can be coached. Made to believe—"

"Don't tell me you're *defending* him?"

Her outburst made Frost flinch back in his chair. In the courtroom, this woman would probably fight like a gladiator, quick to strike, never retreating. Jane thought of young Martin Stanek, twenty-two years old, frightened, and doomed. This was what he faced on the witness stand, this relentless adversary circling in for the kill.

"I interviewed every one of those children," said Erica. "I spoke to their parents. I examined the bruises and scratches on Holly's arms. She's the one who found Lizzie's hat on the bus. She was the one brave enough to tell her mother what was happening at that daycare. Then Billy Sullivan confirmed it, and I knew it had to be true. The Staneks were a nest of vipers, and their victims were so terrified, they didn't dare speak up until Holly and Billy did. It took weeks of interviews, repeated questioning, but little by little the secrets came out. What the children saw, and what was done to almost all of them."

"How many children are we talking about?" said Jane.

"Many. But we chose not to use all the statements."

"Because their stories were even more outlandish?"

"It's been twenty years. Why are you questioning my work on the case?"

"There's a journalist who says you implanted false memories in those children."

"Bonnie Sandridge?" Erica snorted. "She *calls* herself a journalist. She's nothing but a crackpot."

"So you're familiar with her."

"I do my best to avoid her. She's spent the last few years writing some book about ritual-abuse trials. She tried to interview me once, and it felt like an ambush. She has a twisted agenda, thinks these trials are all witch hunts." Erica gave a dismissive wave. "Why should I care what she says?"

"Cassandra Coyle cared, and she wanted Bonnie to correct the record. Cassandra believed the Staneks were innocent all along, and she'd been calling the other children. Asking what they remembered."

"Bonnie Sandridge told you this?"

"Phone records support her story. Cassandra Coyle *did* call Sarah Basterash and Timothy McDougal and Billy Sullivan. We needed to go back almost a year to find those phone logs, which is how we missed it the first time. The only person Cassandra didn't call was Holly Devine, because no one knew how to find her."

"Twenty years go by, and suddenly Cassandra wants to exonerate the Staneks?" Erica shook her head. "Why?"

"Wouldn't it bother *you* if you realized you'd sent an innocent man to prison?"

"Well, I have no doubts. He was guilty, and the jury agreed with me." Erica rose to her feet, a signal that their meeting was at an end. "Justice was served, and there's nothing more to say."

THIRTY-FIVE

"ANOTHER VICTORY FOR THE CRIME-FIGHTING Rizzoli family!" declared Jane's father. He popped the cork and prosecco bubbled out of the bottle, dribbling onto Angela's favorite Tuscan yellow tablecloth.

"Dial it back, Dad," said Jane. "This is not that big a deal."

"Of course it is! Whenever our family name makes it into *The Boston Globe,* it's always worth celebrating."

Jane looked at her brother. "Hey, Frankie, you should go rob a bank. That'll be worth a bottle of *real* champagne."

"You just watch, our Frankie here will be in the news one of these days. I can see the headline now: *Special Agent Frank Rizzoli, Jr., singlehandedly brings down international crime syndicate!*" Frank, Sr., filled a champagne glass and handed it to his son. "I always knew my kids would make me proud."

"Our kids," said Angela. She set the platter of roast beef on the table. "I did have something to do with it."

"Frankie's gonna be in the FBI, and Jane's already in the newspapers. Now, Mikey, well, he still needs to figure out what he's gonna do with his life, but I know he'll make me proud someday. Wish he could be here with us on this fine occasion, but having two of my three kids is celebration enough."

"*Our* kids," repeated Angela. "It's not like you raised them all on your own."

"Yeah, yeah. Our kids." He lifted his glass of prosecco. "Here's to Detective Jane Rizzoli. For taking down another scumbag."

As her father and brother downed their glasses of prosecco, Jane glanced at Gabriel, who gave an amused shake of the head and dutifully took a sip. She'd had no inkling that tonight's Rizzoli family dinner was a victory celebration for her work on "the Eyeball Killer case," as her brother liked to call it. In truth she felt little sense of victory; how could she celebrate when her suspect was dead and too many questions remained unanswered? She couldn't shake the feeling that the job was incomplete, that she'd overlooked something. The prosecco tasted bitter, certainly not the flavor of triumph, and after one sip she put it down. She noticed that Angela wasn't drinking either. Leave it to her dad to buy a bottle of wine so cheap that no one with a functioning taste bud would want to drink it.

That wasn't stopping Frank and Frank, Jr., from guzzling it down as they toasted the Rizzoli triumph. If this was justice, it had come at a terrible price. Jane thought of Earl Devine's cancer-ridden corpse lying on the autopsy table, his tragic secret revealed. She thought of Martin Stanek, who had gone to his grave insisting that he was innocent.

What if he was telling the truth?

"Why the long face, Janie? You should get into the spirit of things," her father said, as he sawed into the slice of beef on his plate. "Tonight's all about celebrating!"

"It's not like I achieved world peace or anything."

"You don't think a job well done is worth a champagne toast?"

"It's prosecco," muttered Angela, but no one seemed to hear her. She sat at the far end of the table, shoulders slumped, the food on her plate untouched. As her husband and son gorged on the meal she'd prepared, Angela had not even picked up her fork.

"It's just bothering me," Jane said. "How this case went down."

"Dead perp, problem solved." Her brother laughed and punched Jane in the arm.

"He hit Mommy!" protested Regina.

"I didn't hit her, kid," said Frankie. "I gave her a victory punch."

"You hit her. I saw it!"

Jane kissed her outraged daughter on the head. "It's okay, sweetie. Uncle Frankie's only playing around with me."

"'Cause that's what grown-ups do," said Frankie.

"You hit people?" Regina scowled at him.

Out of the mouths of babes.

"You've gotta learn to defend yourself, kiddo."

Frankie put up his fists and play-boxed with his niece. "C'mon. Show Uncle Frankie you can fight back."

"Don't," said Angela.

"It's just for fun, Ma."

"She's a little girl. She doesn't have to learn how to fight."

"Of course she does. She's a Rizzoli."

"Technically," Jane said, looking at her ever-patient husband, "she's a Dean."

"But she's got Rizzoli blood. And all Rizzolis know how to stand up for themselves."

"No, we don't," said Angela. Her face was flushed, and there was a volcanic glow in her eyes. "Some of us don't fight back. Some Rizzolis are cowards. Like me."

His mouth stuffed with roast beef, Frankie frowned at his mother. "What you talking about, Ma?"

"You heard me. I've been a coward."

Frank, Sr., set down his fork. "Just what is going on now?"

"You, Frank. Me. It's all one big fucking mess."

Regina looked at Gabriel. "Daddy, she said a bad word."

Red-faced, Angela turned to her granddaughter. "Oh, honey, yes, I did. I'm sorry. I'm sorry." She pushed back her chair and stood up. "Nonna needs a time-out."

"You bet she does!" Frank yelled as Angela vanished into the kitchen. He looked around the table. "I don't know what's gotten into her. She's so moody these days."

Jane rose to her feet. "I'll go talk to her."

"No, leave her alone. She needs to pull herself together."

"What she needs is someone to listen to her."

"Suit yourself," grunted Frank, and he reached once again for the bottle of prosecco.

Mom definitely needs a time-out. If only to avoid a murder rap.

In the kitchen, Jane found Angela standing by the counter, staring ominously at the block of chef's knives.

"You know, Ma, poison would be a lot neater," said Jane.

"What's the fatal dose for strychnine?"

"If I tell you, I'll have to arrest you."

"It's not for him. It's for *me.*"

"Ma?"

Angela turned to her daughter with a look of utter misery. "I can't do this, Jane."

"I hope to hell you can't."

"No, I mean, I can't do *this.*" Angela waved at the dirty pots and pans in the sink, the grease-spattered stove, the pie waiting on the counter. "This is the same trap I was in before. It's the way *he* wants things, but it's not for me. I gave it a shot, I really did. And look where it got me."

"Ready to swallow strychnine."

"Exactly."

Through the closed kitchen door, they heard men's laughter. Frank and Frankie, yukking it up over Angela's tenderly prepared meal. Did they taste the care she'd put into the roast beef and potatoes? Did they have any inkling that right now, behind the kitchen door, a decision was being made that would alter every future meal they'd eat at that dining table?

"I'm gonna do it," said Angela. "I'm gonna leave him."

"Oh, Ma."

"Don't try to talk me out of it. Either I do this or I die. I swear, I'm gonna shrivel up and die."

"I'm not going to talk you out of it. Here's what I *am* gonna do." She placed both her hands on her mother's shoulders and looked her in the eyes. "I'm going to help you pack. And then I'm taking you to stay at our place."

"Right now?"

"If that's what you want."

Angela's eyes misted over with tears. "It's what I want. But I can't stay with you. Your apartment's not big enough."

"You can sleep in Regina's room for now. She'll love having her nonna there."

"This'll only be temporary, I swear it. Oh, God, your dad's gonna make a scene."

"We don't have to say a thing to him. Let's just go upstairs and pack."

Together they walked out of the kitchen. Frank and Frankie were so deep in guy talk, they didn't even notice the women crossing through the dining room, but Gabriel eyed Jane with a look of *what's going on?* Of course her husband would be the one to notice. Gabriel noticed everything. She answered with a shake of the head and followed her mother to the stairway.

In her bedroom, Angela pulled open drawers and scooped out sweaters and underwear. She took only what she needed for a few nights; she would have to return for more clothes when Frank wasn't home to get in her way. Two years ago, when Frank had suffered a brief bout of midlife insanity involving a bleached blonde, he'd walked out on Angela, but he was certainly not going to let Angela walk out on *him,* not without a fight. If they made this a quick exit, he might not even notice that his wife was walking out the door.

Jane carried the suitcase down the stairs, where she found Gabriel already waiting by the front door. "Can I help?" he asked quietly.

"Take this out to the car. Mom's coming home with us."

Gabriel didn't argue, didn't ask any questions. He'd already read the situation and understood what needed to be done, and without a word he carried the suitcase out of the house.

"I need to drive my own car," Angela said. "I can't leave it here. Why don't I meet you at your place?"

"No, you need company right now, Ma. I'll drive with you," said Jane.

"Drive with her where?" said her father. Frank stood frowning at them from the hallway. "What's with all the whispering? What's going on?" he demanded.

"Mom's coming to stay with us," said Jane.

"Why?"

"You know why," said Angela. "And if you don't, you *should.*" She pulled her coat out of the closet. "Dessert's in the kitchen, Frank. Blueberry pie. And there's vanilla ice cream in the freezer. Ben and Jerry's, just like you asked for."

"Wait. You're not walking out on me, are you?"

"*You* walked out."

"But I came back! I did it for the family!"

"You did it because the Bimbo threw you out. I got one life to live, Frank, and I'm not gonna spend it being miserable." She grabbed her purse from the hall table and walked out the door.

Frank snorted to Jane, "She'll be back. You watch."

I wouldn't count on it.

Jane walked out to the driveway and found Angela sitting in her car, the engine already warming up. "Let me drive, Ma. You're upset."

"I'm fine. Just get in."

Jane slid into the passenger seat and pulled the door shut. "You sure about this?"

"I've never been more sure of anything in my life." Angela gripped the steering wheel with both hands. "Let's blow this joint."

As they pulled out of the driveway, Jane glanced back at her parents' house, the house where Angela had raised three children. That she would now abandon it told Jane how desperately unhappy her mother was. These past few months she'd seen that unhappiness in Angela's drooping face, in her unkempt hair and perpetually slumped shoulders. Surely Frank had noticed the signs himself, but he never believed that Angela would act on those feelings. Even now he assumed his runaway wife would come home in a few days. He did not even bother to linger outside and watch her leave but had already walked back into the house and closed the door.

"I promise I won't stay with you any longer than I

have to," said Angela. "I'll be there just long enough to find my own place."

"Ma, let's not worry about that right now."

"But I do worry about it. I worry about everything. A woman gets to be my age and suddenly she's a burden to everyone. Or she's a beast *of* burden. I don't know what's worse. Either way, it's . . ." She glanced at the road sign and gave a soft moan.

"What?"

"That's the turnoff to his place." She didn't need to say his name; Jane knew who *he* was: Vince Korsak, the man who had briefly slipped into her mother's life after Frank walked out. "He must be seeing someone new by now," Angela said quietly.

"Like I said, I don't know, Ma."

"Of course he is. A fine man like Vince."

Korsak? Jane almost laughed. Retired detective Vince Korsak was a walking heart attack, overweight and hypertensive, a man with huge appetites and a painful lack of social skills. But he'd been genuinely in love with Angela and was devastated when she broke off their romance and went back to her husband.

Abruptly, Angela swerved the car around, her tires screeching as she made a mid-street U-turn.

"What're you doing, Ma?" Jane yelled. "That is *so* illegal!"

"I gotta know."

"Know what?"

"If there's still a chance."

"With Korsak?"

"I broke his heart when I left him, Jane. He might not ever forgive me."

"He knew what you were up against. Dad. The family."

"I don't know if he'll even talk to me." Angela's foot came off the gas pedal, as if she suddenly questioned this crazy impulse. Then, just as suddenly, she hit the gas again and the car lurched forward.

All Jane could do was hold on for the ride.

They screeched to a stop outside Korsak's apartment building. Angela took a deep breath as she marshaled her courage.

"How about you just call him on the phone?" Jane suggested.

"No. No, I have to be able to see his face. I need to read his feelings when he looks at me." Angela shoved open the car door. "Wait for me, Janie. This could be a very short visit."

Jane watched her mother climb out of the car. Angela paused on the sidewalk to smooth her coat, run her fingers through her hair. She looked like a girl on her first date, and the transformation was startling—her shoulders no longer slumped in defeat, her chin tilted up to meet whatever might come. She opened the apartment door and vanished into the building.

Jane waited. And waited.

Twenty minutes later, Angela had still not returned.

Jane thought of all the possible reasons, most of them bad. What if Angela found Korsak with another woman, a jealous woman? She could be up there now, stabbed and bleeding. Or Korsak could be stabbed and bleeding. That was the downside of being a cop; her mind always went to the worst-case scenario, because she'd seen bad things happen so many times before.

She pulled out her cell phone to call her mother, then realized that Angela had left her purse and cell phone in the car. She dialed Korsak's phone instead, and after four rings it went to voicemail.

They're both stabbed and bleeding. And you're just sitting out here.

With a sigh, she climbed out of the car.

It had been months since she'd last paid a visit to Korsak's apartment, but nothing about his building had changed. The same fake palm tree was still in the lobby, the floor tiles were still cracked, and the elevator was still broken. She took the stairs to the second floor and knocked at 217. There was no answer, but through the closed door she could hear the TV blaring at full volume, a soundtrack of screams and shrieks accompanied by the ominous thump of drums.

The door was unlocked; she walked in.

The apartment was exactly as she remembered it: black leather sofa, a smoked-glass coffee table, a big-screen TV. Your classic bachelor cave. On the TV, an old black-and-white horror film was playing, and the only light in the darkened living room came from the flickering images of terrified faces staring up at something in the sky. UFOs. An alien-invasion movie.

The sound of voices—real voices—made her turn toward the kitchen.

One glance through the doorway told her more than she needed to know. Angela and Korsak stood with their arms around each other, their lips locked in a kiss, their hands roaming. Jane had been forced to witness many sights in her life, things she did not ever want to see again, and her mother French-kissing Vince Korsak was one of them. She backed away, went into the dark living room, and sank onto the sofa.

Now what do I do?

She sat in the flickering glow of the TV, wondering how long she should wait for this make-out session to end. Should she call Gabriel to bring her mother's suitcase and give her a ride home? She didn't want to interrupt this reunion, but really, how long was this going to go on?

On the TV, a woman was stumbling through the woods, fleeing what looked like a man in a giant rubber ant suit. She remembered that Korsak had a collection of these old horror films because, as he used to say, *There's nothing like a scary movie to make your gal want to cuddle.* As if only fear would drive a woman into his arms.

The ant creature emerged from the bushes in all his rubberized glory. The woman tripped over a tree root and fell. Of course she fell. Every woman who's ever fled through the woods must trip and fall. It was another rule from Horror 101. Now the clumsy woman staggered to her feet, sobbing and hysterical. As Rubber Ant Guy moved in for the kill, Jane was suddenly struck by a memory. Another horror movie. Another young woman running in the woods, pursued by a killer.

She sat up straight, staring at the screen, thinking of *Mr. Simian,* written and produced by Cassandra Coyle. A movie that Cassandra's colleagues said was inspired by a true incident from Cassandra's childhood. *A girl who went missing.*

That girl would have been Lizzie DiPalma.

"Oh, Janie. You're here," said Angela.

Jane didn't look at her mom; her gaze was still on the TV, her thoughts still on Cassandra and Lizzie. On her own misgivings about how the case had been resolved and how many questions had not been answered.

"I'm not going home with you," said Angela. "I'm staying here with Vince. I hope that's okay with you, honey."

"Of course it's okay with her," said Korsak. "Why wouldn't it be? We're all adults here."

"This isn't over yet," said Jane, and she jumped to her feet.

"No, it's definitely not over," said Angela, beaming at Korsak. "In fact, it might be better than ever."

"I gotta go, Ma."

"Wait. What about my suitcase?"

"I'll ask Gabriel to drop it off."

"So you're okay with Vince and me living in, you know . . . sin?"

Jane looked at Korsak's fat hand resting on Angela's hip and shuddered at the thought of what would go on in his bedroom tonight. "Life is short, Ma," she said. "And I have things to do."

"Where you going in such a hurry?" said Korsak.

"To see a movie."

THIRTY-SIX

"IT STILL NEEDS TO BE COLOR GRADED AND there's no soundtrack yet, so there won't be the full emotional boost you get with scary music," said Travis Chang. "But this is our picture-locked version. It's pretty much what the finished film will look like, so I guess we can finally show it to you."

Since Jane's last visit to Crazy Ruby Films, the three filmmakers had tidied up the place. The pizza boxes and soda cans were gone, the trash cans were empty, and the dirty-socks odor was absent, replaced by the savory scent of microwaved popcorn, which Amber was now pouring into a bowl for everyone to share. But no one had gotten around to vacuuming the room yet, and Jane brushed old popcorn kernels off the sofa cushions before sitting down.

Ben and Travis joined her on the sofa, one on each side of her, both of them looking at Jane as if she were an alien who'd plopped into their midst. "So, Detective," said Ben. "We were all wondering."

"About what?"

"Why you changed your mind. You told us you weren't a fan of horror films. And suddenly here you are on a Saturday night, insisting that we show you *Mr. Simian*. Why?"

"Insomnia?"

"Come on," said Travis. "What's the real reason?"

All three filmmakers were watching her, waiting for the answer. For the truth.

"The night I interviewed you, right after Cassandra's murder," said Jane, "one of you told me that *Mr. Simian* was inspired by a real incident, something that happened when Cassie was a kid."

"Yeah," said Amber. "She said that a girl went missing."

"Did she ever tell you the girl's name?"

"No. It was just someone from her school."

"I think that child's name was Lizzie DiPalma. She was nine years old when she vanished."

Amber frowned. "The characters in Cassie's script, the ones who go missing, are seventeen years old."

"I think they're stand-ins for Lizzie, the real nine-year-old girl. I also think the killer in your movie might represent the man who took her."

"Wait," said Travis. "Mr. Simian is *real*?"

"In your movie, who *is* Mr. Simian?"

Travis went to his desktop computer and tapped on the keyboard. "I think the best way to answer that question is to show you the movie. So make yourself comfortable, Detective. Here it comes."

As Amber dimmed the room lights, the Crazy Ruby Films opening logo appeared on the big-screen TV, an image of broken shards joining together to form a cubist image of a woman's face.

"That logo was my idea," Amber said. "It represents all these unrelated fragments joining into a visual whole. It's moviemaking in a nutshell."

"There, you see that?" said Travis. He grabbed a handful of popcorn from the bowl and settled onto the floor near Jane's feet. "That opening shot in the woods ended up taking four horrible days to film. Our original star turned up completely stoned, so we fired her. Had to replace her, like, overnight."

"And I sprained my ankle on that shot," said Ben. "Limped around for weeks. It's like our project was jinxed from the very first day."

Onscreen, a pretty blonde in mud-spattered jeans stumbled through dark woods. Even without any ominous music, the tension was evident in her panicked expression, her gasping breaths. She glanced back over her shoulder and a light flared, the beam illuminating her face, her lips frozen in a rictus of terror.

Smash cut to the same girl, sleeping peacefully in her pink bedroom. The caption read: *One week earlier.*

"That first scene in the woods was just a flash-forward," explained Amber. "Now we go back a week to see how our character Anna ended up in those woods, running for her life."

Cut to Anna's biology classroom, where the camera panned across the students: two girls, giggling and passing notes. A bored-looking jock slouched in his varsity jacket. A pale and studious boy conscientiously taking notes. Slowly the camera swung to the front of the classroom and focused on the teacher. A man.

Jane stared at the wispy blond hair, the round baby face, the wire-rim glasses. She knew exactly why this actor had been chosen for the role. He was the spitting image of a young Martin Stanek.

"Is that Mr. Simian?" she asked softly.

"Maybe," said Travis. He added with a sly smile, "Or maybe not. We don't want to spoil the movie for you. You just have to keep watching."

Onscreen, the students filed out of the classroom and chattered as they opened their hallway lockers. Here were the standard characters of every teen horror flick: The jock. The wallflower. The nerd. The catty cheerleader. The levelheaded brunette. Of course, the brunette would survive; in horror movies, the levelheaded girl usually did.

Twenty minutes into the movie, the brunette lost her head to an ax.

The death scene was a slo-mo gorefest of spurting blood and flying cranium that made Jane squirm on her couch cushion. Jesus, no wonder she didn't watch horror flicks; they reminded her too much of work. She stared at the brunette's headless body sprawled in the woods and remembered seeing just such a corpse lying in a bathtub in Dorchester, a young woman beheaded by her crack-crazy boyfriend. That particular horror was real-life, but at least she didn't have to watch while it was happening, and she'd had the benefit of being warned ahead of time about what she was going to encounter. Usually the warning came in a phone call from a grim-voiced officer at the scene, advising her that *this one's really bad,* and before walking onto the scene she'd brace herself for the sights and the smells, because an audience of patrolmen was always watching and waiting to see if the girl cop was tough enough. She made damn sure she *was* tough enough.

She glanced at the three filmmakers, for whom fake gore was their stock-in-trade. For them, murder was fun. *For me, it's always a goddamn tragedy.*

Onscreen, the killer was just a vague silhouette. No face, no features, only a shadow looming over the brunette's decapitated body. A shovel sliced into the ground. The severed head arced into the night and landed with a thud in the open grave.

Ben grinned at Jane. "Bet you didn't see that murder coming, did you?"

"No," she murmured. What other surprises were lying in store in this film? *What were you trying to tell us, Cassandra?* The story had eerie parallels with the real-life murders to come: Five potential targets. Death after gruesome death. A relentless killer who worked at an after-school center. Had Cassandra somehow foreseen her own fate, as well as the fates of the other child witnesses?

Twenty minutes later in the film, the faceless Mr. Simian struck again, this time his ax chopping through the muscular neck of the jock. No surprise there; in splatter flicks, the jock was almost always doomed. Nor was Jane surprised when the mean cheerleader went down next in an explosion of brains and fake blood. Mean girls were supposed to die; it was every moviegoer's guilty pleasure, revenge against all the snooty girls who'd made their lives miserable.

Travis turned to her. "What do you think so far?"

"It's, uh, engaging," she admitted.

"Have you figured out who Mr. Simian is yet?"

"Obviously it's *that* guy." Jane pointed to the Martin Stanek lookalike, who was now crouched in a dark closet, peeking through a chink in the wall into the girls' restroom. On the other side, the wallflower hiked up her skirt and adjusted her tights. The peeping teacher leered. "He's definitely a creep."

"Yeah, but is he the killer?"

"Who else would it be? Except for the kids and their parents, there aren't any other suspects in this movie."

Travis grinned. "What seems obvious isn't always the truth. Don't they teach you that in detective school?"

Jane flinched as a fresh fountain of blood splattered the wall where the peeping Tom had been crouched. The creepy teacher—the man she'd assumed was Mr. Simian—collapsed to the floor, an ax embedded in his skull. Slowly the figure of the real Mr. Simian moved into the frame, into the light. A killer she'd never suspected. A killer wearing a knit hat sparkling with silver beads.

"Surprised ya, right?" said Travis. "It's just Horror 101. The killer's always the person you least suspect."

Jane pulled out her cell phone and called Frost. "We had it wrong," she told him. "This case was *never* about the Apple Tree. It was never even about the Staneks."

She stared at the screen, where a terrified Anna was running through the woods, pursued by a killer who now had a face. "It's all about Lizzie DiPalma. And what really happened to her."

FOR SEVENTEEN YEARS AFTER HER daughter's disappearance, Arlene DiPalma had remained in the same neighborhood and in the same house that she'd shared with her nine-year-old daughter. Perhaps she'd nursed the hope that Lizzie would someday walk through the front door again. Perhaps the loss of her only child had frozen her in a grief so profound that she was unable to move on, unable to cope with any change. Then, two years ago, change was thrust upon her when her husband collapsed and died of a stroke.

Sudden widowhood was what finally shook Arlene out of her state of suspended animation. A year after her husband's death, she'd sold her Brookline house and moved to this seaside retirement community in East Falmouth, on the elbow of the Cape Cod peninsula.

"I always wanted to live near the water," said Arlene. "I don't know why it took me so long to finally make the move. Maybe I never really felt I was old enough to be in one of these retirement places, although I certainly am." She stared out her living-room windows at Nantucket Sound, where the water was a forbidding gray under wintry storm clouds. "I was forty when Lizzie was born. An old mommy."

Which would make her sixty-nine now, thought Jane, and the woman wore every one of those years on her face. Grief was like an aging pill, spinning the years in fast-forward, graying one's hair, sagging one's flesh. On the mantelpiece was a photo of Arlene as a newlywed, fresh-faced and pretty. That young woman was nowhere to be seen now; like her daughter, Lizzie, the newlywed Arlene had long ago gone missing.

Arlene turned from the window and sat down to face Jane and Frost. "I thought the police had forgotten all about her. After all this time, I was surprised to hear from you. When you called me this morning, I couldn't help thinking that maybe you'd finally found her."

"I'm sorry we had to disappoint you, Mrs. DiPalma," said Jane.

"Twenty years, with so many false leads. But it never goes away, you know?"

"What doesn't?"

"Hope. That my daughter's still alive. That all this time, someone has kept her in his basement, like those girls in Ohio. Or like that poor Elizabeth Smart, who was too terrified to run away from her kidnappers. I keep hoping that whoever took her just wanted a child of his own, someone to love and take care of. That someday my Lizzie will remember who she really is, and she'll pick up the phone and call me." Arlene took a deep breath. "It's possible," she whispered.

"Yes. It is."

"But now you're talking about homicide cases. About four people being murdered. And that takes away any hope I might have had."

Frost leaned forward on the sofa and touched the woman's hand. "They never found her body, Mrs.

DiPalma. Until they do, we don't know that she's dead."

"But you think she is, don't you? Everyone does—even my husband did. But I refused to accept it." She looked straight at Frost. "Do you have children?"

"No, ma'am. But Detective Rizzoli does."

Arlene looked at Jane. "A boy? A girl?"

"A little girl," said Jane. "Three years old. And just like you, I'd never give up hope either, Mrs. DiPalma. Mothers never do. That's why I want to find out what happened to Lizzie. I want you to have your answer."

Arlene nodded and sat up straight. "Tell me how I can help."

"Twenty years ago, when Lizzie vanished, the prime suspect was Martin Stanek. He was sent to prison for molesting children, but he was never found guilty of kidnapping your daughter."

"The prosecutor told me she tried her best."

"Did you attend the trial?"

"Of course. A number of the Apple Tree parents did."

"So you heard the evidence. You were there when Martin Stanek testified."

"I kept hoping he would confess on the stand. That he'd finally tell us what he did to her."

"You believe Martin Stanek took your daughter?"

"Everyone thought so. The police, the prosecutors."

"What about the other parents?"

"Holly's parents certainly did."

"Tell me about Holly Devine. What do you remember about her?"

Arlene shrugged. "Nothing in particular. A quiet girl. Pretty girl. Why do you ask?"

"Did she ever strike you as odd?"

"I didn't know her well. She was a year older than Lizzie and in a different grade, so they weren't friends." She frowned at Jane. "Is there some reason you're asking about her?"

"Holly Devine was the child who found your daughter's beaded hat on the school bus. She was also the first child to accuse the Staneks of abuse. She started the whole chain of events that led to the Staneks being convicted and sent to prison."

"Why is all this coming up now?"

"Because we're wondering if Holly Devine told the truth. About any of it."

That possibility seemed to stun Arlene and she gripped the armrests of her chair, clearly struggling to understand what this might mean. "You don't think *Holly* had something to do with my daughter's disappearance?"

"That possibility has been raised."

"By whom?"

By a dead woman, thought Jane. By Cassandra Coyle, who'd conveyed her message from the grave, in the form of a horror movie. In *Mr. Simian,* the killer had not been the teacher, whom everyone suspected. Like Martin Stanek, the teacher in the movie was merely the distraction, the convenient scapegoat who drew everyone's attention while in the shadows lurked the real killer: the wallflower.

It's just Horror 101.

Arlene DiPalma shook her head. "No, I can't imagine the girl hurting my daughter. Maybe that boy would do it, but why would Holly?"

"Boy?" Jane glanced at Frost, who looked equally bewildered. "What boy?"

"Billy Sullivan. Lizzie despised him. They weren't even in the same grade at school—he was two years older than her. But she knew enough to stay far away from him."

Jane rocked forward, her attention suddenly laser-sharp. Quietly, she asked, "What did Billy do to your daughter?"

Arlene sighed. "At first it seemed like normal schoolyard teasing and bullying. Kids do that sometimes, and my Lizzie was the sort of girl who refused to be a victim. She always stood up for herself, which only made Billy nastier to her. I don't think he was used to not getting his way, and Lizzie wouldn't give an inch. So he got more and more aggressive. He'd shove her at recess. Steal her lunch money. But he was clever about it, never doing it when anyone was watching. Since no one saw it happen, it was always Lizzie's word against Billy's. When I called his mother to complain, Susan didn't believe it. Oh, her Billy was an *angel.* He was brilliant, and my Lizzie was nothing but a liar. Even when Lizzie came home one day with a bloody lip, Susan insisted her son didn't do it."

"Was this the incident on the bus? The reason they found traces of her blood?"

"Yes. Billy stuck out his foot and tripped her. She fell and cut herself. But again, it was Lizzie's word against his."

"Why did none of this come up during the trial?" asked Frost.

"It did, in a way. I told the court there was a reason why they found traces of Lizzie's blood on the bus, but no one asked me *why* she cut her lip. And the prosecutor, Erica Shay, was furious with me for even sharing that information. She didn't want to reveal anything that would hurt her case against Martin Stanek, because she was absolutely certain he abducted my daughter."

"And do you still believe that?" asked Jane.

"I don't know. I'm so confused now." Arlene sighed again. "I just want her to come home. Dead or alive, I want my Lizzie *home.*"

Outside, the storm clouds that had darkened the sky all morning finally unleashed fat snowflakes that swirled into the sea. On a summer's day, this would be a lovely place to lie on the beach or build sand castles. But today the view matched the atmosphere of gloom that hung so heavily inside this house.

Arlene at last managed to straighten again and look at Jane. "No one ever asked me about Billy before. No one seemed to care."

"We care. We care about the truth."

"Well, the truth is, Billy Sullivan was a nasty little shit." She paused, seeming surprised at her own outburst. "There, I said it. I should have said it to his mother, not that she'd ever believe it. I mean, no one wants to think their child is born that way, but sometimes it's obvious who the bad ones are. The kid who likes to hurt other children and then lies about it. The kid who steals. And yet the idiot parent doesn't have a clue." She paused. "Have you met Susan Sullivan?"

"We spoke to her after her son vanished."

"I know it's wrong to talk ill about any mother who's lost her child, but Susan was part of the problem. She had an excuse for every bad thing Billy ever did. Did you know he once skinned a baby possum, just for fun? Lizzie told me he liked to cut open animals. He'd catch frogs in the pond, slice them open while they were still alive to watch their heart beating. If he was already like that as a boy, I can't imagine what kind of man he turned into."

"Did you keep in touch with Susan?"

"God, no. After the trial, I avoided her. Or maybe she was avoiding me. I heard through the grapevine that Billy went into finance. Imagine that, the perfect job for a weasel. He handled millions of dollars of other people's money and bought his mother a great big house in Brookline. A vacation home in Costa Rica. At least he knew how to treat his own mother right." She glanced out the window again, at the snowflakes swirling in the storm. "I know I should send Susan a note and tell her how sorry I am about what happened to Billy. She never bothered to send me a note about Lizzie, but still, it would be the right thing to do. After all, she did just lose her son."

Jane and Frost looked at each other, the same thought on both their minds: *Or did she?*

THIRTY-SEVEN

MY LATE FATHER'S HOUSE IS THICK WITH THE syrupy scent of lilies, and I'd like to throw open the windows and let the wintry air sweep it all outside, but that would not be the hospitable thing to do. Not when thirty-two guests are milling around the living and dining rooms, grazing off trays of appetizers. Everyone speaks in murmurs and feels the need to touch me, and I feel assaulted by all those comforting pats on the shoulder and squeezes on the arm. I respond with somber thank-yous and I even manage to produce a few pretty tears. Practice makes perfect. It's not that I'm heartless about my father's death; I truly do miss him. I miss the comfort of knowing there's someone in the world who loves me and would do anything for me, as he did. To keep me safe, Daddy sacrificed his cancer-ridden body and his few remaining, if miserable, months of life. I doubt anyone else will ever be so devoted to me.

Although Everett Prescott is doing his best to play the part.

Since the moment we came back from Daddy's memorial service, Everett has been practically joined to my hip. He keeps refilling my drink, fetching me little nibbles on plates, and I'm growing a bit annoyed at all the attention, because he won't give me a moment to myself. Even when I retreat into the kitchen to fetch another platter of cheese and crackers from the refrigerator, he follows me and hovers nearby as I peel plastic wrap off the tray.

"Is there anything I can do, Holly? I know how hard this must be for you, dealing with all these guests."

"I can handle it. I just want to make sure no one goes hungry."

"Here, let me do that. And what about beverages? Should I open another few bottles of wine?"

"It's all under control. Relax, Everett. They're just my dad's friends and neighbors. He certainly wouldn't want us to stress out over this."

Everett sighs. "I wish I'd known your father."

"He would've liked you. He always said he didn't give a damn if a man was rich or poor, as long as he treated me well."

"I try my best," Everett says with a smile. He picks up the tray of cheese and crackers and we go back out into the dining room, where everyone greets me with tiresomely sympathetic looks. I replenish the platters on the table and rearrange the vases of flowers. People have brought so many damn lilies, the scent is making me nauseated. I can't help scanning the bouquets, searching for any palm leaves, but of course there aren't any. Martin Stanek is dead. He can't hurt me.

"Your father did a very brave thing, Holly. We owe him a debt of gratitude," says Elaine Coyle. Cassandra's mother stands with a plate of appetizers in one hand and a glass of wine in the other. A few nights ago, her ex-husband, Matthew, finally passed away after weeks in a coma, but Elaine is serenely elegant in the same black dress that she wore to her daughter's funeral last month. "If I'd had the chance, I might have shot the bastard myself. I know I'm not the only one who feels that way." She gestures to the woman beside her. "You remember Billy Sullivan's mother, don't you?"

I have not spoken to Susan Sullivan in years, but she looks no older than the last time I saw her. Her perennially blond hair is upswept and perfectly lacquered in place, and her face is eerily unlined. Wealth seems to agree with her.

I shake Susan's hand. "Thank you for coming, Mrs. Sullivan."

"We're all so sorry, Holly. Your father was truly a hero."

Elaine squeezes Susan's arm. "And how brave *you* are to come. So soon after Billy . . ." Her voice fades.

Susan manages a smile. "I think it's important that we all honor the man who had the courage to finish it." She turns to me. "Your father did what the police never could. And now it's well and truly over."

The two women drift away as other guests come forward to murmur condolences. Some of them I only vaguely recognize. The news channels have been relentlessly reporting the story of my father's death, and I suspect many of these neighbors are here only out of curiosity. After all, my father was a hero who died while delivering justice to the man who'd molested his daughter.

Now everyone knows I was one of the Apple Tree victims.

The looks they give me as I circulate among them are both sympathetic and slightly abashed. How do you meet a molestation victim's eyes without graphically imagining what was done to her? After twenty years, the case had slipped off everyone's radar, but here it is, back on the front page. FATHER WHO KILLED DAUGHTER'S MOLESTER IS SHOT TO DEATH BY POLICE.

I keep my chin up and stare everyone squarely in the eye, because I'm not ashamed. I don't really know what shame feels like, but I do know what's expected of a grieving daughter, so I shake hands, endure hugs, listen to countless murmurs of *I'm so sorry* and *call me if you need anything.* I won't be calling any of them and they know it, yet it's what one must say in these circumstances. We go through life saying things that are expected, because we don't know anything else to say.

It is hours before the house finally empties out and the last stragglers walk out the door. By then I'm exhausted and all I want is peace and quiet. I collapse on the sofa and groan to Everett, "God, I need a drink."

"That I can arrange," he says with a smile. He goes into the kitchen, comes back out a few minutes later with two glasses of whiskey, and hands one to me.

"Where on earth did you find the whiskey?" I ask him.

"It was way back in your dad's kitchen cabinet." He turns off all the lamps, and in the warm glow from the fireplace, I already feel my tension draining away. "Your dad clearly knew his scotch, because this is a top-grade single malt."

"Funny. I didn't know he even liked whiskey." I take a much-needed sip and glance up, startled, when I hear the toilet flush in the powder room.

Everett sighs. "I guess there's still one more guest in the house. How'd we miss that?"

Susan Sullivan emerges from the powder room and glances around in embarrassment at the empty room, at the fire flickering in the hearth. "Oh, dear, I seem to be the last one out the door. Let me help you clean up, Holly."

"That's so nice of you, but we'll be fine."

"I know what a long day it's been for you. Let me do something."

"Thank you, but we're going to leave it all till morning. Right now, we're going to unwind."

She doesn't take the hint to leave, just stands there looking at us. Everett finally says, out of sheer politeness, "Would you like to join us in a glass of whiskey?"

"That would be lovely. Thank you."

"I'll get you a glass from the kitchen," he says.

"You stay right where you are. I'll fetch it myself." She heads into the kitchen, and Everett mouths *I'm sorry,* but I can't really blame him for inviting her to linger when she so clearly wanted to. She returns with her own glass of whiskey, plus the bottle itself.

"It looks like you're both ready for a refill," she says, and politely tops off our drinks before settling onto the sofa. The bottle makes a pleasant *thunk* as she sets it on the coffee table. For a moment we sit in silence as we sip our drinks. "It was a lovely memorial service," Susan says, staring into the fire. "I know I should think about having one for Billy, but I dread it. I just can't accept . . ."

"I'm so sorry about your son," says Everett. "Holly told me what happened."

"The thing is, I can't have closure. He's not dead. He's missing, which means he'll always be very much alive to me. But that's the nature of hope. It doesn't allow a mother to give up." She takes a sip of whiskey and winces at its sting. "Without Billy, I don't see any reason to stay on. No reason at all."

"That's not true, Mrs. Sullivan! There's always a reason to live," says Everett. He sets down his nearly empty glass and reaches out to touch her arm. It is a genuinely kind gesture, something that comes naturally to him. A skill I could learn. "Your son would certainly want you to go on and enjoy life, wouldn't he?"

She gives him a sad smile. "Billy always said we should move someplace warm. Someplace with a beach. We planned to retire to Costa Rica, and we put aside enough money to move there." She stares off into the distance. "Maybe that's where I should go. A place where I can start fresh, without all these memories."

I'm starting to feel light-headed, even though I've had only a few sips. I slide my whiskey toward Everett, who picks it up without even noticing it's mine and takes a gulp.

"Or maybe Mexico. There are so many beautiful homes for sale, right on the water." Susan turns to me, and her eyes are so bright they seem to glow in the firelight.

"A beach," murmurs Everett, giving his head a shake. "Yes, I could use a beach right now. And maybe a nice, long nap. . . ."

"Oh, dear, I've stayed too long. You're both exhausted." Susan rises to her feet. "I'll be going."

As she stands buttoning up her coat, the room suddenly feels warm, too warm, as if waves of heat are blasting from the fireplace. I look at the hearth, half-expecting a conflagration, but there is only the gentle flicker of flames. It's so pretty I can't stop staring. I don't even notice when Susan leaves. I hear the front door close, and the flames give a shimmy as air puffs into the house.

"Feel . . . feel sorry for her," mumbles Everett. "Awful, losing a son."

"You didn't know her son." I keep staring at the flames, which seem to pulse in time with my heartbeat, as if the fire and I have some magical connection. I am the fire and the fire is me. *No one really knew Billy. Not the way I did.* I gaze down at my hands, where my fingertips are glowing. Bright threads emerge in gold meridians, arching toward the hearth. If I move my hands like a puppet master, I can make the flames dance. As wondrous as it all seems, I know this is wrong. This is all wrong.

I give my head a shake, trying to refocus, but the threads are still attached to my fingers and the filaments swirl in the shadows. The whiskey bottle catches the firelight's reflection. I squint at the label, but the words are out of focus. I think of Everett, walking out of the kitchen, carrying two glasses of amber liquid. I never watched him pour it. I never thought to question the drink he placed in my hand or what he might have added to it. I don't look at him, because I'm afraid he'll see the doubt in my eyes. I keep staring at the hearth as I struggle against the thickening fog in my head and I think back to the night I met him. Both of us drinking coffee near Utica Street on the night Cassandra was found dead. He'd said he was meeting friends for dinner in the neighborhood, but what if that wasn't true? What if our meeting was *meant* to happen, all of it leading up to this moment? I remember the bottle of wine he brought me, a bottle that still sits unopened in my kitchen. I think of how he has listened so attentively to every detail I shared about the homicide investigation.

What do I really know about Everett?

All this goes through my head as the fog thickens, as my limbs start to go numb. Now is the time to move, while I still have some measure of control over my legs. I stagger to my feet. Manage to take only two steps when my legs wobble out from beneath me. My head slams against the corner of the coffee table, and the pain cuts through the fog in a jolt that suddenly makes everything crystal clear. That's when I hear the front door thud shut, and I feel cold air sweep in. Footsteps creak across the floor and come to a stop beside me.

"Little Holly Devine," a voice says. "Still causing trouble."

I squint up at the face staring down at me, a man who's been stalking me for the last few years. A man who is supposed to be dead and buried in an unmarked grave. When the police told me that Martin Stanek killed Billy, I believed them, but I should have known better. Men like Billy can't be killed; they keep springing back to life. Even though I've managed to hide from him all these years, even though I've changed my name and altered my appearance, he's finally managed to track me down.

"How is the boyfriend?" asks a second voice, a voice that sends another shock through me.

"He's unconscious. He'll be no problem," says Billy.

I struggle to focus on Susan, whose face has also come into view. They stand side by side, Billy and his mother, eyeing the results of her handiwork. I turn my head and look at Everett, who's slumped on the sofa, even more helpless than I am. Not only did he drink his own glass of whiskey, he also drank mine. I took only a few sips, yet I can barely move.

"I see you're still awake, Holly Dolly." Billy crouches down to study me. He has the same brilliant-blue eyes, the same piercing stare that drew me to him when we were children. Even then I was enchanted by him and easily seduced into doing whatever he asked of me. So were the other kids.

Everyone except Lizzie, because she sensed who and what he was. The day he held a flame to the baby possum we'd found on the playground, Lizzie was the one who knocked the match out of his hand. And when he stole money from a classmate's jacket, she was the one who called him a thief. That made him angry, which is something you don't do to Billy Sullivan, because there are consequences. They're not always immediate; perhaps it takes months or even years before he strikes back, but that's the thing about Billy: He never forgets. He always strikes back.

Unless you make a deal with him.

"Why?" I manage to whisper.

"Because you're the only one who remembers. The only one left who knows."

"I promised I'd never tell anyone. . . ."

"You think I'd risk that now? With that lady reporter and the fucking book she's writing? She already talked to Cassandra. I can't have her talking to you."

"No one else was there. No one else knows."

"But you do, and you might talk." He leans in close and whispers into my ear, "You got my messages, didn't you, little Livinus?"

Saint Livinus the martyr, who is celebrated on my birthday. The saint whose tongue was ripped from his mouth to silence him. While I managed to stay out of Billy's reach, he knew how to send messages I couldn't ignore. He knew the deaths of Sarah and Cassie and Tim would catch my attention and that I'd understand the clues he'd left for me: The palm leaf laid before the burned remains of Sarah's house. The arrows in Tim's chest. Cassandra's gouged-out eyes.

I understood all too well what he was telling me: *Tell no secrets, or you die like the others.*

And I haven't told. All these years, I have been silent about what happened that day in the woods with Lizzie, but my promised silence was not enough. Thanks to the journalist, the truth threatens to surface anyway, and here he is, to ensure that I stay as silent as Livinus with his tongue torn out.

Susan says, "This time it has to look like an accident, Bill. Nothing that will make anyone suspicious."

"I know." Billy rises and regards Everett, who is immobile and utterly helpless. "And we have to deal with two of them. This makes it harder to stage." He scans the room, and his eyes turn to the hearth, where flames barely flicker around a crumbling log. "Old houses," he muses. "They go up in smoke so fast. What a shame your father forgot to change the battery in his smoke detector." He drags a chair under the smoke detector, pulls down the unit, and removes the battery. Then he throws an armload of wood into the hearth.

"I have a better idea," says Susan. "They're tired and they're drunk, so where would they be? The bedroom."

"Let's move him first," Billy says.

They drag away Everett, and as I hear his shoes scrape across the floor toward my father's bedroom, I already know how the death scene will look when we are discovered. The tipsy young couple, their bodies charred on the bed. Just another tragic death due to fire and carelessness.

The fresh armload of wood has made the flames roar back to life, and as I stare into the hellish glow, I can almost feel the heat singeing my hair, consuming my flesh. *No, no, this is not the way I want to die!* Panic sends a surge of adrenaline through my body, and I push myself up to my hands and knees. But even as I crawl toward the front door, I can already hear their footsteps returning from the bedroom.

Hands wrench me backward, and my face slams against the edge of the raised hearth. I feel my cheek swell up in what will be an ugly bruise, but no one will ever see it; all will be cooked in the heat of the fire. I am too weak to resist as Billy drags me down the hall, into the bedroom.

Together, he and Susan heave me onto the mattress, next to Everett.

"Take off their clothes," says Susan. "They wouldn't go to bed with their clothes on."

They are an efficient team, working swiftly to remove my slacks and blouse and underwear. Mother and son, united in this sick striptease that leaves Everett and me naked on the bed. Susan tosses our discarded clothes over a chair, leaves our shoes scattered on the floor. Oh, yes, she has the scenario well thought out, of the young couple exhausted after sex. After a moment's consideration, she leaves the room and comes back with two empty wine bottles, two goblets, and candles, everything wrapped in tea towels. No fingerprints. She arranges everything on the nightstand, as carefully as a set decorator prepping for a stage play. When the candles set fire to the curtains, Everett and I will be intoxicated and asleep. That's why we aren't roused by the smoke. We are naked and drunk, sated young lovers who have been careless with fire. The flames will consume all the evidence—fingerprints, hairs, and fibers, the traces of ketamine in our systems. Just as the flames consumed the evidence of Sarah's murder. Like Sarah, like doomed Saint Joan of Arc, I will be reduced to ashes, and the truth will burn with me. The truth about what really happened to Lizzie DiPalma.

I know, because I was there in the woods when it happened.

It was a Saturday in October, the autumn leaves as brilliant as flames rippling in the trees above us. I remember how the twigs snapped like tiny bones under our shoes as we walked. I remember Billy, already strong at eleven, stamping the shovel into the earth as he dug the grave.

Susan leaves the room again, and Billy sits down on the bed beside me. He fondles my bare breast, pinches my nipple.

"Look at little Holly Devine, all grown up."

Repulsion makes my arm muscles tighten, but I don't move. I don't betray the fact that the ketamine is rapidly wearing off. He doesn't know that I took only two sips of the whiskey that Susan poured into my glass; Everett was the one who finished my drink, who's now bearing the brunt of the full dose. Everett's eyes are open, and he's moaning softly, but I know he's helpless. I'm the only one capable of fighting back.

"You were always special, Holly," he says. His hand moves from my breast, strokes down to my belly. Can he feel me shudder? Can he see the disgust in my eyes? "Always game for everything. We would've made a great team."

"I'm not like you," I whisper.

"Yes, you are. Deep down, we are *exactly* the same. We both know what really matters in this world. What matters is *us* and nothing else. That's why you haven't told anyone all these years. That's why you've kept the secret. Because you knew there'd be consequences. You don't want your life ruined either, do you?"

"I was only ten years old."

"Old enough to know what you were doing. Old enough to make your own choice. You hit her too, Holly. I gave you the rock and you did it. We killed her together." He rests his palm on my thigh, and his touch is so repulsive I can barely remain still.

"I can't find any plastic bags," says Susan from the doorway.

He turns to his mother. "None in the kitchen?"

"All I found are those flimsy grocery sacks."

"Let me look."

Billy and his mother leave the room. I have no idea why they want plastic bags; I only know that this is my last chance to save myself.

I marshal all the strength I have left and roll over the edge of the mattress. I hit the floor with a thud, a noise so loud that they must be able to hear it in the kitchen. I have so little time now; they'll return any minute. I reach blindly under the bed, feeling for my purse. With so many guests in the house this afternoon, I needed a safe place to stash it, because I know how people are. Even a house in mourning is not safe from the sticky fingers of an opportunist. I feel the leather strap and tug it closer. The purse is already unzipped, and I thrust my hand inside.

"She's managed to get off the bed," says Susan. She looms above me, staring down with a look of annoyance. "If we leave her like this, she might crawl away."

"Then we have to finish it now. We'll do it the old-fashioned way," says Billy. He grabs a pillow off the bed and kneels down beside me. Everett moans, but they don't even glance at him. They are both focused on me. On killing me. I will never feel the flames; by the time the fire engulfs this room, I'll already be dead, smothered by linen and polyester.

"It's just the way it has to be, Holly Dolly," says Billy. "I'm sure you understand. You could ruin everything for me, and I can't let that happen." He places the pillow over my face and presses down. Presses so hard that I can't breathe, can't move. I twist and thrash, kicking at air, but Susan throws her weight on top of me too, pinning my hips to the floor. I fight to suck in oxygen, but the pillow is plastered so tightly against my nose and mouth that all I inhale is wet linen.

"Die, goddamn it. *Die!*" Billy orders.

And I am dying. Already numbness is seeping into my limbs, stealing the last of my strength. The fight is over. I feel only heaviness weighing down on me, Billy pressing against my face, Susan against my hips. My right arm is still under the bed, my hand inside my purse.

In my last seconds of consciousness, I realize what I am holding. I have carried it in my purse for weeks, ever since Detective Rizzoli told me my life was in danger, that Martin Stanek would try to kill me. How wrong we both were. All that time it was Billy who waited in the shadows. Billy, who staged his own death and after tonight would vanish forever.

I can't see where I am aiming. I only know that time has run out and this is my last chance before darkness falls. I drag out the gun, press it blindly against Susan's body, and pull the trigger.

The explosion makes Billy jerk away. Suddenly the pillow goes slack and I gasp in a desperate breath. Air fills my lungs and sweeps the fog out of my head.

"Mother? *Mother?*" Billy screams.

Susan is now a deadweight across my hips. Billy rolls her off me and I hear her thump onto the floor. I push the pillow away and glimpse Billy crouched over Susan's body. There is blood streaming from her chest. He presses his hand to the bullet hole, trying to stem the flow, but surely he can see that her wound is mortal.

Susan reaches up to touch his face. "Go, darling. Leave me," she whispers.

"Mother, no . . ."

Her hand slides away, leaving a smear of blood down his cheek.

My arm is shaking, my aim so unsteady that the

second bullet I fire hits the ceiling and knocks off a chunk of plaster.

Billy wrenches the gun from my hand. His face is distorted with rage, his eyes as bright as hellfire. This is the face I saw that day in the woods, the day he picked up the rock and slammed it onto Lizzie DiPalma's skull. For twenty years, I've said nothing. To protect myself, I've had to protect him, and this is my punishment. When you make a pact with the devil, the price you pay is your own soul.

He grips the gun in both hands, and I see the barrel swing toward me like a pitiless eye.

I flinch as the gunshots thunder—a series of explosions that come so rapidly I can't count how many there are. When they finally stop, my eyes are closed and my ears are ringing, but there's no pain. Why is there no pain?

"Holly!" Hands grasp my shoulders and give me a hard shake. *"Holly?"*

I open my eyes and see Detective Rizzoli staring down at me, frantically searching my face.

"Are you hurt? *Talk* to me!"

"Billy" is all I can whisper. I try to sit up, but I can't. My muscles are still not working and I've forgotten I'm naked. I've forgotten everything except the fact that I'm alive, and I don't understand how this is possible. Detective Frost drapes his jacket over my bare torso and I hug it to my breasts, shivering not from cold but from the aftershocks of what has happened. Everywhere I look in my father's bedroom, I see blood. Susan lies beside me, her eyes glazed over, her jaw gaping open. One of her arms is stretched out in a last dying effort to reach her son. Their fingers don't quite touch; instead, it is the pool of blood that connects them, Billy's mingling with Susan's.

Mother and son, united in death.

THIRTY-EIGHT

"THE CLUE WAS THERE ALL THE TIME, IN CASsandra Coyle's movie," said Jane. "The movie I didn't get a chance to watch until last night."

"I'm still not sure what made you think the answer would be there," said Maura, crouching beside the bodies of Susan Sullivan and her son. "I thought it was just a horror film."

Looking down at Maura's bent head, Jane could see a few silver strands peeking out from that sleek black hair, and she thought: We're growing old together. We've both seen too much death. When will we decide we've had enough?

"It *is* just a horror film," said Jane. "But the inspiration for the story came straight from Cassandra's childhood. She was having flashbacks about what really happened when she was a kid. She told Bonnie Sandridge that the Staneks never did anything to her and she was ashamed that she'd helped send innocent people to prison. That shame kept her from talking about it with her friends and family. She shared the story in the one safe way she could: in a film script about a girl who goes missing. A girl like Lizzie DiPalma."

Maura glanced up. "That's what *Mr. Simian* was about?"

Jane nodded. "The group of teens don't realize there's a monster in their midst. And the monster is one of *them.* In Cassandra's movie, the killer turns out to be a girl who wears a beaded cap, exactly like Lizzie's. Cassandra was pointing us to Holly Devine, which turned out to be wrong. But she was right about one thing: The monster *was* one of them."

Maura frowned at the body of Billy Sullivan. "He staged his own disappearance."

"He had to disappear. Over the past few years, he's stolen millions of dollars from his clients at Cornwell Investments, money that he's probably been socking away in the Caribbean. It'll be months before federal investigators find out how much he actually took. They'd just shut down his office when Frost and I showed up that afternoon. We assumed Billy was another one of Stanek's murder victims, buried in some unmarked grave. But it was Billy's way of conveniently vanishing. He ran from his old identity—and from what he did to Lizzie DiPalma twenty years ago."

"He would only have been eleven years old when he did it."

"But he was already a mean little bastard, according to Lizzie's mother. The reason the police never found her body was because they were searching in the wrong places." Jane looked down at Billy and Susan.

"Now we have a pretty good idea of where to hunt for her."

Maura rose to her feet. "You know the drill, Jane. We have another fatal police shooting, and this isn't even Boston PD's jurisdiction. It's Brookline's."

Jane glanced through the doorway at the Brookline PD detective who stood in the hallway, scowling as he talked into his cell phone. A turf battle was brewing, and Jane had some serious explaining to do.

"Yeah, here comes the inquiry," sighed Jane.

"But if there's such a thing as a good shooting, this was it. And you have a civilian witness who'll testify that you saved her life." Maura stripped off her gloves. "How is Holly?"

"When the ambulance took her, she was still pretty shaky from the drug, but I'm sure she'll be fine. I think that girl would survive just about anything. She's full of surprises, that one."

Strange girl. According to Bonnie Sandridge, that's what the other children had called Holly, and Holly Devine *was* strange. Jane thought of the girl's eerie calmness in the face of threat and the coolly analytical way Holly looked at her, as if she were studying a different species. As if humans were alien to her.

"Was she able to tell you what happened here tonight?" asked Maura.

"I got the gist of it. I'll find out the details tomorrow, when she's recovered." Jane gazed down at Susan and Billy again, lying in their mingled pools of blood. "But I think you can see the whole story right here. A nasty little monster of a son. A mother who let him get away with everything. Who even helped him cover up his crimes."

"You always tell me there's no love as powerful as a mother's, Jane."

"Yeah, and here's the proof of how love can go off the rails." She took a deep breath, inhaling the all-too-familiar scents of blood and violence. Tonight it was also the scent of finality, and it was deeply, disturbingly satisfying.

WHEN JANE WALKED INTO HOLLY'S hospital room the next morning, she found the young woman sitting up in bed, finishing her breakfast. Her right cheek was blue and swollen, and her arms were covered in bruises, the vivid evidence of the fierce battle she'd fought last night.

"How are you feeling this morning?" Jane asked.

"I'm sore all over. Do I look horrible?"

"You look alive, which is what matters." Jane glanced at the empty breakfast tray. "And I see you had no trouble cleaning your plate."

"The food here is really awful," Holly said, and added with a wry shrug, "and there isn't enough of it."

Laughing, Jane pulled a chair next to the bed and sat down. "We need to talk about what happened."

"I don't know what else I can tell you."

"Last night you said that Billy admitted killing the others."

Holly nodded. "And I was his last target. I was the one he couldn't find."

"You said he also confessed to killing Lizzie DiPalma."

"Yes."

"Do you know how he did it? Where he did it?"

Holly regarded her bruised arms and said softly, "You already know he's the one who killed her. Do the details really matter now?"

"Actually, they do, Holly. They matter to Lizzie's mother. Mrs. DiPalma is desperate to find her daughter's body. Did Billy give you any idea where he might have hidden it?"

Holly said nothing, just kept staring down at her bruised arms. Jane studied her, wishing she could somehow see through that skull, to crack the mystery of Holly Devine, but when Holly looked up again, Jane could read nothing in the young woman's gaze. It was like peering into a cat's eyes, green and beautiful and utterly enigmatic.

"I don't remember," Holly said. "The drug, it made everything a little hazy. I'm sorry."

"Maybe the details will come back to you later."

"Maybe. If I remember anything else, I'll let you know. But right now . . ." Holly sighed. "I'm really tired. I'd like to sleep."

"Then we'll talk later." Jane stood up. "We still need a full statement from you when you feel up to it."

"Of course." Holly wiped a hand across her eyes. "I can't believe it's finally over."

"It is. This time it really is."

For Holly anyway, thought Jane. If only there were an ending for Arlene DiPalma, but Billy Sullivan had taken the secret of Lizzie's fate to the grave with him, and they might never find the girl's body.

Jane had one more stop to make in the hospital, and

after she left Holly's room, she continued down the hallway to look in on Everett Prescott. Last night, when he was loaded aboard the ambulance, he'd been too stupefied by ketamine to mumble more than a few words. This morning, she found him awake in bed and staring out the window.

"Mr. Prescott? May I come in?"

He blinked a few times, as if coming out of a daydream, and frowned at her.

"You may not remember me. I'm Detective Rizzoli. I was there last night, after you and Ms. Devine—"

"I remember you," he said. And added quietly: "Thank you for saving my life."

"It was a very close call." She pulled a chair to his bedside and sat down. "Tell me what you remember."

"Gunshots. Then you were standing over me. You and your partner. And the ambulance ride. I've never ridden in an ambulance before."

Jane smiled. "Let's hope that's your one and only time."

He didn't share her smile; instead, his gaze drifted back to the window, to a dreary view of gray skies. For a man who'd almost died, he seemed more troubled than happy about this fortunate outcome.

"I spoke to your doctor," said Jane. "He said there shouldn't be any long-term effects from a single dose of ketamine, but you might have flashbacks. And maybe you'll feel a little unsteady for a day or two. But as long as you don't use any more ketamine, the side effects will be temporary."

"I don't do drugs. I don't like drugs." He gave an ironic laugh. "Because *this* sort of thing happens."

He certainly looked like a man with healthy habits. Lean, fit, and clean-cut. Last night they had run a background check on him and learned that he was a landscape architect who worked at a well-regarded Boston firm. No warrants, no criminal record, not even an unpaid parking ticket. Should there be any doubt that the shooting last night was justified, Everett Prescott would be an excellent defense witness.

"You're being discharged today, I believe," she said.

"Yes. The doctor said I'll be good to go."

"We need a detailed statement from you about what happened last night. If you can come down to Boston PD tomorrow, we'll record it on video. Here, let me give you my card."

"They're both dead. Does it really matter now?"

"The truth always matters, don't you think?"

He thought about this for a moment, and his gaze turned back to the window. "The truth," he said softly.

"Stop in at Schroeder Plaza tomorrow, say around ten A.M.? Meanwhile, if any details come back to you, please write them down. Everything you remember."

"There *is* something." He looked at her. "Something you need to know."

THIRTY-NINE

EVERETT IS COMING FOR COCKTAILS.

I haven't seen him since we were discharged from the hospital a week ago, because we both needed time to recover. Certainly I needed time, because I've had so many details to attend to: The reading of my father's will. What to do with my father's dog, who's still in the kennel. The cleanup of his house, with its blood-spattered bedroom. Multiple interviews with the police. I have spoken to Detective Rizzoli three times now, and sometimes I feel she wants to vacuum my brain, sucking out every detail of what happened that night. I keep telling her that there's nothing else I remember, nothing more to share with her, and finally she seems ready to leave me at peace.

The apartment bell buzzes. A moment later, Everett stands in my doorway, holding a bottle of wine. As always, he's right on time. That's Everett—so predictable, but also a little boring. I suppose I can put up with boring, since in this case it comes in such an attractive and affluent package. It never hurts to have a rich boyfriend.

He seems tired and subdued as he walks into my apartment, and the kiss he gives me is only a half-hearted peck on the cheek.

"Shall I open the bottle?" I offer.

"Whatever you'd like." What kind of response is that? I'm annoyed by his lack of enthusiasm tonight. I take the wine into the kitchen, and as I rattle around in the drawer for the corkscrew, he just stands there watching me, not offering to help. After what we've been through together, you'd think he'd be ready to celebrate, but he's not smiling. Instead, he looks as if he's in mourning.

I pop out the cork, fill two wineglasses, and hand him one. The cabernet smells rich and meaty, and it's probably expensive. He takes only one sip and sets down his glass.

"There's something I need to tell you," he says.

Goddamn, I should have known. He wants to break up. How dare he break up with me? I manage to keep my cool as I eye him over the rim of my wineglass. "What is it?" I ask.

"That night, in your father's house—when we almost died . . ." He releases a deep sigh. "I heard what you said to Billy. And what he said to you."

I put down my glass and stare at him. "What, exactly, did you hear?"

"Everything. This wasn't just a hallucination. I know ketamine can fog your mind, make you see and hear things that don't exist, but this was real. I heard what you did to that little girl. What *both* of you did."

Calmly, I pick up my glass and take another sip. "That was your imagination, Everett. You didn't hear anything."

"Yes, I did."

"Ketamine clouds your memory. That's why it's used for date rape."

"You used a rock. You both killed her."

"I didn't do anything."

"Holly, tell me the truth."

"We were only kids. Do you really think I could have—"

"For once, *just tell me the fucking truth.*"

I set down my glass, hard. "You have no right to talk to me that way."

"I do have that right. I was in *love* with you."

Oh, this is rich. Just because he was stupid enough to fall in love with me, he thinks he can demand honesty. No man has that right. Not from me.

"Lizzie DiPalma was only nine years old," he says. "That was her name, wasn't it? I read about her disappearance. Her mother last saw her on a Saturday afternoon, when Lizzie left the house wearing her favorite hat, a beaded cap from Paris. Two days later, a child found Lizzie's hat on the Apple Tree school bus. That's why Martin Stanek came under suspicion. That's why he was accused of kidnapping and killing the girl." He paused. "*You* were the child who found the hat. But you didn't really find it on the bus. Did you?"

"You've reached a lot of conclusions based on absolutely no evidence," I answer, coldly logical.

"Billy handed you a rock, and you hit her with it. You both killed her. And then you kept her hat."

"Do you think this fairy tale would ever hold up in court? You were drugged with ketamine. No one would believe you."

"That's your answer?" He stares at me in disgust. "You have nothing else to say about a little girl who's been missing all these years? About her mother, whose heart must have been broken? *That will never hold up in court?*"

"Well, it won't." I pick up the wineglass again and take an unconcerned sip. "Besides, I was only ten years old. Think of all the things *you* did when you were ten."

"I never killed anyone."

"That's not how it happened."

"How did it happen, Holly? You're right, this will never hold up in court, so you might as well tell me the truth. I don't plan to see you again, so you have nothing to lose."

I study him for a moment, thinking about what he could do with the truth. Go to the police? Blab to the newspapers? No, I'm not that stupid. "Give me one good reason why I should say anything."

"For the sake of that little girl's mother—she's been waiting twenty years for Lizzie to come home to her. At least give her that. Tell her where to find the body."

"And fuck up my own life?"

"*Your* life? It's all about *you,* isn't it?" He shakes his head. "Why the hell didn't I see this before?"

"Oh, come on, Everett. You're making too much of this." I reach up and stroke his face.

He shudders and flinches away. "Don't."

"We had something special together. Good times." I smile. "And *great* sex. Please, let's just put this behind us and forget it ever happened."

"That's the thing, Holly. It did happen. And now I know what you really are." He turns to leave the kitchen.

I grab his arm. "You're not going to tell anyone, right?"

"Shouldn't I?"

"They won't believe you. They'll call you a bitter ex-boyfriend. And I'll tell them how you abused me. How you threatened me."

"You would do that, wouldn't you?"

"If I need to."

"Well, I don't have to tell anyone. Because they're listening to it right this instant. Every word you've said."

It takes me a few heartbeats to process what he's just told me. When the meaning dawns on me, I grab his shirt and wrench it open so suddenly he doesn't have time to react. Buttons fly off and tick to the floor. He stands with his shirt hanging open, and I stare at the telltale wire taped to his skin.

Backing away, I frantically review what I've said, words that I now know the police have been listening to. I never actually *admitted* anything. Nothing I said could be considered a murder confession. While I may have sounded heartless and manipulative, those aren't criminal acts. There are countless people like me in the world, successful CEOs and bankers whose heartlessness isn't punished but rewarded. They are simply behaving like the creatures they were born to be.

Everett is different. He's not one of us.

In silence, he closes his shirt over the exposed wire and I see pain, even grief, in his face. It's the death of an illusion. The illusion of Holly Devine, the girl he loved. Now the real Holly stands before him, and he wants nothing to do with me.

"Goodbye," he says, and walks out of the kitchen.

I don't follow him. I just stand there listening as the apartment door slams shut.

I fling my goblet, and it shatters against the refrigerator in an explosion of glass shards. Red wine drips like blood onto the floor.

FORTY

Two months later

FROM THE BACK PORCH OF MY FATHER'S HOUSE, I can see that something is going on deep in the woods. Parked along Daphne Road are half a dozen police and crime-lab vehicles, and somewhere in the distance a dog is barking. The ground has thawed and they're finally able to probe the soil, but they don't know exactly where to look and they have wasted the first two days searching the property where Billy Sullivan lived as a child. Now they've moved into the stretch of woods just beyond his property. Twenty years ago, investigators didn't search those woods; instead, they devoted all their time to combing the Apple Tree Daycare, as well as the section of road a mile and a half away, where Billy abandoned Lizzie's bike. No one thought to search the woods along Daphne Road, because Billy and I threw them off the scent by directing their suspicions to an innocent man. Everyone believed us because we were children, and children aren't clever enough to devise such a scheme. Or so people think.

The doorbell rings.

I find Detective Rizzoli standing on the front porch. She's wearing hiking boots and a dirt-streaked jacket, and a twig is snared in her wiry black hair. I don't invite her inside. Coolly, we regard each other across the threshold, two women who understand each other all too well.

"We're going to find her body anyway, Holly. You might as well tell us where to look."

"And what will I get for that? A gold star?"

"How about Brownie points for cooperating with us? The satisfaction of knowing you did the right thing for once?"

"There's no gold star for that."

"That's what it's all about, isn't it? *You.* What's in it for *you.*"

"I don't have anything to say." I start to close the door.

She slaps her hand against it, forcing it back open. "I have plenty to say to you."

"I'm listening."

"This happened twenty years ago. You were only ten years old when you did it, so no one will hold you accountable. You have nothing to lose by telling us where she is."

"I also have nothing to gain. What proof do you have that I had anything to do with it? The shaky memory of a witness who was high on ketamine? A taped conversation in which I admitted absolutely nothing?" I shake my head. "I think I'll stick with silence."

My logic is unassailable. There's nothing she can do to force my cooperation. Whether or not they find Lizzie's body, I'm untouchable and she knows it. We stare at each other, two halves of the same coin, both of us tough and clever women who know how to survive. But she's the one who cares too much, and I'm the one who cares scarcely at all.

Unless it's about me.

"I'm going to be watching you," she says quietly. "I know what you did, Holly. I know exactly what you are."

I shrug. "I'm different, so what? I've always known I was."

"You're a fucking sociopath. That's what you are."

"But it doesn't make me evil. It's just the way I was born. Some people have blue eyes; some people can run marathons. Me? I know how to look out for myself. That's *my* superpower."

"And someday it's going to bring you down."

"But not today."

The crackle of her walkie-talkie cuts the silence between us. She snatches it from her belt and answers: "Rizzoli."

"The dog alerted," a male voice says.

"What do you see?"

"Lot of leaf cover, that's all. But the signal's pretty definite. You want to come look at the spot before they start digging?"

At once, Rizzoli turns and strides down the porch

steps. As I watch her climb into her car, I know this is not the last time I'll be seeing her. There is a long chess game ahead of us, and this was only the opening gambit. Neither of us has the advantage yet, but we've both come to know our opponent well.

I return to the back porch and stare across my father's yard to the woods beyond. The trees have not yet leafed out, and through the bare branches I can just make out Daphne Road, where more vehicles have arrived. On the other side of that road are the woods abutting the property where Billy's old house stands. That is where the cadaver dog has caught the scent.

That is where they'll find her.

FORTY-ONE

Lizzie DiPalma emerged from the soil in bits and pieces. A finger bone here, an ankle bone there. Twenty years in a shallow grave had rotted the flesh from the skeleton, but once the skull was unearthed, Maura had little doubt of the body's identity. Cupping the cranium in one hand, she brushed away soil from the upper jaw and looked at Jane.

"This is a child's skull. Based on the partially erupted lateral incisors, I estimate the decedent's age to be eight or nine years old."

"Lizzie was nine," said Jane.

Gently, Maura set the skull on the tarp and clapped dirt from her gloved hands. "I think you've found her."

For a moment they stood in silence, looking down at the excavated grave. The burial was less than a foot deep, which was why the cadaver dog was able to catch the scent, even twenty years later. Two children could certainly dig a grave this shallow, and at eleven years old, Billy Sullivan had been large enough, strong enough, to wield a shovel.

Strong enough to kill a nine-year-old girl.

Maura brushed away more dirt, revealing a depressed fracture of the left temporal bone. This had been caused by more than merely a glancing blow; this blow had been delivered with full force on the side of her head, most likely as she was lying on the ground. She imagined the sequence of events: The girl shoved to the dirt. The boy lifting the rock, slamming it down on the girl's head. It was the oldest of weapons, as old as the dawn of murder. As old as Cain and Abel.

"Holly helped him do it. I know she did," said Jane.

"But how do you prove it?"

"That's what drives me crazy. I *can't* prove it. If we call Everett Prescott to testify against her, the defense will call it hearsay. Worse than that, it's hearsay while under the influence of ketamine. When we had him wired to record her, she didn't admit to a thing. She's too damn smart to slip up, so we have nothing to tie her to this murder."

"She was only ten years old when it happened. Can she really be held responsible?"

"She helped *kill* this girl. Okay, maybe it was twenty years ago and she was just a kid herself, but you know what? I don't think people change. Whatever she was then, she still is. A snake doesn't grow up to be a bunny rabbit. She's still a snake, and she's going to keep striking. Until somebody finally stops her."

"It won't be this time."

"No, this time she gets to walk away. But at least

we've given Martin Stanek some measure of justice, even if it's too late for him. Bonnie Sandridge is gonna make damn sure the whole world knows he was innocent." Jane looked through the trees toward Earl Devine's house. "Jesus, do you ever feel like we're surrounded by them? Monsters like Holly Devine and Billy Sullivan? If they think they can get away with it, they'll slit your throat without a second thought."

"And that's where you come in, Jane. You keep the rest of us safe."

"The trouble is, there are way too many Holly Devines in this world and not enough of me to go around."

"At least you accomplished this," said Maura, looking down at the skull of Lizzie DiPalma. "You found her."

"And now she can finally go home to her mother."

It would be a sad reunion but a reunion nonetheless, one of several that had happened during this investigation. Arlene DiPalma would soon reclaim her lost daughter. Angela Rizzoli was now back together with Vince Korsak. Barry Frost had reunited—for better or worse—with his ex-wife, Alice.

And Daniel has come back to me.

In truth, he had never really left her. She had been the one who'd sent him away, who'd believed that true happiness could only come from rooting out the imperfect, the way one cuts off a diseased limb. But nothing in life is perfect, certainly not love.

And she had never doubted that Daniel loved her. Once, he had been ready to die for her; could she ask for any better proof?

It was after dark when Maura arrived home from the crime scene that evening. Inside her house the lights were on, the windows bright and welcoming. Daniel's car was parked in her driveway, once again out in the open where the world could see it. This was how far they'd come together, to a place beyond caring what anyone else thought about their union. She had tried to live without him, had believed she'd moved on and that love was optional. She had thought that being resigned was the same as being happy, but in truth she'd briefly forgotten what happiness felt like.

Seeing the lights in her house, his car in her driveway, she remembered.

I'm ready to be happy again. With you.

She stepped out of her car, and with a smile on her lips she walked from the darkness, into the light.

FORTY-TWO

THIS, YOU SEE, IS THE WAY OF THE WORLD.

There are people like me, and then there are people who consider me evil because, unlike them, I don't weep at sad movies or funerals or "Auld Lang Syne." But deep inside every bleating sentimentalist lurks the dark embryo of who I am: a cold-blooded opportunist. This is what turns good soldiers into executioners, neighbors into informers, bankers into thieves. Oh, they will probably deny it. They all think they are more human than I am, merely because they weep and I do not.

Unless I have to.

Certainly I am not weeping now, as I stand over the spot in the woods where Lizzie's body was found. It's been a week since the police packed up all their gear and departed, and while the evidence of their excavation is still here—the disturbed soil, the bright scrap of crime-scene tape snagged on a branch—eventually everything will return to the way it was. Leaves will tumble down and blanket what is now bare earth. Saplings will sprout, and roots will tunnel and spread, and in a few years, if left to itself, this patch of ground will once again look like any other spot among these trees.

The way it looked twenty years ago, when Billy and I stood here.

I remember that October day, how the air smelled like wood smoke and wet leaves. Billy had brought his slingshot and he was trying to hit birds, squirrels, anything that had the misfortune to cross his path. He hadn't hit any of his targets, and he was frustrated and hungry for blood. I knew his moods well, knew how he could lash out like a cobra when frustrated, but I was not afraid of him, because in his eyes I recognized myself.

The worst part of myself.

He had just launched another stone, missed another feathered target, when we spied Lizzie on the road, pushing her bike. She wore her pink sweater and her knit cap with the sparkly beads, the one she'd bought during her family vacation in Paris. How proud she was of that hat! She'd worn it to school every day for the last week, and at lunch I'd stared at it, desperately wanting one just like it. Wanting to be like Lizzie herself, so blond, so pretty, so quick to make friends. I knew my mother would never buy me something so dazzling, because it might bring the unwanted attention of boys, who would do to me what her uncle had done to her. *Vanity is a sin, Holly. So is covetousness. Learn to do without.* Now there was that sparkly hat perched on Lizzie's pretty head. She had not yet noticed us in the woods, and she sang as she pushed her bike along the road, sang as if the whole world were her audience.

Billy fired his slingshot.

The pebble thunked against Lizzie's cheek. She screamed and spun around, searching for the culprit. In an instant she spotted us. She dropped her bike on the road and came scrambling into the woods, shouting.

"Now you're in trouble, Billy Sullivan! You're in *big* trouble!"

Billy picked up another stone. Loaded his slingshot. "You're not gonna tell anyone."

"I'm going to tell *everyone*! And this time, you'll—"

The second stone hit her in the eyebrow. Her hat flew off as she stumbled to her knees, blood streaming down her face. Even then, half-blinded by blood, the fight hadn't left her. Even then, she was not going to yield to Billy. She scooped up a clump of earth and threw it.

I remember Billy's howl as the dirt splattered his face. I remember the thrill of watching his rage explode, and I remember the sound a fist makes when it slams into flesh. Then they were both on the ground, Billy on top of her, Lizzie screaming.

But the beaded hat was what I really cared about, and I ran to pick it up. It was heavier than I expected, weighed down with hundreds of pretty beads. A few drops of blood stained the fabric, but I could wash those away. Mama had shown me how easily cold water rinses blood from sheets. I pulled the hat over my hair and turned to show my prize to Billy.

He was standing over Lizzie's body. "Wake up," he ordered, and gave her a kick. *"Wake up."*

I looked down at her head. At the torn scalp, the blood pouring into her hair, into the soil. "What did you do?"

"She was going to tell on us. She was going to get us in trouble, and now she can't." He handed me the fist-sized rock he was holding, a rock that was already smeared with her blood. "It's your turn."

"What?"

"Hit her."

"What if I don't want to?"

"Then you don't get to keep the hat. And you don't get to be my friend."

I stood holding the rock, weighing the choice. The hat felt so good, so right, on my head. I didn't want to give it up. And Lizzie already looked dead anyway; one more blow wouldn't make a difference.

"Do it," Billy insisted. "No one will ever know."

"She's not even moving."

"Hit her anyway." He leaned close and whispered in my ear, "Don't you want to know what it feels like?"

I looked down at Lizzie's head, where there was so much blood that I couldn't see if her eyes were open or shut. What difference would it make now if I hit her?

"It's easy," said Billy. "If you want to be my friend, *just do it.*"

I crouched over Lizzie, and as I raised the rock, a thrill surged through me. A feeling that I could do anything, be anything. In my hand I held the power of life and death.

I smashed the rock against Lizzie's temple.

"There," said Billy. "It'll be our secret. Now you have to promise me you'll never tell anyone about this. Not ever."

I promised.

It took us the rest of the afternoon to bury her in the woods. By the time we finished, I was scratched from brambles, bruised from falling backward onto a rock. The reward for my labors was the hat with the silver beads, which I hid in my backpack so Mama wouldn't see it. That night, after rinsing out the blood, I tried on the hat and looked at myself in the mirror. On Lizzie's head, the beads had sparkled like little diamonds, bringing out the bright crystalline blue of her eyes. The eyes that gazed back from the mirror were neither crystalline nor transformed. It was just me wearing a hat, which had lost whatever magic I'd imagined it possessed.

I stuffed it into my backpack and forgot about it.

Until Monday.

By then, everyone knew that Lizzie DiPalma was missing. At school that day, my fifth-grade teacher, Mrs. Keller, told us to be careful because there might be *a bad man in the neighborhood.* At lunch, the other girls whispered about what kidnappers actually *did* to little girls. Many of the kids were kept home from school, coddled and smothered in parental love, and that afternoon there were only five of us kids who rode the bus to Apple Tree. Everyone was strangely quiet. That silence only served to magnify the thump of my backpack as it slid off the seat and hit the floor.

I had not zipped it up, and everything came tumbling out. My books. My pencils.

Lizzie's hat.

It was Cassandra Coyle who spotted it first. She pointed to the clump of beads and wool lying in the aisle and said, "That's Lizzie's hat!"

I snatched it up and thrust it into my backpack. "It's mine."

"No, it's not. Everyone knows it's Lizzie's!"

Now Timmy and Sarah were paying attention, watching our exchange.

"How did you get her hat?" Cassandra demanded.

I remember all four of the children staring at me. Cassandra and Sarah, Timmy and Billy. In Billy's eyes I saw the cold gleam of threat: *Don't tell the truth. Don't ever tell the truth.*

"I found it over there," I said, and pointed to the back of the bus. "Stuck between the seats."

And that was how suspicion fell on Martin Stanek, who faithfully picked us up every afternoon from Billson Elementary School and drove us to the Apple Tree.

This is how cases are built. On the word of a child, and a hat that belonged to a missing girl. Once you're made to look guilty, everyone assumes you *are* guilty, and so it happened to Martin Stanek, age twenty-two, school-bus driver. From there the guilt spread to his mother and father, whom everyone assumed were part of the conspiracy and equally guilty.

It wasn't difficult to cast suspicion on them after I showed the doctor all the cuts and bruises I got from burying Lizzie in the woods. When Billy joined me with his own accusations against the Staneks, their fate was sealed. From there the tales spread and grew. If you ask young children again and again to remember an event, eventually they will. And so the case was built, child by child, wild story by wilder story.

But the truth is, it all started with a hat that I wanted. A hat that would later appear as the visual clue in Cassandra Coyle's horror film. Cassandra had finally put the pieces together, and she realized that what everyone believed about Lizzie's disappearance was wrong. The truth had been stored in her memory these last twenty years. A memory of me on a bus, holding a beaded hat that did not belong to me.

I look up at the trees, where the buds of spring are swelling and the branches are tinged with green. All the others are dead, but here I am, the survivor. The only one left who knows how Lizzie DiPalma really died.

No, not exactly the only one. Detective Rizzoli has guessed the truth in part, although she can't prove it. She never will.

She knows I am guilty, and she'll be watching me. So for now I must walk the straight and narrow. I must pretend to be the good girl who neither steals nor cheats, who uses the crosswalk and always pays her taxes on time. I must be who I am not. But this too shall pass.

I am what I am, and no one can watch me forever.

ACKNOWLEDGMENTS

MY MOTHER, AN IMMIGRANT FROM CHINA, HAD a shaky command of the English language, but she did understand—and love—American horror films. I inherited her love of the genre, and as a child I spent many happy hours screaming in delight as I watched and rewatched my favorites, including *Them, The Thing,* and *Invasion of the Body Snatchers.* When I finally had the chance to write and produce my own independent feature film, of course it was a horror film. The plot of *I Know a Secret* was partly inspired by my experience of making *Island Zero,* and I thank Mariah Klapatch, Josh Gerritsen, Mark Farney, my husband, Jacob, and the entire cast and crew of *Island Zero* for being part of the adventure. We spilled a ton of fake blood, burned down a house (on purpose), stayed up way too late, and probably drank too much beer, but hey, guys—we actually made a movie! And what I wrote about horror fans is absolutely true: We are one big happy family. We are not scary people. Trust me.

I also thank everyone who helped bring *I Know a Secret* to publication: the incomparable team at the Jane Rotrosen literary agency, my editors Kara Cesare (U.S.) and Frankie Gray (U.K.), Kim Hovey, Larry Finlay, Dennis Ambrose and his team of exacting copy editors (you keep me humble), and my tireless publicists on both sides of the pond, Sharon Propson and Alison Barrow. It has been an honor to work with you all.